THE DARK ONES

BRYAN SMITH

deadite
press

DEADITE PRESS
205 NE BRYANT
PORTLAND, OR 97211
www.DEADITEPRESS.com

AN ERASERHEAD PRESS COMPANY
www.ERASERHEADPRESS.com

ISBN: 1-62105-032-7

Copyright © 2011, 2012 by Bryan Smith

Cover art copyright © 2011 Alan M. Clark
www.ALANMCLARK.com

Printed in the USA.

For Dylan Smith

PROLOGUE

Hollis House
December 1, 1959

A smell so foul it made his eyes water permeated the room. His throat filled with bile as the overpowering odor assailed him, filling his nostrils like poison as wave after hot wave of the foulness engulfed him, making him feel like a man drowning in an ocean of filth. It was impossible to fathom how so vile a stench could issue from the mouth of the woman he'd married almost a decade ago.

Frank Hollis reminded himself that this thing wasn't really his precious Eleanor. It was her body, but there was something else inside her, an evil thing using her flesh like a puppet. The thing was manipulating her flesh in ways that sickened and frightened him, using and abusing the body of its host with reckless abandon. He could only hope Eleanor's poor soul had already departed the ravaged flesh. The possibility that she might still be aware of what was happening, a powerless prisoner in her own head, was too awful to bear. Rage filled him again at the thought of this, but there was nothing he could do.

Frank was lying flat on his back in the bed he and Eleanor had shared since moving into their new home five years earlier. He had made love to Eleanor as recently as three days ago on this bed. Fresh tears welled in his eyes as he realized that would never happen again. His hands were stretched backward behind his head and tied with thick lengths of rope to the headboard. He struggled against his bonds as the thing hovering above him hissed and leered at him.

Thing.

Yes, a thing.

The reminder had to be constant because it certainly still looked like Eleanor. The leering face was the same lovely one he'd kissed so many times. But the expression on that face was so bizarrely alien. The eyes were wide and bulging and hideously bloodshot, almost completely crimson. The lips were peeled so far back from the teeth they had cracked at the corners, causing thin trickles of blood to spill to the point of her chin, where the dark moisture beaded and dripped onto his bare chest.

Frank screamed again as it performed one of its special tricks.

There was a sound of popping vertebrae as Eleanor's neck began to lengthen. Her head stretched toward the ceiling. Her neck now looked like the long, bendable neck of a giraffe or extinct prehistoric creature. The head atop the long, elastic flesh-stick seemed too big and wobbled precariously. It grinned down at him, its lips stretching wider and thinner. More blood spilled from the deepening cracks at the corners of the mouth. Then the magic trick reversed itself, the neck shrinking in a breathtaking instant as the head came sliding back down, stopping with an abrupt wobble. The mouth moved in that weird way it had when the thing was laughing, the lips a shifting blur of impossible to follow motion. Fresh gusts of that hell stench made him gag again.

Then it lifted one of its arms, turning the inner part toward him, displaying the tender, unmarked flesh for him. It waited until it knew it had his full attention. It then flexed the fingers of its right hand, causing the fingernails to lengthen and harden, becoming black, diseased talons.

Frank shook his head. "No. Please. No. Haven't you done enough?"

It laughed again.

The talons ripped at the exposed inner arm, tearing long deep grooves in the flesh. Thick streams of dark blood poured from the new wounds. It held the torn flesh over Frank's face, dripping the blood into his mouth. Frank swallowed every drop. He knew now this was expected of him. The creature enjoyed this extra level of defilement. It enjoyed all the ways it taunted and tormented him.

Its mouth opened wide again and a stream of vomit blasted Frank's face. He gagged and sputtered, coughed out the vileness even as more of it splashed his face and soaked the pillows and mattress beneath him.

He was wailing like a baby now. *"Please! Please! Stop! Oh, please..."*

It wiped the vomit from his eyes with an almost tender motion before shoving one of its pendulous breasts into his open mouth, forcing him to suckle like a mewling baby at the erect nipple. It wriggled its nude body against him, making him hard despite the repulsion he felt for this thing and everything happening to him.

It pulled away from him.

Waited.

He coughed again. "I'm watching, damn you."

The thing raised its left hand again, flexed the fingers and made the nails pop out. But this time they didn't turn into black, razor-sharp talons. It pinched one of the extended fingernails between the thumb and forefinger of its other hand and began to slowly extract it. Frank's stomach twisted as he watched the fingernail slide all the way out of the finger. He grimaced when the thing popped the nail in its mouth and munched on it like candy. The crackling sound as it chewed was awful. It repeated the process with the next nail. And then the next. This went on until all the fingernails on that hand were gone. Then it held the hand in front of Frank's face so he could have a good look at the tender, blood-rimmed flesh slots where the nails had been. The fundamental *wrongness* of what he was seeing was too much. His head snapped to the left and puked again.

When he was done retching, the creature wrapped its fingers around a length of Eleanor's once-lustrous hair and ripped it out, pulling free a bloody piece of scalp with it. This bit of flesh went into its mouth. It chewed slowly this time, relish the taste of the raw, bloody flesh.

Frank sniffled. "Please kill me. Just be done with it. I beg you."

The thing didn't reply. It just grinned and ripped another hank of hair and flesh off Eleanor's head. But the fresh disgust he felt at this was overshadowed in the next moment as he heard the bedroom door creak open. A desperate, tremulous hope stole into heart. Someone, some rare visitor, had at last heard the endless screams emanating from the house and had come to investigate. He hoped whoever it was had a gun. A big gun. A gun wouldn't kill the thing inside Eleanor, but a few well-placed bullets could force it to vacate her body and end this obscene violation. He craned his neck to see past the thing and his suddenly soaring spirits deflated again.

Roger Campbell stepped into full view at the side of the bed. "Hello, Frank."

Frank's face turned stony. "You."

"Yes. I see you've met my special...friend."

"But...this is your doing? Why? How?"

"Oh, I think you know the why part of the equation." He smiled. "As for the how...well, that's more complicated. I plan to make my mark in Ransom, Frank. I'll own this town before I'm done, every goddamn speck of it. But you've been getting in my way at every turn, blocking proposals and property acquisitions." He glanced at the wild-eyed creature sitting astride Frank and smiled again. "I imagine you may have a regret or two about that now."

Frank's eyes glimmered with tears. "I'd kill you if I could."

Roger laughed. "Oh, I'm sure that's how you feel at the moment, but we're going to have a long talk, Frank. A very frank discussion." He grinned, flashing perfect white teeth. He was a handsome man, with his wavy brown hair and blue eyes. "The first thing you need to know is dear, sweet Eleanor was not the adoring, devoted wife you imagine."

Frank stiffened. "Don't you dare."

"Yes, Frank, I had her. Often. Sometimes right here on this bed while you were at work."

"You lie, you son of a bitch."

"She told me she needed all the side action she could get because your tiny cock wasn't enough to satisfy her. She also told me you like it kinky. You like to be tied up and abused. Me, I think that's for perverts and godless commies, but whatever rocks your boat, Frank."

Frank's breath hitched. He sniffled. "No...you lie."

But there was no conviction left in his voice.

The bastard was telling the truth. The thing straddling him leered again and waggled its tongue at him.

"How have you done this?"

Roger reached into a coat pocket and pulled out a pack of Pall Malls. He lit one and exhaled a thick cloud of richly aromatic smoke. He made a sound of satisfaction. "That's better. Doesn't quite mask the demon stench, but it's better. Yes, the thing inside your wife is a demon. A really nasty one, too. I summoned it."

"That's insane."

"It isn't. You believe your own eyes, don't you?" Roger expelled another cloud of smoke. "My ancestors are mostly Romanian. The old country, as my older relations referred to it. Do you know that Campbell isn't my birth name? It's true. My real family name is Antonescu. I got rid of the name, but I've retained a knowledge of secret things passed down through centuries. Family secrets. Old country lore. Including a working knowledge of basic demonology."

"What do you want from me?"

Roger smiled. "Ah, you've hit on it, haven't you?"

He had. And to Frank's amazement, much of his terror had deserted him, even with the demon still astride him. "I'm more useful to you alive than dead."

Roger pointed a finger at him and flipped his thumb down, miming the firing of a gun. "Got it."

"Tell me what you want. I'll do anything."

He meant it, too. Eleanor was lost to him now. He wouldn't have her back even if he could. That filthy, lying bitch. He listened attentively as Roger explained his plans for the town. He was only mildly surprised by how little any of it disturbed him. He hardly felt like the same man he'd been just a few days ago.

In many very essential ways, he wasn't that man any longer.

A fact confirmed a little later when Roger commanded the demon to desert Eleanor's body. He was freed from his bonds as his confused and terrified wife wailed and moaned in agony at the offenses done to her body.

Eleanor extended a shaky hand to him, her bleary eyes pleading for comfort and reassurance. "Frank...I..."

There was a bang and her head blew apart.

Roger Campbell lowered a gun.

Frank closed his eyes and listened to his new master's smug laughter.

PART I:
THEY COME OUT
AT NIGHT

ONE

Something stirred in the darkness, a flickering of awareness after a long, long sleep. A weak fluttering of dormant power as the thing awakened, psychic tendrils reaching out to probe the edges of its surroundings, familiarize itself again with the shape of this place. This dark place. It was trapped here. Imprisoned. Locked down here beneath the earth, condemned to spend eternity alone in this miserable slice of hell.

No.

Not eternity.

Because it could not die. Not really. Not completely. It could not be permanently erased, the way, say, the life-force of a crawling bug could be extinguished irretrievably with such delicious ease, ground to gritty, slimy pulp beneath a heel.

The thing in the darkness could not be extinguished, but it could be banished.

It could be contained.

As it had been contained in this dark place for fully half a century. A flare of rage brought it to a state of almost full consciousness for several moments. A human had trapped it here. A *human*. One of those pitiful, mewling little things. It had been fooled, tricked by a creature so infinitely inferior it was impossible to comprehend how it had happened. Humans able to wield the arcane black magic necessary to bind one such as itself were rare. Almost extinct. And yet one had done just that. First summoned it, then bound it in this deep darkness.

The thing in the darkness longed to be free. Away from the rot and decay of this place, able again to roam among the

13

living things of the world. Its inability to make this happen sparked alternating feelings of despair and anger.

A human had done this!

A *human*!

The thing roared its rage one last time, making the air vibrate.

And then it began to drift back toward sleep. It might not stir again for a period of years, or even decades. And that was fine. Because it knew one day something would happen to break the spell chaining it here.

Someone would come. Some poor, curious fool of a human.

It was as inevitable as the eventual rise and dominion of its dark Master.

Out, it thought.

One day I shall be...OUT.

TWO

The Dark Ones come out at night.

So goes the obscure slogan most residents of the Wheaton Hills subdivision in Ransom, TN fail to ever notice. The words are scratched on utility poles, street signs, rocks, and tree limbs. The few who do note the multiple appearances of the slogan are mostly indifferent to its mysterious meaning. The one or two who do pause to ponder the meaning of the words ultimately chalk it up to harmless teen mischief. Some vague expression of youthful angst. Nothing really worth puzzling over.

There are bigger things to worry about, after all.

Ransom occupies a small corner of a mostly quiet rural community. It is a town on the cusp of fundamental change. New companies, respectably sized, have moved in, bringing with them an influx of upper middle class families from larger cities. Many of these newcomers wind up in sparkling new Wheaton Hills. Their offspring are predictably bored by their new surroundings. There is nothing to do. No movie theaters. No malls. Most adjust and find new ways to have fun and fill time. These are the regular kids. All-Americans. Preppies. Jocks. Geeks. And the just plain average kids existing between the stereotypes.

Then there are The Dark Ones.

It is their name. The label they have chosen for themselves.

The Dark Ones come out at night.

They do not fit easily into any of the usual categories. They are not part of the cool crowd, but the cool kids know to be wary of them. Say you're one of the cool crowd. A star

15

quarterback or head cheerleader. Everyone adores you. You get everything you want, most of the time, and everything is easy. As one of the privileged ones, you sort of see yourself as royalty, a King or Queen, and the other students are your subjects. The unlovely ones are peasants and you treat them fittingly, as royalty would in medieval times. They exist only for your occasional amusement, and it *is* fun to mess with them once in a while.

The Dark Ones come out at night.

You live in Wheaton Hills.

But *they* live there, too. Maybe the adults don't notice, but you've seen that slogan and you remember it. And you know them. Not to talk to, but you know them. You share classes with some of them. They always sit in the back, wearing those dark sunglasses the teachers have given up telling them to take off. Strangely, you see them there more often than in the neighborhood. You do see them at home sometimes, just not during the day. Just now and then when you're feeling restless at night and you get up to take a peek out your bedroom window. You stand there and you watch the empty street, and everything is utterly still, the way any small town neighborhood should be as the hour passes midnight. But you keep watching, waiting, knowing they will come. And they do, eventually they always do. Sometimes alone. Other times in groups of two or three. Slipping like shadows through the night, clad in black as always, somehow always avoiding the direct glare of the streetlights. It freaks you out. It unsettles you. You would never admit it to your friends, but they really sort of *frighten* you. It's a shameful thing. There aren't that many of them. Your crowd outnumbers them by a large margin. Many of your friends are athletes. Large and fearsome, physically powerful.

But it's true. You're afraid of them, and you can admit it to yourself.

Here in the dark. Alone.

The Dark Ones come out at night.

Trip a geek in the hallway between periods and maybe you get to laugh at a quivering pile of terrified blubber scrambling to pick up the textbooks you've knocked out of his arms. But if you decide to tangle with a member of this other set of misfits you won't be laughing for long. If you're lucky, you'll only wind up with a black eye. But you might not be lucky. You might be like the jock who was stomped half to death in the parking lot one morning before school. A handful of incidents like this have taught the bullies to steer clear of The Dark Ones. And yet there is an ongoing tension, a slowly simmering potential for violence. There is talk. Hallway gossip. A fight is coming. A war. Some of your friends are fed up with the intimidation.

But it's so hard to get around just how damn creepy and *weird* they are.

The Dark Ones come out at night.

Every night.

Tonight.

Now.

I'll kill him.

This is what Mark Bell thought as he stared up at the the dark ceiling in his bedroom. Every now and then he glanced at the muted television atop his dresser, where a *South Park* episode was playing on Comedy Central, but mostly his mind was occupied with the fury he felt.

I'll really do it. I'll slit that motherfucker's throat from ear to ear if he ever says that shit about her again.

Pushed far enough, he could really do it. And he was close to that point. Those fuckers simply could not talk about her that way. She was better than any of them.

Kill you, he thought.

Watch you bleed. Watch your fucking life spill out on the ground.

They hadn't known he was there. No way they'd have been running their mouths like that otherwise. He had come up behind them during a break between periods. It was three of those fucking rednecks. *Locals.* Just thinking the word made his lips twist in disgust. He had lived in Ransom more than a year and a half at this point, but he would never think

17

of himself as *local*. This town wasn't his real home. That was Atlanta. Always would be. One day he'd go back there. Or maybe not. Maybe he'd head up to Manhattan instead. Or LA. Or Chicago. Anywhere big and bustling and full of life and possibilities. Anywhere but here. Here felt like death.

The fucking locals would always be here.

Good, he thought.

Let them rot in this nowhere place.

They had been clustered around a set of open lockers in the hallway. Mark's own locker was nearby on the same side of the corridor. The ten minutes allowed between classes was winding down and the hallways were emptying out fast. Yet these three idiots were in no apparent hurry to get to whatever remedial course was next on their schedules. Mark had felt the usual reflexive disgust as he neared them. All were clad in t-shirts advertising wizened classic rock bands and NASCAR drivers and dirty jeans with rips at the knees.

He was maybe twenty feet from them when he heard her name. He tensed immediately, his hand freezing on his locker's combination knob. They still hadn't noticed him. He knew this because he heard her name again. And he heard their barks of derisive laughter. If they'd seen him, they wouldn't have been laughing.

They knew better.

"*Yeah, she's a slut,*" one boy said.

There was more of that stupid laughter and then one of them said, "*Sluts are cool, though. I'd fuck her.*"

Mark's hand came away from the combination knob.

More laughter.

He stood up straight and turned toward them. His blood was boiling.

One of the boys made a sound of disgust. "*You'd fuck one of them city bitches? Your dick'd fall off boy. All them cunts got every STD in the book.*"

Mark's hands curled into fists.

Kill you, he thought.

Fucking kill you.

He started toward them. He cleared his throat. Their

laughter cut off immediately. They turned to look at him, the mirth draining from their stupid faces lightning quick. It was him against three of them. But there was never any doubt how it would go down. One mumbled an apology of sorts and took off down the hallway at once, seeking the safety of a classroom. The other two paused just long enough to slam their lockers shut and then they were running like little bitches, too. Mark derived a small degree of satisfaction from the level of terror he'd elicited from the boys without even voicing a threat. Without uttering a single *word*.

And yet it wasn't enough.

He'd stewed over it all day.

They couldn't talk about her that way.

Even now, many hours later, he couldn't stop thinking about it.

Until a tapping came at his window.

THREE

Three soft taps, with a brief, deliberate pause between each. *Tap. Tap. Tap.* Very light, almost inaudible. There was a reason Mark silenced the TV every evening as midnight neared, and it had nothing to do with appeasing his parents. Their bedroom was at the opposite end of the big house, far enough away that noise was not a concern. The alarm system, however, was another matter, and was the reason for the tapper's light touch.

Mark swung his legs over the side of the twin-sized bed, got to his feet, and crossed the room in three quick strides. At the window, he slid two fingers between blind slats and peered through the narrow gap. It was her. She saw him peeking at her and smiled. He flexed his fingers, widening the gap between the slats, and held up the index finger of his other hand.

Give me a minute, the gesture said.

She mouthed the word *okay*.

Mark stared at her a moment longer. *God, she's so fucking beautiful.* Then he moved away from the window and snatched his keys from the nightstand next to his bed. These he shoved down the right hip pocket of his jeans. He grabbed his black leather jacket from the back of a chair and hurriedly slipped it on. He then dropped to the floor and reached under his bed to pull out a box containing his old collection of Magic: The Gathering cards He'd given the game up years ago, but the loose pile of cards was an effective means of concealing things nosy parents shouldn't see. Things like a quarter ounce of weed in a tightly rolled plastic bag and a half pint bottle of Southern Comfort. He tucked the booze and bag of weed in an inner pocket of his jacket, closed the box, and shoved it back under the bed.

He opened the door to his room and stepped into a small rec room. There was a couch against one wall and a large flat screen television mounted on the opposite wall. The shelves of a single bookcase were filled with board games, and there was a card table upon which these games, in theory, would be played. But it had been a long, long time since the last family game night. At least a year. Maybe longer. There'd been some subtle shift in family dynamics that was hard to define. His parents were no longer as close as they'd once been. Sometimes Mark thought it had to do with the stresses of Tom Bell's corporate job at Stanton Manufacturing. The man worked seriously long hours. Too long. Mark couldn't fathom that kind of time commitment to something that had to be boring as fuck.

Other times Mark was certain the change had something to do with him.

Times when he was sure they just didn't like him anymore and were counting the days until he was out of their hair and out on his own.

It depressed him.

And he didn't want to be depressed right now. There were things to be glad about. The girl waiting for him outside, for instance. He affected an air of jaded cynicism about most things, but this girl made him feel good. The world seemed like a brighter place when she was around. More vibrant. More exciting. And when she wasn't around, all of that went away. Lately she'd been making an obvious effort to spend more time specifically with him, rather than anyone else in their small clique. It didn't take a genius to figure out the interest was mutual. Still, nothing had happened yet and he had a feeling the time to make a real move was at hand.

He was out of the rec room now and standing at the door to the garage. The numbers on the alarm system's keypad glowed a bright green in the darkness. The keypad was mounted on the wall next to the door. Here was the tricky part. The part that put a lump of fear in his throat every night.

21

Just get it over with.

His parents were sound sleepers, but the law of averages said eventually one of them would have a restless, sleepless night around this time. There was an identical keypad mounted on a wall in their bedroom. They might notice the system had been disabled. And if that ever happened...well, he wasn't sure what would happen. Maybe nothing. After all, he was half-convinced they didn't give a damn about him anymore. On the other hand, they might crack down, maybe officially forbid him from going out at night, which would effectively cut him off from his friends.

From *her*.

And that couldn't happen. *Wouldn't* happen. He was beyond their control now. Beyond anyone's control. But that didn't mean he was in any hurry to deal with the drama of a confrontation.

He jabbed numbers on the keypad. Four digits, each accompanied by a beep, followed by a louder beep signaling that the system had been disarmed. He unlocked the door and pulled it quickly open, hurried into the garage, and pulled the door shut again. He felt a little weird leaving the house unprotected by the alarm system, but, really, what was there to worry about? They didn't live in the city anymore. A dead of night home invasion seemed unlikely in sleepy Wheaton Hills.

He had this little inner debate nearly every night.

It was pointless. He was going out and that was that.

He opened the door to the backyard and got the hell out of there.

FOUR

"Alarm's off. The boy's heading out again."

She didn't answer right away. From his vantage point on the bed, Tom Bell could see his wife through the open bathroom door. Clad only in black thong panties and black platform heels, she leaned over the sink to apply a fresh coat of bright red lipstick. He stared at her fit but curvaceous body and felt his pulse quicken. She was wearing the platinum blond wig tonight. It was his favorite. She also had purple, electric blue, and silver wigs, among other shades. When she wore one of those, he liked to pretend he was screwing some hot punk chick.

Lydia strutted into the bedroom. She climbed atop the bed and stalked toward him, the heavy soles of her shoes making deep indentations in the mattress. She stopped when she stood over him at waist level, one shoe planted on either side of his waist.

He stared up at her, his eyes alight with a mixture of awe and desperate excitement. Her face was expressionless, but something in her posture nonetheless conveyed an aloof, almost bored contempt. But that was just part of the game. God, how he wanted to touch her. He groaned and jerked his wrists against the metal cuffs binding him to the bed's wrought iron headboard.

"Be still!"

He flinched. Her tone was harsh and loud. It was the voice of utter authority, implying an infinite capacity for cruelty. She had gotten very good at this part of the game, too So good it scared him now and then when she really got into it. Like the time a month ago when she'd been choking him while he was in this very position, cuffed to the headboard and completely helpless. Just thinking about it made him shudder. She'd had both hands wrapped around his throat and was really bearing down, putting every ounce of her strength in it. He hadn't been able to breathe at all for many long moments. He remembered seeing her nipples stiffen as he struggled for breath. He remembered that single trickle of sweat sliding between her breasts. That had been the thing that spooked him the most at the time, even more than the horribly intent look in her eyes. That tiny, slowly moving droplet of moisture scared the shit out of him. Because sweat meant work. She wasn't playing, not then, and for a few horrifying moments he'd been sure she meant to kill him, a conviction that lasted all the way up to the second she abruptly let go of his throat. She'd scrambled off the bed then, retreating to the bathroom, slamming the door behind her. He remembered listening to her cry.

Tom hadn't really needed an explanation.

It was all his fault.

It all went back to his brief dalliance a year ago with Suzie McGregor. Suzie lived in a big neo-Victorian on Spring Circle, the newest part of Wheaton Hills. They got sloppy and the affair was exposed after only a month. Lydia came damn close to leaving him then. Scary close. Somehow he'd talked her out of it. He cried. He begged. He promised her anything and everything. Somehow it swayed her. They went to marriage counseling. Tom hadn't thought much of the counselor. But one of the woman's suggestions had stuck. She told them they should think of some ways to inject some excitement back into their marriage. Perhaps some role-playing in the bedroom...

Lydia shifted her weight and lifted one foot of the bed. She placed the heavy sole squarely in the center of his chest and applied a bit of pressure.

She showed him a sneer. "You worried about what your son gets up to when he goes out at night?"

"Aren't you?"

"No."

Tom frowned. "Why not?"

"Because I don't care what happens to him."

"Christ, Lydia. He's your own flesh and blood."

"He's a sullen, ungrateful brat."

"Maybe, but it goes with the territory at that age. You know that."

"I don't care. He's a trouble-making delinquent. Fuck him."

Tom couldn't believe what he was hearing. The last year had changed Lydia in a lot of ways, many of them not for the better. And part of that was understandable. She'd experienced a deep betrayal. But Mark was an innocent and shouldn't bear the brunt of her rage. "Lydia—"

She shifted her weight again, pressing the heavy shoe harder against his chest. The point of the spike heel dimpled the flesh below his ribcage. "Shut your mouth."

Tom winced. That heel was really digging in and hurting him. The pain was bad enough, but the things she was saying about there son bothered him more. He knew he didn't spend enough time with the kid, or make enough of an effort to understand him, but he loved Mark.

Lydia did something strange then—she smiled.

He didn't see her smile very often these days.

"I had a very pleasant dream last night."

Tom groaned. The pressure on his chest had increased again. "Yeah?"

"Yes. I dreamed I came home from errands to find you fucking Suzie McGregor on the kitchen floor."

"You know I wouldn't—"

"Shut up. You know what I did when I found you with her in my dream? I got an ax from somewhere and I chopped you and that sleazy little whore into a million tiny pieces. There was blood everywhere. I was soaked in it. It was... *beautiful.*"

Her foot came away from his chest. She wiggled her hips and slid the thong panties down her legs. She dropped the tiny wisp of black cloth on his face and lowered herself to him, gasping loudly once as his engorged cock impaled her.

She leaned close to him. Her voice was a hot whisper in his ear: "*Do you like that?*"

He managed a strangled, "*Yes.*"

She ground away at him rhythmically for several moments before speaking again. "You know what I'm thinking about right now, Tom?"

He heaved a breath. "What?"

She wrapped her hands around his throat and whispered huskily in his ear, "I'm thinking I want to play the choking game again."

She began to squeeze.

FIVE

Mark hoisted himself over the chain-link fence that bordered the rear of the Bell property and came down slightly off-balance on the other side. He wobbled for a few steps as one heel turned at an awkward angle, but he got his feet solidly under him just in time to avoid a clumsy spill.

A black shape came away from the garage door. The shape drew nearer and the faint light of the moon fell across a ghostly pale face. A glossy lock of raven-black hair fell across the girl's forehead and she smiled at him.

"Hey."

Mark loved the sound of her voice. It had a lilting, girlish quality at times, a playfulness, but mixed with that was a clear toughness. You heard it any time she got angry or spoke passionately about something. Like Mark, Natasha Wagner had been uprooted from somewhere else not so long ago, someplace livelier and better than this dead-end shithole.

Funny thing, that. He spent so much time resenting his parents for moving to Ransom. Most among his small circle of friends expressed similar sentiments. There were times when it seemed it was all they could talk about. How much they wanted out. How they were just marking time until the day came when they could leave this godforsaken slice of backwoods hell. And yet...a part of him was definitely glad he was here, mostly because he would never have met Natasha otherwise.

She kicked at a piece of gravel on the driveway. It went skittering across the asphalt and bounced off a rear tire of his beat-up '86 Camaro, which was parked at the top of the driveway. "You got something for me?"

Mark produced the Southern Comfort bottle from his jacket pocket. He screwed the cap off, took a swig, and passed it to her. She put the bottle to her lips and tipped her head back, taking several deep swallows. When she was done, she wiped her mouth with the back of a wrist and passed the now much depleted bottle back to him.

Mark stared at the bottle in mock astonishment. "*Damn.*"

She smiled again. "Thirsty."

"Fuck. I guess so."

He took a smaller swig and screwed the cap back on before tucking the bottle away again. "So what do you wanna do?"

"You."

Mark laughed.

Natasha wasn't smiling now. "Serious."

Marked stopped laughing. This wasn't a joke. "Whoa. Wow."

Now she smiled. Just a little one that dimpled the edges of her mouth. It made him stare at her lips, which looked plumper than usual. And darker. The sweet curve of her mouth had never looked so inviting. He realized she'd applied fresh lipstick very recently, something she rarely did prior to their nighttime excursions. There was a reason for that. Only an idiot wouldn't get it. The deviation in her routine was a conscious thing. Between now and the time he'd seen her last—at the end of the school day—she'd made up her mind about something.

Something involving him.

Holy shit, I'm probably gonna fuck her tonight.

Yes, all signs pointed to Mark Bell getting laid. And that was an infinitely cool fucking thing to happen any time, but with this girl there was something extra special about it. God, she was so beautiful. Those lips. That delicate jawline. The big eyes and meticulously tweezed eyebrows. The cascade of lush black hair over her shoulder. The slender but achingly feminine body. She wore a very short black skirt over tight black leggings, accentuating the shapeliness of her legs and roundness of her ass. The very small Emily the Strange baby doll t-shirt made her medium-sized breasts much larger than usual.

He wanted desperately to kiss her.

To...to...

She put a hand over her mouth and giggled.

Mark blinked. "What?"

She pointed at his crotch. "Your...bulge."

Another giggle.

Mark glanced down and saw what she was talking about. A massive hard-on tented the crotch of his jeans. "Oh...shit."

She laughed again. "It's okay. I'm not offended. It's just...wow."

Mark reached into his pants and adjusted the angle of his erection. She could say she wasn't offended all she wanted, but it was goddamn embarrassing to leave it poking out like that.

Natasha's expression turned solemn with shocking suddenness. "Oh."

Mark frowned. "What?"

"It's just that..." She sighed and looked sad. "...I don't know if all that...will fit in my mouth."

Hysterical feminine laughter.

Mark groaned. "Wow. You are really fucking funny."

She giggled more.

"Wait. This mean you're gonna blow me?"

"We can start there."

He took a step toward her, eager hands reaching for her. She placed the palm of a small hand flat against his chest and stopped him in his tracks. "Whoa. Not so fast. I mean, you can kiss me, whatever. But the fucking has to wait."

He groaned again. "What? Why? We could get in my car—"

She shook her head, adamant. "No. I've got a better idea."

"Yeah?"

"Yeah."

"So tell me."

"You know that creepy old house?"

He knew the house. They all did. Their friend Derek McGregor had stumbled across it during a solo outing one night several months back. Derek liked to venture out alone a lot. It wasn't that he was antisocial. Well, no more than the rest of them. Within the group, though, he was as relatively gregarious as any of them. He had some quirks. Again, it went with the territory. You didn't get to be a Dark One by being Joe or Jane Normal. One of Derek's things was that he liked to go exploring. He would walk out deep into the woods and poke around. He was sort of an amateur archaeologist. Sometimes he found cool things. A rusted canteen with the letters CSA stamped across the bottom. A rusted pistol with the cylinder removed. Another time, way out there, he found a small cluster of ramshackle dwellings that looked barely large enough to have housed actual human beings, but the things he found there—ancient pots and pans, shattered plates, and so on—indicated otherwise.

The house was his latest and greatest discovery. It wasn't as deep into the woods as the slave shacks, but was significantly further down from Wheaton Hills on the other side of Weakley Lane. The house wasn't very big, a typical one-story old Ranch. It was in an advanced state of disrepair. Its windows were boarded-up and heavy bolts with padlocks were secured across the front and back doors. A narrow, wildly overgrown path leading to Weakley Lane had clearly once functioned as a driveway. A broken down old Buick Special sat on blocks in a clearing in front of the house.

But it wasn't the isolation or symptoms of neglect that made the house spooky.

It just felt somehow...*wrong*.

Something in the atmosphere seemed to *shift* any time you stepped into the small clearing. The very ground seemed tainted. It felt like a place where something had gone wrong long ago. It was a place of rot and decay. Of death.

So, of course, it had appealed to all of them instantly.

He certainly wasn't surprised that Natasha had mentioned it now.

"You want to go there."

A statement, not a question.

She came closer to him, reached for his hands, clasped them. "I don't just want to go to the house, Mark."

He swallowed with difficulty. "Y-yeah?"

"I want to go inside."

He frowned. "But—"

"We'll break in."

Her lips grazed his neck, slid across his throat. Mark clenched her hands tighter. "Break...in?"

"Uh huh." She lifted her head and kissed a corner of his chin. "And when we get inside, we'll...well..."

He forced his mouth open and sucked in a great breath. "Yeah?"

"I want you to fuck me in that house, Mark."

"God..."

She tugged at his hand, silently urging him to come with her.

He did not resist.

SIX

Ransom, TN
Hollis House
December 6, 1984

She was bleeding.

Christ, but she was bleeding. Little spurts of red jetted from the ragged gash in her scalp. Norman Campbell wasn't a doctor, but he figured you didn't need to be one to know that couldn't be good. Holy hell, she was either dying, or well on her way to death if he didn't do something about it—and soon.

How had it all gone so wrong so fast?

The call had come in at a little after noon, barely an hour ago. It was pure dumb luck he'd even been there at the time. Norman was president of Ransom Lumber & Supply. The Big Boss Man. He had a couple dozen employees working for him in the company he'd inherited from his own father nine years earlier, after the old man kicked off following a botched bypass operation. On a normal day, he wouldn't be anywhere near the office between the hours of eleven and two. Those were the hours when he would gather with a couple of the other local fat cats for a "business lunch" at the Jackson Steakhouse. Their "business" typically consisted of smoking cigars, drinking whiskey, and telling raunchy stories. And maybe a little flirting with one of the cute waitresses. Norman had been to bed with one or two of the little honeys, bet your ass.

Point was, he should be there right now. Maybe laughing it up with the fellas over the latest tall tales of lewd ladies

32

and close calls with cuckolded husbands (some of which were even true). Or having a halfway serious conversation with Mayor Harper about some ideas for local property development. For damn sure, he should have three or more stiff whiskey drinks in him by now.

He could use a goddamn drink.

Louella Hollis rolled onto her back and reached a trembling hand toward him. He watched a thick trickle of blood spill down her forehead and fork into two thinner crimson streams at the bridge of her nose. The blood began to pool in the corners of her eyes. She blinked slowly, laboriously, unable to clear her eyes as consciousness began to ebb.

"Shit." Norman kicked at a rock on the ground. "Shit and double shit. You dumb little bitch."

Goddamn his work ethic. It was the whole reason he'd been there instead of shooting the shit with the fellas at the Jackson. Ransom Lumber & Supply had recently taken on a big new account, maybe their biggest, and he'd been waiting on a call from the new client's head honcho, Rich Winchester, when the phone in his office rang.

It wasn't Rich Winchester on the other end.

"We need to talk," she told him.

Her morose, almost numb tone made him instantly wary. She didn't sound much like the vivacious young secretary he'd hired only nine months earlier. Back then she'd been bubbly, good-humored, and good-looking, just the way he liked. A good time party girl who knew how to let her hair down and be one of the fellas when the time was right. He was poking her almost daily inside of a month. At first it'd been wonderful. She made him feel young. Made him feel like a stud, like J.R. Ewing on *Dallas,* a real mover and shaker, the cock of the walk.

That all changed three months later.

The first time she suggested he hire a hitman to kill his wife.

Turned out she wasn't satisfied being the boss man's fun fling on the side. She wanted to be a big shot's wife. It struck

Norman as a little funny. A gal into that kind of cold-blooded social climbing would've been better off just about anywhere other than a little bump in the road like Ransom. He told her this, suggesting maybe she'd be happier in Nashville or Memphis. He could giver her some references, maybe set her up in a sweet deal with some likely fellas in a big city...

She wasn't interested.

"I want her dead. It's all I can think about, Normie."

He'd tried to laugh it off again. "Lord, the way you think would spook a man of lesser fortitude. You want to take Audrey's place. Fine. Dandy. There are other ways to make that happen, like divorce. Why you gotta jump straight to murder?"

"Don't make fun of me."

"I'm not."

"You're calling me crazy."

Crazier than a shithouse rat, he thought.

But what he actually said was, "Nonsense."

"Now you're calling me stupid."

He sighed.

This conversation was a long walk down a dark, dark alley, and there looked to be only one way out. It was time to be assertive.

"Darlin', I reckon it's time you start looking into other career options."

He'd allowed himself to hope that was the end of it. He should have known better. No one willing to broach the idea of cold-blooded murder was going to go quietly.

"Talk about what?" he'd asked her an hour ago, playing innocent.

"You know. You and me."

He'd started to get angry. "There is no you and me. Thought I made that clear. Now I'm gonna hang up, and I don't want to hear—"

"I have pictures. Compromising pictures."

His heart almost stopped. "What?"

"I have tape recordings. Listen."

He heard a click from the other end, followed by his own

voice. And then her voice. A goddamn recording. And there was no mistaking what was happening in the recording. Norman was shaken. His whole world was crumbling to pieces around him. Desperation engulfed him.

"Come see me," she told him. "We'll talk."

What choice did he have?

He followed her directions down Weakley Lane, a lonely stretch of two-lane rural road that was mostly just woods on both sides once you got past the old National Guard base. All those tall trees spooked him. He made a mental note to feel out some developers he knew, see if any of them might be interested in knocking out a few hundred acres worth of these damn trees to put in a subdivision or two.

He slowed down as he neared mile marker 6 and kept an eye on the opposite side of the road, just like she told him. And pretty soon he saw the narrow dirt path she'd described as a driveway. Bullshit. Proper driveways were paved. The sight of the dilapidated old house as he pulled into the clearing set the hairs on the nape of his neck to prickling. But it wasn't just the house that stirred the feeling of unease. There'd been a shift in the atmosphere as he'd entered the clearing. It was noticeable even nestled in the warmth of his 1982 Cadillac Seville. It unsettled him and he nearly turned around and left right then. It was what he should have done.

Then he saw her.

She was sitting on the porch of the old house, looking prim in a long skirt and a thick sweater. The attire was a far cry from the revealing outfits she'd favored around the office. He parked the Seville next to an old Buick Special that sat rusting on blocks in the center of the clearing, got out, and approached her warily.

"Damn, darlin', why did you drag me out to this old dump?"

"Family property. It belonged to my grandfather, Frank Hollis. He died a long time ago."

Hollis.

Huh.

Now why did that name all of a sudden ring a dim

bell? Something about it triggered a faint tingle of unease. There was something he couldn't quite put his finger on, an association lurking just beyond the limits of conscious memory.

Screw it.

It'd come to him later.

He nodded at the manila envelope clutched in her small hands. "Let me guess. Some of your dirty pictures. Ain't nothin' lower than a blackmailer. You know that, right?"

She came off the porch and approached him, stopping just a few feet away. "It doesn't have to be like that. You can still do what needs doing."

He scowled. "Once and for all, I ain't killin' my wife." He snatched the envelope from her unresisting fingers and tore it open. His gut knotted up as he shuffled through the large black and white prints. "Oh, lord..."

"Just copies, Norman. I have others hidden away. I needed you to see, so you'd know how serious I am."

He saw, all right.

More than enough.

He hadn't even known he was going to do it. He smashed a fist into her temple and sent her staggering across the clearing. She pitched forward after a few steps and the top of her head slammed into the side of the old Buick. The sound her head made when it impacted the solid metal was sickening.

And now look at her.

He tried to stay calm.

There had to be a way out of this.

He snatched up the handbag she'd dropped, undid the clasp, and rooted around inside. He found her keys right away. An idea began to form. It was risky. But he had to do it. He had too much to lose. He would go back to town. Let himself inside Louella's little house and go over it with a fine-tooth comb, find anything incriminating there and destroy it. Then figure out what to do with Louella and her Fiat Spider, which was parked at the edge of the clearing.

Louella groaned and reached a trembling hand toward

him again. She lifted her head and struggled to sit.

Norman grimaced. "I don't think so, honey."

He scoured the ground around him and found a rock big enough to fit in his fist. He kept her pinned down with a knee and smashed the rock into her head again and again.

There was a lot more blood.

And, finally, a sickening crack as her skull fractured.

Louella Hollis was dead.

SEVEN

It was late October and the air outdoors at this hour was getting a bit nippy. Derek McGregor shivered and puffed on his cigarette as he sat on the top step of the abandoned house's front porch. He exhaled and the smoke plumed in the night air. "Fuck, it's so fucking cold."

His voice sounded strange in the otherwise empty clearing. He rarely spoke aloud when he was alone. Sane people kept their thoughts internalized when not in the company of other human beings. This was a thing he believed strongly. His mother talked to herself so often he frequently overheard her when she believed no one else was around. And a lot of things she said were flat-out fucking crazy. Like, she would maybe drop a plate and start screaming. Just going on and on, like, "YOU DID THAT ON FUCKING PURPOSE! LIKE I HAVEN'T HAD ENOUGH FUCKING SHIT TO DEAL WITH TODAY! YOU FUCKING PLANNED THAT! FUCK YOU!"

The plate-dropping thing had happened just a couple days ago, on Sunday. Derek had just left his room after an afternoon nap and was slowly descending the stairs in his sock feet. He came to a dead stop halfway down the staircase as Suzie McGregor's outburst rang out from the kitchen

His mother was nuts. There was no other explanation. He had no idea who she was addressing in those moments. God, maybe? But she'd never been a particularly religious woman, at least not in his memory. It was more like she believed she was being persecuted or conspired against by some undefined cosmic force. You could call it God, but it could as easily be a demon or other malicious supernatural entity. She never invoked God's name when she was raging like that. But whatever. Derek was content to leave it a mystery. He sure as shit wasn't about to quiz her on the matter. She'd be furious to have her mental state questioned by her son, of all people.

So he had attempted a hasty retreat. He turned around and began to ascend the stairs back to the second floor, but one of the stairs creaked too loudly.

"What the fuck are you doing?"

The words had almost stopped his heart. "N-nothing."

"You were spying on me. Weren't you? Get down here! Now!"

He did as she said. She was his mother. He lived in her house. He started down the stairs and she snagged him by the hair when he got within grabbing distance. She dragged him into the kitchen and slammed him down in a chair, ordering him to lay a hand flat on the kitchen table. He again did as ordered, starting to cry as she went into the pantry and came back with a shiny metal spatula. It was the one his father used for flipping burgers on the grill in the summer. She struck the back of his hand with it numerous times, making him cry out and beg for mercy. But she remained silent and unyielding as she struck him over and over. He lost count of the blows somewhere around twenty.

"Are you going to spy on me again?"

"Never. I promise."

"Are you sorry?"

"Yes."

"Say it!"

"I'm s-sorry."

"Good. Now go up to your room and don't come down until tomorrow."

He'd gone up to his room, all right.

And then out the window and out of the house, staying gone all through the next day. He usually returned at dawn, slipping back in through the window and coming down in a fresh change of clothes after a shower, pretending to have been asleep in his bed all night. But that time he hadn't bothered with the pretense and hadn't returned home until dawn the following day. He'd expected a stern lecture and interrogation, but neither of his parents had said a word about his absence. He wasn't too surprised by this, but it hurt him more than he'd anticipated.

They didn't give a shit about him.

Yet another thing he had in common with most of his friends, sort of a unifying factor kind of deal. He thought of an old saying—*Home is where the heart is.*

It was corny, but true.

His home, his real one, was out here in the dark with his friends, who were more like family to him than any actual blood relative. *We are The Dark Ones*, he thought, and chuckled. It'd started as a joke. A few of them had been drinking and smoking weed. Mark and Natasha had been there. Kevin. Fiona. They had been out all night and it was almost time to part again. They'd all been feeling pretty goofy as the first hint of dawn began to tinge the sky. There was a lot of rambling talk about music and movies. They all liked horror and strange shit in general. They joked about how very *dark* they all were. And it was Natasha who'd intoned in a low, darkly sinister voice, sounding like some cheesy late night horror host, "*We...are...the...DARK ONES.*"

A joke, yes.

But it struck a nerve. The name stuck.

Derek stubbed out his cigarette, shook another from the pack, and struck a match. He was applying the flame to the cigarette when he heard the crunch of booted feet trampling twigs somewhere near the edge of the clearing. He didn't look up right away. He knew who it was.

A fact confirmed a moment later when a voice called out to him: "Aren't you fucking cold?"

Derek shrugged. The smoke was lit. "I am impervious to cold. I am a fucking super Eskimo."

"Eskimos wear fucking parkas and shit when it's cold, dumbass, not just some fucking t-shirt."

Derek blew out a cloud of smoke. "You know not the ancient ways of the wise super Eskimos. Give me a beer."

Jared Kelly hefted the case of Budweiser cans by its cardboard handle. "Stuck this out in the drainage ditch by my house yesterday. At least it won't be puke warm like last time."

"Yeah. Lucky it didn't rain, lardass."

A broad grin stretched across Jared's slightly doughy face. He was a good thirty pounds or so overweight, but he was also tall and large of frame, with big biceps and thick wrists. No one outside his circle of friends would ever dare give him shit about his weight.

"A lardass I may be, but I can lose weight and you're *always* gonna be ugly, son."

Derek laughed. He knew he wasn't ugly. Girls liked him, despite his strangeness. "I don't know about that, man, but I do know I'm way too fucking sober. Beer me."

Jared approached the porch and set the case of Bud down on the top step. He ripped a corner of the big carton open, pulled out a can, and said, "Help yourself." He knocked back a slug of Bud and made a sound of satisfaction. "You know what I like about beer?"

"What?"

"Everything."

Derek opened a can. "I'd kill for some pint of vodka, though. I like to get fucked up faster."

Jared laughed. "You want to commit murder, do it just for kicks. Campbell will get you the booze."

Clayton Campbell was the older guy they hung out with sometimes. He had a house in the neighborhood. He sold them pot now and then and sometimes bought them booze, usually at jacked up prices. Which was a ripoff. The guy had plenty of cashola. He just did it because he could.

Derek frowned. "Can't afford the surcharge."

Jared tilted his head back and gulped down the rest of his first brew. "Shit, I'll give you the money. Or just pay Clayton for it myself."

Derek shrugged. "Cool, whatever."

Jared's father was CEO of Stanton Manufacturing. He gave his son a generous weekly allowance. Which was sort of putting it mildly. Jared had more money coming in on a weekly basis than any minimum wage-earning student at Ransom High School. He was as messed up as any of them, but he had one up on the rest of his friends in one significant way—his parents didn't loathe him.

Jared popped the tab on his second beer and glanced up at the half-gabled hip roof on the left end of the old house. He shivered. "Fucking creepy."

Derek twisted his neck to get a look at the house from Jared's perspective. The window up there was boarded, like every other possible means of entry. Someone had painted a pentagram on the board covering the window long ago. The black spray paint was nearly as faded as the blue paint flaking away from the outer walls.

"Makes you wonder."

Jared grunted between sips of beer. "Wonder what?"

Still staring at the pentagram—which the moonlight rendered dimly distinguishable amidst the shadows cast by the roof's angles—Derek said, "Makes you wonder what happened here." His head swiveled back toward Jared. "That fucking pentagram's there for a reason, I can feel it."

Jared snorted. "Right. Maybe you shouldn't watch so many horror movies."

"Fuck that. And anyway, you can feel it, too. Tell me I'm lying."

Jared glanced at the pentagram again. "I feel something, but whatever. Show me an abandoned old house out in the woods that's not a little bit creepy. Ain't any such thing. It's just a house. And it's been here fucking forever. You think you were the first to find it? No way. Maybe some Black Sabbath-listening stoner from 1973 or whatever painted that thing." He nodded. "Yeah, I can see that."

Derek didn't reply.

It was too easy to imagine. So easy he could see the scene vividly in his head—some lanky longhair with a head full of acid and Sabbath tunes crawling around up there on the roof with a bucket of black paint.

"BOO, BITCHES!"

Derek shot to his feet as Jared dropped his beer and whirled toward the source of the sound. Derek turned in the same direction, unconsciously positioning himself so that Jared's bulk was between him and the intruder. A dark form moved out of the shadows near the side of the house. It was carrying something long and dangerous-looking.

Then Derek got a look at the intruder's face and groaned. "You asshole."

Smug laughter. "Scared ya, huh?"

Derek showed Kevin Cooper a middle finger. "Fuck you, douchebag. Hold on. Is that what I think it is?"

"Yeah, if you think it's a fucking sledgehammer. If you think it's a bag of fluffy bunnies, I don't know what to tell you."

Kevin approached the porch with the sledgehammer propped over one shoulder. He grabbed a brew from the Bud carton and popped the tab.

Derek frowned. "Where in fuck did you get a fucking sledgehammer?"

Kevin knocked back half his first brew in one go and belched loudly. "You know that shed behind the Carlton place?"

"Uh huh."

"Broke into that. Found some funny shit. The most massive collection of Playboy magazines you've ever fucking seen. Snagged a few of those. And there was a mannequin. Like a full-sized lady mannequin. Weird shit. And there was this." He lifted the sledgehammer off his shoulder, set the heavy end on the ground, and leaned on the handle. "A fucking monster-ass sledgehammer."

Derek grabbed another beer. "So why'd you take it?"

Kevin smiled.

"Oh." Awareness dawned. Derek looked at the house. The shadows at the far end of the porch, where the boarded front door was located, seemed more sinister now, as if something malign lurked there. Some kind of...*thing*.

But that was ridiculous.

Wasn't it?

Kevin climbed the steps to the porch and turned to face them. "I'm getting up in this bitch tonight. Who's with me?"

"Um..."

"Don't be a pussy."

The magic words. What guy his age wouldn't rise to that provocation?

He sighed and glanced at Jared, who shrugged.

Jared looked unperturbed. "Whatever. "

They joined Kevin on the long porch and approached the door.

EIGHT

A little earlier...

Her husband's snoring brought Suzie McGregor out of her light doze. She glanced at the clock on the nightstand and saw it wasn't yet midnight. Kurt turned over in his sleep. The shifting of his bulk caused the headboard to thump the wall. Suzie looked at him. Even in this darkness, his form a dark outline beneath the heavy blanket, she felt that familiar reflexive disgust. He'd been a real stud before they were married, powerfully built and fit, but over time all that muscle had turned to mush and he'd become immensely fat. As always, she couldn't help comparing him to Tom Bell. They were the same age, but Tom worked out and kept himself in shape. It was a rotten shame that bitch wife of his had found out about them. Tom wasn't just fitter and better-looking than Kurt, he was an infinitely better lay. Suzie clenched her fists in frustration. She needed a man again.

She glanced at her husband.

A *real* man.

She thought of Tom again and slipped a hand between her legs. She closed her eyes and moaned softly.

Yes, here we go...this is nice...

She shifted her hips and moaned again.

What the hell—self-love is better than no love at all...

A loud creak snapped her eyes open. She lifted her head and stared at the closed bedroom door. Several silent seconds passed. She lifted her torso, propping herself on her elbows. Her heart was racing. The sound could have been just the house settling, but it was possible there was an intruder.

45

They didn't have an alarm system. Stupid Kurt. He thought he was the only line of defense they needed against anyone foolish enough to invade his territory. Typical example of his self-deluding ways. He was a big old pig of a man, but he imagined he was some kind of badass. Suzie almost hoped there was an intruder. A naughty—but undeniably arousing—scenario came to life in her head...

The bedroom door crashes open. A muscular man dressed all in tight-fitting black and wearing a ski mask comes into the room. Tom gets up and tangles with the intruder, but the brute knocks Kurt out with one powerful blow and spots Suzie cringing beneath the blanket. He licks his lips and yanks the blanket away to stare at her shapely form, which is clad only in the very small silk nightgown. He climbs onto the bed and reaches for her, tears the flimsy garment from her sweat-sheened body, and—

The creak came again, louder than before, and this time her head snapped toward the large window overlooking their back yard. She looked at Kurt again to see if the sound had stirred him. He was facing her now and she could see his slack, doughy features in refracted moonlight. A thin stream of drool leaked from a corner of his mouth to stain the sheet. Jesus. He was so gross. It was so unfair. She was sexy. Men gave her long looks all the time. She deserved better than this giant bucket of goo masquerading as a man. The universe conspired against her in a lot of ways, but the most blatant of all was the way it'd stuck her with this asshole.

And now there was another sound from outside.

A loud thump as something hit the ground.

Suzie eased the blanket away from her body and slipped out of bed. The hardwood floor was cool beneath her bare feet as she padded over to the window and slipped a finger between the drapes, pulling the edge of one back far enough to get a glimpse of a dark-clad form scaling the high, slatted wooden fence. The figure was moving fast. Its speed and the darkness made identification impossible. It was gone in seconds. A tall oak tree with thick branches stood just outside the window. Her son's bedroom was directly above their own. One of the tree's thickest branches was close to the window up there.

Was Derek sneaking out of his room at night?

She didn't know whether she should feel fury, concern, or some mixture of both. Something within that spectrum would be a normal parental reaction, especially considering it was also possible the form she'd glimpsed hadn't been Derek. Perhaps there'd been an intruder, after all, someone who'd specifically come to harm Derek. Her son was a good-looking boy, despite his absurd "outsider" posing, a tempting target for a certain kind of sexual predator. She thought instantly of Clay Campbell. Campbell was about forty and lived alone in a house at the top of steep Laural Hill Drive. He was a frequent subject of neighborhood gossip. Kids in the neighborhood were often seen hanging around his house. There was something not right about him. He didn't seem to work, for one thing. Suzie was certain he was some kind of pervert.

She pictured it in her mind. Clay Campbell going up the big tree, then crawling out that short distance along that thick branch to Derek's bedroom window. It wasn't an easy thing to envision. Campbell was on the chubby side. But that wouldn't matter if he was determined. She imagined him sliding the window open and slipping inside unheard by her sleeping son. Or...and this hadn't occurred to her until now...what if Derek had been waiting for him? Suzie felt a flutter of disgust. Was her son a homosexual? The notion disturbed her more than the possibility of an assault. She didn't like queers. That wasn't the correct way to think anymore. It wasn't a thing she could say out loud to most people. But it was how she really felt. She simply could not have a gay son.

Suzie moved from the window and crossed the room to Kurt's walk-in closet. She took one of his belts from a hook and wound one end of it twice around her right hand. The buckle end dangled, brushing the floor. She slipped out of the bedroom, electing not to wake her oblivious husband. He wouldn't have the balls to do what needed doing. If her son was queer, she was going to whip the perversity right out of him.

Upstairs, she tried the doorknob, but it was locked and wouldn't turn. Of course. The boy wouldn't risk being caught in the act of something perverted. Well, tough shit. She had some tricks of her own.

The room on the other side of the hall was used primarily for storage. It was crowded with boxes and miscellaneous junk. She entered the room and flicked on the light switch. She negotiated her way through the haphazardly stacked boxes and came to a small desk wedged into a corner. The top drawer contained an array of mostly useless items. She rooted through the assortment of crap and soon found the perfect thing at the bottom—a hairpin.

The lock on her son's bedroom door was simple and not designed for heavy duty security purposes. Suzie slid the hairpin through a hole in the center of the knob and probed for the latch. She found it, pushed, and heard the lock pop open.

Smiling, she pushed the door open and stepped into the room. The smile faded when she flipped on the light switch and saw that her son wasn't in the room.

Derek was sneaking out, after all.

She felt a strange disappointment at not having caught him in some compromising situation. She'd been looking forward to whipping the boy with the belt. She had a lot of anger. A lot of frustration. She needed a way to vent some of that. Her son happened to be a handy target sometimes. It wasn't a normal thing. A lot of people would think there was something wrong with her if they could hear her thoughts. Luckily, most people could not hear thoughts, and she tried to avoid the ones she suspected of possessing the ability.

She closed the door behind her and walked further into the room.

"It's okay, DeeDee." Her smile returned. "You'll be back. We'll deal with you then."

Because he still needed to be punished. The boy was still a minor and he would live by her rules as long as he lived under her roof. Sneaking out of the house in the middle of the night—on a school night, no less—merited some level of correction. Of discipline.

She sat on the edge of her son's twin-sized bed. She plucked at the hem of her silk nightgown and was surprised by the abrupt sound of her own laugh. She looked like a woman dressed for seduction rather than a concerned mother come to punish her wayward son. What would Derek have thought if he'd actually seen her like this? It might have done him some good. She was his mother, yes, but she was very attractive. She had a curvaceous, womanly figure. A boy his age should see a full grown woman in bedroom attire at some point.

She smiled and began to feel naughty again.

Maybe the belt wouldn't be necessary.

Maybe something other than an act of discipline would occur when her son returned. After all, there was no real evidence her son was anything other than heterosexual. And she would hardly be the first mother to...

She frowned.

It was happening again.

Those thoughts she knew would upset or horrify anyone who heard them. She experienced a moment of deep anxiety. But the moment passed and the anxiety eased. She was alone. No one was around to tune in to her thoughts. And the cosmic forces that were always fucking with her couldn't hurt her so long as she just sat here quietly and waited.

So she sat right there on the edge of his bed and studied his things. The walls were adorned with rock band posters. Hatebreed. Killswitch Engage. Slayer. There were stacks of paperbacks on his desk. *Fear and Loathing In Las Vegas. The Electric Kool-Aid Acid Test. The Anarchist's Cookbook.* And several other titles obviously inappropriate for a young child. There were bad influences everywhere she looked.

Something else to have a long talk with him about when he returned.

Suzie scooted backward on the bed, stretched out, and turned onto her side to stare at the dark window and the pale branches of the tree outside.

She let go of the belt and slid the tips of her fingers over a bare hip.

The bad, forbidden thoughts surfaced again, more vibrant and vivid than before.

She hoped Derek would be back soon.

NINE

Kent Hickerson was having a restless night. This lying wide awake and staring up at the ceiling for hours business was not normal for him. It was annoying and frustrating. It was now almost midnight and he was as awake and alert as he normally was at school in the middle of the day.

He sighed. "This is fucked."

Maybe he should just surrender and get up for a while. Maybe find something cool to watch on cable. Have a midnight snack. The notion had an unexpected appeal. Kent was a guy who appreciated a sense of order in all things. Nighttime was for sleeping. A good night's rest was crucial for excelling during the day. He planned to be a successful man one day. A rich man. To make that happen it was necessary to adhere to a rigid self-discipline. The mindset had paid off so far. His grades were stellar, yet he wasn't some uncool egghead. He was popular with the girls because he was very conscious of the importance of proper grooming and wearing the right things. He always looked well put together, but with just enough safe pseudo-edginess to avoid the curse of coming off like a straitlaced bore. He was one of Ransom High's most popular seniors, a status he was certain would set the tone for the rest of his life.

And yet...

He kept thinking of that midnight snack.

His stomach growled.

"Fuck it."

Clearly the only viable way of dealing with this crazy impulse was to indulge it. He would get up and have a sandwich. Roast beef. Some crunchy chips. Tomorrow night

50

he would slip back into his normal routine. Tonight had to be a one-time deviation from the norm. He reached for the lamp on his nightstand and switched it on, blinking his eyes against the sudden glare. He tossed the blanket aside and swung his legs over the side of the bed. His intent was to go directly to the kitchen, but a random impulse caused him to get up and go to his bedroom window.

He tugged at an edge of the curtain and peered outside.

He saw nothing remarkable at first. The neighborhood was quiet, undisturbed by sirens or the constant sound of car engines and horns, which had constituted the nighttime soundtrack of his city life as a child. Wheaton Hills went to sleep at night. It was very still and peaceful. But what was this? He glimpsed movement just outside the sphere of light projected by the closest street lamp, on the other side of the narrow residential street. He kept his eye on the street, hoping to see whatever he'd seen again. Several seconds passed. Nothing happened.

Then there they were.

Two people, a boy and a girl, stepped into the light. Their features were clearly defined beneath the glare of the street lamp for perhaps as long as two seconds before they continued down the street and again became two indistinct forms moving through the night. The boy was Mark Bell, who lived in the house directly across the street. Mark's dad was a big deal, an executive at Stanton. The girl was Natasha Wagner. He was pretty sure she lived in Wheaton Hills, too, a few streets over in one of the newer sections. He saw her in the hallways of Ransom High now and then and was always struck by her beauty. But she was the wrong sort for him. Too edgy. And it wasn't just a pose. Her body language was rife with suggestions of potential violence and danger. You couldn't mess with a girl like that. Besides, she was always hanging out with the wrong type.

Like Mark Bell.

Tom Bell was an important man, no doubt about it.

But his son was a world class troublemaker. There weren't many people who actually frightened Kent Hickerson, but

Mark Bell did. He was big and muscular from years of lifting weights. He had an athlete's physique, but no apparent interest in sports, which just added to his already high weirdo quotient. Seeing him out there wandering the streets of Wheaton Hills at an hour when any decent person was in bed unsettled him.

The Dark Ones come out at night...

Kent had seen the slogan. And he'd heard the rumors about those kids. But he'd never taken them seriously.

Until now.

Seeing them out there offended his belief in the necessity of adhering to a set of rules and regulations. They'd been heading away from Mark's house, off to who knew where, and he doubted they'd be back any time soon. Did they do this every night? It was what he'd heard But when did they sleep? He saw them in school nearly every day. They weren't ditchers. It was a mystery. And he didn't like mysteries.

He moved away from the window and grabbed his cell phone from the nightstand. He selected a recipient from his contacts list and keyed in a text message: ARE YOU AWAKE? I SAW SOMETHING.

He hit the Send button.

He sat there and waited for a reply, knowing it might not come. It was possible they wouldn't be able to discuss this until the next day. But the phone buzzed in his hand a few moments later as the reply came through: AWAKE. CAN'T BELIEVE U R THO. WHAT'S UP?

Kent keyed in his response: I SAW THEM. THE DARK ONES. OUT IN THE STREET.

The reply came almost immediately: THE DORK ONES? REALLY? LMFAO! WHAT ABOUT THEM?

Kent hesitated. He didn't need the kind of trouble the thing he wanted to say might start. But he thought of Mark Bell's face illumined in the light of the street lamp and felt that unsettled feeling winding through his guts again.

The hell with it.

He punched buttons on the keypad.

WE HAVE TO DO SOMETHING ABOUT THEM.

TEN

"Did you see that light come on?"

"Yeah."

"And that shape at the window?"

"Yeah."

"Who lives over there?"

Mark laughed. "The Hickersons."

"What's so funny?"

Mark shrugged. "You know who Kent Hickerson is, right?"

"Know *of* him, don't know him."

"But you know his reputation."

"King of the douchebags."

Mark smiled. "That's right. He thinks he's fucking perfect. But he's so fake."

"How so?"

"You can tell he spends hours every day thinking about what clothes to wear and how to style his hair. He poses a lot. Like he thinks he's a model or pop star, indulging the fucking paparazzi. It's fucking hilarious. I just burst out laughing at the guy at school one day and he got all upset."

"Home come you never told me that before?"

"Because nothing happened. He's a pussy."

"You think that was him in the window?"

"Don't know. Maybe."

Mark took out the Southern Comfort bottle again. He spun the cap off and took a generous swallow. The alcohol was already acting on his system, igniting the first little tingle of intoxication. He took another swallow and passed the bottle to Natasha, who, as before, knocked back an even

53

bigger helping. He wondered about that. Either she really loved Southern Comfort or she was showing off, maybe demonstrating what a tough chick she was. A girl who could handle her booze, as much as any guy, maybe more. The idea that she might want to impress him was kind of cool.

"You're staring."

Mark blinked. "What?"

"You're staring at me. Like you're in a trance. Look." She touched a corner of his mouth, wiped away a speck of moisture with the ball of a thumb. "You're drooling."

She giggled.

"*Ma-ark likes me. Ma-ark likes me.*"

She was making fun of him. But it didn't bother him. "Yeah. I do."

"Of course you do. I'm awesome."

"I know."

She grabbed him and kissed him sudden enthusiasm. He staggered a bit and wrapped his arms around her to keep from falling over. She pressed into him, continuing to kiss him, her mouth working against his with a hunger that made his whole body feel electrified. She broke the kiss off just as abruptly and they stood panting in the middle of the road, eyes locked, her hands hooked around the back of his neck.

"Holy shit."

Natasha made a purring sound. "Mmm. You taste like bubble gum and liquor."

"Uh...yeah. Had a stick of Doublemint earlier."

She pushed against him again. "You should see a doctor. There's a lump in your pants."

He held her tight and said, "You're the only cure for that." His eyes widened. "Oh, shit!"

Her face twisted with confusion. "Mark? What—"

No time to break it down for her. A police cruiser was at the far end of the block. Its blue lights weren't on and it was possible they hadn't been spotted yet, but that wouldn't last long. He seized Natasha by a wrist and dragged her into the closest yard. She yelped once, but quickly fell into step with him as they pounded across the grass and passed beneath the long and low-hanging branches of an old tree. In the darkness, the branches looked like the extended limbs and talons of some scary creature. It didn't take long to orient themselves. This was the Smith property. The house abutted a small field cleared out by bulldozers some time ago. Nothing had been built there yet and it was overgrown. Several huge slabs of rock had been pulled out of the ground from the field and placed along one side of the Smith property and down a small stretch along the edge of the front yard, forming an L-shaped barrier of granite. Neighborhood kids liked to play on the rock barrier. They would pretend to be soldiers storming a beach or ancient warriors guarding a stone fortress. There was a deep depression in the part of the field where the rocks had been excavated, but because the field was so overgrown, the depression wasn't obvious to the naked eye.

Mark risked a quick glance over his shoulder just before they reached the rock barrier. The cruiser's blue lights still weren't on, but its spotlight was. It was closer by half now, and the slowly rotating light was just beginning to turn in their direction.

They vaulted over the rock barrier and landed in the narrow dirt path between the rocks and the field, ducking as a wash of light approached. In the next instant they were plunging into the field and sliding down into the depression. Natasha gasped when Mark piled into her at the bottom of the hole. She twisted around in discomfort and got her body straightened out as he stretched out beside her. He put his face close to hers and started to speak: "Do you think—"

She clapped a hand over his mouth and shook her head.

He nodded and held his breath, waiting.

He turned his head in the direction of the road and stayed very still as he listened for the cruiser. Its engine soon became audible. The soft rumble indicated it was just sort of creeping along. This wasn't an unusual occurrence. Bored cops would occasionally make slow sweeps of the neighborhood because they had fuck all else to do. Ransom wasn't exactly a hotbed of criminal activity. So the local law liked to hassle the kids, especially newcomers.

Fucking asshole cops...

But the sound of the cruiser's engine faded at last. "Shit. That was close."

He braced his hands on the ground and started to push himself up.

Natasha grabbed the front of his shirt and pulled him back down.

"Hey. They're gone. What's—"

"I know."

She slid a cool hand inside his waistband and down the front of his jeans. Her hand curled around his dick and he instantly grew hard. He looked into her eyes, able to see her more clearly now that his eyes had adjusted to the deeper gloom of the hole. Her eyes looked very intent.

"I don't want to wait for the house."

"You mean..."

She nodded. "Yes. Right here. *Now.*"

Mark grinned.

Yes. Why not here?

She raised her mouth to kiss him even as her hand retreated from his cock to undo the button of his jeans. She tugged his underwear down and he uttered a shuddering moan as his erection sprang free and twitched in the cool air.

Then her hands came away from him as she started tugging at her own clothes.

He helped her.

ELEVEN

It sensed them.

The thing in the darkness.

For the second time in less than a day it stirred toward wakefulness, toward something close to full awareness. This was unusual, considering that very frequently years passed between stirrings. There had been shorter gaps, of course, times when weeks or only months passed. But this degree of frequency was almost without precedent. One other time, a decade or so back, it had stirred three times within a matter of hours. A volatile energy had emanated from the place above its prison. A wild, heady mix of anger, panic, and desperation.

And violence.

And death.

Someone, a human, had died somewhere in the vicinity.

Alas, the energy waned and the creature slipped back into its silent slumber, resigned to the dreary likelihood that a similarly energizing event might not occur for many more years or decades, if ever.

But something was happening now.

Somewhere...up above.

Humans had come to this blighted place again. It opened its inner eye—the one that felt rather than saw—and detected their unique psychic markers. It probed at the edges of their minds, which was the limit of its reach in the absence of some psychic upheaval (or removal from its prison).

It sensed something.

The humans...they were trying to come closer.

To come inside the house.

57

The air in the basement grew warmer and vibrated with demonic laughter.

Yes, it thought.

Come inside.

Come...to me.

Kevin slammed one blunt end of the sledgehammer against the heavy bolt fastened across the front door several times. The bolt didn't budge.

"Goddammit." Kevin wiped a sheen of sweat from his forehead. "Goddamn door might as well be a vault at Fort fucking Knox."

Jared shot a smirk at Derek. "Let me give it a try."

Derek smiled.

Now we get in.

Kevin shrugged. "Be my fuckin' guest."

Jared took the sledgehammer from him and twirled it easily in his hands, like a baseball slugger practicing his stance in an on-deck circle. The sledgehammer had been Kevin's find, so of course they'd deferred to him in the beginning, despite how obviously futile his efforts would be. Kevin wasn't exactly a weakling, but he lacked Jared's raw physical strength.

The muscles in Jared's arms bulged as he flexed his fingers. His face twisted as he brought the hammer down. There was a ferociously loud *CLANG!* The bolt sagged on the first blow as the thick screws holding it in place pulled partially free from the wood. Jared hefted the sledgehammer again and brought it down one more time. The bolt came all the way free and hit the porch with a clatter.

Kevin's grin was sheepish. "I, uh...loosened it for you."

Jared's belly heaved as laughter boomed out of him. "Yeah, man. Of course you did. That's what we call fuckin' teamwork."

Derek snorted.

That's what we call fuckin' bullshit.

Jared propped the sledgehammer's handle on one of his broad shoulders and slid the fingers of his right hand along an edge of the thick sheet of plywood nailed over the front door. "Knocking the bolt loose was the easy part. What we really need is a crowbar. And some flashlights."

Kevin popped the tab on another can. "Why do you need a fuckin' crowbar? Why not just bash your way in?"

"I could do that, I guess."

"So what the fuck?"

Jared looked at Derek and indicated the Bud carton with a tilt of his chin. "Beer me?"

Derek grabbed a beer out of the carton and tossed it to Jared, who snatched it out of the air in a one-handed grab and popped it open. "Bashing the plywood to pieces would be a lot of work. A lot of messy work. Splinters and shit flying everywhere. A crowbar is cleaner and simpler. We just pry the plywood off and then I knock the lock off the goddamn door."

Kevin was nodding. "Okay. Yeah. I can see that. But... flashlights?"

"It's gonna be dark in there, man. Like, really, seriously dark. I'm talking blackest pit of hell dark. And you can call me a pussy if you want—"

"Pussy."

Jared showed Kevin the middle finger of the hand gripping the Bud can. "Think about it. There'll be boards on every window in this place. And I'm not about to take them all off, man. I came out to party tonight, not work my fuckin' ass off. I also wanna see where I'm going once we get up in this motherfucker."

Derek glanced at Kevin. "Man's got a point." He swung himself over the porch railing and hopped down to the ground below. "I can get everything we need from my dad's work shed. And my house ain't that far. Don't you motherfuckers drink all that beer while I'm gone."

Kevin snickered. "I take that as a challenge. I'm drinkin' all these motherfuckers."

Jared shook his head. "Like hell you will. " He looked at Derek. "Hurry back."

Derek turned away from them and continued across

the clearing into the woods, where the darkness swallowed him. The fear he felt then surprised him. He knew his way through these woods better than anyone, could negotiate his way through them with nearly equal ease during the day or night. So why did it feel like the darkness was pulling at him tonight? Like it was a living thing and it was trying to wrap him up in its spiderweb-sticky embrace?

Fuck.

He knew it was crazy and irrational, but he couldn't fucking help how he felt.

He picked up his pace.

TWELVE

The doorbell rang.

Clayton Campbell was sitting on his sofa and watching *Doctor Who* on BBC America. He groaned and leaned forward to set his beer on the coffee table. The coffee table was overflowing with an accumulation of magazines and unsorted mail. He shoved a stack of unopened envelopes aside and set the bottle down on the heavily stained wood. He didn't use coasters, which meant the wood was imprinted with countless overlapping condensation rings from the bottles. It didn't matter. The only company he ever entertained tended not to be too picky or judgmental about such things. Most of them were kids coming to him for some favor or other.

They almost always came calling at night.

It was as if they were allergic to sunlight. If Clayton hadn't known better, he might have suspected they were vampires. They weren't vampires. Of course not. No such thing. Ditto for any other goddamn thing that supposedly went bump in the night. Just a bunch of made-up nonsense, despite the crazy things his cracked-in-the-head father used to tell him.

Despite his skepticism regarding all things supernatural, Clayton loved horror movies. Every now and then the so-called 'Dark Ones' (a name that never failed to make him chuckle) would hang out at his place for an all night marathon of splatter cinema classics. They had a special taste for the cheapest and sleaziest gorefests from his vast collection of movies, things like *Frankenhooker, Blood Feast, Blood Diner, The Driller Killer, Ilsa: She Wolf of the SS,* and *The*

Gates Of Hell, all of which had been made many years before any of his young guests had been born.

Sometimes he worried some of their parents would put together a lynch mob and come after him, determined to put an end to his negative influence. But the kids stayed out all hours of the night and slept when they got home from school. The goddamn parents obviously weren't involved in their lives in any meaningful way.

The doorbell rang again.

Still, it never hurt to be careful. Clayton got up with a grunt and winced at the creak of his knees as he walked out of the living room and into the foyer. A Louisville Slugger was propped in a corner next to the door. The fat end of the bat was heavy and solid. One good blow from that bad boy would lay out any intruder. Okay, so it wouldn't be much good against someone with a gun, but Clayton hated firearms. His father had committed suicide by blowing his brains out with a Smith & Wesson .38. A gun in the house would be a constant and unbearably painful reminder of that decade-old tragedy. But there was more to it than that. A gun in the house would also be a dangerous temptation. Clayton liked to drink. He liked to get high. He did these things alone a lot. And sometimes he got weepy and started feeling sorry for himself and regretful over the way his life had worked out. It was too easy to imagine opting for the same kind of exit his father had chosen.

He picked the bat up by the handle and put an eye to the peephole.

He set the bat down again and opened the door. "Hey, Fiona."

The girl standing on his porch smiled at him. It was chilly out and she was shivering slightly. Her hands were shoved down in the pockets of her black hoodie. "Hey, Clay. Can I come in?"

"Sure."

He stepped aside and held the door open for her. The slim girl slipped through the opening and stood shivering in his foyer. He closed the door and listened to her teeth chatter. She bounced up and down on her toes and nodded her head. She had a nice face. Really cute, with big eyes and high cheekbones. The dark eyeliner she wore made the eyes especially compelling. Long, dyed-black hair framed her pale, delicate features. The only flaw was a faint speckling of acne across her chin. And she was almost too skinny, with no real figure at all.

She smiled again. "You look like The Dude."

Clayton frowned.

Then a light went on in his head.

Oh, yes. *The Big Lebowski.*

His long, scraggly hair and the fraying bathrobe he wore over his pajamas made it an obvious comparison. "I swear, it's not intentional. I, just, uh..."

She laughed. "Yeah, sure. You got any weed?"

Ah.

The reason for her visit. It was usually either this or booze. He didn't mind hooking them up with what they needed. He knew what it was like. Again, he'd been much like them at their age. You had to get loaded and you needed a reliable way to procure your poison. The kids were commendably circumspect regarding where they got their stuff. More than one of them had gotten into some trouble over some foolish thing they'd done while under the influence, but so far, knock on wood, no cops or irate parents had ever come calling. He trusted them and didn't think they'd ever narc on him. Maybe it was stupid, but he believed it.

"I might be able to help you out."

"Cool, man. I appreciate it."

"What do you want?"

"I was thinking an eighth?" Her voice rose on the last word, turning the statement into a question. "But I've only got ten dollars on me. Could I owe you?"

Clayton scratched the stubble on his chin. "Don't you still owe me for the last bag?"

Her face scrunched up and she bounced again on her toes. "Come on, man. I'll pay you back. You know I will." She laughed. "Hell, I'll blow you for it, if you want."

"Uh...that won't be necessary. I'll just spot you again."

Fiona came closer to him, pressed herself against him. She looked up at him, her expression coy and playful. "You like me, don't you?"

He smiled. "Of course I like you. It's just...I, uh..." He struggled to concentrate. Her slender body felt nice snuggled up against him. But she was so young. Too young. He couldn't go there. Not with her. Not with any of them, regardless of how painfully tempting it could be. He pressed his hands gently on her slender shoulders and backed her off a few paces. She frowned. Then he pointed to the staircase behind Fiona. "I'm going up there for a few minutes. Make yourself at home. I'll be down shortly."

Her face brightened. "Awesome! Can I have a beer?"

"Help yourself."

"Cool."

She took off, disappearing through the archway into the kitchen. Clayton stared at the empty space where she'd been standing, then turned away and headed for the staircase.

THIRTEEN

It had been awkward at first, there in the dark, on the uneven ground, with the undergrowth scratching at their flesh as they moved. The logistical aspect of getting enough of their clothes removed and their bodies properly positioned was also a challenge, but they managed to make it happen. He didn't have a condom. She didn't care. He could just pull out. He asked her if she was sure. Maybe they should wait. No, she was sure.

So it happened.

And it was wonderful.

Better than anything fucking ever. Except...he'd been so caught in the grip of ecstasy he'd started to come inside her before he even realized it was happening. He apologized profusely. Even cried a little. Visions of unplanned pregnancy and a forced early entry into adulthood assailed him like scenes from a nightmare. He would have to marry her. Get a job. He saw himself stuck in Ransom, forced to give up his dreams of escape and success elsewhere in order to provide for a new family. He would become just another local. A small town nothing.

"It's okay," she told him, holding him down there in the dirt and the darkness. "Really. You'll see. The universe isn't so fucked up that I'd get knocked up the first time we ever did it."

Mark didn't know what to say to that.

The universe was plenty fucked up. Just turn on CNN any given day for proof aplenty. But he didn't say that, either. What was done was done. He couldn't take it back. So instead he just said, "I love you. I can't stop thinking about you."

Any other time she might have laughed at him for saying that. They were the Dark Ones. They didn't believe in anything so stupid and fleeting as love.

She kissed him and told him she loved him, too.

They stayed down there in the darkness for some time after the lovemaking was over, locked in each other's embrace. The wind sighed above them. Living things, probably squirrels, occasionally scampered through the foliage around them. Slowly, the impression of a significant block of time passing began to penetrate the languor of afterglow.

"Maybe we should get up out of here."

"Yeah."

Mark lifted himself off of her and scooted out of her way as she pushed her skirt down and began to pat the ground around her. He pulled his pants up and fastened the button. "What are you looking for?"

"My fucking panties. I can't find them."

Mark got on his hands and knees and helped her look for a few minutes, but the flimsy scrap of fabric proved difficult to locate amid the bramble in the darkness.

Natasha made a sound of exasperation. "Fuck this. They're lost."

He clasped hands with her and they carefully climbed up out of the depression, keeping their heads down as they shouldered their way through the overgrowth. In moments they emerged from the hole and stood on the narrow dirt path that acted as a buffer between the field and rock barrier that bordered the Smith property. Natasha brushed at her hair and clothes, plucking away bits of dead leaves, grass, and bramble. Mark did the same.

Natasha picked a small thorn from a tear in her leggings. "Next time we fuck, let's please do it on a bed or the back of your car. Anywhere other than a giant hole in the fucking ground."

"Hey, it was your idea."

She smiled. "Yeah. And I'm glad we did it. And at least we got all that first time bullshit out of the way interestingly."

"What do you want to do now?"

She chewed on her lip and thought about it a moment. She shrugged. "I don't know. Maybe go see what Campbell's up to. Get high, watch some stupid movie."

"I thought you wanted to go to that spooky old house."

She kicked at a rock and sent it skittering down the path. "Yeah. We could still do that, I guess."

"Something wrong?"

"Did you really mean it?"

Mark frowned. "Mean what?"

"You know...that love thing." She raised her head and looked him in the eye. "You weren't just fucking with me."

"No."

She smiled. "You sound so fucking solemn."

"I just..." He looked away from her, stared out at empty Austin Avenue. "You're really fucking important to me. I wouldn't joke about that. I love you. Maybe that makes me stupid."

"It doesn't make you stupid. Well..." She smiled. "Picking me to fucking fall in love with *is* kind of stupid. I'm pretty messed up."

He looked at her. "Well, I'm messed up, too. So I guess we're a perfect fucking match."

They stared at each other in silence for a few minutes. The intensity of the connection between them seemed to be strengthening by the moment. The spell remained unbroken until Mark glimpsed something at the periphery of his vision. His head snapped back toward Austin Avenue. A slim figure was moving along the edge of the road, taking care to stay out of the bright glare of the street lamps.

One of us.

"Someone's coming."

Natasha looked.

"I think that's Fiona. Let's see what she's up to."

"Okay."

Mark followed her down the path to the road, but they stopped short as the figure saw them and hesitated. But then the girl saw who they were and came across the Smiths' yard toward them, climbing atop one of the huge rock slabs. Perched on the rock, the slight girl seemed to tower above them. "You guys look all dirty and shit. You go rolling around out in the fucking field?"

"Yeah. We fucked down in that big fucking hole."

Natasha, blunt as ever.

Fiona laughed. "Cool. I just came from Campbell's place."

"Anyone else there?"

"Just Campbell. Got some weed. You guys got anything?"

Mark withdrew the pint of Southern Comfort from his jacket pocket. Remarkably, it had survived the tumble into the depression intact. "Got this. Some weed, too."

Fiona hopped down from the rock slab and approached them. "Hook me up?"

Mark let her have the bottle and frowned at the several huge swallows she took. Jesus, what was it with chicks and Southern Comfort? Between the two of them, they were going to polish off all his booze before he could get a decent buzz on.

Fiona chewed on a fingernail and looked out at the field. "We should do something. This standing around shit is boring."

Mark reclaimed the pint bottle and tucked it away. "We were thinking of going out to that house?"

"The abandoned one?"

"Yeah."

Fiona nodded. "Okay. You think Derek will be there?"

Fiona had a thing for Derek, but he didn't seem interested in her. It made things awkward sometimes when they were all together. She would stare at him and focus almost entirely on him, but he would barely acknowledge her. She had a little thing for Campbell, too. Also awkward.

Mark shrugged. "I don't know. Probably."

"Cool. I'll tag along if you guys don't mind."

Natasha laughed. "Why would we want *your* company, skank?"

Fiona flipped her off. "Bitch. Mark, why do you hang out

with this slut?"

Mark opened his mouth to reply, but Natasha beat him to the punch.

"*Because* I'm a slut. Not like you, you little cocktease."

"Better a cocktease than a cunt."

"Dyke."

"Whore."

Mark tuned them out after a few rounds of insults. They were both proficient at rattling off seemingly endless strings of nasty and degrading things just about anyone would find offensive. It didn't bother Mark most of the time. But it did disturb him to hear Natasha refer to herself as a slut. It made him flash back to that near showdown at school earlier in the day. He got mad all over again just thinking about it, so much so he didn't immediately notice the girls had stopped trading verbal jabs.

Natasha slugged him in the shoulder. "Hey."

Mark gave his head a hard shake. "What?"

"What's wrong with you?"

"Huh? What do you mean?"

Natasha's brow furrowed. "You had this crazy look in your eyes. Like you wanted to beat someone to death."

Fiona smirked and rocked backward on her heels. "Yeah, man. You looked like fucking Charlie Manson there for a second. Like any second you were gonna wig out and cut up some pigs."

"No. I just—"

"Because I gotta tell you, man, I'd be down with that."

Natasha laughed. "Hell, yeah."

Mark shook his head. "Dare you to say that shit at school."

Fiona rolled her eyes. "Right. Because I totally want to get interrogated by some dumb fucking cop who thinks I'm gonna go all Columbine on Ransom High. Like I'd let anybody know I was gonna pull some shit like that ahead of time. I'm not stupid. I'd just keep that shit to myself, then show up one day and start blazing, surprise the shit out of everybody."

An unexpected silence descended.

Fiona did the eye roll thing again. "Oh, come on. I was joking."

Mark coughed. "Anyway..."

Natasha clasped hands with him and steered him toward the road. "Awkward silences piss me off. Let's go check out that house."

The trio started toward the road.

FOURTEEN

Derek was on Spring Circle now, about a block down from his house. When he reached the house, he circled around to the back and quickly scaled the high wooden fence. It felt weird to be coming back home so far ahead of his usual pre-dawn return. He didn't like it. He swung his legs over the top of the fence and dropped to the ground, a scattering of dead leaves crunching beneath his feet as he landed in a crouch. He came out of the crouch fast and started toward the shed at the rear of the yard.

But he stopped in his tracks when he glimpsed the light emanating from the second floor bedroom window.

Shit.

He stood there frozen in indecision for several moments. He was trembling. It made him feel like a pussy. But he couldn't help it. He'd been caught. In all the time he'd been going out at night, it'd never happened. Right now, while he stood here shaking like a bitch, his parents were up there in his room, staring at an empty bed. He had two options. He could go back inside and take his medicine now. Or he could get his ass back up over that fence and run like the devil until he made it back to the old house. He was sort of leaning in that direction. He could have one more night of fun with his friends before his parents brought the hammer down. He was so pissed. He was about to lose the only thing that kept him sane and he couldn't understand how it had happened. There was no good reason for his parents to check on him at this time of night. Whatever. It didn't matter. It had happened, and one way or another, he had to deal with it.

It occurred to him there was a third option, a variation

on the second.

He tore his gaze away from the second floor square of light and stared at the shed. The shed was never locked. He could get inside it and gather the things he needed while making only a minimal amount of noise. The only risk involved would be a chance glance out the window by one of his parents at the wrong time. He was already caught. There was no way around that. He thought about the old house with its boarded up doors and windows. There might be nothing inside, or there might be all manner of unexpected treasures. It would be a kind of adventure, perhaps the last real adventure he'd have for some time.

He took a deep breath and started toward the shed.

Derek carefully pulled the shed's door open. It made only a slight creak. He left the door open as he walked into the shed. The open door made him nervous, but it was necessary. He wouldn't be able to see in the cramped and crowded shed without the benefit of moonlight.

Even with the moonlight, it wasn't easy to see. There was an overhead bulb, but the light would just heighten the risk of being caught. He banged a knee against a leg of a big worktable and bit back a cry of pain. He moved around the table and examined the tools hanging off a row of pegs on the wall. The crowbar was where he remembered seeing it. He tucked it under an arm as he shuffled over to the far right wall, where there was another work bench with a set of drawers beneath it. The heavy Maglite flashlights were in one of those drawers. He was almost done here, thank fuck.

The overhead bulb popped on.

Derek let out a gasp. The crowbar slipped from his arm and landed with a clatter on the wood plank floor. He whirled around with his heart galloping, but his terror at being caught quickly gave way to astonishment and confusion. His mother stood framed in the open doorway, attired only in a very tiny and flimsy nightie.

She smiled and stepped into the shed, closing the door behind her.

"Hello, DeeDee."

Derek frowned. "Mom? What's..."

Suzie McGregor had a belt coiled around her right hand, the buckle end dangling. He tried and failed to hold in a whimper as he backed a few steps away from his mother.

"Mom...please. I..."

Suzie was still smiling. "It's okay, sweetie. Mommy has to punish you. But after I've whipped you, I'll make you feel better." She licked her lips and smiled again. "I promise."

Derek didn't care for the way his mother was staring at him. At all. It was almost...lustful. Also, her nipples were erect and swollen against the fabric of the nightie.

Derek felt sick.

Oh, Christ...

"Mom...what's wrong with you? You..." His stomach started knotting up. "I don't...what are you..."

Suzie laughed. "Nothing's wrong with me. You're the one who's been naughty. And you know what happens to bad boys, DeeDee. They get spanked. Now get over here and take your medicine."

Derek didn't move. He felt paralyzed. He wanted out of this shed and away from his crazy mother. But he was too intimidated by her to force his feet into motion.

She snapped the belt against the edge of the worktable. *"GET OVER HERE!"*

Something inside Derek compelled him to obey. He gripped the edge of the work table to keep from falling over as he approached her.

Suzie was smiling again. "There. Was that so hard? Now drop your pants and bend over."

"What?"

"You heard me. Now do as you've been told, or I'll make it worse. And you know I can."

Derek did know that.

He also knew he couldn't let this happen. If he allowed his fear to control his actions here, some very bad things would happen. Things that might scar him forever. So instead of reaching for the snap of his jeans, he moved away from her and picked up the crowbar. He stood up and saw that his mother's expression had darkened considerably.

"You little shit. Put that down and get back over here."

"No."

He shifted his attention to the workbench. He pulled a drawer open and found the Maglites. There were two of them. He pulled out both, tucking them under an arm as he turned to face his mother again. "I'm going back out. If you try to hit me with that thing..." He nodded at the belt. "I'll hit back." He hefted the crowbar. "With this."

Suzie sneered. "You wouldn't dare."

Derek smiled. "Maybe. Maybe not. But we're gonna find out."

He started toward her.

The shadow of fear that crossed her face in that moment was gratifying. It gave him the last little bit of strength necessary to call her bluff and see this thing through. He wasn't even shaking now. It was amazing. At school, he was fearless. He never backed down from a fight. But at home it was different. He reverted to scared little kid mode every time. Until now. The loss of his fear filled him with sense of elation. By the time he stepped past his mother, he knew she wouldn't lash out at him with the belt. Not this time. And not ever again.

"Stay."

Her voice was lower now, the single syllable a plea rather than a command.

He shook his head. "No. I don't care what happens after tonight. You're not gonna hurt me anymore."

Her face crumpled. "DeeDee, please..."

He reached for the door. "No."

"Stay and I'll fuck you. Wouldn't you like that?"

"There's something really wrong with you, mom. You know that, don't you?"

He opened the door and stepped out into the night.

FIFTEEN

The narrow path that had once served as the abandoned house's driveway was now so overgrown that any passing motorist was unlikely to spy it. The little break in the trees was easy to miss, unnoticeable to most, and hard to pick out even if you knew where to look. Naturally, it was even trickier to find and negotiate in the dark. Even if you got on the path and started out in the right direction, you might go wandering off the wrong way, winding up deeper into the woods rather than closer to the house.

It was what had happened to Mark the last time he'd come out here at night. But he had been alone that time. It was easier to get lost in the woods when you were on your own. This time, though, he had Natasha and Fiona with him and they were making relatively rapid progress. Jared and Kevin were sitting on the porch. They stood up to greet them as the trio came into the clearing.

Jared nodded at Mark as they came closer. "Yo."

"Yo."

"Want a beer?"

"You like pussy?"

Jared squinted. "You're saying it's a stupid question?"

"Yeah."

"Fucker."

Mark grinned and fished beers out of the Bud carton, passing two of the cans to Fiona and Natasha. They popped the cans open and the five of them stood around shooting the shit and talking about maybe getting inside the house until they heard a crunch of booted feet on dead leaves. They turned toward the source of the sound and saw Derek

75

McGregor striding into the clearing. He was carrying some flashlights and something else. It took Mark a moment to recognize the heavy iron implement as a crowbar.

Derek grinned as he came closer. "Yo, Kevin. You didn't drink all the fucking beer, did you?"

Kevin smirked. "Saved one or two for ya."

Jared tilted his chin in Derek's direction. "Hand me that fuckin' crowbar."

Derek passed the crowbar to Jared, who went to work on the boarded-up door right away, wedging the pronged end into the paper-thin space between the board and the door frame. The rest of them stood there sipping their beers as Jared threw himself into the job with a determination that approached frenzy at times. He paused occasionally to insert the pronged end in a different spot, then went immediately back to work, cranking the tool back and forth with gusto, the savage twist of his features reflecting the magnitude of the effort. The board began to grudgingly come away from the frame on one side. The nails that had been used were thick and very long. The wood creaked and splintered in places as it came loose. Jared grunted louder with each crank of the crowbar. Sweat glimmered on his face and rolled down his forehead into his eyes. He blinked the moisture away and kept at the job, soon shifting his focus to the other side of the door. He stopped briefly at one point to strip off his flannel shirt, revealing a black Cannibal Corpse t-shirt beneath. But he otherwise didn't slow down as he neared completion of the task. Derek snapped on one of the Maglites and aimed the bright beam at the door, causing Jared's sweat-dripping, flushed face to stand out in stark relief. At last, he let the crowbar fall out of his hands and land with a clank on the porch. He then carefully inserted his big hands into spaces between the nails and began to push the board away from the frame.

He glanced at the others. "Everybody back!"

Mark and the others shuffled back down to the opposite end of the porch. They watched the board come away from the frame. Jared let go of it and the top end landed with a

76

thump on the porch railing. He bent to grip it by the bottom end and grimaced as the ball of a thumb was pricked by a nail.

"Damn!" He shook his hand and then sucked the small welling of blood from his thumb. "Hope I don't get fucking lockjaw."

Mark sipped beer. "Tetanus."

"Whatever."

He gripped the bottom end of the board again, with much more caution this time, and lifted it up, heaving it over the railing to land nail side down on the ground. After taking a moment to catch a breath and palm sweat away from his forehead, he reached for something propped in the darkest corner of the porch and hefted it.

A sledgehammer.

Mark didn't bother asking where it had come from, knowing one of them had stolen it from somewhere, loot from one of their occasional smash and grab expeditions into someone's work shed. Jared set one end of the sledgehammer head against the doorknob, took another deep breath, and lifted it over his head. Mark gripped Natasha's hand as Jared brought the sledgehammer down. His excitement was growing. They were actually going to see the inside of this place tonight. The doorknob gave way with one blow and the door popped open.

Everyone moved closer as Jared kicked the door the rest of the way open. Mark peered through the open door and his nose crinkled as stale air wafted out. The place didn't exactly stink, but the air carried with it slight undertones of rot and mustiness. He could dimly discern the outlines of various pieces of furniture, which struck him as strange. He had been sure the former owner would have emptied the place before sealing it up like this. It was possible they could find some pretty interesting things in here.

Jared glanced at Derek. "I'll take one of those flashlights."

It wasn't a request. And considering the amount of work Jared had put into getting them inside, Mark figured he was entitled. Derek stepped past Mark and handed one of the Maglites to Jared, who snapped it on and became the first of the Dark Ones to enter the house. Derek offered the remaining Maglite to Mark, deferring to him the way he usually did, seeing him as the group's de facto unspoken leader. It usually annoyed Mark. His instinct was to wave off the offer, but he knew Natasha would want him to take it, so he did.

He smiled and glanced at Natasha. She wasn't smiling. She seemed sort of...distant. His own smile faltered as he thought again of his failure to pull out earlier. He knew she was thinking of the same thing, and he experienced a renewed twinge of the dread he'd felt in the moments just after it had happened.

It can wait, he reminded himself. *Whatever happens, if anything, we'll deal with it.*

He gave her hand a squeeze and they entered the house.

The thing in the darkness sensed them much more clearly now. They were closer. Oh, so much closer. And there were more of them. It opened its inner eye and reached out again, probing, feeling...

Six of them.

Six little souls to feed from and ravage.

The air in the closed space vibrated again with sub-audible demonic laughter. They were inside the house now, walking across the creaking floorboards above its prison. It sensed their youth and reveled in it. Young humans were the easiest to exploit and manipulate, and their souls were imbued with an intoxicating energy most adults lacked. Energy that would make it strong again, perhaps stronger than ever, once it was able to feed from them.

Though still imprisoned, they were close enough to touch in subtle ways.

It reached out to them, probing again, searching for the weakest link among them.

Derek.

Oh, Derek, I'll be taking you so very soon.

It could not yet make Derek do as it wished. The binding

magic was too strong. But it was able to plant a seed in Derek's mind. A suggestion.

It would be enough.

The young were too curious. They wouldn't be able to resist. The young were also more apt to take risks than adults, occasionally doing things they would later see as very stupid. Things like breaking into a sealed up piece of private property. Of course, they couldn't know the true degree of risk they were taking. Nor could they have any way of knowing they had broken the first of the binding seals the moment they had knocked that door open.

The air in the basement vibrated subtly again as the demon laughed and awaited the inevitable arrival of its liberators.

SIXTEEN

Clayton aimed the remote at the 51-inch high definition screen and paged through the channel guide listings. TBS had several consecutive episodes of *Family Guy* scheduled. He'd come back to that if he found nothing else of interest. There were a lot of channels and a lot of possibilities. Yes, a lot of possibilities. So why was he paging so rapidly past many very interesting-looking programs without pausing to click the info button for any of them?

Well, here was the answer to that question.

He'd reached the pay-per-view porn section of the channel guide. He scrolled slowly through the selections, pausing the longest on *Lesbian Summer Camp Sluts*. That'd probably get the job done. He ordered the movie and settled back on the couch, getting comfortable for his masturbation session. The sooner he got it over with, the better. He could then resume his normal late evening habit of frying his brains and watching random shit on the tube until he passed out. He untied his bathrobe, pulled it open, and slid a hand into his pajama pants to grasp his already swelling cock. The action on the screen had barely begun and he was already about to pop. Which wasn't surprising, considering all the unspent erotic energy bubbling inside him in the wake of Fiona Johnson's abrupt departure.

Fuck.

He didn't want to think about her. He should have continued shooting down her repeated sex-for-dope offers. It was what anyone with brains would have done. But a long unquenched thirst for physical intimacy with another warm body made him weak.

And, hell, here he was, going over it all again in his head. *Damn...*

She'd cuddled up with him right here on the couch after they'd shared some of the weed. He made one token, half-hearted effort to push her away, but she giggled and clung to him, leaning into him to nuzzle and kiss his neck. One of her delicate hands reached through the fly of his pajama pants to grip him through his underwear.

She draped one skinny leg over his knee and and laughed softly. "Like that?"

"Yeah."

He remembered feeling a combination of lust and despair at what he saw in her expression. Her face, so pale and achingly pretty despite the sprinkle of acne across her chin, conveyed an exciting amount of actual desire, but this thrill was leavened by an obvious contempt that showed in her eyes and in a smile that was trying hard not to be a smirk.

"Would you like to put this thing in me?" she'd asked him as she continued to stroke him through his underwear. "Would that be nice?"

"Oh, God..."

She giggled then. And the next words out of her mouth were the pin that popped the balloon. "When was the last time anybody fucked you, Clay?"

He didn't say anything. His hard-on instantly shriveled.

"Clay? Is something wrong?"

Ten years ago, he'd thought. *It was ten years ago and you even look a little like her, but you don't need to know that. It was ten years ago that my father blew his brains out and everything changed forever, and you don't need to know about that, either.*

"Get out."

"What the fuck is wrong with you?"

"Just leave. Please. I'm sorry, but...please, just go."

She'd stared at him for a long moment, disbelief etched in her features. Her eyes turned shiny, but then she blinked away the excess moisture, scooped up the bag of weed he'd dropped on the coffee table, and stood over him. "I'm not

81

paying for this."

"Okay."

"I mean it. I figure the little thrill you just got is payment enough. Am I right?"

"Okay."

"*Okay.*" A sneering, mocking tone. "Fuck you, you fat fucking old asshole."

She kicked him hard in the shin then and left.

Her harsh words cut deep. He liked Fiona. He liked all of them. But he knew his relationship with the so-called Dark Ones had an expiration date and it was coming up soon. They were growing up. Graduation was around the corner. There might be other kids to replace them one day, other young troublemakers, but odds were they wouldn't be half as interesting as these kids. He thought of them as friends, but in his rare sober moments he recognized this as foolish. Soon they'd move into a new phase of their lives and he'd never see any of them again.

"What the fuck am I doing?"

He was getting depressed and when he was depressed he couldn't bear to watch porn. He aimed the remote at the screen again and clicked over to *Family Guy*.

The doorbell rang again.

His first—and only—thought was that Fiona had come back to apologize for being mean. He'd ordered her out, but the self-pitying turn of his thoughts made him eager to see her again. Which was why he failed to exercise the usual degree of caution. The Louisville Slugger stayed propped in its corner as he pulled the door open without a glance through the peephole.

"Hey—"

A huge fist crashed against his jaw and made him stagger backward. He tripped over his feet and crashed to the floor. The tip of a boot slammed into his stomach, blasting the air from his lungs. He wheezed and rolled onto his back, looking up through a blur of tears at his assailant.

The man towering over him wore a blue uniform and a badge.

Cop.

Clayton had just enough time to start being really scared. Then the beating began in earnest.

When it was over the cop stood over him and sneered at his quivering, huddled form. "Consider that a warning, Campbell. That's how I deal with sickos like you. I hear you got away with a lot for a long time because of your daddy. But daddy's dead and nobody cares anymore. Your days of living about the law are over. You give that girl trouble again and it's your ass, you hear me?"

Another boot to the stomach. "YOU HEAR ME!?"

"Y-yes."

The cop left.

Clayton stayed where he was for a long time, holding his stomach and shaking from the pain. Then he got to his hands and knees and made his way back to the living room. He grabbed a rum bottle from the coffee table and sat with his back against the sofa. Fat tears spilled down his cheeks as his body quaked with sobs.

He drank most of the rum before he passed out.

SEVENTEEN

The Hollis House,
December 6, 1984

The top of her head was a pulpy mess. Norman sat on his knees next to her, his hands shaking as he stared at her empty face. The stillness of her features was horrible. His stomach churned as spasms of remorse ripped at his conscience and warred with the instinct for self-preservation. He knew the latter would eventually prevail. It was, after all, why he'd done this awful thing in the first place. He wasn't a killer by nature. He hadn't actually meant to kill her, really. Just maybe beat a bit of sense into the bitch and scare her into giving up any additional blackmail materials. But then she had to go and bust her head open after he popped her one.

It was all her fault.

She was no angel. That was important to remember. She had wanted to kill his wife. His dear, sweet Audrey. In a way, what he'd done was a virtuous thing. He'd been acting to protect someone he loved. He couldn't let himself think of this dead thing leaking blood on the ground as a human being. It had been a threat, an invading cancer, and it had to be excised. But he looked at her unmoving lips and remembered how soft they had been, how nice they'd felt giving him teasing little kisses up and down his body. She'd had her good points, for sure. Another twinge of remorse made him grimace.

No.

I did the right thing here. She brought this on herself.

He grabbed the corpse by the wrists and dragged it over

to the Fiat Spider. After getting the trunk open with her keys, he hauled Louella's body up off the ground and wedged it in the trunk. He then covered her with a tarp and slammed the trunk shut, mercifully removing the grisly vision from his eyes. He would leave her here for now and get back to town in his own car. Maybe go home and change out of these bloody clothes before heading over to Louella's place to purge it of anything investigators shouldn't see.

No. That was no good. Audrey would be there. And Clayton, who was home sick for the day. The boy was home sick a lot. Only he wasn't really sick most of the time. Unless being allergic to school counted as being sick.

He couldn't go home. Not yet.

There was one person in town he could count on to help. It wouldn't be a no questions asked or no strings attached kind of situation, though. There would be plenty of both. The mayor would take care of this for him. They were drinking buddies. Business partners and friends. They had done favors of questionable legality for each other before. Not anything as severe as this, perhaps, but certainly things that could land either of them in jail for a good stretch if state investigators ever became privy to the information.

The mayor might scold him something fierce, but in the end he'd help.

And that would be the end of this nightmare.

The decision made, Norman turned and ran flat-out for his car.

He didn't stop shaking until he reached the mayor's house.

EIGHTEEN

Lydia Bell let go of her husband's throat and watched with satisfaction as he coughed and spluttered. She felt his chest heave beneath her as his lungs worked hard to draw in fresh oxygen. His cheeks were flushed a deep red and covered in sweat. He gasped and whimpered, staring up at her with eyes that were wide with terror. She loved the choking game. It made her feel powerful and in control, the opposite of the way she'd felt after learning of his infidelity.

"Lydia...you...have to...stop this..."

"Why?"

"Because..." He sucked in another big breath. "You're going to...kill me."

She cocked her hand back and snapped it across his face.

He was actually crying now and that was good. That was *very* good.

"Please..."

"You betrayed me, Tom."

"I know. Jesus, I know." He whimpered again. "How many times do I have to say I'm sorry?"

"You'll never be sorry enough. Never."

She slapped him again.

"Let's get a divorce." His eyes radiated desperation. "I won't contest anything. You can have it all. The house. Custody of Mark. As much money as you want. Let's just end this misery."

He didn't get it. He could never give back what he had taken from her. Her dignity. Her sense of herself as a woman. She was intelligent and desirable. The whole package. Until earlier this year, the notion of her man straying would have struck her as absurd.

But Tom had done just that.

Lydia wrapped her hands around his throat again.

"No." He sobbed. "Please..."

She smiled. "We're not getting divorced. Ever."

She tightened her grip on his throat.

The truth was, this wasn't just a game.

It was practice.

One day she'd keep the pressure up until the cheater had breathed his last. Because why go through the hassle of divorcing him when she could simply put an end to him forever?

Yes. He really didn't get it. *At all*.

The room was spinning again. She grabbed the edge of the bathroom sink to keep from toppling over. That would be bad. She could crack her head open on the hard tiles. She had a fleeting vision of her bleeding and very still body on the floor. She let go of the sink with one hand and touched the top of her head, feeling for a gash that wasn't there.

Silly, Suzie McGregor thought.

That didn't happen. That was just an idea in my silly head. A visualization of something that could happen, but I won't let it. No, I won't let you do that to me. You want that to happen, don't you?

"Don't you?"

Her voice emerged soft but steady, belying how she really felt.

It wasn't enough that the force that controlled the universe was maliciously messing with her in the usual insidious and hateful ways. Oh, no. And it wasn't enough that it had planted that awful image of her split-open noggin in her head. That was its way of saying, *Look, Suzie, there you are dead. Doesn't that look about right to you?*

Wouldn't you be better off not alive anymore?

She sneered at her reflection in the mirror, knowing the powers working against her could see it. "How subtle. Fuck you. FUCK YOU! Go to hell! You can take your stupid little subliminal suggestions and shove them up your fat fucking cosmic ass!"

She thrust an upraised middle finger against the mirror. "FUCK YOU!"

No.

This...nonsense...was par for the course. This was Standard Operating Procedure. It was Situation Normal, All Fucked Up. She had been dealing with it nearly all her life. She was used to it. The thing that had her perhaps seconds away from a total meltdown was the lingering psychological sting from the confrontation with her son. It hurt to even look at herself, knowing the galling degree of weakness that lurked within her. She didn't know how she could face Derek again. Hell, she didn't know how she could even be in the same *room* with him.

There's something really wrong with you, Mom.

"There's nothing wrong with me, boy. *You're* the problem."

She watched her lips move and it occurred to her what any casual observer would think upon viewing this scene...

...something really wrong with you...

"*Nothing* is wrong with me."

She watched her face harden again and felt anger at the tears that spilled down her cheeks.

"I'll teach you, child. Learn you a permanent lesson."

He would have to come home at some point. All his stuff was here. And he was a minor. There was no way around it, unless he ran away, and he was too much of a weakling to fend for himself out in the world just yet. His little show of defiance tonight was an anomaly and did nothing to change that essential fact. He'd be back. And she'd be ready for him.

I am going to kill my little boy. So help me, I am.

The notion filled her not with sorrow or self-disgust, the things one might expect, but rather with a sense of glorious exultation, of freedom within reach.

Yes, she thought. *Death is the answer.*

She would start with her son.

And then move on to her husband. Stupid, useless Kurt.

And she'd top the dance of death off by killing herself.

She began to smile. "Yes. Die, die, die, my darling, we're all going to fucking die."

She laughed.

There was a knock on the door.

"Hon?" came the muffled voice of her husband. "Is something...wrong?"

Suzie hated it when stupid Kurt intruded on one of her little dialogs with the adversary. He would express the usual concern and suggest she "see someone." Oh, it made her so mad. When it happened, he always had that same wary look in his eyes, a look that reminded her very much of the expression she'd seen on her son's face earlier. That look was meant to convey concern, of course, but that was just a lie. *You're crazy*, was what that look really said. *You're simply out of your skull...and I'm better than you.*

She would not have anyone looking down on her, especially anyone in her own family.

What right did he have to pry? And why was the useless pig of a man out of bed anyway? She gripped the edge of the sink and forced her voice to remain steady. "Nothing is wrong, Kurt. Go back to bed. You have to get up early, remember."

She heard him sigh.

Asshole.

"I know, hon. It's just..."

He trailed off and Suzie quirked an eyebrow, waiting for him to finish.

It's just that I worry about you, hon. I think you should see someone.

But Kurt McGregor never finished his thought.

A heavy crash from the other side of the door made Suzie gasp. She let go of the sink and staggered over to the door. She grabbed the doorknob and hauled the door open. Her husband's big body was sprawled on the floor. Suzie stared down at him in uncomprehending confusion for a moment.

Then she laughed.

"Holy shit, Kurt. I was just thinking about killing you

and your stupid ticker went and did the job for me."

It was probably just a coincidence, but she couldn't help thinking...maybe she'd killed him just by thinking about it hard enough. Perhaps she'd become strong enough through her decades of psychic struggle to focus and direct her thoughts in a lethal way.

Yes.

It made sense.

She'd submitted herself fully to the forces of darkness in that moment when she'd decided to kill her family. The adversary was no longer the adversary. Now it was a conspirator. She'd shown herself worthy and now it would assist her, starting with knocking off Kurt.

Perhaps now she wouldn't have to kill Derek right away.

This development did open up some interesting possibilities. She could play the heartsick widow and he would have no choice but to play the role of the consoling son. It would be the role society expected of him, and, being the weakling he was, he'd fall numbly into it. He'd put on a good show tonight, but she knew the real truth about him. He was a plastic rebel, a suburban wannabe playing at being tough and non-conformist. Also, his defenses would be down in the wake of his father's death. Breaking him again was going to be easy.

A *lot* of people would be consoling her in the coming days.

One of them might even be Tom Bell. It wasn't at all unrealistic. She knew he wasn't really happy with that witch Lydia, no matter what he said in their private texts and emails. The fact that those remained ongoing was proof enough of that.

She stood there and stared at Kurt's unmoving form for perhaps another ten minutes. When she was certain he was beyond any hope of resuscitation, she picked up a phone and punched in 9-1-1.

A low hissing sound emanated from the spray paint can as Kent held the button down and aimed it at the side of Mark

Bell's old Camaro, slowly spelling the word FAG in large, looping letters.

"Bell is gonna freak when he sees what you've done to his car."

Kent Hickerson glanced over his shoulder at the person hovering behind him. "That's the idea."

"I don't know, man. I don't like these assholes, either. But I've seen this guy in action. He's no joke. He hit this one dude in the parking lot at McDonald's harder than I've ever seen anyone get hit. It was jut POW! Like in the movies. One punch. The other guy went down hard. A tooth came out of his mouth." Brett Hogan shook his head. "I'm just saying."

"You're saying you're afraid of...hell, I don't know what he thinks he is. Some weird combination of goth, metalhead, and old school greaser. None of it's real anyway. Bottom line, he's a fake. A pathetic phony."

"A phony with fists of steel."

Kent sighed. "I'm telling you, you're giving this guy too much credit. High school's gonna end soon and guys like him always give up their stupid little poses when they have to start dealing with the real world."

"When they have to fucking work for a living."

"Exactly. Not much call for brawlers in the modern job market."

"Well...there's the UFC."

Kent chuckled. "Maybe, but his realistic options are limited. He'll find that out soon enough. Meanwhile, it's about time he got knocked down a peg."

"And you're big plan to do that is to spray paint 'fag' on his car?"

Kent shook the can again and painted a crude rendering of a penis. "This is just the opening salvo in a war, my friend. I'm gonna talk to Moose tomorrow—"

Brett groaned. "Oh, man..."

"I know, I know. He's a Neanderthal."

"That's an insult to Neanderthals."

"I know, okay? But Moose likes me. He's always laughing like a goddamn hyena at every little thing I say.

Point is, I may not have fists of steel...but I know people who do."

Kent took a step back to admire his handiwork. The red spray paint against the car's faded black paint job would be hard to miss in daylight. The thought of Mark having to drive the old heap to school with FAG painted in big bold letters on the door made him crack a grin. But the grin faltered as he had an annoying thought.

He'll probably just skip.

Fuck it. It didn't matter.

This is just the opening salvo.

Every righteous struggle needs a leader and Kent knew he was the only student at Ransom High up to the task. The defacing of Mark Bell's car proved that. A good general knows when the time has come to meet the enemy on his own turf and terms. This was a shining example. He'd come out late at night, just like them. Had committed a petty criminal act, just like them. Things so out of character they would shock anyone who knew him.

Brett clapped a hand on his shoulder. "Let's get gone before they get back."

Kent shrugged the hand away. "Not yet. There's more work to do."

Brett groaned again. "Are you serious?"

"Dead serious. Do you know where Natasha Wagner lives?"

NINETEEN

The musty living room was fully furnished. Mark aimed the Maglite's beam at a long sofa and stepped further into the room. Natasha stayed right beside him, clutching loosely at his left arm. The hardwood floor groaned as they moved, sagging a little with each step. This place had been closed up a long time. It was possible the wood beneath their feet was rotted to a dangerous degree. There could be extensive termite damage. But it was holding up so far and he wasn't about to be the one to suggest they abandon this expedition over safety concerns. Everyone else seemed cool with the risk, so what the hell.

Mark shifted the arc of the flashlight's beam, revealing reveal more of the room's interior. There were end tables to either side of the sofa. A lamp sat atop the one nearest them. Natasha let go of his arm and reached under the lampshade to turn the switch. Nothing happened, of course.

Fiona arched an eyebrow. "Did you really expect that to come on?"

Natasha shrugged. "No. But I thought of it and just had to try it."

"Like Mount Everest, it was there?"

"Yep."

Mark turned away from them and spied a dark shape sitting opposite the sofa. He pointed the flashlight at it and saw an old-fashioned television atop a wooden swivel stand. A set of rabbit-ear antennas sat perched on top of it. A plate affixed to the wood just beneath the screen revealed the brand name—Admiral. Taking a cue from Natasha, he pushed the power button. Nothing happened. It was there. He did it. The old television was sort of cool. Other than the coating of dust, it looked pristine. It could have been a museum piece. He considered returning in daylight to haul it out of here.

Natasha nudged him. "Why do you think all this stuff was left behind?"

"I don't know." He turned away from the television and aimed the beam against the far wall. The light revealed a large roll-top desk with its top down. "It's weird. All this stuff must have been pretty valuable when the place was abandoned."

Fiona laughed. "Shit, it's valuable *now*. We should come back during the day sometime and see what we can scavenge. Haul *all* this shit out to a pawnshop."

Mark found the idea initially tempting, but something about it didn't feel quite right. It felt sort of like grave robbing. And there was something else. Something sort of crazy. He felt like something was watching him. Something other than his friends.

Something.

He shivered and tried to shake the off the bout of paranoia. It wasn't easy. This place did feel sort of like an open tomb. Like a graveyard, this was the country of the dead. They didn't belong here. *Especially* at night. That feeling of being observed, irrational as it was, didn't help matters.

He feigned a yawn. "This place is sort of lame. Anybody else bored of this shit?"

Natasha grunted. "No."

Well, that settles that.

Mark would no sooner skip out on Natasha than he'd chop off his own hand. He wasn't surprised she wanted to stay. She was likely enthralled by the deeply spooky vibe of the place. They were all into horror and metal, but for Natasha the interest went deeper. It was her life. Her obsession. She wanted to be involved in the horror business somehow someday. Most would consider this a fanciful aspiration that would soon give way to more realistic goals. But Mark didn't think so. Maybe it'd be like that for most people, but not for Natasha. Anyone who spent any time *really* listening to her hold forth on the subject would know better. For her, a trip through a spooky old house must be like a trip to Disneyland.

He looked at her pale, angular face. The way the shadows played over her features as the light cast by the Maglite shifted made her look like a vampire from an old black and white movie. Her plump lower lip was painted a dark shade of scarlet. He had a nearly irresistible urge to chew on it. He noted again the way the swell of her breasts stretched the tiny Emily the Strange t-shirt and felt a tightness in his groin.

"You look sort of like a vampire."

"Oh no. My secret. It's out." Her playful tone made it clear she liked this. "What gave me away? Was it my fangs?"

"That, and your insatiable thirst for blood."

Natasha's expression was speculative. "I think I know what's really on your mind."

"God...I want you so fucking bad."

She kept smiling. "I know."

Fiona had wandered back from an inspection of the roll-top desk. "Desk is locked. Hey. Stop looking at each other like that."

Natasha feigned innocence. "I don't know what you mean."

"Like fuck you don't. I'm feeling pretty frustrated right now so I'll get all pissy if you guys go at it while I'm around."

"Well, you do have options." Natasha paused a moment. A bit of boisterous bantering audible from one of the other rooms filled the silence. She smiled. "Three of them."

Fiona rolled her eyes. "No fucking way. They're cool and all, mostly, but no. It'd be too much like fucking my brother. If I had one, I mean."

Mark piped in: "I thought you were into Derek."

"I am, man, but he ain't into me. I'm not gonna keep sniffing around his ass like a bitch in heat."

Natasha chuckled. "You *do* sound frustrated."

"Tell me about it."

A voice boomed out from somewhere else in the darkness, making them all jump: *"Yo! Markus, get in here, man!"*

Mark aimed the Maglite's beam in the general direction of the voice, which had emanated from the opposite side of the living room. Another room was visible through a wide archway. He glimpsed the legs of a table. The kitchen, maybe?

A big shape came charging through the archway. Too big to be anyone but Jared. "*Mark!*"

Mark swung the flashlight's beam up, splashing light across Jared's face and making him squint. "Dude, we found something weird. Well, Derek found it."

"Found what?"

"See for yourself. Come on."

They followed him through the archway and into the kitchen, which was much smaller and humbler than the kitchen in his Mark's parents' house. There were no expensive fixtures. No high tech ovens or wine refrigerator. This kitchen appeared modest but highly functional. There wasn't a lot of clutter. This was evident despite the layers of accumulated dust everywhere. Mark imagined a 50's housewife pottering about the place in a frilly white apron with a duster always at hand, ever ready to whisk away any hint of dirt. It all seemed painfully ordinary. The only thing that piqued his curiosity was the table. A checked tablecloth was spread neatly over it. Four white plates were arranged around the table, as well as an accompanying set of silverware for each plate. It was a little creepy.

What the hell happened here?

Why was everything left like this?

Jared and the other boys were clustered around the entrance to a walk-in pantry. The source of the excitement had to be in there. The girls followed Mark to the pantry, where he paused at the door and looked at Jared. "So what's up?"

Jared glanced at Derek. "You found it, dude, you show him."

Derek shrugged and sidled past Jared into the pantry. He glanced over his shoulder at Mark as he followed him into the space. "It was kind of weird. I was poking around in the kitchen, opening cabinets and drawers, looking for...hell, I don't know what. Something made me look over here. The pantry was closed, but I had a really strong feeling I should check it out."

Mark took a quick look around and saw shelves to either side of him. They were stocked with various goods in cans and jars, ancient food stuffs gone to rot. There was a sour tang to the air in here. He didn't see what all the fuss was about until he shifted the Maglite and got a glimpse of the wall at the back of the pantry. Another door was back there. It was covered with writing and crudely drawn pictures, as well as a lot of arcane symbols. One he recognized as a pentagram. Though he couldn't identify the others, gut instinct told him these also held some kind of occult significance. Above the symbols was a picture of a fearsome animal that resembled a large black wolf. Astride the wolf was a winged humanoid figure with the head of a raven. Mark approached the door for a closer look, his brow furrowing deeply as he read the words painted below the symbols: *DANGER. Hazardous materials stored within. DO NOT ENTER!*

The others crowded around him, craning their heads and wiggling their bodies for a better view. Fiona pressed herself against him a little harder than was necessary to get a good look. He knew it was an intentional provocation and it bothered him, but it was something he could deal with later. He was too captivated by the mystery of the door to care about anything else just now.

Derek gripped the rust-flecked doorknob and rattled it. "Locked."

Kevin Cooper snorted. "No shit. And what if it'd been unlocked?"

Derek shrugged. "Dunno. Would've gone in, I guess."

"You do see that bit about 'hazardous materials', right?"

"Yeah. So?"

Mark coughed. "I don't know if I believe the warning. Somebody went to a lot of trouble to seal this place up tight. I bet at least part of the reason why is on the other side of that door. I think the warning is a kind of last line of defense, a way to scare off anyone who gets this far."

They were all silent for a long moment as they thought about that.

Then Natasha spoke for them all when she said, "It's really kind of freaky."

Jared laughed. "Freaky as a motherfucker. Everybody out of my way. We're checking this shit out."

Fiona pivoted away from Mark and thrust her ass against his crotch as she made room for Jared. He worried for a moment that Natasha had seen this, but her gaze was riveted to the door. He pushed Fiona away and she laughed. He recalled what she'd said about feeling frustrated and guessed, if anything, she'd been understating it. He hoped she'd knock it off soon. The last thing he needed was any drama between the girls.

Derek got out of Jared's way and the rest of them shuffled back a few steps. Jared planted one foot firmly beneath him and launched the other at the door. It was a mighty kick and the door popped open amid a spray of wood splinters, a vertical rectangle swinging backward into deep darkness.

The thing in the basement exulted.

Yes!

Come closer, children. Just one seal remains.

Come to me.

Come down.

Come down.

Come down...

Jared poked his head into that dark space, staring down for a silent moment before glancing back at them. "Stairs."

Mark frowned at the darkness. He didn't believe in any kind of supernatural phenomena. There were no horror movie spooks lurking in the shadows here, waiting for just the right moment to spring at them from the shadows. Even so, it was apparent that whoever had lived here *had* believed in such things. The symbols on the door could be wards, part of a spell designed to keep evil things out.

Or in.

Mark frowned.

Now where had *that* disquieting thought come from?

Derek took a look through the open door. "Basement."

Natasha clasped hands with Mark again. Her skin felt cold against his and she was trembling a little. But Mark knew she didn't share his trepidation. The trembling signaled not fear but mounting excitement. She leaned against him and the heat of her breath against his throat was a stark contrast to her cool flesh. A nice contrast. Because, just for a moment, he'd felt he was clutching hands with a dead thing. He felt a sudden prickling of something close to real fear. Something just didn't feel right about this place. At all. It was a bad place. It flew in the face of his disbelief in the supernatural, but sometimes you had to listen to your gut.

"We should leave."

The words just came out.

Natasha tensed next to him. "What? Why?"

"I just—"

Jared's booming laughter made him wince. "Are you shitting me? Are you scared?"

"No."

"What then?"

Natasha let go of his hand. "Yeah, what?"

Before Mark could reply Jared stepped through the darkened doorway and started down the stairs.

Mark's heart lurched. "Wait!"

Jared stopped just a step or two down and turned back to look at him. "Dude, seriously. Stop acting like a bitch."

Mark sighed. "Look, it's not that I'm scared. I'm not, okay? But this place is fucking old. Those stairs are probably rotten. You could fall and break your neck."

Kevin tittered and threw his words back at him in a lisping, mocking tone: "Yeah, you could fall down and break your necks, fellas."

The others were laughing now. Even Natasha, which was the worst. That really stung.

Mark seethed. He wasn't accustomed to having his

courage called into question. And in any normal situation it would never happen.

Jared's voice cut through the laughter. "Doesn't matter anyway. Check it out." He stamped a foot up and down, a flat, slapping sound that suggested unyielding solidity. "The stairs are fucking concrete. I'm going down. See ya there. That is..." He grinned. "...if you're not too *scared*."

He started down the stairs, the light from the Maglite he was holding bobbing as he descended. Derek was right on his heels, following Jared's lead instead of Mark's for once. And then Natasha strode rapidly ahead and stepped through the doorway without so much as a glance back.

Shit.

Keven hurried after her.

Fiona smiled. "It's just you and me, I guess."

Mark grimaced. "Yeah."

"Let's go outside." She touched his hand. "Who wants to go banging around some smelly old basement anyhow?"

He didn't say anything. All he could think of was Natasha's back turned to him. Of course she'd want to check out the basement, but to leave without a word like that? It felt like a judgment. How could she do that so soon after making love with him for the first time?

Fiona took his silence as encouragement. She wrapped her arms around him, raised herself up on her tiptoes, and pushed a thigh up against his crotch. She kissed his chin and then his lips, making a soft moaning sound low in her throat.

Mark placed his hands on her shoulders and pushed her back a little—but not all the way. Their bodies were still touching.

"Stop."

She laughed softly and pressed her thigh against him again. "Doesn't feel like you want me to stop. Besides, that bitch totally blew you off. Get back at her by taking me outside and fucking my brains out."

"This doesn't sound like you."

She laughed again. "It's an all new me. New and improved."

"Natasha's your best friend."

"Doesn't mean I'm above stealing you from her. Come on." The press of her thigh was more insistent this time, the need in her voice more pronounced. "I am so fucking horny. Please."

Mark's pride was wounded. It was tempting to just let it happen. But the intensity of his feelings for Natasha wouldn't allow it. He had to go after her and make this right.

"I'm sorry."

He pushed her away again—all the way, this time—and went to the open door. He stared down into the darkness and caught glimpses of the others in the herky-jerky shifting of Jared's Maglite. He saw other things. A chair. Stacks of boxes and crates against one wall. A table and another chair in a corner. And, in the approximate center of the small room was a circle painted on concrete. Another fucking pentagram. He didn't start down until he felt Fiona touch him again. He cringed at the sound of her boot heels on the steps behind him as she followed him down. He'd hoped she'd elect to stay behind in the wake of his rejection, but he supposed that hadn't been realistic.

Jared turned his beam toward them and barked laughter. "Well, look who decided to join the party after all."

Mark gave him the finger and crossed the room to where Natasha was standing in front of a bookcase, the shelves of which were lined with thick, leather-bound volumes. She glanced at him. "Some strange stuff here."

"Hey, look...I'm sorry."

"For what?"

"You know, for saying we should leave. For acting like..."

She smiled. "Like a pussy?"

"Yeah. Like that."

Her smile broadened. "It's okay. I forgive you. I—" She tilted her head to look past his shoulder and her eyes went wide. Then she burst out laughing. "Holy shit."

Mark turned around. He echoed her comment: "Holy shit."

Derek and Fiona were inside the pentagram. He was

101

on top of her and they were clawing at each other, grinding against each other. Most of their clothes had already been discarded. Derek ripped at the Skinny Puppy t-shirt she'd worn beneath her hoodie, tearing the fabric and exposing her pale flesh to the light. It looked so tender juxtaposed with Derek's harder, more muscular flesh. Mark felt a tightness in his throat at the sight of it.

And another kind of tightness in his jeans.

What's wrong with me?

It was a good question. He couldn't understand why he was getting turned on by this. And that wasn't all. He'd known Fiona was desperate to get laid, but that didn't explain why Derek had suddenly lost his previous disinterest in her. Now he looked like he wanted to devour her. And the air in this basement was too warm, whereas the air in the rest of the house had seemed unnaturally cool. Sweat beaded in Mark's eyebrows and spilled down the sides of his face. He knew something very wrong was happening, yet even in the midst of this awareness, he was unable to shake his fascination with the erotic scene playing out in the circle.

Fiona's bra was off now and the thick nipples at the tips of her small breasts stood erect and glistening, bathed in the light from the Maglites. It was only then that Mark realized he was aiming the beam of his own flashlight directly at the couple in the circle, holding it at just the right angle to provide optimum illumination. Jared, on the other side of the circle, was doing the same. This was a show. A performance. And they were the rapt audience. Mark knew he should look away, had the sick sense that what was happening here was not right, but he was helpless. The last of Fiona's clothes came away from her body, leaving her writhing naked in the middle of the circle. Derek, also nude now, fell atop her again and penetrated her. A shrill scream ripped out of her lungs as her thin legs shot into the air. She clawed at his bare back, tearing crimson gashes in the white skin. They writhed against each other with astonishing ferocity, both of them growling and grunting like animals as they copulated.

From a distance, Mark heard the door at the top of the

stairs slam shut.

The air vibrated. It felt like...*laughter*?

A voice like crackling hellfire spoke in his brain, *I am Andras, killer of men. I am a Grand Marquis of Hell and I have been a prisoner. But you have set me free.*

Then more of that demonic, sub-audible laughter.

Mark knew he should feel nothing but terror, but the erotic charge in the air was too intense. He was under a spell of some type. Something that was relentlessly massaging the pleasure centers in his brain, rendering him incapable of responding to anything but physical impulse and need. In the next instant, he was kissing Natasha with an intense hunger that felt like it could never be sated. He needed to be inside her now, wanted to feel her nude body pinned to the concrete floor beneath him. They fell to the floor, groaning and tearing at each other's clothes. The clothes came away in tatters. And then he had what he wanted. What it wanted. Andras. He screamed as he felt his cock plunge into that delicious, moist softness. Then he was pounding her for all he was worth, arching his back and screaming again and again into the darkness overhead, the sounds reverberating in the enclosed space as they intermingled with the screams of his friends. It seemed to go on endlessly, with the release of orgasm always just out of reach. Mark would look down at Natasha's undulating body for a time, and then he'd look at what Derek and the others were doing to Fiona. He knew they were all under the same kind of spell. That what they were doing would leave psychic scars that might never be erased. But right now all that mattered was the demands of the flesh. The other boys were taking turns with Fiona, turning her over and rearranging her body to be penetrated from different positions. And she screamed in ecstasy through it all, urging them on. Later he wouldn't be aware of when the transition had occurred, but eventually Mark had a turn with Fiona and the others all had a go at Natasha.

At various point through this, Mark perceived flashes of bright light at the periphery of his vision, little stuttering blips like static in the fabric of reality. These were followed by occasional glimpses of some other place. *Blip*. A fiery place. Great, billowing columns of fire radiating incredible heat. *Blip*. Back in this world, watching the tips of Natasha's outstretched fingers clawing at the concrete floor, her voice hot in his ear, begging him to fuck her into oblivion. *Blip*. Another horrid glimpse of that awful place. He saw piles of body parts stacked to the sky, trailing ribbons of intestines and other organs. He saw blood like a river flowing over a cobbled street. Then *blip* one more time, returning again to this world, seeing Fiona beneath him now, her eyes wide and full of tears. And as he fucked Fiona, he felt his own tears begin to flow, already experiencing the shame that later would haunt them all. He saw tears on all their faces. There was no pleasure in any of these acts for any of them, at least not beyond those initial few moments of raw, aching need.

He knew the deepest despair in that moment.

This was never going to end. They would go like this until they were dead, all of them, until their hearts had exploded from the relentless, forced exertion. The thing that had been imprisoned here—that they had inadvertently released—was never going to let them go.

But then it did.

All but one of them.

PART II: UNBOUND

TWENTY

Five days later...

There was something wrong with her son. Something more sinister than the infuriating spark of rebellion he had shown the night Kurt keeled over. It had certainly started that night, though. He wouldn't talk about it, but something bad had happened. She sensed this every time she made uneasy eye contact with him. That hard, knowing stare of his made her feel like he was seeing right into all the nooks and crannies in her brain, making him privy to all those dark, secret things lurking there.

I know you, that look said. *I know every sick thing about you.*

You're pathetic.

Pitiful.

And I am better than you.

That perceived judgment made her seethe with rage and resentment. But she'd had to keep a tight lid on those feelings with so many of Kurt's relatives around the last few days. And now, in the aftermath of the service and subsequent reception, she was being made to feel like a bad parent by Kurt's insufferable witch of a mother.

"You should go check on the boy. He's feeling lowly."

They were standing in her kitchen, both of them still dressed in funeral black. Ella McGregor held a coffee mug in her wrinkled, liver-spotted hands and sipped from it with an irritating daintiness that made Suzie want to swat it away from her. Her right pinkie stuck straight up, making her look like a proper society lady enjoying a spot of tea. She was very prim and ladylike, an impression undercut somewhat by her black mourning dress, which was shorter and more form-fitting than was proper for a woman her age, in Suzie's opinion. She had a nice figure for such an old cunt, though. The dress did made her look sort of sexy. Sexy for a woman of sixty-one, anyway. But it was not at all appropriate for a funeral service. Suzie supposed the old bat had been hoping to hook up with one of the older gentlemen in attendance.

Disgusting.

And now this.

Don't you tell me what to do, you fucking hag. He's my son, not yours.

Suzie blew out a cloud of cigarette smoke. "The boy's father just died, Ella. He needs time. He'll be more upset if I bother him."

Ella waved at the haze of smoke. "I wish you wouldn't do that in here."

"My house. I'll do what I want."

Ella sniffed. "How childish. You know those things are deadly. And if you don't care about your own health, at least think about your boy. You're all he has now."

If you don't start minding your own business soon, I'll put this thing out in your goddamn eye, you hag.

Suzie reminded herself she would only have to endure the woman's company for one more night. Just one more night of playing the somber, grief-stricken widow. One more night of getting an earful of Ella's advice on how to deal with sudden widowhood. Suzie needed none of that. She already knew exactly what to do. She dimly heard her Blackberry buzzing in her purse, which was propped on the island in the middle of the kitchen. It would be Tom again.

She snatched the phone out of her purse.

Sure enough, there was a new message from Tom.

Must see u soon. Safe to call now.

Suzie flashed her mother-in-law a phony smile. "Excuse me. I just need a minute."

She ducked out of the kitchen before Ella could reply and made her way to the opposite end of the house, where she slipped into her own bedroom and shut and locked the door behind her. She pulled up Tom's number and put the call through.

He answered on the first ring. "Hey."

She smiled as she sat on the edge of the bed and pulled at the hem of her black dress He had such a sexy voice. "Hey yourself."

He sighed. "I'm so glad to hear your voice."

She laid back on the bed and lifted her ass to pull the hem of the dress up over her thighs. She settled her ass on the mattress again and touched herself through already wet cotton panties. "Where are you? I wish I could see you."

Another sigh, the regret and horniness in it palpable through the phone. "I'm at home. Lydia's gone to the grocery store. But she won't be gone long. If I have to hang up suddenly, it's because she's back."

Suzie wriggled a little on the bed. "You meant what you said, right?"

"Um...about what?"

"That you love me."

"Of course."

She smiled again, liking how fast the reply came. She needed this thing with Tom to happen. Kurt had left behind a significant amount of money and there was a generous life insurance policy that would be paying out at some point. She had more than enough to pay the bills and be comfortable for the foreseeable future. But she needed a provider in her life. She wanted to be more than comfortable. She wanted luxury and the endless indulgence of a handsome man who worshiped her. Tom could give her all that and more.

"I want you, baby. So bad."

He coughed. "I want you, too. I can't take Lydia anymore. She's fucking crazy. She's never been able to get over, you know...you and me."

"You poor thing. It must be hard, living with that."

"You don't know the half of it."

"Some people just aren't as strong as us, baby. They can't get past their own insecurities. I'm sure she's made life a living hell for you. I'll make you happy again, I promise."

But even as she uttered these reassurances, she was thinking how a man who strayed while married to one woman could surely do so again with another. Once they were married, she would make the potential consequences of cheating on her very clear.

"Tom?"

"Yeah?"

"You're the man of my dreams. I want to be with you forever."

"You will be. You're all I've been thinking about the last few days. And...hold on. Shit. I have to go."

The phone went dead in her ear. She sighed and for a moment felt an aching emptiness. No matter. Tom would belong to her soon enough.

She returned to the kitchen.

Which was empty.

Thank fuck.

She'd not been looking forward to resuming the maddening conversation with Ella. She realized how exhausted she was. A nap would be nice. She started back toward the bedroom, but stopped at the archway separating the kitchen from the living room and foyer. She quirked an eyebrow, thinking she'd heard something strange. A gasp. Or a moan. She poked her head through the archway and stared up the flight of stairs leading to the second floor. It was dark up there, but there was a slice of dim light visible through the slightly cracked door to Derek's bedroom. The gasp came again.

You naughty boy.

It sounded like he was masturbating up there and trying to keep quiet about it.

Why, Derek...jerking off on the day of your father's funeral...my, my...I guess you're not better than me after all, eh?

All thoughts of rest were quickly forgotten. She stepped out of her two-inch heels and began to ascend the carpeted stairs in her stockinged feet, treading lightly to avoid warning creaks. Instinct told her the act of voyeurism she planned was a bad idea. She was still concerned by the strange change in his demeanor. But the residual erotic charge from her conversation with Tom overrode her common sense. She was remembering her original plans for Derek on the night of Kurt's death. She very much hoped to catch him in the act. And there was that cracked door to consider. It was almost as if he *hoped* to be spied on.

Oh, I'll spy on you, darling.

And maybe it won't stop there.

But she paused again halfway up the stairs, frowning as she remembered more about that night. He had returned home shortly before dawn, shimmying up that tree to crawl through the window to his room, where she had been waiting. Her intent had been to hit him with the news of his father's death right off the bat. She would reassert her authority over him while he was off balance, berating him for not being there in her hour of need. And then she would punish him, giving him the thorough thrashing he should have received hours earlier. The cops and paramedics were long gone by then, Kurt's bloated corpse gone with them. The boy needed to be corrected, and there was no one around to prevent her from using any means she deemed necessary to adjust his behavior.

But she abandoned this plan as soon as he entered the room, the color draining from her face as she got a good look at him. His clothes had been reduced to shredded rags that barely hung on his slim frame. Most of his body was visible through huge holes in the fabric, and much of the flesh she could see was bruised and scraped. He had cuts on his face and all over his arms and back. A closer look at the dark clothes showed they were stained with blood. Once she got past the initial shock of seeing him like that, she assumed he'd been in a brutal fight, had maybe been lucky to escape with his life.

His eyes looked darker than they should, almost black. He didn't say anything, but that moment was when she first realized something was wrong. Something deeper than the obvious physical abuse he'd endured. Then his eyes rolled back in his head and he toppled over, a dead weight crashing to the floor, rocking the hardwoods and causing his guitar to fall off its stand. The Les Paul landed with a jangly, discordant thud. She had screamed then, certain he had died. He hadn't died, though, and his breathing had seemed regular. But he didn't wake up for hours. She wavered for a time over whether to call 911 again, but in the end she decided to wait it out. She stripped his ruined clothes from his body and wrestled him into his bed. It wasn't hard. He didn't weigh much. She covered him with a sheet and left him there. The next she called his school to let them know he wouldn't be in for several days due to bereavement.

He slept until late afternoon. As planned, she hit him with the news as soon as he was awake. "I'm sorry, Derek, but your father died this morning. A heart attack."

He'd nodded. "Okay."

That was it.

No expression of grief. No questions. He accepted all her instructions about how to behave around the relatives and what to wear to the funeral. He didn't say much at all in the ensuing days. He just watched her with those too-dark eyes and that smug expression.

She gave her head a hard shake and started up the stairs again.

Probably a lot of it was just her imagination. She had a lot to deal with, after all. And Derek was a typical sullen teenager, prone to a lot of the usual weird mood shifts.

She reached the second floor landing and heard more muffled gasps emerging from his room. And then a low moan. She smiled. *Definitely sexual.* But there was something about those sounds...some subtle variations in the timbre. It almost sounded like a couple trying to keep quiet about fucking rather than one person masturbating. But that made no sense. None of Derek's few friends were here today. In fact, they hadn't been around at all.

It didn't occur to her to wonder again about Ella's whereabouts until she peered through the crack in the door.

The old cunt was in the room with Derek.

Suzie slapped a hand over her mouth to stifle a gasp. Her first instinct was to retreat, get back down the stairs as quickly and quietly as possible. But she felt rooted to the spot. The reality of what she was seeing was impossible to accept for several moments, but it just kept going on, affirming that it was not a hallucination. They were on Derek's narrow bed. Ella was beneath him, with that little black dress hiked up over her waist. Suzie spied a scrap of black cloth on the floor. Thong panties. Most of Derek's funeral outfit was also on the floor. The polished black shoes, the dark gray trousers. He still wore the crisp white shirt, but the front of it hung open. She saw a scattering of white buttons on the floor. He was positioned directly above Ella, his hands braced flat on the mattress on either side of her, arms locked and rigid at the elbows, upper body arched high. Her legs were spread wide, the slender white limbs looking ghostly pale in the dim light. The light was dim because someone had tossed another shirt over the nightstand lamp. Ella's head was turned to one side, and a corner of the pillow beneath her head was in her mouth. She was using it to muffle her gasps.

Oh my God...

Suzie's mind reeled.

Despite the twisted fantasies she had entertained herself, her mind was temporarily incapable of processing this on any level. Ella was a little shameless in her flirtations with men her own age, but these were all normal interactions. Hell, she was a regular grandmother in most ways. A fucking cookie baker.

She could think of no way to explain it.

She only knew she had to get away *right now*.

She backed up one step.

And that was when Derek's head snapped toward her. There was that horrible, knowing grin again. And his eyes weren't just too dark, they were black. *Entirely* black. He snarled and bounded off the bed, crossing the room in two leaping strides.

Suzie was able to take one more backward step.

Then the door was open and he had her by a wrist. His grip was impossibly strong, like iron.

There were tears in her eyes. "Derek...DeeDee...I... please..."

He laughed and then snarled as he hauled her through the door. She screamed as he tossed her across the room. She bounced off the wall and struck the nightstand. She managed to stay upright, but the lamp tumbled to the floor and the light went out.

But she could see Derek stalking toward her in the gloom.

She felt hands grabbing her from behind.

Ella. You bitch.

Then Derek was on top of her, pushing both of them backward onto the bed. She screamed again when she felt Ella's bony hands ripping at her dress.

Derek backhanded her and the world went dark for a time.

TWENTY-ONE

Two weeks after Kurt McGregor's funeral, Natasha Wagner awoke at dawn feeling nauseated and achy. She rolled onto her side seeking relief from a pain in her lower back and winced as her stomach did a queasy roll. She stuck a knuckle in her mouth to stifle a low whimper. A sheen of sweat broke out on her forehead as she suddenly felt too hot beneath her covers. She tossed the blankets aside and lay there breathing rapidly in her black Corpse Bride pajamas. It was November now and a seemingly permanent chill had settled into the air outside, but she was soaked in sweat. Her teeth chattered as sudden tears stung her eyes.

Please, a desperate voice in her mind implored. *Please just let me be sick with the flu. I can't do the other thing, I just can't. Please...*

The flu would make sense. It was getting to be that time of the year again. Her father had just gotten over a nasty cold. Perhaps he'd passed the bug on to her. But the flu wouldn't explain the strange new tenderness in her breasts or the episode at the dinner table last night. Her mother had served up grilled chicken with broccoli, which was usually one of her favorite meals. But one whiff of the chicken had sent her scrambling to the bathroom to heave her guts out. That had led to some uncomfortable questions from Colleen Wagner. Luckily, she had lots of practice at deflecting parental concerns.

She wished she had someone to talk to about what was happening to her body. Someone other than a judgmental adult. A girlfriend. Fiona, preferably. But she hadn't talked to Fiona at all in the last two weeks. Same went for the rest of her friends, including Mark. *Oh, Mark.* She missed him so

115

much, but she couldn't bear to be around him. She still loved him fiercely, but she simply couldn't look him in the eye. She couldn't interact with any of them in any significant way without feeling a deep, soul-crushing shame. When she was around them at school, she could think only of all the awful, degrading things they'd done together in the basement of that house. She had performed sexual acts with every one of them. It might not have been so bad had the episode merely been a wild but consensual experiment in group sex. But something had been guiding them, a malevolent thing that delighted in their debasement. There had been no choice in any of it. Natasha had prayed for death near the end of the ordeal.

Another, stronger surge of nausea accompanied the vile memories.

Knowing she could contain the sickness inside her no longer, Natasha lurched off the bed and staggered across the room to her bathroom. She groaned again as dropped to her knees in front of the toilet. She leaned over the bowl and felt her throat swell as a rush of hot vomit blasted up from the depths of her tortured stomach. Her teeth chattered again and a fresh sheen of sweat made her pale face glisten in the bright light. She continued to kneel there for a time, breathing hard as she prayed this was the end of it.

She glanced up at a framed poster mounted on the wall above the toilet. It was for the original version of *The Texas Chainsaw Massacre.* It showed Leatherface with his chainsaw and a girl dangling from the business end of a meat hook. The tagline on the poster read, *Who will survive and what will be left of them?*

"Yes," she said, smiling grimly through her tears. "What will be left of us?"

Another framed poster was mounted on the wall by the glass shower stall. Janet Leigh in *Psycho.* Her parents didn't understand her interest in morbid things, but they tried. When it came to parental acceptance and tolerance, she had it a lot better than most of her friends. During one of many conversations with Colleen Wagner on the subject, Natasha had said, "Horror is my life." Her mother didn't scoff or admonish her to pursue more practical interests. Natasha loved her for that. Only now she wished she'd never uttered those words, because now the statement seemed more like prophecy than an expression of her fondest dreams and desires.

Yes, she thought. *Horror is my life, for real now. And I don't see a happy ending to this fucking movie...*

She stayed there in front of the toilet until she was sure her stomach had settled. Then she pushed the flush handle, got up, and had a look at herself in the mirror. She looked like hell. There were dark smudges under her eyes. She had been sleeping more now that she'd stopped going out at night, but somehow she looked more tired than ever.

I look like shit.

Feel like it, too.

She couldn't bear looking at herself any longer, so she traipsed tiredly back to her room, her shoulders slumped and her head hanging down, the cuffs of her too-long pajama bottoms dragging across the carpet.

She sat on the edge of the bed and debated whether she should start getting ready for school or have her mom call in sick for her. School was another thing that was harder to deal with now. As if being violated by some kind of demon or ghost wasn't enough, the very same night some asshole had vandalized her car, painting nasty words on the doors. Something similar had been done to Mark's car. Under any other circumstances, she would have been livid, barely able to contain her fury. And Mark would have been on the warpath. But in the wake of their harrowing shared experience, it had amounted to little more than an afterthought. So someone wanted to be an asshole, so what? She had bigger things on her mind, including an increasingly tenuous grasp on her sanity. Still, things were undeniably tenser at school. The spell of intimidation she and her friends had cast as a group was broken. She felt the smirking stares of her classmates every time she walked the halls of Ransom High. It was annoying, but she remained too numb to care most of the time.

She noticed the glowing screen on her cell phone, which she'd left on the nightstand the night before. Someone had texted her within the last minute. She knew this because the screen always went dark again less than a minute after receiving a message.

She picked up the phone and cringed as she recognized Mark's number.

The message read, *Come out tonight. Please?*

She deleted the message without sending a reply and set the phone down again. At least not as long as she still lived in Ransom. Her breath hitched as an intense sense-memory of kissing Mark assailed her. She could almost feel his strong arms wrapped around her waist, holding her so firmly against her body. It had felt *wonderful*. She started crying again. It was almost like he was in the room with her right now.

Only he wasn't.

And never would be again. She'd made up her mind.

She was wiping more tears away as a knock sounded at her door. "Tasha? Honey? It's getting late. Are you ready for school yet?"

Natasha cleared her throat, "I'm not going, mom. I think I've got that bug dad had."

"Oh, honey." Colleen Wagner's voice was full of concern and devoid of reproach. "You stay in bed. I'll call the school for you."

Natasha sniffled. "Thanks, mom. I love you."

"I love you, too, sweetie. Oh, honey, I have some good news."

Good news? How novel.

"Oh, yeah?"

"Your father told me he spoke to the boys at the paint shop. Your car will be ready today."

Natasha sighed. "Cool."

And then Colleen Wagner was gone, leaving Natasha alone again with her tortured thoughts. She slipped beneath the covers again, crying some more as she thought of Mark and the life she suspected was growing inside her.

The life she could never tell him about.

She buried her face in her hands and cried hard enough to shake the bed.

TWENTY-TWO

Somebody was knocking on the door. Check that. It was more like a *hammering* on the door. A heavy, loud, relentless pounding. Clayton could hear the door rattling in the frame as he slowly became conscious and blinked against the glare of the TV screen. He sat upright with a groan and pressed the heels of his palms into his eyes to massage them.

BAMBAMBAM

Perhaps a half second of blissful silence.

Then...

BAMBAMBAMBAMBAMBAMBAMBAM—

His hands came away from his eyes. "STOP DOING THAT YOU COCKSUCKING MOTHERFUCKING ASS-HOLE SON OF A FUCKING WHORE!"

This was followed by a sob.

And then laughter.

Wow, I have seriously gone off the rails. This is probably how your average psycho asshole sounds before heading out to shoot up a mall or church social.

BAMBAMBAM

"Fuck this." He pitched his voice a little higher. "Knock it off! I'm coming, goddamn you!"

He heaved himself to his feet and staggered out of the living room. He was still feeling the beers that had put him under a few hours back. He hadn't checked the clock on the cable box before departing the living room, but a rough guess put the time at around midnight. He was in the foyer now, standing at the front door, with one shaking hand poised above the doorknob.

He pulled the hand back.

Hold on. Midnight?

Things hadn't gone so well for him the last time he'd answered a late night knock at his door. Parts of his body still ached from the beating dished out by that jackbooted thug. At least he wasn't pissing blood anymore. That had been scary as hell and had almost been enough to make him actually go to a doctor, a thing he hadn't done in...what... decades? Luckily the red in his urine gave way to a pinkish tinge by the second day and was back to its usual bright yellow by the third. He was hopeful his body would continue to recover well enough without outside help. One obvious and excellent way of making sure of that was avoiding any contact with a certain Nazi pig with a badge.

BAMBAM

There's no way that jackass has a search warrant. I have nothing to hide. I've done nothing wrong, and I'm not letting him in.

Clayton frowned.

His self-righteous outrage was immediate and instinctive. But some of it wasn't quite based in actual fact. He did have some things he wouldn't like agents of local enforcement to see. Some dope and some of the more embarrassing bits of his porn collection. And, okay, sure, he'd done some things that were technically wrong. Selling dope to minors, for instance. Selling illicit substances to *anyone* was a crime, but he thought maybe there was a stiffer penalty for selling it to the underage and impressionable. His frown deepened as he scratched his chin and thought about it. Huh. Was that right? He shrugged. He didn't know. And it didn't fucking matter. He'd step in front of a speeding bus before going to prison.

BAMBAMBAMBAMBAMBAMBAMBAMBAMBAM!

The horrendously loud banging—by far the worst burst of it yet—left his head pounding. Anger started to override his fear. Then something hit the door again, a softer sound. Instinct told him it was the sound of a body slumping against the door. Then there was another sound.

A low, hitching sob.

Then he heard it again. It was the sound of a person in deep pain. A bereft sound. Whoever this was, it wasn't that cop. That man was a vicious monster. And he for damn sure wouldn't be weeping on Clayton Campbell's doorstep.

One of the kids. Has to be.

He hadn't seen any of them in weeks. Not since that terrible night. Something had happened. Something that had changed everything. He had no proof of this. No one had told him a thing. But he felt it in his heart. There had been evil in the air that night and it had touched more than just him. The death of Derek's father the same night reinforced this opinion. And he was positive their absence had nothing to do with the bogus assault story Fiona had fed the cop. A tale like that wouldn't fly with the other kids. They would see right through her self-serving line of bullshit.

At least he hoped so.

Despite everything, he still wanted them to like him. Even Fiona.

He turned the doorknob and eased the door open. A stench of booze wafted through the cracked door before he opened it the rest of the way and saw a slightly stooped-over Mark Bell standing on his porch. His eyes were red and wet and his head wobbled woozily on his shoulders. A liter bottle of some liquor was clenched in his right fist, a crinkled brown paper bag obscuring the brand.

Mark looked Clayton in the eye and began to weep openly, his shoulders going up and down as the force of his emotions shook his body. Clayton was flabbergasted. The Mark Bell he knew was tough. Was maybe the toughest kid he'd ever met. He grimaced and beckoned the boy inside with a tilt of his head. Mark wobbled inside, nearly toppling over as one of his feet slid awkwardly over the threshold. Clayton caught him by a shoulder and kept him upright.

Clayton peeled the liquor bottle from Mark's fingers. Mark groped for it, mumbling a protest, but Clayton held the bottle out of reach and moved away from the kid to throw the door shut. "You've had enough. I don't know what's going on with you, but I *do* know that."

He steered the boy into the living room, where he collapsed on the sofa and struggled to keep his eyes open. He was probably moments away from passing out. Clayton was okay with that. The kid needed to sleep his drunk off. It was strange. They usually only started drinking around this time, but Mark had evidently been at it for hours.

This kid's parents aren't paying any fucking attention to him at all.

It made Clayton angry, largely because of how closely it paralleled his own youth.

What's wrong with those assholes? Hell, I'm *a better parent to these kids than their own flesh and blood.*

Clayton knew he was a lousy role model, too, but it felt fucking true, dammit.

Mark wasn't ready to pass out yet, though. He sat there with his head back on the headrest for a few moments. His eyes fluttered some, but he did not lose consciousness. Eventually he gave his head a hard shake and scooted to the edge of the sofa to stare up at Clayton through red-rimmed eyes. "Dude, please...can I have a beer? I know I've had enough of the hard stuff."

Clayton studied the kid a bit longer before replying. His eyes, while still nowhere close to sober, possessed a surprising steadiness. There was something he wanted to talk about and he was determined to stay conscious until he'd vomited all the words out. "Okay. Hang tight. Don't go falling off the edge of the world while I'm gone, okay?"

Mark managed a woozy smile. "Yeah. Okay."

Clayton went to the kitchen, where, he paused in front of the magnet-and-note-covered refrigerator door to peel the crinkled paper bag off the liquor bottle, grimacing when he saw the Bacardi 151 label.

Boy wasn't kidding—this is definitely the hard stuff.

He crumpled the brown bag and dropped it in the trash can. He then screwed the cap off the bottle and took a deep swig, his face twisting at the burn in his throat. It was good shit, but better mixed with something, both to soothe the palate and dilute the serious kick of the booze. Somehow the kid had downed nearly a third of the big bottle without slipping into a coma. Odds were good he'd be dead to the world by the time Clayton returned to the living room.

He cleared his throat. "You awake in there, son?"

The reply came back sooner and clearer than he'd expected: "Hell, yes. Hurry back with that beer."

Clayton took one more drink from the bottle and screwed the cap back on. He set it on the counter and opened the fridge. The top shelf was dominated by a few dozen loose bottles of beer, an eclectic mixture of brewing styles and brands. When it came to beer, Clayton liked variety. There were pales ales, lagers, pilsners, stouts, porters, and various creative variations on those styles. There was also one bottle of Bud Light, a leftover from a previous visit by Mark Bell and friends. He grabbed the bottle of Bud Light and pushed aside some of the other bottles to grope around in the back. Just as he began to suspect the object of his search had gone missing, he spied it in a corner, wedged behind a big bottle of Dead Guy Ale. The bottle of non-alcoholic O'Doul's was a relic of his latest, halfhearted effort at sobriety.

Doomed from the start, he thought with a rueful smile. *You'll never dry out, because there's no part of you that really wants that.*

Clayton popped the caps off both bottles and dumped the contents of the Bud Light bottle in the sink. Still standing over the sink, he used both hands to carefully refill the empty Bud Light bottle with the non-alcoholic brew. He then dropped the O'Doul's bottle in the trash can, grabbed a bottle of Snake Dog IPA for himself, and returned to the living room.

Mark accepted the bottle with a wry smile. "What, I'm not good enough for one of your beer snob brews?"

Clayton dropped into a recliner positioned at an angle that allowed it to face both the TV and the sofa. "You wanted a beer, there ya go. I figured you should have a weak one."

Mark took a tentative sip. "Ugh."

Clayton shrugged. "It is what it is."

"That's fucking brilliant, man."

Clayton smiled. "I know. I coined that phrase. Little known fact."

"You're full of shit."

"I know." Clayton took a sip of his own beer. "Now why don't you tell me why you look like death warmed over."

Mark smirked. "Death warmed over, huh? You coin that one, too?"

"This is what your typical social worker son of a bitch would call an avoidance tactic. Cut the shit and tell me what's up."

Mark's smirk withered. His face seemed to crumple. The tears came hard and fast. Rivulets of moisture ran down the boy's forearm. As he watched the kid cry, he felt a heaviness in his chest, a swelling of dormant emotion. *You've been an idiot. These are just kids. Really just kids. Savvier and tougher than most, but really just kids when you get down to it.*

He didn't know what to do. Had not the first idea what to say.

But he had to try.

"Kid...come on. It'll be okay."

"*NO IT WON'T!*" he wailed. He angrily swiped moistures from his eyes and glared at Clayton. "I fucking love her, man. I love her *so* much. She won't answer my goddamn calls or messages. She avoids me at school. I even went up to her house today and knocked on her door. I've never done that. Her parents don't even know me. How fucked is that? Her mom answered, said Natasha doesn't want to see me."

"Hold on. How did she know that? You said she doesn't know you."

Mark threw up a hand in exasperation. "Shit, I don't know, man. I guess Natasha gave her a fucking good description. She said I was to never show up there again or she'd call the fucking police."

Clayton nodded. "Uh huh. Okay. So, and I'm not making light here, I just want this clear in my head—the reason you're all tore up is your girlfriend has dumped you. That's all that's going on?"

Mark visibly fought for control and when he had at least

a semblance of it, he sipped from the Bud Light bottle. "No, man." His voice was lower now, almost somber. No. Not that. *Scared.* "There's something else. Something happened. Something so fucked up it's got me wanting to fucking kill myself so I can stop thinking about it."

Clayton took another drink. "Okay. So tell me about it."

Mark heaved a breath. "There's this house. Old and abandoned. Way back in the woods on the other side of Weakley Lane. We broke in, you know, just something to do. Something was there. Something...bad. It made us do things. Terrible, horrible fucking things."

One phrase hit Clayton hard.

Something was there.

The Snake Dog bottle slipped from suddenly numb fingers and cracked open on the hardwood floor. "Shit."

Mark squinted at him. "Dude...are you all right?"

Clayton didn't say anything. A deep chill insinuated itself around his heart.

An idea appeared to penetrate the thick cloud of inebriation engulfing Mark's brain. "Hey...do you know something about that house?"

Clayton forced himself to swallow and take a deep breath. "It's the Hollis house. What I know about it is what my father told me before he killed himself. I never believed any of it. Too crazy. But my father believed it. It's *why* he killed himself. And if any part of that craziness was even a little bit true, it would explain why you're acting this way, especially if you did something as completely fucking stupid as breaking into that house."

The kid definitely looked scared now. "I wish we could take it back. Never go in that fucking place."

Clayton groaned. "But you did."

"Yeah."

"You idiot. All of you. Fucking idiots."

"Yeah."

Clayton heaved himself out of the recliner and went to the kitchen. He came back with a dustpan and a little hand broom. He swept up the broken glass, returned to the kitchen to dispose of the pile of brown shards, and grabbed two more beers from the fridge.

In the living room, he shoved a bottle of Guinness at Mark. "Take that."

Mark looked confused. "I still haven't finished the first one."

"It's fucking O'Doul's in a Bud Light bottle. I was trying to be responsible and shit, but fuck that. Take it."

Mark took it.

Clayton settled in the recliner again. "Fuck. Okay. Look. You're gonna need to be sober for this, so I'll save most of it for later. Tomorrow night, say. And try to get as many of your friends over here as you can."

"I'm not really talking to any of them right now."

Clayton jabbed a finger in Mark's direction. "It's important."

Mark nodded. "Okay. I'll try. Do my best, whatever."

"You do that. Now just tell me this—did you also manage to get your stupid asses down inside that basement?"

Mark's jaw began to quiver at the mention of the basement.

It was all the answer Clayton needed.

"Right."

Tears were leaking from Mark's eyes again. "What did we do? Oh my God, what did we do?"

Clayton's mouth was a grim, hard line. "Well, I'm still not saying I believe any of this, but..."

"But?" Mark prompted.

Clayton drained the rest of his beer in a single, long pull. "Be careful when approaching your friends about coming over here tomorrow."

"Careful...how? You can trust them, Clay. They're not gonna tell anybody about this shit."

"That's not what I mean. When you talk to them tomorrow, I want you to pay real close attention to how they act. Watch for any sign of something...off. It could be something subtle, or it could be something really fucking obvious right off the bat. I don't know. All I have to go on is what my father told

126

me when he was drunk that last night, babbling craziness about demon possession."

Mark shivered. "You think one of my friends is possessed by a fucking *demon*?"

Clayton shrugged. "I don't know, you tell me. You were the one there that night. *Something was there*. Remember? What do *you* think?"

"Andras."

Clayton felt an unaccountable chill at the mention of the name. "Who is..."

"He says he's a Grand Marquis of Hell. I heard him speak in my head. We all did. I hoped I was imagining it...group hypnosis or some shit."

Clayton snorted. "Group hypnosis, my fat ass. You're not some slimy government agent covering up a UFO sighting. But just to eliminate any other alternate theories...I know you kids like to party...you sure you weren't on anything hallucinogenic? Acid or mushrooms, shit like that?"

Mark shook his head a single, emphatic time. "No. Just the booze. A little weed, maybe."

"I believe you. Had to ask, though. Well, if this shit is for real, maybe my father wasn't so crazy after all. Which means there's a good chance you and your idiot pals may have released a fucking demon from its prison. And, yeah, one of you is probably fucking possessed." A humorless laugh. "Congratulations."

Mark set the Guinness bottle down and buried his face in his hands again.

"Like I told you, watch your friends, Mark. Watch them close. You get any kind of wrong vibe, you shut your mouth about this meeting and get away from them. Got it?"

Mark lifted his tear-streaked face again.

He still looked scared and broken-hearted, but there was another quality there now, too, a hint of something like hope. The kid was putting his faith in Clayton Campbell.

Which, in Clayton Campbell's informed opinion, was a hell of a fucking thing.

"Got it."

TWENTY-THREE

December 6, 1984

The mayor's mansion in Ransom sat at the top of a gently rising hill. The enormous lawn was a neatly tended lush expanse of green. A crew of landscapers worked the lawn tirelessly to keep it looking as resplendent as any golf course on the PGA tour. The big plantation-style house was set a hundred yards back from the road and was surrounded by a tall wrought-iron privacy fence with a security gate at the foot of the driveway. Technically, of course, it wasn't a private residence. On paper, the property belonged to the town. But everyone in Ransom knew the mansion essentially belonged to Luke Harper, who had occupied the office of mayor for close to thirty years.

After being buzzed through the gate, Norman Campbell sped up the long, semi-circular driveway, bringing his Cadillac to a screeching, rubber-peeling halt alongside a high, many-stepped marble porch that looked nearly as grand as the Lincoln Memorial in DC. Norman huffed and puffed as he flew up the steps. A stiffening wind lifted his tie and blew it backward over his shoulder. He was out of breath by the time he reached the door and jabbed a thumb at the round doorbell. He was still breathing hard and palming sweat from his forehead when the door opened. Frederick, a very proper English butler straight out of the pages of a Wodehouse story, greeted him with a look of intense dismay.

The butler opened his mouth to say something, but Norman cut him off with a wave of his hand. "I have to see Luke...the mayor...right now."

Frederick's expression remained wary. "I'm afraid the mayor is busy at the moment. You may wish to call his office and arrange an appointment."

Norman fumed. He wasn't some common Joe Blow with some kind of crackpot grievance against the city. "Don't fuck with me, Freddy. This is a goddamn emergency and the mayor *will* want to hear about it. Believe me, it's your ass if you drag your prissy little heels on this. Now hop to it, goddammit."

Frederick's expression darkened. Probably wanted to punch him in the face. Fat chance of that. The prick knew his place. He was the help. Nothing more. "I will apprise the mayor of your arrival. Wait here, sir."

Norman smiled. "Sure thing, Freddy."

Frederick disappeared through a tall archway to their left and Norman heard the heels of his polished black shoes clicking down the hardwood floor of a hallway. Left alone, Norman went into a kind of trance as his mind again fixated on the events leading up to the death of Louella.

He jumped when Frederick reappeared. "The mayor will see you now, sir. If you'll follow me..."

Norman clapped a hand to his chest. "Goddamn, Freddy."

The butler lifted an eyebrow approximately one millimeter. "Sir?"

"I'm a big ol' bundle of nerves today, Jeeves. You don't want to go sneaking up on a man like that." He thumped his chest again. "Jesus goddamn Christmas. All right. Lead the way."

In a few minutes, he was seated in Luke Harper's private study. He had a glass of whiskey in one hand and a freshly lit Cohiba in the other. The booze and the tobacco helped take the edge off his nerves, but that didn't stop him from squirming beneath the considerable force of the mayor's unflinching gaze. He listened to Norman's grim tale in attentive silence. When Norman was finished, Harper used his desk phone to make a call. He hung up after issuing terse instructions. "I've sent some men to retrieve the corpse. So... the bitch meant to blackmail you?"

129

Norman gulped more whiskey. "Oh, yes. Definitely. And wait...what do you mean 'retrieve'? They're not bringing her back here?"

"Don't concern yourself with that. This woman also asked you to hire a man to kill Audrey?"

"Yes. I...look, I know how crazy it sounds, but—"

Harper raised a hand to cut him off. "I don't care how it sounds. You did what needed doing. A woman has to know her place, Campbell. What concerns me about this incident isn't that you killed a gold-digging whore, but rather the location of the incident."

"It was just a boarded-up old house."

Harper shook his head. "No. It is much more than that. And this issue is so much more complicated than you know. For instance, are you aware that your father also committed acts of murder on that property?"

Norman frowned. "Um...what? But he's..."

"Yes, he's been dead a long time. And this happened a long time ago."

"Wait...you said murders, as in more than one?"

Harper's smile was strained. "Your father killed a number of people. Two of them at the Hollis house.. The other concerning aspect of this matter is the identity of the woman you killed. She is...was...a descendant of Frank and Eleanor Hollis...who were murdered by your father. This cannot be coincidence."

Norman drained the last of his whiskey. "This is crazy. You're telling me my father was...what...a serial killer?"

"He was a man interested in power, a trait he passed on to you. And he had some...arcane ways of acquiring power."

"Such as?"

Harper folded his fingers steeple-style as he leaned over his desk. "Your father was a practitioner of what some would call black magic. He was capable of summoning and binding demons. Powerful entities he used to intimidate and bully his adversaries."

Norman laughed. "This is a joke...right?"

"No."

"So...he was crazy?"

"No."

Norman puffed on the Cohiba and grinned broadly as he pointed an index finger at Harper. "All right, old buddy. You had me goin' pretty good there, but—"

The mayor abruptly stood and circled his desk to stand before him. Norman's grin faded as he stared up at the man's face. He had an uneasy, stomach-clenching sense of being in the presence of a dangerous stranger rather than a trusted old friend. The feverish intensity of the man's gaze made him cringe. Jesus, but everything about today was wrong and upside down. He couldn't understand how his entire life had gone so far off track in the course of a few hours. Until today, he'd been happy and successful, utterly content in nearly all aspects of his existence. Now he was a murderer and his best friend was spouting lunatic nonsense. Harper started talking again at some point, but Norman's high state of agitation was such that he heard none of what the man said.

"Are you listening to me?"

Norman blinked. "What?" He stubbed the cigar out and wiped sweat from his forehead. "I don't feel so good."

Harper's mouth twitched. His eyes bugged out in a strange and disturbing way. "Do you feel it?"

"Uh..." Norman scooted to the edge of his chair. *Time to get the hell out.* "I don't know what you're talking about. I don't feel shit. And, uh, you know, I'm starting to think maybe I should, uh...leave. I shouldn't have burdened you with any of this this anyway. A man should clean up his own messes, after all. So I think I'll just be on my way."

He started to rise from the chair.

Harper grinned.

Something in the expression stopped Norman. There was something wrong about it. It looked somehow...inhuman. Almost...feral. It looked a bit like the look you'd expect to see on the face of some savage wilderness predator cornering prey. It was a *hungry* look. A wild and gleeful flash of long-hidden madness.

Norman gulped.

Harper laughed. "You *do* feel it. The presence of the demon."

Norman didn't know what to say. "Uh..."

You are a crazy son of a bitch. Lord, please get me out of here. I'll never sin again, I swear.

Harper abruptly whipped his coat off and flung it across the room. Norman's face twisted in confusion as the man tugged at the tie knotted around his neck. The tie came free and Harper began to rip at the front of his shirt. Buttons popped free of the knitting and went bouncing across the carpeted floor. Norman no longer had any doubt he was in the presence of a deeply insane person. The mayor of Ransom stood panting in the middle of the room, his muscled chest heaving mightily with each big breath. A chest, in fact, that looked a good deal more muscled than it should. Harper had never been a fat slob, but he was soft in the way of many men of his age and position. But now his physique resembled that of a dedicated gym rat, with rippling, hard muscle in evidence all over. Just as inexplicable was the scar tissue on the man's stomach. Norman saw intersecting lines of raised, puckered flesh in a circle. Someone had branded the man with a pentagram.

The same symbol he'd seen painted on one of the boarded-up windows of the Hollis house.

"My God..." Norman was shaking. "What's...wrong with you?"

Harper flashed another savage grin. "Your father shared his demonology secrets with me. Together we raised the demon Andras and his henchman Flauros. In the old days, Andras was called 'the killer of men.' He was among the deadliest of all demons. Your father and I became rich men by harnessing his powers, but Andras was too powerful. We could no longer control him. Something had to be done."

Norman nodded. "Yes. I see. That sounds...sensible."

Harper laughed. "You don't believe me."

Norman shook his head several emphatic times. "No, no, no, I believe you. I mean, I can see how serious this is and, um..." He frowned and scratched his head, unable to think of the right thing to say to pacify this maniac. "Ah..."

Harper slapped his stomach. "*This* was done. Your father seared my flesh to bind Flauros inside me forever." He laughed again. "Well, forever is relative. Flauros is locked away in a corner of my mind." He pointed at his head. "In *here,* where the demonic cocksucker will stay until the day I die. You see, we didn't have much time. They were getting harder to control and we had to do something before they became unbound. They'd kill us if they got loose. We had to bind them in a more permanent way, and we had to separate them because they're stronger together. Sticking Flauros inside me was an imperfect solution, but your father believed it was the best option available at the time. He swore he'd transfer the vile thing to a more permanent prison after the immediate danger was removed. But it never happened. For all his knowledge, he couldn't figure out how to do it. And I can't just release Flauros. It would be suicide."

"Uh huh. So this Flauros fella is in your noggin?"

"He is. He can't control me. The binding magic your father performed was very effective. But his influence bleeds out."

"And that's why you look sorta like that green asshole on TV right now, right? All hulked up?"

The hard muscles in Harper's arms visibly swelled. "Yes."

Norman didn't know what to think. All this demonology stuff had to be nonsense. But Luke's body was transforming right in front of him. There was something not natural happening here. He didn't want to believe it, but he was seeing it and he wasn't the sort to hallucinate. "Okay. So what happened to the other one?"

"Andras." Harper's expression darkened again. "We imprisoned him in the basement of the Hollis house using layers upon layers of binding spells. He is there still, asleep in the darkness and imprisoned underground. Even so, you must have felt his presence when you were there today."

Norman thought of the unnatural chill that had emanated from that house. And that strange sense of being observed.

133

He shrugged. "There was...something."

He jumped at a knock on the door.

Harper's huge muscles rippled like waves as he turned toward the door. He bared his teeth and raised his voice to address the person on the other side: "*Yes?*"

His tone was huskier now, a deep, low down rumble. A wisp of what looked like steam drifted out of his nostrils. His ears twitched and thickened, changing shape to become almost pointed. Norman glanced at the big window to his left. He knew it overlooked the rear of the property, but he couldn't recall whether it was positioned over the hard cement pool deck or the adjoining acres of lush green grass. A leap through the second-story window to the ground below would mean a world of pain either way, but he might just survive a tumble to the ground whereas an impact with the deck would surely mean at least one broken limb. It was something to think about, because this demonology business no longer seemed like such a steaming load of horsehit.

Instinct brought Norman to his feet. He backed away from the mayor and glanced again at the window, psyching himself to take a possibly suicidal dive through the glass. A voice from the other side of the door stopped him cold. "Luke?"

Norman's heart almost seized up. He recognized that voice.

A throaty chuckle rumbled out of Harper's throat. "Come in, dear."

The door opened and Audrey Campbell came into the room, stopping short when she glimpsed Norman's stricken expression. "Oh. I thought I saw your car outside."

Audrey was wearing a sexy red dress that accentuated her lithe curves, the thin fabric clinging to her body like an extra layer of glistening skin. Her high heels raised her shapely ass in a provocative way and emphasized the jut of her large breasts. It was a far cry from the frumpier outfit she'd been wearing this morning. She generally only dressed to kill for the more important social events.

He forced the words out: "What are you doing here?"

Audrey smiled. "Why do you think, Normie?" She went to Harper and draped herself around his still-shifting physique. His thighs had grown huge and were straining the fabric of his khaki trousers. Audrey leaned into the man's massive erection and writhed like a harlot, wanton and shameless. She shot a leer at her husband. "You want to watch, baby?"

Norman's hands curled into fists. "You...*bitch*."

Audrey tossed her head and laughed. "Please. You think I don't know about your all your whore-fucking?" She dragged a red-painted fingernail down the length of Harper's sculpted torso. "Well, I do. So you can take your jealousy and shove it up your tight little ass."

She laughed again.

Harper snarled, sounding more like an animal than ever, and ripped the red dress from her body, exposing generous breasts that jiggled and glistened in the harsh overhead light. The thing that now only vaguely resembled the mayor of Ransom threw her to the floor and fell on top of her. The remaining clothes came off and in seconds Harper was violently fucking his wife on the floor.

Norman reeled.

He couldn't deal with this. At all. It was just too insane. He stumbled toward the door and then through it. He wobbled down the long hallway, pitching from wall to wall until he reached the second floor landing, where he took a moment to gather his wits. He winced as he listened to Audrey's high-pitched shrieks of ecstasy. It was that damnable sound that at last drove him down the stairs.

He was just starting toward the big double front doors when they burst open and Frederick came through them wielding a chainsaw.

Norman screamed and toppled over.

Everything went fuzzy for a time.

When he came to, he was in the mansion's large garage. He saw Frederick and again felt the urge to scream. The man was still wielding the chainsaw, but the power tool wasn't on. His coat was gone and in its place was a thick leather apron. He didn't much look like a proper English butler just now. His gleeful grin made him look like something from a nightmare. At first he was certain Frederick meant use the chainsaw on him, but a glimpse of something else familiar drew his still slightly foggy vision to the floor and this time he did scream.

It was that woman. That blackmailing bitch.

She'd come back from the dead to exact her revenge!

Except...no...she was still dead. Norman struggled to calm down. He was close to hyperventilating. The woman was there, but she was a corpse. He made himself focus on that fact and that alone for a few moments. Then he saw that a large, clear sheet of plastic had been spread beneath the body.

It all suddenly clicked.

The chainsaw.

The leather apron.

The sheet of plastic.

Holy fucking shit!

Norman surged to his feet, whirled about, and ran smack into a brick wall. He teetered and stumbled backward, realizing seconds later that he'd run not into a brick wall but a man built like one. He was a large and powerfully built thuggish brute. He was dressed all in black. Black jeans. Black shoes. Black turtleneck sweater. Black watchcap. Black leather gloves. The man's eyes were a hard, pitiless blue and his prominent jaw looked carved from granite.

Frederick laughed. "Say hello to Sasha."

"Ain't that's a girl's name?"

Sasha's nostrils flared.

Frederick smiled. "I'd advise you to keep any further comments impugning the masculinity of dear Sasha's name to yourself, Herr Campbell."

Norman's head just kept spinning. "*Herr*? What in tarnation? You're *German* now?"

Frederick barked more insane laughter and yanked the chainsaw's starter cord. The big McCulloch sputtered and roared to life. He lowered the spinning blade to dead

Louella's fragile neck. The blade bit into the flesh and made an instant, sickening mess of it, sending bits of flesh and gristle flying everywhere. Then the head came off with a pop and went spinning like a top across the plastic sheet.

Norman barely felt the pain as his knees hit the hard cement floor.

He wanted to shut his eyes against the scene of butchery, but he couldn't. He felt nothing but repulsion. Nothing but the most intense loathing and disgust. It didn't matter that he had killed the woman in the first place. That had been instinct. An act of self-preservation born out of desperation. This was something else entirely.

Harper's butler—or whatever the hell he really was—was doing this for *fun*.

Holy Jesus...

Through it all, he remained unable to look away, something inside him compelling him to watch and bear witness as the revving chainsaw reduced his former mistress bit by bit, turning her into unrecognizable piles of bloody meat.

After a seemingly endless time, the act of butchery was at last over.

But Norman knew the horror that had invaded his life was far from over.

He was afraid it might never end.

TWENTY-FOUR

The doorbell rang. Lydia Bell looked up from the latest issue of *Entertainment Weekly* and scowled in the general direction of the front door, which wasn't visible from her current position, which was curled up on the leather sofa in the living room. The doorbell was an unwelcome intrusion. She was used to having the house completely to herself in the morning. With Tom at work and Mark possibly at school (or at least off drinking somewhere with his fellow delinquents), the house was normally quiet this time of day. She never had the television on or listened to music. The silence was sheer bliss. It allowed her some measure of peace in a life that perpetually felt on the edge of collapse.

The doorbell rang again.

"Goddammit!"

It was rare that anyone came calling this time of day. She had distanced herself from her friends in the neighborhood over the last year. The last time any of them had tried to reach out to her had been months ago. Apparently she'd snubbed them one too many times and they'd simply given up, which was fine with Lydia. She no longer desired human interaction or company of any kind.

She got up and stalked out of the living room. As she entered the foyer, the doorbell rang a third time and then a fourth. Each new tone felt like a knife through her skull. Her caller was impatient and obnoxious. Lydia hated whoever it was already. She unlocked the door and yanked it open, a curse dying on her lips as she saw who was standing on her porch.

"Hi!"

Suzie McGregor's voice was bright and chirpy, a perfect match for the broad smile that showed off her perfectly white and straight teeth. Lydia's mouth dropped open as her mind went into a frenzied overdrive. A wide array of conflicting thoughts and emotions bounced around in her head, making it impossible to respond or think straight for several long moments. The gall of this woman! Her instinct was to scream and curse at her, but she didn't want the slut to have the satisfaction of seeing her lose her cool. As she stared in gaping amazement at the woman who had ruined her marriage, a detached, analytical part of her mind began cataloging other odd details. Suzie's hair was perfect, a sleek and stylish cut that made her look like she'd just come from the beauty shop. She was wearing a very short and flattering green dress and high heels. Not exactly typical attire for a chilly fall day. On her ring finger was a diamond ring so big it looked like it should be adorning the finger of a queen. Her bubbly demeanor was odd for a very recent widow. Lydia felt self-conscious and inadequate in her rumpled sweatpants and t-shirt. There was one other strange thing. Suzie had a piece of luggage with her, a black suitcase on rollers with an expandable handle. Lydia hoped the fucking cunt was leaving town forever, but something in the woman's hideously happy smile hinted otherwise.

She gripped the doorknob tighter. "What are you doing here?"

Suzie kept smiling. "Is Tom here yet? He said he'd be here around lunch time."

Lydia's brain did the overdrive dance again. This time it was so intense it propelled her backward into the house. She couldn't understand what was happening. Tom was talking to this woman again. That was all she understood. All the implications that went along with this fact temporarily eluded her. The son of a bitch had broken his solemn vow to never communicate with Suzie McGregor again. She was stunned at how deeply this stung her. She had been thinking seriously about killing the man, so why should her eyes be filling with these damnable tears now?

Suzie followed her into the house and threw the door shut.

The loud sound made Lydia jump. Then her face turned hard. "Get out of my house, you fucking homewrecker!"

Suzie laughed. "I'm not going anywhere. At least not until Tom gets here. Then we'll go away together, leaving you all alone." Her voice pitched higher on *all alone*, then she laughed again. "Which is only what you deserve. Tom tells me you don't know how to satisfy a man. He says he has to think of me to stay hard when he's fucking you, which, by the way, he'll never do again."

Lydia knew her rival was baiting her by preying on her deepest insecurities. She knew damn well she could still take care of her man in the bedroom, but this knowledge did nothing to calm her growing fury. Her hands curled into fists as she considered leaping on the woman to pummel her. The only thing that held her back was noting how physically fit Suzie looked. She looked young and vital and projected strength and a surplus of confidence. Lydia was confused. The bitch looked as if a decade had magically been shaved off her chronological age. She had never been out of shape, not exactly, but she'd carried around the few extra pounds you'd expect of a woman nearing forty.

Suzie noticed her scrutiny and smiled broadly again. She let go of the luggage handle and did a slow twirl, showing off her new physique. "You like? Isn't it amazing? I look like I'm twenty-five again."

Lydia frowned. There was no denying it. She thought of how haggard she must appear next to the new and improved Suzie McGregor and experienced another surge of self-conscious bitterness. "But...how is this possible?"

"Do you believe in the devil, Lydia?"

Lydia's eyes widened at the seeming non-sequitur. There had been rumors in the neighborhood about Suzie. Whispers that she wasn't quite right in the head. Lydia had dismissed this as meaningless gossip, but perhaps there had been an element of truth to it all along. "What the fuck are you talking about?"

"I'm talking about our lord Satan. Do you believe he exists?"

"I believe you might be batshit."

Suzie's big smile did a slow fade. "You shut your mouth."

Lydia couldn't help the instinctive satisfaction she felt at wiping the woman's smug smile from her face. It felt too good after the humiliations she'd already endured. "People talk about you, Suzie. Did you know that? They say there's something wrong with you. Some have even said you should be locked up in a mental hospital."

This last bit was a total fabrication, but the abrupt flare of Suzie's nostrils told her it struck a nerve. "You lie."

Lydia chuckled. "Do I? You're the one raving about the devil."

Suzie surprised her then, recovering her composure almost immediately rather than getting angrier. The big smile returned. "That's because I believe in the dark lord with all my heart. I know this because right now my son is possessed by one of his most powerful servants. His name is Andras, and he is a Grand Marquis of Hell."

Lydia tilted her head. "Um...what?"

There could no longer be any doubt about the woman's mental condition. She wondered if Tom had any idea how deeply unbalanced the bitch really was. She hoped not, because if he was really leaving her for this lunatic, then he deserved whatever hell Suzie would eventually put him through. But that was something she could think about later. She was suddenly certain Suzie was a serious threat in more ways than one. She took a tentative step backward in the general direction of the kitchen, where she could at least grab a knife or find some other form of protection.

Suzie kept smiling. She seemed not at all bothered by Lydia's increased wariness. She ran a hand over the front of her body in a slow, deliberately sensual way. "Ask yourself, how is this possible? You and I both know it would take a lot of expensive cosmetic surgery over a long of period of time and even then I couldn't possibly look this good. So let's rule that out. No doctors performed this miracle." She squeezed her breasts and groaned as her erect nipples became apparent through the thin fabric of her flimsy dress. "No, baby, *this* miracle is a result of Satan's exquisite grace, which deepens within me each time Andras fucks me."

"What?"

Suzie grinned. "You heard me. I'm fucking the demon."

Lydia squinted. "But...didn't you say your son is possessed by this...Andras?"

"Yes."

A wave of disgust carried Lydia backward another few steps. "But...that means..."

Suzie giggled like a naughty schoolgirl. "Yes. Isn't it wonderful?"

"Oh, God."

Lydia ran for the kitchen. She heard the clack-clack of Suzie's high heels following her. The woman had made no move to attack her yet, but that didn't matter. The bitch was chasing her at high speed. That alone was proof her fear was justified. Lydia banged a hip on the kitchen table, sending a sharp stab of agony down her leg. She managed to stay upright and hobbled as fast as she could toward the kitchen counter. The wooden knife block was finally within reach. Her fingers were just brushing the handle of the longest carving knife when Suzie grabbed hold of her ponytail and jerked her roughly backward.

She screamed.

Suzie laughed.

She screamed again as Suzie twisted the ponytail painfully enough to make her knees buckle. Suzie's other hand curled into a fist and drilled into the small of Lydia's back, making her cry out and drop to her knees. Suzie was laughing again as she drove her the rest of the way to the floor. She flipped Lydia over with astonishing ease and straddled her across the waist, pinning her to the floor. Lydia flailed weakly at her. Suzie giggled as she knocked each limp blow aside. Then she started slapping Lydia across the face, whipping her head side to side in a frenzy of hard blows. Lydia soon ceased struggling. She could only weep and endure it.

She had no idea how long it went on.

Backhand blows followed slaps followed backhand blows followed slaps. Her face became very sore and at some point her bottom lip split open, leaking a thin trickle of blood that spilled down her chin and then down her neck, staining the collar of her Amnesty International t-shirt.

Dimly, she heard the sound of a door opening somewhere in the house and felt a faint spark of hope. It had to be Tom coming home. She would be all right now. He might have betrayed her, and he might even have been planning to leave her for Suzie, but she knew he was a decent man at heart. No way would he let this continue.

Heavy footsteps entered the kitchen. Lydia's eyes flicked in the direction of the sound. She saw the lean, masculine form of her husband through a mist of tears. He was in the business suit he'd put on this morning and his briefcase dangled from his right hand. He calmly set the suitcase on the kitchen table and began to loosen his tie as Suzie continued to slap her.

He cleared his throat. "What's going on here?"

Suzie at last stopped hitting her and shot a radiant grin at Tom. "Darling! I came by to help you pack like we planned, but you weren't here. So I decided to kill some time by beating the shit out of your hag of a wife." Her expression became an exaggerated pout, a mock showing of sorrow for her transgression. She put a finger to her mouth and nibbled on a fingernail. "Oh, dear. Did I overstep my bounds?"

Lydia stretched a hand in his direction. "Tom...please... help....me..."

Tom started toward them and Lydia felt another brief flicker of hope.

Then he lifted his foot and stepped on her hand with the thick heel of one of his Oxfords. Lydia cried out again and stared up at him with an expression full of hurt and anguish. Even after all they had been through, how could he do this to her? She noted the huge erection tenting the front of his trousers and understood at last how completely dead the love they'd once shared was.

143

She wanted to die.

She also understood, belatedly, the real reason she'd never been able to kill Tom. Some unspoken part of her had known she wouldn't be able to bear a life that didn't include him.

Suzie said, "We should kill her. It would be fun."

"No, there'd be too many questions. It'd be too messy. We should take her to Andras."

Lydia whimpered.

Somehow Suzie's delusion had infected her husband. Could mental illness really be contagious?

"Yes!" Suzie nodded emphatically. "We should offer her to him. It would make him love us even more. But before we do that..." She looked down at Lydia and her grin seemed broader and madder than ever. "...we should have some fun."

Tom chuckled. "Good idea. Let's take her to the bedroom. There's some things in there we can use. Isn't that right, Lydia?"

Lydia's only answer was another helpless whimper.

Suzie stood and jerked Lydia to her feet.

They each took her by an arm and steered her through the house to the bedroom.

It was a long time before they took her to Andras.

TWENTY-FIVE

When the end of the day bell rang at three that afternoon, Kevin Cooper bolted from his usual seat at the back of his Sociology class and was out of the room before anyone else. He banged through the door and took off down the hallway at high speed.

Mr. Harris, standing behind his desk at the front of the classroom, glanced at the door as it began to swing shut. Then, smirking, he peered at the rest of his still-seated students over the top of his reading glasses. "I'd like you all to finish reading chapter eight from your textbooks tonight and write a one page summary of the material. I won't ask any of you to pass this information along to Mr. Cooper as he clearly has more important business to tend to today."

Several of his students laughed dutifully as they began to gather their books and wander out.

Kent Hickerson stayed seated a moment longer, turning around and leaning backward to speak in hushed tones to Brett Hogan. "You wanna watch Cooper get his ass kicked?"

Brett smiled. "So it's finally happening?"

Kent stood, slinging his book bag over his shoulder. "Oh, yeah. It's totally on. Let's go."

Brett followed Kent out of the classroom.

Kevin got to his locker in record time, legs pumping hard as he ran through hallways and passed through the wide, open lobby that adjoined the front offices and the cafeteria. He then vaulted a short set of steps that led down to another hallway on the other side of school. Banks of lockers lined both sides of the hallway. His was located right next to

145

an open set of double doors. He heard voices emanating from the auditorium as he twisted the dial on his locker's combination lock. He jerked the lock as he turned the dial to the third number in the combination and slammed the base of a fist against the locker door when it didn't budge.

"Fuck!"

He forced himself to take a deep breath and slow down. He put his fingers to the lock and stared at them until they stopped shaking. The school was coming alive with the sounds of student chatter as classrooms began to empty. Soon the halls would be filled with warm, jostling bodies. Things were different now. These days a crowded hallway often meant he could count on at least one deliberate elbow to the ribs or punch in the back. The worst of this so far had occurred a week ago. He was punched and elbowed multiple times, all of which he endured with a tight-lipped stoicism. But then someone tripped him and he crashed to the floor. Someone else stepped on his back and walked over him before he could get to his feet. He heard laughter from several sources as he scrambled to get upright, fighting to hold back tears as he turned in a wobbly circle in the hallway and glared at the people around him. He'd been so sick with fury he was ready and willing to fight any of them. It didn't matter that he could no longer count on his friends to back him up in a conflict, none of whom had been anywhere in the immediate vicinity anyway. He longed to strike out at his tormentors, but he held back, knowing he would just be ganged up on and kicked half to death in the hallway.

This time the lock popped open smoothly. Kevin heaved a sigh of relief and opened the locker. He tossed the Sociology book inside, snagged his keyring off a hook, and shut the locker. As usual lately, he was departing empty-handed, without a single textbook. He didn't give a damn about his grades anymore and was thinking of dropping out. His parents would be pissed, but he didn't fucking care. He just couldn't take this place much longer. Yeah, his job prospects would be few, but so what? He had a car and the open road was available to him at any time. He could probably lay his hands on enough cash to get himself to the nearest big city, where anything could happen.

He passed the open doors to the auditorium and came to a dead stop, a frown twisting his features. He could swear he'd heard a familiar voice issuing from inside. The after school chatter was growing louder and in a few moments this hallway would be swarming with departing students, but he figured he could still spare a moment to satisfy his curiosity. He moved closer to the open doors and peeked inside.

"Huh."

It looked like the drama club was rehearsing something on the stage. They were running through some bit of dialog he didn't recognize, reading from sheets of paper. Natasha Wagner was down there with them, several pages clasped in her own slender hands. A guy finished reading a line and glanced at her. She smiled and recited her next line. She delivered the line with conviction and her body language was less stiff and more natural than some of the other actors. She was good. But Kevin was baffled by Natasha's involvement with these people. Had she always been a part of the drama club? He didn't think so. She'd always been like the rest of their clique. Straight to home from school to sleep the day away so they could stay out all night.

Only none of them were doing that anymore, so far as he knew.

Things had changed, and, apparently, Natasha had reacted by making some changes of her own. He felt a strange sense of reflected pride at the thought. He'd always liked her. She was awesome in all sorts of ways. She was smart and smoking hot. Quick to anger at times, but also funny as hell. In truth, he'd always been deeply jealous of her obvious interest in Mark. Seeing how she was trying to move on and maybe change her life made him feel bad about his own thoughts of throwing everything away. It was...cowardly. As he listened to her speak her next lines, he had another thought that shamed him—*maybe I could have a shot with her now*.

It was common knowledge by now that she was keeping her distance from Mark.

So maybe...

But as he stared at her, his mind flashed back to that awful night in that dank old basement. He saw himself on top of Natasha, pounding into her naked body, savoring that exquisite wetness at the center of her despite his anguish and terror of the unseen thing manipulating them. They had all taken turns with her. And she'd squirmed and moaned through it all, that thing forcing her to enjoy the degradation on a physical level even as the tears streamed endlessly down her quivering face.

"Shit."

Kevin forced himself to look away from her.

The truth was clear.

Natasha wasn't just done with Mark. She was done with all of them. And Kevin couldn't blame her one bit. Whatever they'd all had together, it was over. Completely. That spark of magic that had united them had been extinguished. A deep, aching emptiness brought tears to his eyes.

The hallway began to fill with noise and he sensed bodies moving past him. He had lingered here too long. Keeping his head down to hide the tears, he hurried down the hallway, exiting the school from a door that opened onto the smaller parking lot at the rear of the building. This was where he parked every morning due to its proximity to his locker. It was sunny today, which took the edge off the chill in the air as he hurried through the lot. He slowed down as he began to near his old Eclipse, which was parked in the farthest corner of the lot, behind a row of tall hedges separating the lot from the road. Two big football players were leaning against the back of a weatherbeaten Toyota parked next to his Eclipse. He recognized Moose Hendrickson right away and thought the other one was called Zack or Jack. There was no reason to think they were waiting specifically for him. That was just paranoia. He had no beef with either of these guys and knew they weren't the ones who'd been tormenting him in the hallways. So he picked up his pace again, anxious to be in his car and on his way away from this fucking place.

Too late, he realized he should have been more wary.

The Toyota they were lounging around belonged to some skinny geek. Jason something.

Moose and Zack or Jack flashed predator grins and grabbed him. Kevin fought against them with all his might, but they were just too strong. They wrestled him down onto the asphalt and worked him over with savage speed and efficiency, their hard fists drilling into all the soft spots of his body. They left his face alone until near the end when one particularly ferocious blow pulped his lips and sent blood spilling down his chin and the front of his shirt. At some point during the assault, Kevin heard laughter from someone nearby. The sound wasn't coming from the football players, who were too intent on the task of beating the living shit out of him. He twisted his head and tried to see who the laughing asshole was through the flurry of oncoming blows.

Kent Hickerson sneered at him from his position several feet away. Brett Hogan was standing next to him. They were effectively blocking the view of anyone who might happen by. Kevin understood then that this whole thing had been planned out in advance. It was a trap and he'd walked right into it. So stupid.

The beating took only a few minutes. The final touch was provided by Moose, who twisted his arm behind his back and leaned close to his ear to whisper a threat. "You tell anyone who did this and I'll fucking kill you, bitch."

Kent came a little closer. "You might even want to think about never coming back, faggot." He smiled. "Who knows what might happen next?"

Then they were gone.

Kevin heard them laughing as they walked away. Hatred and shame consumed him. He stayed there sobbing on the ground for several minutes. He rolled onto his side and curled into a fetal position, shaking from the pain. He screwed his eyes shut and stayed like that until he felt a foot nudge his ass.

He forced his eyes open and rolled over with a groan.

Fiona Johnson was standing over him. She was wearing her usual loose jeans and hoodie. The acne around her chin

149

seemed a little redder than usual, as if she'd been unable to keep from scratching at it. It was the first time she'd approached him since the night in the basement. He and the other boys had abused her body every bit as thoroughly as they'd used Natasha's. Though there had been no free will involved in any of it, some part of Kevin had felt like a filthy rapist ever since that night.

Fiona came closer and knelt next to him. "I'm sorry, I saw it happen. I...there was nothing I could do. They..."

Kevin managed a smile despite the pain. He clasped hands with her. "I know. It's okay."

"No, it isn't."

Kevin didn't have a reply to that. She was right. It wasn't okay. Nothing was okay anymore. They stayed there like that a while, listening to the sounds of revving car engines as the lot slowly emptied.

Then Fiona said, "I know where I can get a gun."

Kevin's grip on her hand tightened.

She lowered her face to his and lightly kissed his bloodied lips. "Would you like that?"

Kevin sobbed one more time. "Y-yes."

Another kiss, this one with a touch of passion.

"Good."

TWENTY-SIX

Ella didn't know if she could go through with it. But *he* had commanded it. Andras. The beautiful dark thing living inside her grandson's body. She could not return to the house without completing the task. She despaired at the thought of never being in the demon's presence again. She felt deliciously alive and renewed whenever she was around him. Young again. Not just in spirit, but in body. Like her daughter-in-law, her she looked younger every day. She had lived a span of sixty-three years, but today she looked no more than forty. Perhaps by tomorrow she'd be as gorgeous and youthful as Suzie. It would be awful to lose this restoration of youth, and Andras had assured her this would happen should she disobey him or leave his sphere of influence.

She looked at her face in the Bentley's rear view mirror and again admired the almost flawless countenance that stared back at her. The skin was smoother and fresher-looking than it had been in many years. Some faint worry lines remained around her eyes and at the edges of her mouth, but most of her wrinkles were gone. She was a vain woman, but the improvement in her appearance was not the only thing binding her to Andras. The other thing was the sex. She couldn't imagine never being ravished by the demon again. She shivered at thought of how he was able to electrify her with a relentless chain of explosive orgasms. It didn't matter that the demon was using her grandson's body to do this. The flesh was just a vessel. Derek wasn't really there at all. And, hell, if anything, it only enhanced the delicious, sweet decadence of it all. It made her want to wallow in sin and offer her soul to Andras and his master in Hell. So what if she was Damned in God's eyes now? She would spend eternity in Hell as one of Andras' chosen acolytes.

Until today she had felt no qualms about embracing this dark path. But now the path was taking a darker twist. He had assigned her the task this afternoon in the immediate aftermath of yet another wild sex romp. He had been on top of her, his cock still huge inside her, making her quiver and whimper again every time it twitched. His eyes were dark and intent. "I want you to do something for me, Ella."

She whimpered and writhed on the bed, barely noticing as Lydia Bell rolled up against her and drew one of her nipples between her teeth. "Anything...anything..."

She frowned. "What? Why?"

He laughed and told her. "Promise me you'll do it."

So she had made the promise to the powerful supernatural entity. It wouldn't be wise to disappoint the demon. Still... she wasn't sure she could go through with it.

She had spent the last half hour or so cruising the narrow back roads that skirted the boundaries of Ransom, deliberately avoiding places with a lot of people around. But when she reached the next intersection, she turned right, a direction that would lead her to a more populous area. The thick woods became less dense. She saw little businesses along the sides of the road. Most were ramshackle and looked as if they had been there forever. When she spied a more modern-looking convenience store a few more blocks down on the right, she pulled in at once. The store looked very new. It was probably one of many businesses popping up to service the influx of people brought in by Stanton Manufacturing.

People like Kurt.

She parked and shut the car off, frowning as she thought of her deceased son.

He's dead, she thought. *Really, truly dead.*

She hadn't thought about Kurt's death much lately, mostly due to her preoccupation with Andras. For days now her whole world had revolved around an ecstatic sensory overload pumped into her mind and body by the demon. There had simply been no room for anything else. But now...

She sniffled. "I miss you, sweetheart."

She got out of the car and walked into the convenience store, swiping at her eyes. The door opened ahead of her and two young men came swaggering out. They looked to be in their early twenties, blue collar laborers of some sort with the muscular builds of athletes. Each was carrying a case of cheap beer.

One of them grinned wolfishly at her while the other held the door open. Ella thanked the one holding the door and shot a lustful look back at the one leering at her. She welcomed the resurgence of her libido as it dampened the sadness caused by the sudden flare of grief. The boy was wearing tight jeans and a t-shirt that looked molded to his muscular upper body. Her nipples stiffened as she continued into the store and stared back at him over her shoulder. As she watched, he spread a finger on either side of his mouth and waggled his tongue between them. Ella couldn't remember the last time someone so young had ogled her so openly. It felt good. Really, *really* good. Part of it was her newly youthful appearance, but some of it was the way she was dressed. Her outfit consisted solely of a flimsy black dress with a very short hem and some sexy, strappy heels.

Ella asked the clerk at the counter for a pack of Marlboro Lights. She paid for the cigarettes and went back outside. The young men were waiting for her. Ella wasn't surprised. She peeled the cellophane off the pack and dropped it on the sidewalk. She tapped a cigarette out of the pack and accepted a light from the man in the tight t-shirt.

She blew a puff of smoke in his face and looked at them each in turn. "So how would you boys feel about double-teaming me in the back of my Bentley?"

The men gaped at her, glanced at each other, then guffawed.

"No? Okay."

She turned away from them and began to strut back toward the Bentley, exaggerating the sway of her hips as she walked.

"Hey, wait!"

153

They hurried after her, one of them grabbing her by a wrist as her hand reached toward the driver's side door. She glanced down at the big, muscled hand encircling her thin wrist. She smiled. "Let go."

The man in the tight t-shirt let go of her and moved back a step, holding up his hands in a placating gesture. "I'm sorry...we just...well..."

His friend coughed. "We didn't think you were serious."

Ella unlocked the car, opened the door, and slid in behind the wheel. She smiled up at them. "Get in the back, boys."

One of them frowned. "Uh...what about my truck?"

"We'll come back for it."

Ella held back a laugh.

Or not.

They got in and within moments Ella was guiding the Bentley toward the back roads again. The men ripped into their beer cartons and popped the tops on aluminum cans. Ella accepted one of their beers when it was passed up to her. It was cheap swill, but she could use a drink.

She was about to fulfill her promise to Andras. She supposed there had never been any real danger that she'd do anything other than what she'd sworn she would do The indecision had been nothing more than first time jitters caused by reflexive, ingrained moral qualms. It was good to know she was truly beyond that now.

She parked on the shoulder of one of the quiet little roads and turned in her seat to stare at the boys over the headrest. "Either of you feel kinky?"

Tight t-shirt guy shrugged. "Depends what you have in mind."

Ella grinned. "I adore making love in the great outdoors, don't you?" She nodded at the overgrown field on the other side of a low-slung barbed-wire fence. "Over there should do. What do you say?"

Another exchange of glances in the back, followed by another pair of shrugs.

"Then it's decided. I'll grab a blanket"

Ella pulled the trunk latch and got out of the car.

The guys followed her out of the car with beers in hand, watching with mildly curious expressions as Ella opened the trunk and leaned inside to search for something. For the blanket, ostensibly. She didn't flinch when one of them lifted the hem of her dress and pressed his crotch against her exposed ass. They laughed and one of them popped the tab on another can of beer. Ella lifted the blanket she'd used to cover the implement Andras had given her for this expedition. She paused for a moment with her hand wrapped around its handle and wiggled her butt against the boy's swelling crotch.

"You like that?"

"Oh, yeah."

The other one said, "I gotta get me some of that."

Ella giggled. "Well, I wonder how much you'll like this."

She bumped the boy away with a thrust of her ass and whirled suddenly around, raising the meat cleaver high above her head, her face contorting with a wild, manic glee as she brought it around in a wide, vicious arc.

I want you to go out today and kill someone for me, he'd said.

Anyone at all. It doesn't matter who.

It's time to spill some blood.

The cleaver's blade slammed into his throat, severing his carotid and nearly decapitating him with the one blow. She yanked the blade out and a gout of blood splashed her face and the front of her dress. He was already dying but raised a shaky hand to ward her off. She whipped the blade around and cleaved off three of his fingers. The other one screamed and dropped his beer, stumbling backward and falling into the ditch. Ella cackled and pounced on him immediately. She buried the blade in his belly and tore it open, dragging out a length of intestine as she yanked the blade back out. He screamed and clutched at his stomach, sitting bolt upright and pushing her away with the last of his strength. She came right back at him and silenced his scream with a chop to his throat. He gurgled a blood froth from his mouth. Ella pushed him to the ground and lapped at the blood, drinking it up like sweet nectar. When he was finally dead, she chopped off his head and put it in the Bentley's trunk.

Make your kill and bring back a piece of your prey.
Make me proud by showing me what you've done.
Ella stared at the head and smiled.
That should do.
I love you, Andras. Now you'll see how much.

She slammed the trunk shut, rolled the other body into the ditch, and drove as fast as she dared back to her demon lover.

TWENTY-SEVEN

He felt like some kind of shady character hunched down and lurking behind the bushes along the side of the Wagner residence. A thief scoping the place out or, worse, a rapist waiting to pounce on prey. He had to keep fighting the impulse to just give it up and dash.

The thing was, he didn't have a choice. He *had* to see Natasha. Not being able to talk to her or just be in her presence was killing him. He'd never felt so desperately alone, and her seeming total indifference to his mental anguish was only making the pain worse. She still wasn't answering his emails or texts, and every time he dialed her number his call was routed straight to her voice mail, indicating she'd added his number to her auto reject list. So he was reduced to this, lurking and waiting. But he was getting impatient. She usually came straight home from school. Ransom wasn't a big town, so she should be here any minute. Hell, she should be here already. He pulled out his phone to check the time again.

3:31.

Shit.

More than half an hour since final bell. What the hell? He felt more conspicuous with each passing minute. These bushes were large and sported an impressive profusion of brittle green leaves in spite of the advancing fall season, which reduced the chances of being spotted by a passing motorist. On the other hand, he would be immediately visible to anyone who might come traipsing through from the adjoining Weaver property. He glanced at the Weavers' unfenced back yard and was relieved to see there was still no one there, but he knew he needed to be ready to run like hell at any second. The last thing he wanted was to wind up in the back of a police car. Things were already weird and tense enough at home without adding an extra element of drama to the mix.

More minutes passed.

The narrow residential road the Wagner home faced was devoid of traffic. *Damn.* But just as he was about to finally give up, a car appeared at the far end of the street. His heart raced as he recognized the outline of Natasha's silver PT Cruiser. He checked his phone again. 3:51. Nearly an hour after final bell. He couldn't imagine what had kept her so long, but it didn't matter now. He was about to talk to the girl he loved for the first time in weeks. He was excited and anxious. He knew she wouldn't be happy about him sneaking up on her like this, but it was a chance he had to take.

The PT Cruiser slowed and turned in at the driveway. Mark shifted on his haunches, rising slightly and holding his breath as he prepared to come out of his hiding place. He wanted to step out smoothly rather than jump out and startle her. He began to stand as the car reached the top of the driveway and came to a stop.

He held back a moment longer, waiting for her to come out of the car. He cursed the car's tinted windows, wishing he could see her already. He frowned when doors on both sides opened and two people emerged from the vehicle. Mark felt a tightness in his throat and in his chest. His heart felt like a cold, strong fist had closed around it. He saw Natasha come around the front of the car. She was as breathtaking as ever, attired in a plain black t-shirt and tight jeans that emphasized the lovely shape of her legs. She had dyed her again. It was the darkest shade she'd ever used, black as the heart of midnight. Her lips were painted a shade of red that looked like freshly spilled blood, a stunning contrast to her pale features.

The other person said something to Natasha, making her laugh. A helpless fury ignited inside Mark and he came bursting out of the bushes just as they were starting toward the house.

Natasha yelped and splayed a hand across her chest.

Mark jabbed a finger at the vaguely familiar-looking boy standing next to her. "Who the *fuck* is this? What the fuck, Natasha? You're already hooking up with some other fucking guy?"

Her expression shifted quickly from startled and frightened to the stony, emotionless mask she'd shown him every time he'd tried to get her attention at school. Her eyes looked hard and focused. Her body language was stiff and guarded. She was not at all happy to see him. He'd expected it, but the reality of it hit him hard and silenced the next barrage of accusations before he could utter them. He experienced a moment of intense vertigo, as if the world had turned upside down or he was falling through a hole in the fabric of existence. She had been so into him a very short while ago. Had wanted to be with him and talk to him all the time. She had made him feel like he mattered. Didn't she understand how cruel it was to yank something like that away from a person so suddenly?

The boy edged a little closer to her in a sort of half-assed protective gesture. He was toothpick thin and he was trying hard not to show how terrified he was of Mark. His legs were shaking, but he puffed out his chest and put himself between Natasha and a perceived threat. Knowing he could snap the little prick in two only made Mark feel worse.

The guy looked right at him and said, "You stay away from her. Show some respect."

Mark snorted. He couldn't help it. "*Respect?* Are you fucking serious?"

The boy started to say something else, but Natasha touched his arm and said, "Enough. Chris, go on inside. I'll be in in a minute."

Chris frowned and kept staring at Mark. "I'm not sure I should leave you alone with him."

Natasha allowed a small smile to slip through the rigid mask of her features. "It's okay. I can take care of myself." She gave him a gentle nudge toward the house. "Go on."

Chris started toward the house with obvious reluctance.

"Okay." His eyes locked on Mark. "Don't you upset her or threaten her. I'll be watching."

He turned away from them then and entered the house through the garage.

Threaten her? Had it really come to this? Jesus.

Mark sighed. "Natasha—"

She held up a hand. "Shut up."

"But—"

"Shut the hell up!"

She snapped the words at him. And the way she was glaring at him made his heart feel like it was being squeezed again. A single tear rolled down one of his cheeks. Seeing it seemed to briefly soften something inside her and for a second her face lost that hard, unyielding look. But then it was gone and the mask was back in place.

"You need to leave, Mark."

"Why are you doing this to me?"

"You know why."

"But..." He sniffled and cursed his weakness as his eyes filled with more tears. "I thought you cared about me. I know what we went through was horrible, especially for you and Fiona, but that wasn't us, not really. You've gotta see that."

She stared at him in silence for many long, uncomfortable moments. Then she sighed. "I'm only going to say this once. This is about more than that night in the basement. It's—"

"Jesus, I almost forgot, I have to talk to you about that. I'm sorry, but Clayton—"

She made a loud sound of exasperation and clapped her hands to the sides of her head.

Mark shut his mouth. Her obvious annoyance and lack of patience with him pierced his heart again. He thought of how they used to talk for endless hours about everything under the sun. Deep things. Silly, meaningless things. And everything in between. But now, apparently, she couldn't even stand to hear his voice.

His eyes brimmed with tears yet again. "I'm sorry."

She dropped her hands and shook her head. "Just listen to me for a minute. You're right. That wasn't us. I don't blame you or Jared or Kevin for any of it. But everything changed for me that night, Mark. *Everything.* You understand? There are things I want to do with my life. Things that take a lot of work. And I won't be able to have those things if I stay on that path." She laughed without humor. "I can't be a 'Dark One' anymore."

Mark thought he saw a small glimmer of hope. "But... if it's just about all the partying and all, I can give that up. I mean..." He strained for the right thing to say. "Look, I love you. I'd, you know...support you." He forced a weak smile. "No matter what."

She didn't reply right away. Minutes passed as they stood there staring at each other. As the silence lengthened, her hard mask began to crack and her eyes grew wet. "You'd try. I don't know." She looked away from him, stared out at the empty residential street. "I need time. A lot of time. I need to think. I won't say we're done forever, but I won't promise you anything either. All I know is I can't go on like we were. So give me some time, okay?"

Mark swallowed another thick lump in his throat. "Yeah. Okay. Of course." He glanced at the house, frowning again. "That guy..."

She laughed. "Chris Harknell. He's cool."

"Huh."

Natasha laughed. "He's also gay."

Mark blinked. "Oh."

"He talked me into joining the drama club." She smiled. "Can you believe that? I'm in the goddamn drama club."

"That's cool, I guess."

"Damn right. I'm gonna make movies someday, you know."

Mark nodded. "I know. Look...I hate to change the subject, but you really need to come out tonight."

Natasha groaned. "Have you not listened to a word I've said?"

"No, no, it's not like that." He strove for a tone solemn enough to show her how serious this was. "That night in the basement...you know it wasn't natural. Hell, it was *super*natural. And Clayton, I shit you not, knows something about it. Something to do with his dad."

"Isn't his dad dead?"

"Yeah, but listen, he says we let a demon out of its prison that night and now it's, I don't know, possessing one of us."

Natasha gaped at him. "Mark...are you serious?"

Now it was his turn to be impatient. "Yeah, I'm goddamn serious. You were there, Natasha. You know what happened. It's no goddamn joke. Clayton says the thing that put us through all that rode out of there inside one of us. And we have to, I don't know...*do something* about it."

"No."

"Huh? But—"

"I'm not Buffy the fucking Vampire Slayer, okay? I'm not about to go chasing demons or whatever. You're right. I was there. I know something fucking evil happened. I'm not about to go looking for it again. And you shouldn't either. You know we can't fight something like that."

Mark knew he was losing the battle, but he wasn't willing to give up just yet. "I'm gonna be at Clayton's tonight to hear what he has to say. You should come. What harm is there in just listening?"

She shook her head. "I'll think about it. No promises. I probably won't come, but...I'll think about it." She moved away from him and started toward the house, pausing a moment to glance back at him over her shoulder. "I've got things to do, okay? So...goodbye."

She hurried into the house before he could reply.

There was so much more he wanted to say to her, but it would have to wait. And he would just have to hope she would have a change of heart about tonight. Maybe she would come, maybe she wouldn't. Either way, he felt like he'd won something. A little something. A *chance*. But that was okay. Compared to what he'd had only a few minutes earlier, it was everything in the world.

He took his leave of the Wagner residence via the open Weaver back yard and continued through their front lawn to the street beyond. He turned right when he hit the street, continuing up a long and sharply rising straight stretch of Spring Circle. The steep hill was the best place for sledding in the winter. There had been a good bit of snow last winter, more than usual for Tennessee, and he and his new friends had spent several late nights taking plunge after plunge down the hill. They only had two sleds, so they would take turns, the others standing at the top of the hill and sharing around a bottle of Southern Comfort while waiting for the sledders to reach the bottom and trudge back uphill. It had been a lot of damn fun, too much for anyone to care much about the bitter cold. What did cold matter when you had the amazing good fortune to have such cool friends? He started to smile at the memory, but it faded and he began to feel depressed again.

Their circle was broken, the unique bond shattered. Maybe forever.

Shit.

The Kelly house was near the top of the hill on the right, close to where the road curved to the right and looped around until it became Washington Avenue. The house looked like a mini-mansion, with plantation-style columns bracketing the wide front porch and a long, ornate second story balcony overlooking the front yard. Jared answered his knock, closing the door behind him as he stepped outside and stood on the porch.

"What's up?"

Jared's demeanor wasn't as guarded as Mark had expected. The guy had been playing the avoidance game as hard as any of them, so this was surprising. Mark eyed him closely for a moment, not knowing quite how to start. "Um... are you, uh...okay?"

Jared scowled. "Don't get all emo on me, man."

Mark nodded. "Right. But...are you?"

Jared shoved his hands into his pockets and shrugged. "Yeah. I won't lie. Those first couple nights...I had some seriously messed up nightmares. Could barely look at myself in the mirror, dude. But then I decided to stop being a pussy and got over it. So...what brings you here?"

Mark took a deep breath. "Can you come out tonight?"

Jared tilted his head. "Dunno. Maybe. Why?"

Mark told him about the meeting at Clayton's house and the possibility that the thing they'd released was possessing one of their friends. "So...can you come?"

"Yeah. I'll be there."

Mark couldn't help the grin that spread across his face then. The gratitude he felt in that moment was overwhelming. At least one of his friends was joining him in this—and without any obvious reluctance. The feeling of intense loneliness that had been gripping him for days eased just a little. "Cool. I already talked to Natasha. Not sure if she's coming, can't count on it, but she might. I'm heading over to Fiona's after this and then to Derek's."

Jared glanced up at the sky and squinted. "Weird being outside this time of day."

"No shit. Feel like I've been cured of vampirism."

"Yeah." Jared looked at him. "I'd steer clear of Derek."

Mark frowned. "Why?"

"Pretty sure he's the one got hijacked by your fucking demon."

"But how do—"

"I know. Trust me." The troubled set of his features was more obvious now. His eyes looked haunted. "I went over there. To offer my condolences. And...I got as far as the front door. I heard screaming. I started looking in windows. I couldn't see anything. I went around to the back and hopped the fence. I was thinking maybe I should call the cops, but I don't know why, I felt like I should check it out myself first. I peeked in through a window. This time I saw something."

"What did you see?"

Jared visibly shivered. "I think if they'd spotted me I'd be dead now, or I'd be a part of whatever fucked up shit is going on at that house."

Mark was getting impatient. "Would you just tell me what you fucking saw?"

Jared grimaced. "You asked for it, remember that."

He told Mark every detail of what he could remember from that brief glimpse through the window at the back of the McGregor house. It was more than enough to convince him that Jared's suspicion was probably true. "Holy shit."

Jared nodded.

They stood there in silence for a time, each of them wrapped up in their own hopeless thoughts.

Then Jared said, "Fuck it. I know where we can get some beer. Wanna go for a ride?"

Mark didn't hesitate. "Hell, yeah."

TWENTY-EIGHT

She couldn't think of any realistic way out the situation and was again beginning to wish they'd just kill her and be done with it. But that wasn't about to happen. Andras, the infernal thing walking around inside Derek McGregor's skin, was having far too much fun with her. Lydia's mind boggled at the wide array of sickening and perverse acts she'd been forced to either witness or participate in since being dragged away from her home earlier in the day. The demon delighted in cruel acts of humiliation and torture. The sense of shame she felt in the wake of some of these acts was bad. The occasional moments of nerve-shredding agony were very bad. But the very worst part of it was how he was able to make her enjoy every second of it. He could make her body convulse with orgasm after orgasm even as she lay bleeding in a pool of her own vomit. Those moments of having no control over her own body stretched her sanity very near to the breaking point.

And now she was hogtied on the floor in Suzie McGregor's living room. All the furniture had been pushed out of the way to form a large open space in the center of the room. Her hands were stretched behind her back at painful angles, her wrists tied to her upraised ankles with electrical cords. The hardwood floor felt cold and uncomfortable against her nude body. Blood was still leaking from the dozens of places where Andras had nicked her flesh with a knife. She could feel it pooling between her breasts and forming a sticky puddle against her abdomen. None of the wounds were lethal, not even combined, but they hurt like hell, causing her to whimper now and then as Andras walked in a slow circle around her and stared down at her.

He knelt next to her and plucked at one of the taut electrical cords, making her arms vibrate with pain again.

She screamed.

He laughed.

Tears dripped from her eyes to the floor. She quivered as he went to one knee next to her and began to caress her bare back and ass, his hand gliding smoothly over the soft, delicate flesh. The touch was gentle, almost loving. She knew better than to trust this impression...but it felt so good.

"Do you like that?"

She sighed. "Yes."

He plucked at the cords again, eliciting another scream.

"What about that, woman? Do you like that?"

She sniffled. "Y-yes."

He pressed his fingers between her legs and probed at her pussy, causing it to become instantly wet again. He pushed his fingers inside her, deep inside, and flexed them, making her cry out and writhe on the floor. She was helpless to prevent her body's physical reaction, despite the pain that came with each little twitch. The muscles in her shoulders, thighs, and calves felt like they were on fire. She nonetheless writhed some more and screamed some more as he continued to work at her with his fingers. The sensations became so intense that she forgot all about how he was degrading her and gave herself over to shameful ecstasy. After many minutes of pain intermingled with bliss, he untied her and flipped her over. She spread her legs wide and screamed louder than ever at the penetration that followed. Her eyes went wide and her long nails clawed at his bony shoulders as he began to thrust against her. Her fingernails tore into him, drawing blood as his rhythm increased. She yelped and thrashed and tore at him as her body shook in the grip of cascading orgasms. Her hands were sticky with his blood by the time he shot his seed deep inside her.

He pulled out of her and moved away. A powerful sense of loss brought tears to her eyes. She wanted him back inside her. Wanted him there permanently. She didn't ever want to stop feeling like that. Andras was beautiful. He was perfect. How could she have ever thought there was anything wrong with this? She lay there panting for several minutes, feeling delirious and dizzy as she stared up at the ceiling. The high didn't begin to fade until she heard voices and knew the others had returned.

Tom and Suzie.

And Ella, Suzie's mother-in-law.

They had departed separately, dispatched by Andras to perform various tasks. Ella went out alone, Tom and Suzie together. She propped herself up on her elbows and stared at them through eyes that were still a little bleary. Ella and Suzie were still in the tiny, sexy dresses they'd been wearing upon departing. Suzie looked as sexily immaculate as she had prior to embarking on her errand, but Ella's little black dress was torn in places and the front of it was soaked with a sticky, dark substance that could only be blood. There was more blood smeared across her face and chest. The severed head of a young man was cradled in the crook of her left arm. The dead man's face was frozen in an expression of agonized shock. A short piece of his spinal column protruded from the ragged, bloody stump of his neck. Lydia experienced a brief moment of revulsion, but it passed quickly. This had been done by her new master's bidding. It was his will. And that made it right. That made it good. She suddenly longed to prove her own worth by taking a life, too. She imagined plunging a knife into the trembling body of a terrified victim. The image excited her. She made a husky sound low in her throat and pushed a hand between her legs.

The others stopped talking and watched her.

Her excitement grew by leaps and bounds as they watched her masturbate. She rotated her pelvis as she furiously rubbed at her clit. She was thrilled when she saw how excited she was making the others. Ella lifted the hem of her dress and fingered herself. Suzie separated from the group, staggered awkwardly across the hardwood floor in her heels, and dropped to her knees between Lydia's spread legs. Suzie's rapt expression was equal parts desire and hatred.

Lydia knew exactly how she felt. She arched her back and slid her butt across the floor.

Suzie wiped away a strand of saliva hanging from a corner of her mouth. "Bitch."

Lydia leaned forward and grabbed the other woman by the back of the neck. "*Cunt.*"

Then she pressed her rival's face down to her sex.

And she screamed at the first expert flick of Suzie's tongue.

The trunk of the Lexus was dark and uncomfortable. And too small by far. Greg Fox was trying not to hyperventilate. He had always had a moderate issue with close, tight spaces. Just a little touch of claustrophobia that wasn't a big deal at all during the normal, daily course of his life. But there was nothing normal about being forced at gunpoint into the trunk of a stranger's car.

He clawed at his shirt collar, tearing at the thin fabric.

Christ, I'm gonna suffocate in here.

He pounded a fist against the closed trunk.

"*Yea, though I walk through the valley of the shadow of death, I will fear no evil, for thou art with me. Thy rod and they staff, they comfort me...*"

Greg wanted to laugh.

Did she really think her fucking prayers would save them?

But then he felt bad for thinking that. Carrie was seeking the only comfort available to her. Her boyfriend had failed to protect her and was too much of a pitiful wreck to provide solace of any kind. She was a religious girl, and it only made sense she would look to God for answers.

"*Thou preparest a table before me in the presence of mine enemies; thou anointest my head with oil; my cup runneth over...*"

Greg screamed and pounded his fists against the closed trunk again. "*Let us out!*"

"It won't help, honey."

Greg sobbed.

"Pray with me."

He shook his head. "That won't help, either."

His breath caught in his throat as heard a sound from somewhere outside the car. It had been ominously quiet for a while. So quiet he suspected the car was parked in a private garage rather than some public place. He clapped a hand over Carrie's mouth to stifle another snippet of scripture and cocked his head, straining to hear any evidence of a presence outside the car. For long moments, there was nothing. Carrie was perfectly still next to him, listening, apparently not so resigned to her fate that she didn't still hold out some hope for divine deliverance.

Then the sound came again.

Footsteps on concrete, followed by another sound—the jangle of car keys. Greg tensed, thinking maybe he'd take a shot at being a hero after all by leaping out at their captors. Maybe he'd get lucky and somehow manage to disarm the man with the gun.

The trunk lid came opened and the man who'd taken him pointed the gun in his face.

So much for playing the hero. Again.

The man backed off, waving at them with the gun. "Get out."

It was just him. His partner, the woman in the sexy green dress, was out of picture for the moment. The guy's appearance remained as incongruous as he remembered. He was handsome and fit, with a chiseled jaw and perfect movie star hair. In his Brooks Brothers suit, he looked like one of those male models from the glossy ads in GQ. Or an extra from the set of *Mad Men*. He radiated confidence and self-assurance. He didn't look like someone who made a habit of randomly kidnapping people at gunpoint. So maybe this wasn't random. Maybe it was a case of mistaken identity. Maybe Mr. GQ and his hot lady friend thought they had money, or thought they were the offspring of rich people. The idea might have made him laugh had he not been staring straight down the barrel of a gun. If this was some sort of ransom deal, their abductors were in for a serious disappointment. But it couldn't be a ransom thing.

The guy obviously wasn't hurting for money.

Which could only mean this was about something far more sinister.

The truth of the situation hit home again.

We're going to die. They're going to torture us. Then they're going to kill us.

The guy cracked a smug smile. "Get out of the trunk or I'll shoot you in the dick." He aimed the gun at Greg's crotch. "I imagine that'd hurt. A *lot*. So you'd better move."

There was no way around it. Greg shifted his body, raising up at the waist and grimacing at the stiffness in his joints. He took a look around, saw that his hunch about a garage had been correct. He couldn't see it from this vantage point, but he suspected the garage door was closed. So even without the prospect of a bullet in the back to dissuade him, the possibility of making a run for it was out of the question. He could maybe scream for help, but he doubted anyone who could help would hear him. Again, the looming presence of the gun was the deciding factor in the equation.

Greg really didn't want to get shot.

In the dick or anywhere else.

He climbed the rest of the way out of the trunk and helped Carrie climb out after him. They clung to each other, shaking as their legs cramped from the long hours in the trunk. Carrie pressed her face into his shoulder and her mouth continued to move, the words coming faster now and at a lower volume, a ceaseless string of half-intelligible bible verses.

Mr. GQ waved the gun at her. "You. Bible girl. Look at me."

Carrie looked at him.

The man smiled again. "Do you want to live, bible girl?"

She shuddered. "Y-yes. God have mercy."

"God has nothing to do with this." He waved the gun at them. "If you want to live, do exactly as I say. Don't hold back or hesitate. Understand?"

She nodded. "Yes."

"Cool. Here's the first thing I want you to do. Slap your boyfriend. *Hard*."

Greg's brow wrinkled in confusion. *What the hell is this?* He didn't really expect Carrie to obey the command. She was a very proper, church-going kind of girl. A *nice* girl. And definitely about as non-violent as a person could be. So he was more than mildly surprised when she eased away from him and whipped her hand across his face. *Hard,* as commanded. He staggered away from her, bumping his ass against the Mercedes SUV parked next to the Lexus. He stared at Carrie in a look of wide-eyed shock and saw something else that surprised him. She didn't look scared anymore. Her expression was the cunning look of an animal desperately pursuing the only way out of a dangerous situation. The difference between this girl and the girl clinging to him only moments ago was stunning, almost impossible to comprehend.

Mr. GQ laughed. "Good. Now kick him in the balls."

Again, there was no hesitation. Carrie came straight at him, planting her left foot solidly on the concrete as she pivoted at the hip and slammed the heel of her shoe into his crotch. The pain was immediate and world-obliterating, robbing him of his breath for a long moment as he dropped to his knees and clutched at his abused privates. He began to wail as he caught his breath, the pain doubling back on him and bringing forth fat tears that spilled in hot streams down his quivering cheeks.

"Kick him in the face."

The pain rendered him incapable of scuttling away or acting to defend himself. This time the hard heel of Carrie's shoe smashed into his jaw. His head snapped backward and thumped against the side of the SUV. Blood filled his mouth and he felt something sharp pricking at his tongue. He gagged and spat something out. The pain again was immense. A tide of nausea caused him to pitch forward and brace his hands against the cold concrete floor of the garage. Now he was staring straight down at the thing he'd ejected from his mouth. It was a piece of one of his teeth.

He lifted his head and stared up at his girlfriend. "I thought you loved me." It hurt to talk. Every movement of his jaw sent a sizzling flash of agony through his skull. "How could you do this?"

Her expression still had that animal aspect. There was no softness there at all. And no mercy. "I want to live. That's all."

Mr. GQ came up next to her and draped an arm over her shoulders. "It's funny how they turn on you, isn't it?" He laughed. "You're young, so I suppose you didn't really understand about that yet. There's no such thing as true loyalty anymore. In the modern world it's a big game of fuck over whoever you need to fuck over to get ahead."

Greg glared at him. "Fuck you."

The man smirked. "Oh, so *now* you're brave. Now that you think you've got nothing left to lose, you think it's time to show some balls." He disengaged himself from Carrie and aimed the gun straight at Greg's face. "Get up."

Greg looked into the man's eyes and saw his own death reflected there. He got his feet planted under him and started to rise, as instructed. But, instead of standing straight up, he launched himself into the man's midsection, ramming the top of his head into his stomach and knocking the breath out of him. This brought a fresh burst of agony, but it was worth it when he heard the gun go clattering across the concrete. He slammed the man against the side of the Lexus and fell against him. The man tried to shove him away, but Greg stayed slumped against him, somehow finding the strength to pepper his sides with punches. In his peripheral vision, he saw Carrie going after the gun. And now she had it. It was a miracle. They were going to get out of this nightmare. And then it wouldn't matter what Carrie had done. He would forgive her, just as God would forgive her. She was a victim, nothing more.

The sense of elation lasted right up to the moment when she pointed the gun at him. "Stop."

Greg's shoulders sagged. His fists fell to his sides.

The man shoved him away and snatched the gun from Carrie.

Greg gaped at her. "Why?"

173

She smiled. "I don't know. I...felt something. It felt like God talking inside my head. He told me what to do."

Greg groaned. "Fuck."

Well, this is just fucking great. My girlfriend is fucking fucked in the head. Thanks, God. It would have been nice to know this sooner.

The man grinned. "Got news for you, honey. That's not God talking to you. That's my buddy Andras, and he's really looking forward to meeting you. I think you'll dig him. I'll tell you this. He's a hell of a lot more fun than that God of yours."

Carrie smiled. "Cool."

Cool?

Carrie wasn't herself right now. Obviously.

Not that knowing that could change anything.

The man waved the gun at an open door. "That way."

Out of options, Greg started toward the door. A scream issued from somewhere inside the house. His throat tightened and his bowels clenched.

What kind of horror show am I walking into here?

TWENTY-NINE

The Ransom Lanes bowling alley had a largish parking lot that was always filled on weekends, and business was robust even on school nights. The young people of Ransom didn't have a wealth of other entertainment options. There were no movie theaters. The few places that occasionally hosted live music acts were shitty little country bars that didn't allow underage patrons. No, if you were a teenager in Ransom in a mood to socialize, Ransom Lanes was pretty much it. The bowling alley's interior was spacious, with lots of room for mingling, and the owners made sure to keep all the recent big hits pumping over the loud sound system. If you got bored of bowling, there was a small billiards room and an even smaller adjacent room that housed a few ancient arcade video games.

Kevin Cooper knew none of these things firsthand. Fiona, however, had hung out here a time or two. It was a long time ago, she told him, maybe a year since the last time, but it seemed unlikely anything significant had changed in that time.

"I still don't get why you ever came here. I mean...it's lame."

"I guess. It was before I knew you guys." Fiona bit down on a black-painted thumbnail and stared at the entrance to the bowling alley, her dark hair falling across her face. "Mostly."

They were in his Eclipse, which was parked in an angled slot facing the front of the building. After nearly thirty minutes of sitting there, Kevin was beginning to feel conspicuous. He doubted anyone had noticed them or given them a second thought if they had. There was too much activity. Too many people entering and leaving the building. But it was hard not to be a touch paranoid every time his eyes flicked back to the gun. The .38 revolver was wedged into the little tray beneath the radio. And it wasn't just paranoia he felt every time he looked at the gun.

There was also doubt.

Yes.

A lot of fucking doubt.

He shifted in his seat. "I'm not sure about this."

Fiona flipped her hair from her face. "What do you mean?"

He lifted his chin. "That. The fucking gun. I don't really wanna kill anybody."

Fiona's features folded into a look of withering contempt. "Are you serious?"

He sighed. "Yeah. I am."

Fiona slugged him in the shoulder. "You fucking pussy."

He grimaced. "Ow. Jesus, Fiona."

She slugged him again. "You can't pussy out on me now. You have to do this."

He shook his head. "No. Look, I hate those motherfuckers. I wouldn't shed a goddamn tear if something bad happened to them, but I'm not gonna murder anybody. I just can't. That makes me no better than them."

Fiona looked disgusted. "That's not what you were saying a few hours ago."

"I wasn't in my right mind, okay? I'd just gotten the shit beat out of me. And I'm still pretty fucked up from that. But think about it. We do this thing and it'll be just like saying they were right about us all along. I don't wanna be one of those pricks you see on the news, with the interviews with neighbors and shit, all of them saying, 'Oh, yeah, they were weird kids, all into metal and goth shit, we really should've seen this coming, maybe done something about it.' Fuck that, Fiona. Fuck that right in the ass."

Fiona stopped looking at him about halfway through this speech. She went back to chewing her thumbnail and watching the bowling alley's entrance. The ensuing silence became uncomfortable as it stretched through several long minutes. Kevin was close to just starting the car and driving away. It would be the smart thing to do. Another smart thing would be to take that gun and stash it somewhere. He stared at the keys dangling from the Eclipse's ignition, psyching himself up to just go on and do it. Fiona would be pissed, but she would get over it. Or she wouldn't. It didn't matter either way. He had come so close to making the biggest mistake of his life. A thing he wouldn't be able to take back or make amends for, ever. All that mattered was he'd made the decision to pull back from the brink.

Fiona picked up the gun and pointed it at him.

Kevin held his hand and put his back against the driver's side door. "Jesus. Fiona—"

"Shut up."

Kevin's mouth clamped shut. He was shaking. He didn't think Fiona would shoot him, but it was far from a certainty and that bothered him nearly as much as the possibility of being shot. She was his friend. More than that. They were comrades. Allies against all the bastards in the world. It *should* have been a certainty and the fact that it wasn't filled him with despair.

Fiona used her free hand to angle the rear view mirror toward him. "Look at yourself. Look what they fucking did to you."

Kevin glanced at the mirror, winced at the now familiar sight of his pulped bottom lip and swollen eye. He still hurt like hell all over. The painkillers Fiona had swiped from her mother's vast supply of subscription drugs had dulled the pain only slightly.

Fiona's harsh expression softened some. "This shit is what always happens to people like you and me sooner or later. We don't fit in. We're different. And the normal motherfuckers can't stand it. So they have to put us in our place. Knock us down. Beat the shit out of us. Make sure we know we can't go through life being different. That we've gotta conform or get knocked down in the dirt again and again."

Kevin shook his head. "No. It's just...you know, it's shit that happens in a small town. Cliques fighting cliques. None of it will really matter when we're older."

"We're not getting older."

Kevin's eyes went to the barrel of the gun. It was eerie how steady her hand was. He looked her in the eye again. "Please don't kill me."

"I'm sorry. It wasn't supposed to be like this."

Kevin's eyes misted. "Please."

"We can't go on. You have to see that."

A light went on in Kevin's head. Of course. He should have seen it sooner. This wasn't just about payback for the beating he'd taken. Hell, that was the smallest part of it. This was about that night in the basement. That was the thing she couldn't face anymore. The real adversary. Those dark, twisted memories. It was why she'd been so quick to nudge him toward the murder-suicide scenario, knowing he'd be most susceptible to it while the beating was still fresh in his mind.

She smiled, seeing it in his eyes now. "It has to be this way. It's okay, Kevin. It's my fault, really. I should have known you weren't strong enough for this." She pushed the barrel of the gun against his stomach. "I'm sorry. I'll see you on the other side."

It all seemed so crazy now.

If things had gone according to the original plan, he would have killed her fist, then he would have gone inside to blow away Hickerson and his friends. And then himself, thus sealing the pact. He cursed his stupidity. How could he have gone along with it even for one second, even in the depths of his humiliation?

Fiona jumped at the sound of a fist loudly pounding the window on her side.

Kevin gasped as the gun barrel pressed harder against his stomach. He cringed, expecting her to squeeze off a shot in surprise. But her finger stayed off the trigger as she turned her head to glance over her shoulder at the intruder. Kevin craned his head and saw Mark Bell's grinning mug peering through the glass. He looked sort of fucked up. Somebody else was standing near him. Somebody big. Had to be Jared.

Kevin waved.

He kept his eyes on Mark as he addressed Fiona. "Put the gun down, okay? You don't wanna do this now, not with them here."

Her head swiveled back toward him. "Okay."

She let go of the gun. Kevin took it from her and dropped it in the little storage slot at the bottom of the door on his side. He was pretty sure the angle of Fiona's body had shielded the gun from sight. Which was good. He didn't want the others knowing how close Fiona had come to killing him.

He hit a power window switch and the window on Fiona's side rolled down.

Mark poked his head inside. His breath reeked of alcohol. He grinned. "I knew this was your fucking Eclipse, Cooper. Am I interrupting anything?"

Fiona smiled. "Well, I was about to go on a murder spree. You interrupted that."

Mark laughed.

He lifted his head slightly and bumped it against the top of the door frame. "Ow. Damn." The guy was really hammered. "What are you guys doing at fucking Ransom Lanes?"

Kevin shrugged. "I could ask you the same fucking question."

Mark laughed again. Bumped his head again. "Touche. We were just driving around, man. This may come as a big fucking surprise, but there ain't a lot to do in Ransom, even during the day, so we decided to cruise by..." Some of the drunken high spirits drained from his features as he took a longer look at Kevin's face. "Man...what the fuck happened to you?"

Before Kevin could say anything, Fiona launched into a fast-paced and luridly detailed account of the beating he'd taken at the hands of Hickerson's jock pals. Her delivery was hyper verging on manic, with a lot of hand gestures and twisting around in her seat. By the time she was done recounting the tale, Mark no longer looked sloppy drunk. His eyes were clear, his features strained with fury. Jared had bent at the waist to peer in at her as she talked, and his expression was the same. Kevin became nervous as he observed the transformation in Mark's demeanor. The air was again thick with the palpable threat of violence.

Mark jerked a thumb at the building. "And that Hickerson motherfucker is in there now?"

Fiona nodded. "They're *all* in there. Every last one of those assholes."

Mark stared at Kevin's face a beat longer.

Then he and Jared exchanged a glance.

Jared said, "Wanna fuck some people up?"

Mark's only a reply was a nod.

He and Jared moved away from the Eclipse and began to walk rapidly toward the bowling alley. Kevin twisted in his seat to watch them. They were already halfway across the lot. There was no hesitation at all in their gait. This was not going to be pretty. "Oh, shit. What should we do?"

Fiona reached for the door handle. "Our part, that's what."

She opened the door and climbed out, hurrying after them.

"Fuck!"

Kevin banged a fist against the steering wheel. This was happening too fast. He knew he couldn't just sit here in the car like a bitch while his friends went after the people who'd attacked him. He got out of the car and jogged fast across the parking lot, drawing near his friends just as they were stepping through the front door and entering the lobby.

Bang through the doors and then the oppressive thump and blare of the latest from Lady Gaga. The thunderous music was just one part of an overall assault on the senses. The bowling alley's interior was darker than Kevin had anticipated. There were flashing disco lights and the lanes were lit up in neon colors. A fog machine was pumping out a low-lying mist. The sign out front had referred to something called Cosmic Bowling. The floor area was choked with limber young bodies flailing to the dance beats. The faint crash of bowling pins was barely audible through the din. Hard to believe this was what passed for fun for so many people. On the plus side, there was a chance a fight in so chaotic a setting might go unnoticed by the building's security staff, at least long enough to have at the bad guys and make a quick getaway.

There was one problem with that.

Mark Bell.

The guy wasn't the hit and run type. He was more the go completely ballistic fucking psycho type. That was his default setting for dealing with people he perceived as enemies. Add in the fact that he'd been drinking heavily, and this situation had the potential to turn really ugly really fast. Mark and Jared bulled their way through the throng of dancers. Kevin's stomach did a slow, queasy roll as he and Fiona followed in their wake.

Mark and Jared came to an abrupt stop at the partition that separated the floor area from the recessed area where the bowlers sat waiting their turns. Their heads swiveled on their necks as they searched the area. There were a lot of lanes and the flicker of the strobes made it hard to pick out individual faces. Kevin reached the partition and took a look around. Only the faces of the people sitting in the area directly below where he was standing were occasionally visible. One or two of them looked vaguely familiar, but none of them were Hickerson or his friends. Good. Maybe they had slipped out unnoticed at some point while he'd been arguing with Fiona.

But Mark abruptly leaned over the partition and pointed to the left.

Jared leaned over the partition, peering in the same direction.

Then they took off running.

Kevin grimaced.

Shit.

He and Fiona trailed after them again, the knot in Kevin's stomach tightening as he saw Mark and Jared disappear through one of the openings in the partition down to the pit

181

below. By the time he and Fiona joined them down in the pit, Mark was shrugging off his leather jacket and bearing down on a very surprised-looking Moose Hendrickson. The football player was a bit bigger than Mark, but this did not make him more imposing. The endless hours Mark spent pumping iron in his garage was obvious even in the bad lighting. Thick, corded slabs of muscle strained the fabric of his t-shirt. Kevin couldn't see his friend's face, but he had no doubt there was pure murder in his eyes. The football player saw this immediately and started backing off. No hint of bravado there at all. Just fear. Despite the sick feeling in his gut, it made Kevin happy to see that.

The other kids sitting in the same area came out of their seats fast and scrambled out of the way. Kevin recognized Kent Hickerson and his friend Brett. That other football player, Zack or Jack, who'd participated in his beating, was there too. Some of them had girlfriends with them. The girls screamed in unison as Mark launched a fist at Hendrickson. The blow connected. Hendrickson flew backward, crashing into empty chairs as a spray of blood flew from his broken nose. Before he could recover, Mark seized the football player by the throat and started punching him repeatedly in the face. Zack or Jack made a half-hearted, hesitant move to intercede, but Jared intercepted him, slamming him to the floor with a ferocious body blow. He fell atop Zack or Jack and started pummeling him with his meaty fists. More blood flowed. There were more screams.

Kevin drew in a big breath.

Released it.

And took a step forward, poking Kent Hickerson in the center of his back. The boy flinched and whirled around. His face blanched when he saw Kevin standing there, grinning at him. Kevin launched a blow of his own, giving it everything he had. The feeling when his fist connected with Kent's soft lower lip and split it open was the most gratifying thing he'd ever felt. Pain shot up his arm and turned his hand almost instantly numb.

But he didn't care.

He had tasted of blood and vengeance and it felt good.

He kicked Kent in the face when the boy tried to stand, snapping his nose and sending him howling in pain back to the floor. The adrenaline was sizzling through his system now and he pressed the attack. In the midst of the melee, he failed to notice Fiona melting backward into the crowd of onlookers and slipping away. The frenzy continued for just a few minutes more. At some point the music stopped and the strobe lights stopped flickering as the regular overhead lighting came on.

Then he felt other hands on him, pulling him roughly away from the bloodied face of the boy beneath him. Kevin laughed even as his arms were twisted painfully behind his back, the wild exhilaration of the moment still gripping him like a kind of madness. He savored the looks of shock on the faces of everyone around him, especially those familiar faces. He knew he was in some serious trouble here, but he knew one other thing just as clearly—no one at Ransom High would ever fuck with him again.

The cops arrived and slapped on handcuffs.

They were hauled out of the bowling alley and shoved into the backs of police cars.

Yeah, they were definitely in some trouble. Big trouble.

But it was hard to care at the moment. Later, sure, he'd care. But not now.

Because Kevin Cooper felt better than he had in a long time.

Maybe ever.

THIRTY

Mark Bell felt like shit when he was let out of jail the next morning, his joints all stiff from a night of trying with little success to sleep on a tiny, uncomfortable cot. His shoulders hurt and his hands were still throbbing, aftereffects of the beating he'd given Moose Hendrickson. His father had come down to pay bail. Finally. He hadn't been able to reach either of his parents the previous night and had been forced to leave halting, awkward messages about his situation.

He signed the things he needed to sign and was processed out at just after 9 am. They returned his belongings, including his phone, wallet, and keys. He checked the phone on the way out of the building for messages. He'd missed a call from an unknown number during the wee morning hours. That had to be Clayton Campbell, wondering why no one had showed for the meeting. There were texts from Jared and Cooper, who were both already out. There was nothing from Natasha, which saddened but didn't surprise him. By now she knew all about what had gone down at Ransom Lanes and had probably reverted to her hardline stance against him. He suspected the problem had grown beyond his ability to solve. He had come close to swaying her with his impassioned words and promises before, but more than likely they were done forever now.

His father was waiting for him by his late model blue Lexus in the parking lot. He was dressed for work, but he had his suit jacket off and was holding it slung over a shoulder by a thumb. Tom Bell's expression was predictably stony as he watched his son cross the parking lot. His parents had never been strict disciplinarians, but they would probably take a stab at it now.

It was bullshit and more than a little late in the goddamn game. Fuck that. He wasn't many months removed from being a legal adult. What were they gonna do? Ground him?

Yeah, right.

Mark went right to the passenger side door and waited.

Tom looked at him across the hood of the car. "Well. What do you have to say for yourself?"

Mark matched his father's stony stare. "Nothing."

His father shrugged. "Okay."

Mark "*Okay*? Really? You sound like you don't give a shit."

Another shrug. "You're right. I don't. So you were in a fight. So what? I got in the same kind of trouble when I was your age. It's meaningless. I'm out a hundred dollars, ten percent of the bond, but I don't care about that either. It's chump change."

Mark laughed. "Chump change?"

Tom Bell shrugged into his suit jacket and straightened the fine material with his palms. "Yes, Mark, chump change. I make a lot of money by average Joe standards. It's the reason you have so many nice things, things most kids your age can only dream of having. All your little electronic gadgets. All the newest and latest and most expensive things. This may come as a shock, but most seventeen-year-olds don't get a hundred dollar weekly allowance. Point being that, yes, that hundred bucks was nothing to me. But there'll come a time when I can't coddle you any longer. A time when you'll have to start making your own way in the world. Do you think you're ready for that?"

Mark sighed more than once throughout this speech. It was exactly the sort of thing he'd expected to hear. "I think I'm ready to get the hell away from this goddamn police station."

His father nodded. "On that we can agree. Let's go."

They got in the car and Tom drove them away from the Ransom police station, steering the luxury car through the center of the town's small main drag. As usual, there wasn't a lot to see.

"Where are we going?"

His father's eyes flicked toward him, then went back to

185

the road. "I have a bit of business I need to take care of. Mark..."

Mark didn't care for the tentative tone of his father's voice. It was how he always sounded when he was about to broach an uncomfortable subject. "Yeah, dad?"

"I love you, you know that, right?"

Mark squirmed a little in his seat.

Shit. Here we go with the touchy-feely bullshit.

"Uh...yeah, dad. Sure, I know that."

Tom slowed the car as they neared a traffic light. "Good. I'm glad." He sighed. "Listen...son...there are some things happening you don't know about. Things haven't been... right...between your mother and I for a long time."

Mark bit down on a bitter laugh.

No shit, dad.

Traffic was light and the light stayed red for just a few seconds. It turned green and they started through the intersection. "I had an affair with another woman a while back and, well, things all kind of went to hell after that. Your mom found out and I had to fight like hell to keep the marriage alive."

Mark grunted. "Well...that explains a lot."

"Thing is, son, I don't think the effort was worth it. We've both been distant from you for a long time, mostly because of this situation I caused." His voice became steadily more hoarse as he talked. Mark realized with growing alarm that his father was on the verge of a crying fit. "And I know how...how fucking hard it's been for you. We haven't been involved in your life and I'm so goddamn sorry."

Mark's eyes began to mist. "Dad...it's okay. Seriously."

Tom Bell gave a single, adamant shake of his head and stared hard at him. "No, son, it is not okay." They turned down a side street that took them out of the center of town. They were out of the main commerce section of Ransom and were coming up on the small hospital and post office. There was another building further down, a three story thing that looked depressingly drab. Tom guided the Lexus past the hospital and turned left into the drab-looking building's mostly empty parking lot. He parked in a slot near the front of the building and turned in his seat to look directly at his son. "Mark, I've felt lost for a long time. I even thought about killing myself a time or two, but now I'm glad I didn't do that."

Mark read the plaque on the wall outside the building's entrance.

EVERGREEN ASSISTED LIVING FACILITY

"Uh...dad...what are we doing at a nursing home?"

"That business I mentioned earlier. There's a man I have to see here."

Mark glanced at the sign again. "Who could you possibly have to see here? We don't have any older relatives in Ransom. Um...do we?"

Tom shook his head. "No. I'm here to kill a man I've never met. His name is Luke Harper. He was the mayor of Ransom a long time ago."

"Uh huh. Did you just say you were here to kill this guy?"

"Yes."

"Right. That's what I thought. Dad...have you lost your fucking mind?"

"Lost it? No, not really. It's not entirely my own anymore, though."

Mark was still chewing over the strangeness of that statement when his father reached across him and opened the glove box, taking out a handgun and a thick, sealed envelope. He offered the envelope to Mark, who took it in his numb, shaking fingers and stared wide-eyed at his father. The gun was an automatic of some kind. Mark knew nothing of guns, but it was clear this was no toy.

It's not entirely my own anymore...

His father really wasn't acting like himself at all. And this thing about killing this stranger was pure craziness. Could it be that someone or something else was forcing him to do this?

A demon, for instance?

"Dad—"

"There's ten thousand dollars cash in that envelope. The

title of this car is also in there. I've signed it over to you."

"Uh...I already have a car."

"That old beater?" A fleeting smile tugged at the edges of his mouth. "Yes, a ride like that, a young man like yourself...I can see the appeal. But it is old and this car is new. I'm giving you something of value, son. Something you can use...something..."

"Dad, listen, seriously, you can't do this. You don't—"

"I can and I will. It's nothing to me to kill this man. I'm doing it in service to Satan and to Andras."

Oh, fuck.

Oh, fuckfuckfuck.

"Things are different now, son. I'm not the man I was. I serve a higher purpose now. A darker purpose. By the time I come out of this building I won't really be your father anymore."

Mark's cheeks glistened. "Dad, don't do this. *Please.* This Andras, we were the ones who let him out. It was a mistake. But we—"

"I know that, Mark. You and your friends did a great thing that night."

"No. It was a bad thing. And we have to fix it. We—"

Tom laughed. "There is no fixing it, son. There's nothing *to* fix. Please understand. Most of me belongs to Andras now. But while I'm away from him, his influence is a little weaker, maybe just enough to save the only person I still care about. Take that money and this car and get the hell out of Ransom."

"What? Where would I go?"

"You can't stay here. Your mother is with us, too. Go to Knoxville. My brother lives there. I called him before I bailed you out. You can stay with his family a while. And listen to me. This is my last piece of advice to you. This goes back to what I was saying about money. You play the role of the tough guy pretty well, but a lot of the reason you get away with so much at school and in this town is because of who you are. You're a rich kid. The leather jacket, the long hair, the ripped jeans...it's all just a disguise. Which is fine for when you're young." He leaned closer to Mark, those blue eyes drilling into him, emphasizing the point. "But be careful you don't wear the disguise so long it becomes who you actually are. Get smart. Go to college. Accomplish things. Give yourself the tools to take care of yourself after I'm gone."

Well, that sure had the ring of a *goodbye forever* speech to it. Mark shook his head. "No. Fuck this. I'm not letting this happen."

He made a grab for the gun, but his father rocked him back in his seat with a punch to the jaw. The blow wasn't delivered with full force, but it was enough to daze him for a moment. He heard a door open and slam shut. By the time his vision cleared, his father was already entering the building.

"Fuck. Goddammit!"

He got out of the car and staggered into the building. Inside the lobby, he saw a man in white clothes lying unconscious on the floor, blood leaking from a broken nose. The man had to be an orderly or worker of some sort, being clearly too young by decades to be one of the residents. Other workers were standing around screaming and pointing. Something jerked Mark's gaze to the left and he saw his father running down the hallway. Tom Bell banged through a door at the end of the corridor and started up the stairway to the upper floors.

"Dad!"

Mark hurried after his father. A nurse came out of a door on the right and bumped him, throwing him off stride. He stumbled and went to his knees, cracking them on the hard tiles. He screeched in frustration and staggered to his feet again. Another man in white orderly garb grabbed him by a shoulder and spun him around.

The bushy-haired man was heavyset with a florid, jowly face. "Hey, kid—"

Mark popped him in the mouth. Hard.

The big man fell over, crashed into a cart containing cleaning supplies.

Like father, like son.

Boom, out go the lights.

More people were coming down the hallway. More men

in white and a security guard. He couldn't knock them all out and didn't have time for this shit anyway. He turned away from them and continued down the hallway, banging through the same doors his father had disappeared through moments before. He vaulted up the stairs to the second floor landing, heard screams from the other side of the closed door there. He pulled the door open and stepped into another hallway awash in pandemonium. Panicked old people in gowns were milling about everywhere, choking the hallway. A lot of people were crying and wailing.

Unfortunately, there was no time for delicacy.

Mark started shoving his way through the crowd. The wrinkled and frail oldsters cursed him and pushed back as he made his way through the corridor. He saw his father enter a room near the end of the hallway and stepped up his efforts, ramming his way through the ranks of the elderly without regard for any harm he was inflicting. He hated to hurt them, but there wasn't time for delicacy.

At last, he reached the room his father had entered. Tom Bell glanced over his shoulder as his son came stumbling into the room, a wide, mad grin stretching the corners of his mouth grotesquely.

"I should have known you wouldn't do the smart thing and go. I'm glad, actually. You should be here to see this, to witness the glory of my ascension."

Tom Bell was pointing the gun at the head of a very frail-looking old man sitting in a chair by the room's only window. The man's expression was blank, his eyes hollow and unfocused. He probably wasn't seeing the gun at all, or if he saw it, his brain didn't recognize it for what it was—the instrument of his death.

Mark started across the room. "Dad, please don't."

Tom squeezed the trigger.

It was *loud*.

The bullet punched a hole through the center of the old guy's forehead. Blood and brain matter flew out the back of his head and splattered the wall behind him. Mark gagged, felt bile rise into his throat. He was dimly aware of more screaming from the hallway.

The old man's body began to violently convulse. Mark couldn't grasp what he was seeing at first. The guy's head had been fucking *emptied*. His essence, whatever had made him Luke Harper, ex-mayor, was all over the goddamn wall. So his body shouldn't be jerking like that, like a man riding the lightning in an electric chair. And, holy shit, what was this? The front of his gown was burning and starting to catch fire. A pattern formed, visible for just a moment. A pentagram.

What the fuck?

The old man's head blew apart in an explosion of gore and bone fragments. Mark felt wetness splash his cheeks. A brief and brilliantly intense flash of light bloomed toward the ceiling from the space formerly occupied by the man's head and flew into Tom Bell's wide open mouth.

Tom grinned again. "Goodbye, son. You really should leave now. Flauros is here."

His body began to shake.

Mark had only a small inkling as to what was happening here. A demon had been inside the old man. A different demon, not the one they'd released.

And now it was inside his father.

He didn't need to know anything else.

He backed out of the room in a hurry and started shoving his way back through the crowd. Hands grabbed at him. People tried to slow him down, ask him questions. He had to knock some of them down. He had no time for their questions and couldn't stay here. He sure as hell couldn't deal with the cops, who were sure to be on the scene within minutes.

Back in the Lexus, he started the engine and peeled out of the parking lot.

He could think of only one place to go. One possible sanctuary.

Keeping one hand on the wheel as he drove away at high speed, he dug his phone out of his pocket and called up his list of missed calls.

He hit the button to dial the unknown number.

Clayton Campbell answered on the first ring.

191

THIRTY-ONE

A monster walked the streets of Wheaton Hills that morning, enjoying the chance to really stretch its borrowed legs for the first time since the night of its release. The cool breeze carried with it a scent of burning leaves mixed with a ripe odor of decay. The latter emanated from the corpse of a dog slowly rotting in a drainage ditch at the far end of the street. Maggots squirmed in the dead animal's various orifices, feasting on the bloated remains. It was the dying time of the year. The time when green gave way to brown, when the warmth of the sun yielded to plummeting temperatures and morning frost. The ominous pause before the deeper harshness of winter.

It was not possible to truly appreciate these things without a human host. Too many years had passed since the demon had known the joy of physical sensation. How incredible it was to *feel* again. Even something as simple as the texture of a blade of grass or crumbling leaf rubbed between his host's fingertips. The feel of the wind on his face. Every little thing was a new revelation.

The streets of the neighborhood were quiet this time of day. All the little children were off learning useless things. Most of the fathers and many of the mothers labored elsewhere, endlessly performing dreary tasks that brought little joy but provided food and shelter. It was a safe and comfortable place. A place for good people to raise happy families.

At least that was the idea.

Andras had a vision. A glorious, crimson-stained vision. These falsely idyllic streets awash in blood, the screams of the dead and the dying echoing in the night.

It was more than a vision.

It was a promise. A prophecy of things to come.

He left the street and crossed a well-manicured lawn to climb the front steps of a house his host had visited only once. He had access to all his host's memories. The one time was enough.

This was the place.

He jabbed the doorbell and waited.

Colleen Wagner opened the door seconds later, her features drawing into an expression of confusion at the sight of the boy standing on her porch. A thin boy in jeans and black jacket, strands of long blond hair protruding from beneath the wool hat atop his head. A boy with a dangerous grin and eyes alight with demonic delight. Something primitive inside Colleen sensed she was in the presence of genuine evil.

She screamed.

Tried to shut the door.

Andras, laughing, kicked it open and walked on in.

The day felt like it dragged on forever. Natasha wasn't in the habit of spending her days fretting over time or watching the clock, but this day was an exception. This day couldn't end one second too soon. Ransom High was abuzz with gossip about the bowling alley fight. It seemed like the whole school wanted to hear what she had to say on the subject. Friends and acquaintances. Teachers and administrators. *Everybody*. A lot of them didn't believe her when she said she didn't know anything, but it was true. The first she heard about it was when she showed up at school in the morning. Chris Harknell intercepted her on the way in and told her all about it. What he knew of it, at least.

Mark was in jail. Under arrest for assault.

Ditto Jared and Kevin.

It explained the incessant buzzing of the cell phone in her tote bag. She'd figured it was Mark going all obsessive again and had been ignoring it. The first thing she did after getting the news was turn it off. All the unwanted extra attention would have been bad enough on its own, but it was made worse by how awful she felt. She felt bloated and tired, the way she did during a heavy period. But she was not having a period. She had a home pregnancy test kit in her bag, but she had not yet worked up the nerve to use it. She was afraid of what it would say. She did not want to be pregnant. It would screw up all her plans. She was too young. She wasn't ready for it. She didn't know who the fucking father might be. It was all that was on her mind in the moments when she wasn't being hassled about Mark. By the time the final bell rang, her head was pounding. She got the hell out of there as fast as she could.

She made it home in record time, drastically exceeding posted speed limits and terrifying numerous other motorists the whole way back. After parking the PT Cruiser, she stumbled out of the car and puked in the grass beside the driveway, heaving and heaving long after her guts felt empty, her body straining painfully as tears streamed down her cheeks.

The sickness finally passed and the shaking mercifully began to ease.

At last, she was able to stand.

The garage was open, so she entered the house through the back door. After shutting the door, she stood very still for a moment in the short hallway next to the laundry room. Something wasn't right. The house was quiet. Her mother always had either the television on or music playing during the day. A deep sense of unease settled inside her and gooseflesh pebbled her bare flesh. Her heart was beating faster and her throat felt tight. She tried to tell herself she was being silly. There was nothing solid on which to base this...unease. Just the quiet. That uncharacteristic quiet. But maybe she wasn't the only one with a terrible headache. Maybe mom was just lying down somewhere.

She should have known better.

As soon as she entered the kitchen, that sense of something not right amplified. There was still no sound, save for the ticking of the grandfather clock in the adjacent living room. It only took a moment of intent listening to realize this wasn't exactly true. There *was* another sound. It was intermittent and very soft. There was something...sneaky about it. It was a furtive and secretive sound. A very low and, well...*rhythmic* exhalation of breath. It was a sound she knew. A rhythm she knew. Someone was having sex somewhere in the house and was trying to be quiet about it. Her father's car wasn't in the garage and, anyway, he wasn't due home for hours yet. The thought that her mother might be screwing someone else astounded and horrified her. So far as she knew, her parents were happily married. So what the fuck?

Then she heard a sound like a whimper.

Something in the timbre of that sound confirmed it was her mother. The sound cut off, as if it had been suddenly stifled. A hand slapped over a mouth, maybe? So maybe her mother wasn't banging some other guy behind her dad's back. Maybe she was in trouble. The back door had been unlocked. Which meant nothing in and of itself. It was usually unlocked. It was something they never thought about. This wasn't the city. Homes didn't get invaded in Ransom. Unfortunately, the lack of caution meant anyone could get inside the house during the day.

A murderer, for instance.

Or a rapist.

Her mind flashed on images from that night in the basement.

Or worse.

She grabbed a carving knife from a cutlery drawer and set her tote bag on the kitchen counter. She then began a slow, cautious exploration of the house, holding the knife in front of her in a shaking hand as she edged up against the frame of the archway leading to the living room. She peered around the frame and saw that the living room was empty.

The sound came again.

That slow, slow rhythm and shuddery exhalation of breath, accompanied this time by a very faint squeak of bedsprings. This time she was able to follow the direction of the sound.

Upstairs.

She stepped out of her shoes and began to ascend the stairs to the second floor, moving as quietly and as lightly as she could manage. The sound was coming from her own bedroom, the door to which was standing open. She paused as she reached the top of the stairs, unable to decide whether she should beat a hasty retreat or press ahead to see what was what. The thought that got her moving again was knowing her mom wasn't stupid. Even supposing she was fucking some dude in her daughter's bedroom, she would be aware, at least vaguely, of the time. She would know Natasha was due home and would likely catch her in the act.

Which brought her right back to the most logical conclusion.

Something terrible was happening.

She had to help her mom.

She edged up to the door to her bedroom and peered inside.

They were on her bed, naked and rutting. The sheets were a tangled mess. The black comforter had spilled off the bed onto the floor. They were positioned facing the doorway, Colleen Wagner on her back, her head hanging off the edge of the bed. Derek McGregor was atop her, his pelvis grinding slowly as he thrust in and out of her. The air was thick with the stench of sweat and sex. Their bodies glistened. Her mother's grin was apparent even with Derek's hand over her mouth.

Natasha dropped the knife and staggered backward.

Her back thumped against the wall behind her.

Derek removed his mouth from Colleen's neck, glanced through the open door, and smiled when he saw Natasha. "Hello. We've been waiting for you."

Colleen twisted her head around to look at her daughter, dislodging the hand from her mouth. "Come here, baby. Mommy wants to undress you."

She cried out as Derek thrust into her yet again.

Natasha listened to her instincts this time.

She couldn't save her mother. Nor did she have the words to coax her out of whatever dark magic was keeping her under the spell of the thing inside her friend's body. She knew it wasn't really Derek. One look into those strangely glittering eyes was enough to confirm that.

She ran at top speed back down the stairs. The only thing that mattered now was getting gone as fast as she could. She had to get to Mark and let him know what was happening. Maybe have that meeting with Clayton and hope like hell the old guy actually knew a way to fix this fucked up shit.

The demon caught up to her just as she reached the back door and dragged her screaming back into the kitchen. The demon pressed her to the floor and ripped open her t-shirt. She screamed and flailed at him. He backhanded her, putting nearly enough force in it to knock her out. The world went gray. When everything came back into focus, her tattered shirt had been removed. The demon's face was closer now. Its hard-on pressed against her belly, the length of it still slick with her mother's vaginal secretions. Her stomach knotted and her throat filled with bile. She tried again to shove the demon off her, but it didn't budge. Everything went black for a time. This time consciousness was slower to return. When it did, she was completely nude and the demon was positioned between her spread legs. She could feel the hard-on prodding her again. Her mother was kneeling next to her head, her heavy breasts hanging near her face. She was stroking her daughter's hair and giggling.

The demon's breath was hot on Natasha's mouth.

"I smell the life stirring inside you. It's mine. It belongs to me. I put it there."

Natasha's eyes filled with tears. "No."

"Yes."

Another adamant shake of her head. "Fuck you. No."

The demon laughed. "Deny all you wish. You feel the truth of it. I know you do."

Natasha began to sob.

"I've come to claim you as my bride. To take possession

of what is rightfully mine."

Natasha squeaked out the words between sobs: "Y-y-you c-can't...do this. It's w-wrong."

"Oh, but I can do anything. Watch this."

The demon flicked its right hand. The fingernails elongated, becoming sharp, black talons. It whipped the hand at Colleen Wagner, raking the talons across her face, tearing the flesh to bloody ribbons.

Natasha screamed.

The worst of it was that her mother wasn't trying to defend herself. She fell onto her back, but did not retreat. The demon pounced and raked the talons across her throat. Blood pumped from the wide gash. The demon lowered its head to the wound and drank deeply of Colleen's life force. The older woman's body began to convulse. Still, the smile never left her ruined face.

Natasha found the strength to turn over and get up.

She tried to run.

Only her feet weren't moving.

She dropped to her knees next to Andras, pressed her head against his as she was filled with an all-consuming need to imbibe the still gurgling blood. It wet her face and filled her mouth. The taste was wonderful. She raised her face from the wound and grinned at Andras, blood dripping from her lips.

The demon grinned back at her.

And then it pounced on her.

THIRTY-TWO

She shoved the gun back into his mouth and said it again.

"Say you love Satan! Say it, bitch!"

The middle-aged fat man trembled and wept as he tried to speak around the cold steel wedged against the back of his throat. Carrie yanked the gun out and whipped it across his face, eliciting a shriek followed by yet another plea for mercy. Greg wanted to tell him not to waste his breath, but what was the point? Nothing he could say would ease the poor bastard's suffering and it would just piss Carrie off again. And he absolutely did not want that. Before Andras, he never would have imagined she possessed such a deep capacity for sadism. But she did. She loved hurting people. It was obvious in the way her face lit up with every scream. And it wasn't just the influence of the demon driving her. That had merely been the trigger. This need to hurt had been inside her all along, just waiting to be brought into the light.

She pressed the barrel of the gun against the man's forehead.

"Say you love Satan, you fat fuck. *Say it!*"

The man's head sagged against the gun barrel as he started in with the sobbing again. He was tied to a chair in his kitchen. The house was across the street from the McGregor house. It had been Carrie's idea to come here after hearing from Suzie that the man who owned it lived alone and was a shut-in due to poor health. The dude was short but enormous. He wore gray sweatpants that looked stretched to the snapping point and a white t-shirt big enough to double as a tent. The clothes stank, as if he hadn't washed them in weeks or months. The house was a mess, with trash and debris everywhere and huge piles of

199

Bryan Smith

dishes in the sink. The nightstand next to his bed was crowded with pill bottles. Also in the bedroom were several large oxygen canisters in a rack. Whatever was wrong with the guyt had to be something pretty severe. Life-threatening, maybe. The possibility made what was happening here marginally less horrible. You could almost see it as an act of mercy.

Almost.

Sort of.

One thing he had to admit. And it was sort of shameful, but it was the truth. The new wildness in Carrie had transformed her in more than one way. Before she'd been pretty but demure. But the way she carried herself was different now. She was freer with her body, with the way she moved. This insolent pose she was striking right now, for instance, with her hip cocked out and her pointy chin jutting forward, the big gun held so confidently in her small hand. She wasn't cute anymore. That wasn't the right term at all for a girl like this. She looked hot. Almost literally *hot,* as if just touching her would scorch your fingers.

She thumbed back the hammer on the revolver. "Last chance. You should really say it."

The man's breath hitched. "I love Jesus Christ, my savior—"

The hammer came down and Greg jumped at the blast, expecting to see brains and blood fly out the back of the man's head. But he was still alive, weeping and wailing louder than ever. She'd shifted her aim subtly before pulling the trigger, the bullet blasting harmlessly through space inches from the side of his head. The slug shattered the transparent door of a microwave oven propped on a cart in a corner of the kitchen. Dude wouldn't be warming up any more Big Macs in that thing.

Carrie laughed. "Listen to yourself. You fucking baby. You're not shot, you dumb cunt. Not yet. But you are seriously trying my patience, big boy. I think you need the hammer again."

She glanced at Greg, arched an eyebrow.

"The hammer, baby."

Greg sighed.

He hefted the hammer and approached the bound man, who looked up at him with bleary, pleading eyes. "Please...I'm begging you..."

Greg cracked the hammer against an already pulped knee. The man screamed.

Carried smacked the back of Greg's head with her free hand. "Stop with the fucking love taps. Smash him. Fucking ruin him. Hit him as hard as you fucking can."

She smacked the back of his head again.

"Now!"

Greg did it. He brought the hammer down with all his might, then again, crushing the knee, reducing it to something less than useless. The man wailed and rocked against his bonds. Carrie shoved Greg aside and silenced the man with a few more rapid pistol whips across the face.

She smiled. "I was just kidding last time. This really is your last chance."

She pressed the barrel against his forehead, pushing his head back.

"Say it."

The man's shoulders sagged. "I-I...love...S-Satan."

Carrie's posture became less rigid. The smile on her face was softer than the mad grin Greg had seen so often since yesterday. You could almost imagine a trace of actual benevolence in that expression. "There. Was that so fucking hard?"

He sniffled. "N-no."

Carrie gripped one of his ears and twisted it, making his face contort. "You did mean it, didn't you? You weren't just saying it to get on my good side, right? Tell me you really love Satan. I want to hear the truth of your love ringing in your words. Can you do that?"

The man raised his face and nodded, wincing slightly because she was still twisting his ear. "I-I do. I really, really love Satan." He sniffled again. "So much."

Carrie let go of his ear and stroked his sweat-slick hair. "Awesome. That's really fucking cool. I'm glad to hear you've come over to our side. Did you ever read that book?"

The man frowned. "Huh?"

Carried nodded. "*Say You Love Satan*. I saw it at a garage sale a long time ago. Never read it, but that title...it stayed with me. I had *nightmares* about it. These bad fucking dreams where bad people would force me to say that shit. This shit today, right here and now with you, this fun little game? It's fucking *cathartic*."

Yep, Greg thought. *Crazy from the start. But she hid it so well.*

Not that he cared anymore. He wasn't as gung-ho as Carrie, but he was a willing participant in this atrocity. It was what Andras wanted. The demon existed to spread death and cause suffering. And it wanted them to do the same. So here they were, honoring their new master. It was good to please the demon because the demon could make them feel so good in turn. Even if some small part of him harbored a tiny bit of regret every time he struck this man with the hammer, it was okay because Andras would reward them so well.

He had promised them all an honored place among his 30 infernal legions in Hell.

It reminded Greg of something he'd heard once.

Better to rule in Hell than serve in Heaven.

Carrie aimed the gun at the center of the man's face. "Congratulations, you've passed part one of the test. Now here's part two. Say you love Andras."

The man's brow furrowed as he stared up at Carrie. "Who?"

Greg couldn't help it this time—he smiled. "Uh oh."

Carrie made a tsk-tsk sound. "Sorry. You don't get a second chance in this part of the game."

The man's eyes went wide with fear.

He tried to rock the chair over. Wouldn't have done him any good had he succeeded, but Greg couldn't blame the guy. He was human. Sick or not, his survival instinct was intact. He fought like hell to get out of the way of the bullet.

Carrie allowed him a few more seconds of struggle.

Then she smiled. "Time's up."

This time her aim was true.

This time the blood and brains did fly.

THIRTY-THREE

Things were getting a little dicey over at the McGregor house. People kept showing up unannounced. First it was that weird old English guy in the black suit. He drove up in an old Bentley shortly after Tom left to deal with his delinquent son and do that thing for Andras. He was tall and gaunt and very old, with these icky folds of loose flesh hanging beneath his chin. He looked like an elderly undertaker. Super creepy. Suzie's first instinct had been to slam the door in his face.

Then he had to go and say, "I am Frederick. Andras has summoned me."

Shit.

Suzie had no choice but to let him in. "What Andras wants, Andras gets."

Turned out Frederick wasn't alone. There was an old woman in the trunk of the Bentley. Not quite as old as Frederick, because holy crap, who was? Her name was Betty Hoover and she was Frederick's next door neighbor. Frederick intended to offer her as a sacrifice to Andras. Suzie understood why after they hauled her inside and removed the gag stuffed in her mouth. She was a snooty old cunt, full of threats and demands despite the dire nature of her predicament. The gag went back in and they stashed her in a closet.

A little later a representative of Ransom High showed up to inquire after Derek. The man was very lean, the kind of skinny you saw in those vegan pussies. His khaki trousers and blue button-down shirt hung loosely on his ultra-slender frame. He was young, no more than maybe mid-twenties. He looked sort of nerdy with his wire-rim glasses and tousled hair. Nerdy in a sort of cute way, though. His name was Rick

Armstrong. The surname made Suzie giggle. The guy looked sort of uncomfortable to begin with, but Suzie's reaction to his name caused him to blush and tug at the tie knotted around his shirt collar. "I'm, uh, sorry to bother you, Mrs. McGregor, and I of course want to offer my condolences for your loss."

"My what?"

"Your loss."

"What did I lose?"

Tim tugged at his tie again. "Um...your husband?"

Suzie grinned broadly and smacked her forehead. "Oh, right. Yes, my husband's dead. I totally forgot. I've been sort of, uh...busy."

Right about then was when Tim got that wary look in his eyes, the one she knew from long experience meant the person suspected she was perhaps a bit unstable. "Uh huh. So...as I said, I'm a counselor at the school and I just wanted to, well, check in on your son and see how he's doing. I've left several messages on your voice mail and grew concerned when I didn't hear back from you."

"I don't really check my voice mail anymore."

"Oh. Well..." Tim shuffled his feet a little and crossed his arms. He didn't seem to know what to do with himself. He shot a quick glance at the little red Toyota parked behind Frederick's Bentley. His car, presumably. The poor guy was obviously already regretting coming out here. "That's, uh... understandable. I guess. The death of a loved one causes a lot of upheaval. Things can seem confused and often there's a problem with coping and moving forward. Your son—"

"Would you like to fuck me, Rick?"

He blushed. "W-what?"

"It's just that you keep staring at my tits."

It was true. She was wearing cut-off denim shorts, very short and very tight, and a skimpy little tank top without a bra. And she had big tits. You couldn't help but fixate on them.

He stared at her in shock for a moment, but quickly recovered. "Mrs. McGregor, I'm sorry, but this is highly inappropriate. I should—"

She stepped out of the doorway and grabbed him by the crotch. "You should let me suck this, that's what you should do." She gave him a hard squeeze and his cock, unsurprisingly, sprang to life. She leaned against him and stroked him through his trousers. "Imagine how good it'd feel to have my mouth wrapped around this, all hot and wet and sliding up and down, all velvety smooth and soft."

Rick groaned.

Then he surprised her by bracing his hands against her shoulders and pushing her firmly away. "I have to leave now, Mrs. McGregor. I can't allow myself to be seen as possibly taking advantage of a vulnerable widow. Please have your son call me or come by the school to talk."

Suzie smiled.

Then she balled up a fist and punched him in the face. There was an audible pop as the cartilage in his nose snapped. He staggered backward and stumbled over the edge of the porch. There was another loud pop as he hit the sidewalk below. Suzie moved to the edge of the porch and looked down.

"Oh, damn."

The young school counselor had landed at an awkward angle. His neck was broken.

Lydia joined her on the porch. The other woman was nude save for a pair of pink panties. He brown nipples stood erect in the cool air. "He's dead."

"No shit."

"What should we do?"

The door creaked behind them as Frederick came outside. He stared at the corpse for a long moment, a creepy smile twisting his thin lips. Then he looked at Suzie. "Do you happen to own a chainsaw?"

"Uh...yeah. Why?"

Frederick told her.

"Oh. Yuck. You want to do this in my garage?"

"Yes, madam."

"Whatever." Suzie stared again at Rick's unmoving form. "A shame, though. Look at that wiry little body. I could have had some fun with him."

Frederick chuckled. "I concur."

Suzie looked at him. "Frederick, I don't want you to take this the wrong way, but you are a strange fucking dude. And coming from me, that's really saying something."

"Madam, you don't know the half of it."

"And who are you to Andras? I don't think you told me."

"A faithful servant. It is all you need to know."

"Whatever."

They dragged the dead school counselor into the garage and placed the body on a tarp. The old guy revved up the chainsaw and went to work while Suzie and Lydia got rid of Ricks car. Lydia, now fully clothed, drove the Toyota out of Wheaton Hills while Suzie followed in her SUV. They ditched the Toyota in a field on the outskirts of town and drove back together in the SUV.

On the way back, Lydia started fiddling with the radio. She found a classic rock station and turned the volume up loud.

Suzie turned the radio off.

Lydia turned it back on.

Suzie turned it off again. "This is my car, bitch. The radio stays off."

Lydia grunted. "Well, I sure don't want to talk to you."

"So don't."

"I still fucking hate you, you know. I love Andras and all, and I'll do whatever he says, but that hasn't changed."

"I'm not the president of your fucking fan club either, bitch."

They drove in silence for several moments, neither of them looking at each other as the SUV sped along the rural back road. There wasn't much to see out here. Just trees and the occasional open stretch of scrubby field.

Suzie cleared her throat. "So...do you want to pull over and get it on right here or wait until we get back?"

Lydia grinned. "Right here."

"Awesome."

Suzie pulled over and they scrambled into the back seat and went at each other for a while.

The remainder of the drive back was less tense.

Back up front, Lydia checked her hair and makeup in the rear view mirror as Suzie drove. "It's crazy how horny I am all the time now."

Suzie nodded. "I know, right? I'm not sure if it's just being around Andras, some kind of mind control, or something to do with fucking him or drinking his blood, that exchange of bodily fluids. Maybe it's a combination."

"I don't really care why it is, I'm just glad. If I'd known consorting with demons was this hot, I'd have been doing it all along. I haven't had this much fun in years."

"Yeah."

"It's like being a kid again." Her eyes flashed mischievously as she smiled. "A devil-worshiping kid."

"Hail Satan."

"Hail Andras!"

They both giggled.

Their renewed high spirits faded some as Suzie turned down the street leading to her house. A white USPS truck was parked in the street outside her house. The chubby mailman was walking toward her front porch, a package tucked under his arm, something too big to fit in the box by the driveway.

"Oh, hell."

The mailman climbed the steps to the porch and rang the doorbell.

Ella opened the door and came at the startled mailman with a rolling pin. He staggered backward and threw up an arm to protect himself. The rolling pin smashed against his forearm. The next blow connected with the side of his head. The mailman crumpled on the porch, still clinging to the package as Ella fell atop him and commenced to bashing his skull in with the rolling pin.

Lydia shook her head as they pulled up. "That's really uncalled for."

Suzie sighed. "But not unexpected. The old bitch is fucking bloodthirsty."

"I'm just pissed about having to clean up another mess. This is starting to seem like work."

Suzie shrugged. "Let's just get it over with."

207

They got out of the car and hauled Ella off the battered mailman. The older woman's whole body was vibrating with manic energy, her eyes wide and sparkling with delight. "I smashed his head! Smashed it like a fucking melon!"

Wild laughter ensued.

There was a spreading pool of blood beneath the mailman and the shape of his skull looked all wrong. "Yes, I guess you did," Suzie said. "And look at the mess you made."

Frederick joined them on the porch again. "Oh, dear. Another one."

Suzie nodded. "You up for some more chainsaw work, Frederick?"

Another of those creepy smiles. "Always, madam."

So they hauled the dead mailman off to the garage and Frederick again went to work cutting a dead man down to size. Suzie donned some nondescript clothes, a tight-fitting sports bra, and put her hair up under a cap. People were expecting their mail and there was only thing to do—finish the route. At least the Wheaton Hills part of it. That way, hopefully, the missing mailman's trail wouldn't lead back to her doorstep. She was able to more or less properly finish the Wheaton Hills stretch of the mailman's route. An envelope here or there may have gone into the wrong box, but that happened all the time anyway, so big fucking deal. When she was done, she abandoned the mail truck outside an apartment complex on the other side of Ransom and gave Lydia a call to come pick her up.

Lydia wasn't alone when she rolled up in the SUV.

Tom Bell was sitting in the front passenger seat. Only this man wasn't really Tom anymore. Was there a hint of sulfur in the air or was that just her imagination?

Suzie climbed into the back and Lydia twisted in her seat to glance at her. "Sorry it took so long. Got a call from this guy. Uh...apparently we'll be hearing about a nursing home massacre in the news soon."

The demon wearing Tom's flesh laughed softly. "They are all dead."

Suzie pulled off the cap and shook out her long, blond

hair. "Uh huh. All dead. And did you get away without being seen?"

"They are all dead. There is no one to tell the tale. The building has been consumed in the flames of an infernal fire."

Suzie's squinted. "Say what now?"

"I summoned Hellfire, infernal flames that will not be extinguished until the entire building and everything in it is reduced to useless ash. There are no witnesses. No surveillance images. I will not be identified."

"Huh. Okay then."

Flauros did not respond to further attempts by the women to engage him in conversation. The ride back to Wheaton Hills passed in uncomfortable silence. It was a strange thing. This Flauros was supposedly subservient to Andras, but both women found him significantly more intimidating. Andras was a remorseless killer and a shameless manipulator, but he clearly enjoyed playing with the humans he'd drawn into his web. Suzie had the sense his henchman felt nothing but contempt for them.

We're like bugs to him.

Filthy, mindless, crawling, insignificant things.

The realization made her sort of angry. She consoled herself with the thought that it didn't really matter. Andras was the one calling the shots. That was the important thing. That and the promises he'd made.

Thinking about that, Suzie smiled and felt some of her anxiety slip away.

She couldn't wait to begin serving her new master in Hell. But first, of course, there remained much work to do. Work, the word Lydia had used to lament the complications caused by Ella's murder of the mailman. But the work didn't bother Suzie. It was *dark* work. And that made it *good*.

Andras had said the streets of Wheaton Hills would flow with rivers of blood.

Suzie hoped he was right.

She couldn't imagine anything more beautiful.

THIRTY-FOUR

Earlier in the day...

Clayton Campbell was pretty sure he'd never been this tired in his entire life. But maybe it just felt that way. There had been many sleep-deprived nights in those first months after his father's suicide. Back then he hadn't wanted to sleep because of the bad dreams that awaited him any time he finally did succumb to exhaustion and slip into unconsciousness. In the dreams, he would relive that moment of walking into his father's study and discovering his corpse. The reality of it had been bad enough. All that blood splattered all over Norman Campbell's treasured collection of baseball memorabilia. Bits of crimson-stained bone slivers and brain matter clinging to framed pictures. The horrible slack expression on the old man's face, with the gun still hanging from his mouth. All that and the horror of not being able to do a damn thing about it. Yeah, all that was pretty goddamn terrible. His relationship with his father had been complicated, most of it admittedly because of Clayton's apparent inability to fit into society in any meaningful way. But they were father and son and they loved each other. It hit him hard, threw his world off its axis. It was the worst hurt he'd ever known. But the dreams took that already hard reality and twisted it, shaped it into something darker and more sinister. He would see it actually happen instead of walking in after the fact. He'd see his father wink at him before pulling the trigger. Other times his father would come to him as a walking corpse, a shambling zombie like in the movies, drooling and moaning with the back of his head blown out.

Yeah.

Not a lot of sleep in those days. However, after the worst aspects of the dreams at last began to fade, he became rather an accomplished sleeper. He inherited enough money from his father that he didn't have to work and, without that motivation to get out and interact with the world, it was easy to embrace a lifestyle that centered around being unconscious a lot of the time. The other defining aspect of this lifestyle was the hours he kept. Just like his young friends, he stayed up during the night and slept through the day

Hence his current dilemma.

He had remained awake long past his usual crash time. By the time eight in the morning rolled around, he finally accepted that something had gone wrong and the kids wouldn't be coming over for the meeting. He'd forced himself to stay up on the off-chance one or more of them would put it in an appearance to explain what had happened. He put on some coffee and stayed up a bit longer still, hoping against hope. At one point he called the number Mark had given him, but no answer.

He finally gave up and headed off to bed.

About five seconds after he at last closed his eyes, the phone rang and he snatched it up.

Guess who?

And now they were seated across from each other at the table in his kitchen. His account of all that had happened to him since last night had come out in an explosive rush, leaving him almost breathless. He was antsy. He kept fidgeting, squirming around and rocking in that chair so much it made Clayton's head hurt just to watch him. He looked more like a kid than usual. Vulnerable and scared. Based on the story he'd told, it was understandable.

Mark abruptly ceased fidgeting. "You got any beer?"

"What kind of fucking question is that? Of *course* I've got beer."

Mark shifted in his seat and crossed a leg over a knee. "I mean can I have a beer?"

"You think that's wise?"

"No. Still want one."

Clayton rubbed at his bleary eyes then waved a hand at the refrigerator. "Help yourself."

Mark lurched out of his chair, nearly knocking it over in the process. He opened the refrigerator and glanced at Clayton. "You want one?"

Clayton considered it, then shook his head. "No, I'm a zombie already. I need to wake up and get my head clear. Uh...you don't happen to have any coke, do you?"

Mark still had the refrigerator door open. He frowned at its contents. "Well...there's, like, one can of Diet Coke way in the back on the bottom shelf."

Clayton laughed.

"What?"

"Nothing. The Diet Coke will be fine."

Mark came back with the drinks, sliding the soda can over to Clayton as he sat down. "Why do you need to wake up?" He popped the cap off a bottle of Heineken with the bottle opener attached to his key chain. "You should get some rest before we really have to get down to business with this fucking demon situation."

"Can't. Have things to do. Miles to go and all that noise."

Clayton popped the soda can's tab and drank deeply, wincing at the sharp diet taste. Funny. He couldn't remember buying diet soda at any time in recent memory. No telling how how old this thing was. Oh, wait. The expiration date. He lifted the can and peered at the numbers printed across the curved bottom of the can. "Kid, this can's been sitting in my fridge somewhere in the neighborhood of six years."

Mark grimaced. "And you're chugging it."

Clayton drained the rest of the can and crushed it in his fist. He belched. "Excuse me." He tossed the crumpled can at the tall wastebasket that sat in a corner of the kitchen. It went right in. Mark whistled in appreciation at the shot. Clayton shrugged. "Practice. Lots and lots of practice. Anyway..." He stood, groaning at the very loud creak of his knees. "I'm gonna get dressed."

"Aren't you dressed now? I only ever see you in a robe

and sweats."

"Today I will don jeans. I have one pair that still somewhat fits. I will complete the ensemble with a selection from my vast collection of t-shirts."

"What's the occasion?"

Clayton's expression turned sour. "I have to go...out. To a place where my usual sartorial splendor won't cut it."

"I'll come with you."

Clayton shook his head. "No. I have to do this on my own. I'll tell you about it later. Stay here and keep trying to contact as many of your friends as you can. See if you can get them over here tonight. Or earlier, actually. And it's best if you stay in at this point, what with this other demon riding around in your dad's body now. You'll want to stay under the radar until we're ready to...uh...do what we're, uh, gonna... do."

Mark knocked back more beer. "And what's that, exactly?"

"Later, okay? Get started on those calls."

He walked out of the kitchen before the kid could ask any more questions.

THIRTY-FIVE

Mark puzzled over Clayton's cryptic comments for a few moments after the guy walked out of the kitchen. It seemed strange to hold anything back at this point, but maybe he had some good reasons. Normally he was a pretty unflappable dude. Very mellow. Part of that was all the booze and pot. It was hard to really rattle a guy who walked around in a semi-permanent haze. Part of it was just the way he was. But whatever he was venturing out to do was taking him out of his comfort zone. He seemed uptight. Apprehensive. But he also seemed pretty determined to deal with it on his own. Mark would just have to trust that he'd be ready to provide some answers later in the day.

If he had any answers, he better damn well come across with them.

Mark's mind kept going back to that image of his dad pointing the gun at the old man's face. It kept playing on an endless, blood-stained loop in his head. He'd give anything to cast the memory out of his head, but the sad, hard truth was he was stuck with it for life. *Goddamn.* He hadn't been close to his father for a while, but there was a part of him who was still the little kid who idolized his dad. They'd had some great times together in the old days. The ball games. The family vacations. All those goofy little father and son moments. It seemed forever ago sometimes, but other times it felt like just a few seconds ago. He hoped like hell Clayton had some secret hoodoo voodoo knowledge for casting out demons. He wanted both his parents back, wanted to feel like part of a real family again, their home a sanctuary again rather than a place he needed to escape.

It was hard to be patient. He wanted answers and he

214

wanted them *now*. He decided the only way to deal with the frustration was to do as Clayton had asked. Mark checked his phone for messages. Nothing from Natasha. The now familiar pang he felt at that absence pricked at him again, but it was a duller ache this time. It felt like the thing between them was already over, finished before it'd had a chance to really get going. Sucked, but he needed to stop being such a bitch about it, at least until all this other crap was resolved. There were a few more messages from acquaintances, but the lone pertinent message simply read, *CALL ME*.

Mark hit the call button and put the phone to his ear.

Jared Kelly answered on the second ring. "Hey."

"Hey."

"So...how much shit you in?"

Mark leaned back in his chair and felt a deep weariness settle over him. The adrenaline rush brought on by his flight from the nursing home had faded and he was on the verge of crashing hard. "I'm in so much shit..." He paused for a yawn. "I'm in so much shit I feel like I'll never get clean again."

"Talking about the fight and getting arrested or this other shit going on?"

"The other shit."

Jared sighed. "Damn. After last night and getting my ass chewed out by my folks today, I was kind of hoping the rest of it'd just go away. Knew it fucking wouldn't, though."

"Yeah. We've gotta talk about that. Can you come over to Clayton's tonight?"

"Shouldn't be a problem."

"Really? Your parents aren't in lockdown mode?."

"They are, but it ain't no thing, really. I think my dad was even sort of proud of me after he got the whole story, fucked up as that sounds. So, yeah, I'll be there."

"Cool, cool. Hey, uh..."

A pause. "Yeah?"

"You haven't heard from Natasha, have you?"

Another pause. "Aw, no, man, I haven't. Sorry."

Mark looked up as Clayton came back into the room. He had indeed put on a pair of jeans. Old and very tight jeans of the outdated acid-washed style popular when hair bands ruled the radio. His fresh t-shirt was a solid shade of dark blue. Gone was his perpetual five o'clock shadow. His hair still looked sort of wild, but he'd combed it and overall looked presentable. Mark was sort of shocked.

Clayton acknowledged him with a nod as he passed through the kitchen and opened a door next to the pantry. The cluttered garage was visible through the open door.

"Hold on." Mark pulled the phone away from his ear. "Yo, Clayton. Listen—"

"I told you—later."

Clayton left, slamming the door shut behind him.

"No need to be rude, motherfucker." Mark put the phone to his ear. "Clay's off on some urgent fucking errand. I think he has some super mojo scheme to save our asses."

Jared laughed. "Clayton?"

"Yeah."

"Damn. So that's what it's come to."

"Yeah."

"We are so fucked."

Mark's beer was empty. He got up and walked over to the fridge again, pulled the door open and stared inside. "Seriously, though, I think he's got something in mind. Maybe it'll help, maybe it fucking won't, but whatever it is, it's gotta be worth a shot at least. He was gonna tell us about it last night, I think, but...well, you know. Damn, but Clay's got a lot of fucking beer. I think I'm gonna drink it all just for being all secretive and shit. Show his ass."

"That's a brilliant plan. I'll be over in, like, five minutes to help."

"Seriously?"

"Seriously."

The line went dead.

Mark took a beer back to the table and sat down again, taking a deep drink of the cold brew before calling up the next number on his list and hitting the call button again.

A woman's steely voice answered. "Who is this?"

"This is Mark Bell calling for Fiona."

The woman harrumphed. "This is Fiona's mother. What do you want with my daughter?"

"Uh...just to talk."

Mark frowned. Why in hell was Fiona's mom answering her daughter's cell?

"Is it you then? Are you the son of a bitch who violated my baby and got her pregnant?"

Mark's heart almost stopped. "What did you say?"

Mrs. Johnson's voice became shrill. "You heard me perfectly well, young Mr. Bell. Fiona is pregnant. *At seventeen!* And if you think you're—"

Mark hung up.

Holy fucking shit!

The phone immediately started ringing. He glanced at the display and was unsurprised to see Fiona's number. He turned the phone off and drank the beer down in several long swallows. Then he went back to the fridge and got another bottle. And then another.

The revelation laid on him by Fiona's mother had rocked him.

The implications were obvious and shocking.

Holy shit.

Holy, holy fucking shit.

Unable to stop thinking about it, he kept drinking to calm his nerves. He kept at it until the knock on the door came. That would be Jared, showing up a bit later than promised.

He opened the door.

It wasn't Jared.

Mark stared at Fiona in stunned silence for a moment. "Oh. Hey."

Her hands were shoved down into the pockets of her hoodie. "What are you doing here? Where's Clay?"

"Clay went...out. Not really sure where. And I'm here because I'm sort of hiding out. What's your story? Kind of shocked to see you, you know Just tried calling and had this fucking weird conversation with your mother."

"I know. I heard. She wasn't letting me answer my phone."

Mark felt a twinge of unease at her use of the past tense.

"Huh."

She started to pull one of her hands out of the pockets. "I wanted to start this shit with Clay, but you'll do."

There was a gun in her hand now. A revolver. Fiona backed him into the house and thumbed back the gun's hammer. "I'm sorry. There's no other way."

Mark held up his hands. They were shaking. The seriousness of her intent was obvious. He didn't understand it, but that made it no less real. She meant to kill him. "Why are you doing this?"

She smiled sadly. "It's the way it has to be."

His hands abruptly ceased shaking. Anger began to displace the fear. "That makes no goddamn sense. What are you talking about? What's wrong with you?"

She laughed. It was a delicate, fragile sound. The sound of a broken soul. It made Mark ache to hear it, even as he stared down the barrel of the gun. "You know what's wrong with me. Same thing's wrong with all of us. But you know what? If you hadn't come by the bowling alley last night, it would've been just me and Kevin and those jock fucks. But it's a good thing you came along and fucked that up. I've had some time to think. We all have to die. We weren't meant for this world."

"That's bullshit."

Her expression hardened. "It isn't. It's something I've been thinking for a long time. That night in the basement just gave me an excuse. People like you and me weren't built for this world. It's too hard So fuck the world. And fuck life."

Mark stared at her and calculated. She was maybe a foot out of grabbing distance. But he was almost out of time and knew he'd have to make a grab at her anyway. He'd probably just wind up shot, but it'd be better than just standing here and taking it like a pussy.

He looked into her eyes. There was maybe one way left to distract her and perhaps give himself a little edge. "Fiona... did you kill your mother?"

Her breath hitched.

Mark made his move.

Fiona pulled the trigger.

THIRTY-SIX

The garage door rattled up on its tracks and Clayton Campbell backed the old Cadillac out of the garage. The engine sputtered and stopped about halfway down the driveway. He cursed the old car and took a moment to hit a button on the garage door opener clipped to the visor over his head before attempting to start it again. The garage door clanked back down. That done, he shifted his attention back to getting the car properly started. The Caddy had once belonged to his father and was more than a quarter century old. It could be temperamental at times. He twisted the key in the ignition. The engine made some of those annoying grinding noises before finally sputtering and catching again. He revved the engine several times. When it sounded like it was running smooth, he put it in gear again and backed the rest of the way out of the driveway.

He drove away from his house, which actually predated the Wheaton Hills development. It was one of a handful of homes built by an earlier developer who went bankrupt. The Wheaton Hills people came in several years later and began building around them. It was crazy how many homes there were in the neighborhood now. It used to seem so lonely out here, like living on the edge of a frontier. But now he was surrounded by young professionals and their families, none of whom much liked him.

Not that he could really blame them.

And with that thought, melancholy threatened to descend. There was only one certain cure for that—some vintage tunes. Local radio was crap, so that was out. What he needed was a serious jam. There should be something

219

appropriate in the CD player. He switched inputs and began to click through the selections in the CD changer as he pulled out of Wheaton Hills onto Weakley Lane. Pink Floyd. No. Too mellow. Television. No. Too art punk. Not really the right vibe. He knew he should catch up with the rest of the world and get an MP3 player. All the music you could ever want housed inside a little square of plastic and microscopic gizmos. Crazy. The Ramones. Closer, but still not quite what he wanted.

He clicked over to the last selection.

Here we go.

The scrape of a guitar pick up the length of a string, followed by the slam of power chords.

And then again. Scrape, slam.

Clayton shook a fist and banged the base of it against the rim of the steering wheel in time to the song.

"*Shout!*"

Scrape, slam.

"*Shout!*"

Clayton indulged in a bit of old school headbanging as the tune continued. The old Motley Crue track was too absurdly appropriate and he had an unexpected attack of the giggles. *Shout at the devil, indeed. I'll get right on that, Mr. Sixx.* Still giggling, he reached across the seat and opened the glove box. The car weaved a little as he rummaged through the assortment of junk inside, but Clayton course corrected by instinct. He had a lot of practice at skillfully driving like a maniac, a legacy of his hard-partying youth. In those days, he'd had friends his own age. His own group of like-minded comrades and kindred spirits. He had lost touch with them all long ago. Best not to think of that. It was another surefire route to depression.

"Aha!"

Clayton's fingers closed around the thing he was looking for. He flipped the glove box shut, put the slightly mangled old joint between his lips, and stabbed in the dashboard lighter. As he waited for it to heat up, he reached the traffic light at the end of Weakley Lane, where it intersected with

Luke Harper Boulevard, the long, looping road that fit like a mangled horseshoe around the approximate center of Ransom. The lighter popped out as the light changed. He accelerated, turning to the left as he applied the glowing lighter coil to the joint. He puffed it to life, then coughed a little and thumped his chest. It was good weed and not too old. He'd have a good buzz on here in a few minutes.

He groaned, abruptly remembering the need to keep his head clear.

Whatever. Too late now.

The sprawling new industrial complex loomed on the left as he took the Caddy around a wide curve in the road. This was the home of Stanton Manufacturing, Ransom's vaunted economic savior and the reason most of his young friends had come to Wheaton Hills. People like his dad had tried to woo a company on the magnitude of Stanton to Ransom for years and now here it was, his dad's dream come true. The Stanton complex was vast and sparkling and very modern-looking. It didn't look like it belonged in sleepy old Ransom at all. Except that Ransom was becoming less sleepy all the time. A time was coming when he wouldn't much recognize the place he'd grown up in at all.

He soon slowed and turned right off of Luke Harper down a narrower side street. This route would cut straight to the heart of the commerce district and the place he had to visit. The joint tumbled from his fingers as he worked the wheel one-handed.

"Ah, damn."

He peered down at the floorboard between his feet, searching for the fallen joint. The Caddy weaved a little and he heard the stuttering, high-pitched burp of a police siren.

Oh, no.

Clayton glanced at the rear view mirror and saw flashing blue lights.

Damn.

He thumbed down a power window button as he pulled over to the shoulder of the road at the edge of a quiet three-way intersection. Traffic was lighter here than on Luke

221

Harper, so there were stop signs in place of a traffic light. He waved his hand in discreet little motions, hoping to dissipate some of the pot smell before the cop came up to his window. Probably a futile effort, but he didn't know what else to do. The police cruiser pulled up behind him and parked. Clayton's heart raced and he began to panic. In the old days, this would be no big deal. The cop would see who he was and let him go. Or Norman Campbell would have the ticket torn up and the cop reprimanded. But this wasn't the old days and he was still hurting from his last run-in with an officer of the law.

A blue-uniformed cop stepped out of the cruiser.

Clayton's heart nearly seized.

It was the same fucking pig who'd beaten him almost to death.

Christ, come on, what are the fucking odds!?

"Oh, man, this is so not fair. Fuck you, God. Seriously."

The cop approached the Caddy and bent slightly at the waist to peer in at Clayton. "You."

His voice dripped acid. His hate was palpable.

He pulled his gun, aimed it square at Clayton's head, and backed up a few steps into the road. "Out of the car, asshole. You're under arrest."

"For what?"

"OUT OF THE GODDAMN CAR!"

Clayton cringed. The cop was out of line. He had no reason to arrest him at this point. Maybe when he found the joint, but there was clearly no just cause yet. There were procedures, steps to follow, but none of that was happening. That couldn't be a good sign. And yet Clayton knew any disobedience or contrary statements on his part would just make things worse.

He was reaching for the door handle when he caught a glimpse of the big red pickup truck at the edge of his vision. It came whipping out from the side street just ahead of where he was parked, rear end fishtailing, its tires screeching as the driver ignored the stop sign and tromped the gas pedal to the floor again. The cop turned toward the truck just in time to see its big grille bearing down on him. Clayton felt the crunch of the impact down to his bones. The truck's big tires thumped over the cop's body before skidding to a halt.

Clayton craned his neck to peer out his window and saw scared young faces looking down at the body in the road. There were a few of them in the cab of the truck and a few more in the bed. Local redneck kids out joyriding. He heard the clank of a beer bottle rolling down the trunk bed. Drunk. Of course. He saw the terror in their faces and felt sympathy for them. They were just dumb kids out for some fun. They'd done a stupid thing, a thing that would haunt them for the rest of their lives. He could almost imagine the thoughts racing through their heads. How would they explain this to their parents. How—

The truck sped off.

"Huh."

With great reluctance, Clayton got out of the Caddy and shuffled closer to the body for a look. Maybe he could administer CPR or...nope, dude was completely fucking dead. No doubt about it. His neck was twisted at a hideous angle and the back of his head had impacted the asphalt in a really rather resounding way, essentially crushing it. The big truck had driven right over his midsection, undoubtedly rupturing many vital organs. So, yeah...totally dead.

He glanced at the empty cruiser and thought about footage he'd seen of traffic stops on television news shows. Usually the non-routine kind where something had gone horribly wrong. So this cruiser might have some kind of onboard surveillance technology. Of course, any footage would show he wasn't the responsible party here, but the law might take a dim view of him just driving off while one of their own lay bleeding in the road.

He cleared his throat and pointed an unsteady finger at the fallen cop. "For the record, this man is no longer alive. He is as dead as it is possible to be. I have important things I have to take care of, like life and death important, otherwise I would stay, I swear. If there were any chance he might be saved, again, I would stay. Such is not the case. Therefore...

oh, fuck it. You'll want to be looking for a red Ford F150. Bunch of kids. Local tags. First part of the license is LCX. Uh...goodbye."

He got back in the Caddy and drove away at high speed.

In a few minutes, he pulled into the lot of the Ransom Southtrust Bank. Considering that he'd just fled the scene of a hit-and-run, he felt remarkably calm. The incident had focused things for him. He had something crucial to take care of here. Lives really were at stake. Maybe a lot of them.

He got out of the Caddy and walked into the bank.

After several minutes of discussion, he showed the required proper identification and a bank official led him back to the safety deposit boxes.

THIRTY-SEVEN

His sudden lunge startled her, causing her to jerk her hand up as she squeezed the trigger. The bullet slammed into the ceiling somewhere over his head. He got his hand around her slender wrist and gave it a savage twist. She cried out but somehow managed to hold onto the gun long enough to squeeze off another shot that also went astray. He kept twisting her hand even as he pulled her closer and grabbed her by the neck with his other hand. The gun finally shook loose and hit the floor with a heavy thunk. Mark turned her around and yanked her arm up hard behind her back. She thrashed and struggled against him, the fingers of her free hand extended and reaching for the fallen gun. But Mark had too strong a grip on her and she couldn't reach it. Despite this, he kicked the gun across the floor for additional piece of mind.

A big shape filled the open front door.

Fiona cried out. "Jared! Help! Mark's trying to rape me."

She kept trying to twist out of his grip, but Mark held her firm. "She's lying. She just tried to kill me."

"Fuck you, Mark! He's the liar. Why would I do that? He's fucking crazy. Help me, you fat piece of shit."

Jared came the rest of the way into the house and calmly shut the door and locked it. "A fat piece of shit I may be, but that's about the only thing you said that sounds true. It's funny...I could swear I heard something like gunshots a minute ago. The kind of thing you'd hear if, I dunno, somebody was trying to kill somebody else."

Mark grunted. "Like I said—"

Fiona slammed a foot down on his instep. The sudden pain caused him to let go of her and she dove for the gun.

225

Jared was in motion at nearly the same time, launching himself into the air a split second later. He crash-landed on top of her just as her hand was closing around the revolver's handle, causing her to scream in sudden agony. Keeping her pinned beneath him, he crawled forward a little and seized the hand wrapped around the gun. He lifted it and slammed it against the floor repeatedly until she let go of it again. Fiona twisted her head and sank her teeth deep into the meaty flesh of his forearm. And now it was Jared's turn to scream. She started to reach for the gun again, but Mark came hobbling over and scooped it up.

He moved back a safe distance and aimed the gun down at them. "Enough of this shit. Stop fighting, Fiona. It's over."

She went still and glared up at him. Her mouth was bloody. "Fuck you. You're stupid. That's what everybody thinks. They just won't say it to your stupid face."

Jared got to his feet and stared in disgust at the ragged wound on his arm. "You rotten little bitch. Look what you did. What's wrong with you?"

She spit long strands of dyed-black hair out of her mouth. "You're a pig. Pigs are for eating."

She made oinking noises.

Mark shook his head. "I feel sorry for you."

She stopped making the noises and glared at him again. "What?"

"You heard me. I feel sorry for you. You're just trying to hurt us any way you can. But you're still my friend and I want to help you."

"I don't want your help."

"Tough shit. You're getting it anyway."

Her smile was bitter. "You can't. No one can. You were right. I did kill my mom. My little sister, too."

Jared's eyes went wide. "Whoa? What?"

Fiona started sobbing and said nothing further on the subject. Mark and Jared stared at her in shocked silence for several moments. Both boys wore similar expressions of sick resignation. She was right. There really was no meaningful way they could help her now.

Jesus.

"How could you do this, Fiona?" Mark asked.

She lifted her head and wailed at him: "*I told you why. There's no other way! We have to die!*"

She resumed her sobbing.

Jared held his wounded arm and scowled at her. "What the hell kind of fucked up bullshit is that? You do know you've crossed a line, right? This isn't just some regular fucking mistake kids make. You're not gonna get to just say you're sorry and have it all be better. There's no coming back from this. You're a murderer."

Fiona rolled over and sat up. Mark moved back a couple steps, keeping the gun's barrel carefully aimed at her chest. "No sudden moves."

She wiped moisture from her eyes and laughed. "*No sudden moves,*" she said, pitching her voice deeper in a mockery of machismo. "Tough guy. You sound like you're on a stupid cop show."

She got shakily to her feet and started toward the front door.

"Hey. Hold up."

"Fuck you."

"You can't leave."

"Watch me."

Jared moved to intercept her, putting himself between Fiona and the door. "No way. You're not going anywhere."

"Get out of the way."

"No."

She threw herself at him, clawing at his eyes with her fingernails.

Mark groaned. "Jesus Christ."

Jared wound up a fist and sent a hard blow crashing across her jaw. She took a few rapid staggering steps backward and tumbled to the floor again. She rolled onto her back with a moan, but she didn't get back up. She looked woozy, on the verge of unconsciousness. Jared's face was bloody from where her nails had torn into his flesh. "The bitch does not give up. Goddamn."

Mark nodded. "Yeah. I don't know what to do with her."

Jared pushed away from the door. "I do."

"You do?"

"Yeah."

He scooped the semi-conscious girl up in his arms and carried her into the kitchen. Mark followed him and watched him dump her in one of the chairs by the kitchen table. Her head drooped forward when he let go of her, but she didn't fall out of the chair.

Jared moved away from her then, crossing the kitchen to the door by the pantry. "Gonna check the garage for some shit. She comes to and tries that running away shit again, do what I did and knock her ass out. I know she's a girl and all, but the time for playing nice is over. You got that, right?"

Mark gave a terse nod. "Yeah. Go on."

Jared disappeared into the garage.

Mark unloaded the gun and set it on the kitchen counter, well out of Fiona's reach should she regain full consciousness. He just didn't feel comfortable holding it. He didn't relish the idea of forcing her to stay put via physical force, but pointing a loaded gun at a live human being made his stomach churn. He felt better with the bullets in his hip pocket.

Fiona was awake now and smiling at him. "Where did Jared go?"

"He's looking for something."

"He really walloped me."

"Yeah."

"We should leave while he's gone."

Mark frowned. "What?"

She began to stand.

Shit.

"Sit down, Fiona."

She got fully to her feet and took a few shaky steps toward him. One side of her face was swelling slightly from where Jared had struck her. "We should go off together. You were right. This is a stupid thing I was doing. I see that now. But we really don't belong here, Mark. In Ransom." She was close now, almost within touching distance. "Let's go. Right now. I'll be better to you than Natasha ever was, I promise."

The door to the pantry opened and slammed shut again.

Jared grimaced as he came into the kitchen. "Goddamn."

He grabbed her by an arm, steered her back to the chair, and forced her to sit again. Then he removed the thick coil of old rope slung over his shoulder and went to work tying her to the chair. When he was finished, he stood and glared at her. "There. That's one problem solved."

Mark's expression was grim. "For now. We still need to figure out what to do with her."

Fiona laughed. "You could untie me and take turns with me. It'll be just like that night, except nothing will be forcing us." She licked her lips. "Come on. You know you wanna."

Jared said, "I'll look for a gag. Be right back."

He walked out of the kitchen again.

Mark went to the fridge and grabbed a beer. He drank it down. It helped only a little. He suspected there weren't enough beers in the world to make this situation any better.

But he kept knocking them back anyway.

What else was there to do?

THIRTY-EIGHT

The McGregor house had become a hive of Satanic activity by early evening. Throughout the day, various members of the growing Congregation of Andras took turns venturing out and retrieving more neighbors. Methods of retrieval varied. Carrie and Greg bagged their catches through a combination of force and terror. Most of the people they brought in arrived bloodied and battered. One of them, a woman in her early thirties who'd lived alone in a Tudor-style home two houses down, expired soon after being dragged through the front door. Other luring methods included seduction and feigned medical emergencies. Ella alone brought in several men and women apparently incapable of resisting the temptation of her newly youthful and ripe flesh. Most of the new arrivals reacted with horror upon entering the house. Most tried to flee. A few got a look at all the squirming, copulating naked flesh and joined right in, apparently not bothered by the ample evidence of carnage amidst all the writhing bodies. The ones who tried to get out were unsuccessful. Andras reached into their hearts and minds. He soothed and seduced them. Many of these became his most eager converts. A few he saved for play. For his own dark amusement and as a way to stoke the fires of degradation burning in the souls of his acolytes.

Andras walked through the house, surveying it all with demonic delight. So much time had passed since he'd last enjoyed so rich a feast of twisted human souls. The heady stew of corruption and suffering was an intoxicating tribute to the mission Satan had assigned him after his fall.

That mission was simple.

He was the Killer of Men. The bringer of death and sorrow and suffering.

For so long he'd been chained in that place, locked beyond the reach of his master. Imprisoned by men. It was galling. The specific men responsible were, unfortunately, dead. But no matter. He would visit his vengeance upon the people of this pathetic village instead.

The main event was still ahead, but his revenge was already underway.

In the garage, some of the men held down a struggling nude woman while Frederick revved up the chainsaw and lowered the whirring blade to one of her breasts. Her ululating screams formed a kind of wild music in concert with the buzz of the chainsaw as the blade bit into her nipple and chewed.

In the kitchen, Carrie chopped off a young man's hand with a meat cleaver and laughed hysterically as his flailing wrist stump sprayed blood everywhere. She and Greg then cauterized the wound by wrestling the man over to the stove to apply the stump to one of the red-hot burners. The sizzle of burning flesh filled the air with a delicious, stomach-rumbling aroma.

In the living room, a mass of writhing bodies. A lot of moist, smacking sounds. Kissing, slurping, sucking, grunts, moans, and screams. An orgy of quivering flesh. Much of the sex was consensual, but not all. There were whimpers and pleas for mercy as men and women not under Andras' spell were repeatedly violated with cocks and fingers and fists and various inanimate objects.

In the back yard, Flauros, housed in his virile new body, was preaching the gospel of Satan to a group of eager young converts. The people in this group would serve as some of Andras' most vicious soldiers in the battle ahead.

The walls inside the house had been redecorated. There were pentagrams everywhere, most drawn with freshly spilled blood. They all knew the pentagram. But there were other symbols as well, the ones he'd shown them through visions. Here was a four-horned goat inside a pentagram-like symbol. Over there on the front door was another variation on the pentagram, with the point down and a lightning bolt in the middle. On a foyer wall was a detailed rendering of Andras himself astride a huge black wolf, the head of a foe clutched in one of his hands, his sword held aloft in his other hand. The symbols were a necessary element in the conversion of the house. This was no longer a home. It was a black church. A place of dark worship.

Congregation of Andras.

Church of Satan.

On the stairs were more fornicating humans. A man taking a woman from behind near the bottom of the staircase. Further up the stairs, Lydia Bell sat with her ass on the edge of one of the steps, with Ella McGregor kneeling between her splayed legs. Suzie was perched on the step directly behind Lydia. Suzie's arms encircled her former rival, her hands sliding over the front of her body, groping and kneading her breasts and occasionally dipping between her legs. They all turned glazed expressions his way as he passed them on his way up the staircase. They moaned and reached for him, their desire for him so intense it sounded like anguish. The moment he was gone they resumed plying each other's bodies in desperate search of some elusive, final release, a release that remained always tantalizingly out of reach. Playing with their libidos, ratcheting up the normal desires they already possessed to an almost unbearable state of constant need, remained one of the most effective ways of manipulating and controlling humans. It worked just as well today with these ostensibly more civilized peoples as it had thousands of years ago with their primitive ancestors.

Up here was another example.

Yet another pentagram adorned the closed bedroom door. Andras opened the door and entered a room still filled with the artifacts of a young boy's interrupted life. Derek's electric guitar and band posters were all still in place. Andras closed and locked the door behind him. The room was Andras' sanctuary. All but one of his acolytes were forbidden from entering.

"Hello, Natasha."

"Hello, master."

Andras shrugged off his jacket and joined her on the bed.

She curled her nude body around him and kissed his neck, suckled hungrily at his flesh. His cock stiffened, straining his jeans. He rolled her over and climbed atop her. He kissed her mouth and neck, eliciting whimpers. "Remember how you resisted me the first time I took you?"

She tugged at the snap of his jeans. "I remember. I was stupid. I didn't understand yet."

He chuckled. "And now you do?"

"Of course."

"What do you understand?"

"That you are my master and I am your bride. And that Satan is my lord."

"Do you remember drinking your mother's blood?"

"Yes."

"And how did it taste?"

"Wonderful."

He ran a hand up the length of one of her long, lean legs. She unfolded it for him, lifting it high into the air, extending her painted toes toward the ceiling. "Your father is with us now. My people were waiting for him when he returned home and saw what we had done to his beautiful wife."

"My dad? Here?"

Andras smiled. "Yes."

Natasha smiled. "Good."

"You're going to kill him for me. A gesture of your allegiance and obedience."

Natasha resumed tugging at his jeans. "Yes. Please. I want you again."

"Of course you do."

He removed his clothes and gave her what she wanted. She screamed and clutched and clawed at him. Her eyes filled with tears from the intensity of the pleasure. When it was over, he dressed again and moved to the door. "Remember, you are not to leave this room while I'm gone. You are my bride. No one else is to touch you."

"Where are you going?"

"To fetch my other young bride."

"Fiona."

"Yes."

Natasha pouted. "But I thought—"

"Don't think. Just obey."

The pout lasted another second or two, then gave way to another smile. "Yes, master."

Andras left the room and closed the door behind him.

Downstairs, he saw flashing blue lights visible through gauzy sitting room curtains. Someone pounded on the front door. "Open up! Police!"

Andras tossed his head back and laughed heartily.

The pounding came again. "Open up! This is your last warning!"

Andras opened the doors. There were two uniformed cops on the porch, both standing there with their weapons drawn and pointed right at him.

"Good evening, gentlemen."

The cop closest to him snarled and said, "Hands in the air! We've had reports of screaming coming from this house and...what the hell is happening in there?" The cop's scowl gave way to a look of astonishment as he peered around Andras and got a glimpse of what was happening on the staircase.

Andras knocked the gun out of the cop's hand and seized him by the throat, making the man gurgle as he lifted him off the ground. "We're having a party of sorts. And guess what? You're both invited! Come on in!"

Andras backed into the house and dropped the wheezing cop on the floor.

The other cop had already lowered his gun. He started to follow them inside, but Andras held up a hand. "You. Turn off those lights. Tell your superiors the reports you had were unfounded."

The cop holstered his gun. "Yeah. Okay."

He turned and walked back out of the house. Andras was not concerned by the arrival of the cops. It had been inevitable. And it was good it had happened at this stage. These men could prove useful in any number of ways.

Meanwhile, he still had this other task to tend to.

He left the house and traversed the streets of Wheaton Hills until he arrived at the Johnson residence.

He was not pleased by what he found inside.

Or, rather, what he did not find.

THIRTY-NINE

A powerful sense of precognition hit Clayton as he turned down the street to his house. Something had changed in his absence. Something he couldn't quite pinpoint, an elusive sense of *wrongness*. The air in Wheaton Hills felt strangely charged. He was more intensely aware of his heartbeat. He didn't much care for the way the irregular thump-thump resonated in his chest. His teeth were on edge and his skin was crawling. Paranoia encroached as he scanned the yards and the windows of the houses he passed. He didn't see anyone, but he could almost feel unseen eyes tracking him as he continued down the street. The really fucked thing was he couldn't just attribute the feeling to nerves or a runaway imagination.

He was on the edge of a nervous breakdown by the time he pulled into his garage and reached overhead to stab the button on the garage door opener. The door started to rattle down but got stuck about halfway down. He sighed. *Of fucking course.* Another push of the button caused the door to roll back up. He glanced at the rear view mirror and bit down on a shriek as he watched a police cruiser roll slowly by in the street.

They're coming for me!

But the cruiser kept rolling and was soon out of sight. Clayton scrambled out of the car and sidled over to the edge of the open garage, where he carefully peered out at the receding back end of the cruiser as in continued its slow crawl through Wheaton Hills. Then it turned down another street and was gone from view.

Clayton felt almost sick with relief. "Holy shit. Thank fuck."

Hours had passed since the hit-and-run death of the officer who had stopped him, but the memory was still nauseatingly fresh in his mind. The guy was a dick, true enough, but that didn't make what had happened to him any less horrible. And Clayton doubted his fellow officers gave a damn that he'd been an asshole. He was a fellow member of the fraternity, that fabled thin blue line. So he'd been dreading the return home, so certain was he there'd be a bunch of cops waiting to clap him in handcuffs and drag him off to jail for a rough-and-tumble round of "routine questioning."

On the other hand, there was a lot going on in Ransom today.

A lot of bad craziness.

So maybe they were just super busy and merely hadn't gotten around to dealing with him yet. Or maybe today was just his lucky goddamn day. Whatever the case, he didn't have time to stand here and speculate. Mark was waiting for him. He'd want to hear the explanation he'd been promised. Clayton had one, but whether it amounted to anything truly helpful was yet to be determined.

He got the garage door closed on the next attempt. He then retrieved some things from the car and entered the house. The first thing he noticed was Fiona Johnson. She was tied to a chair and there was a strip of duct tape across her mouth. One side of her mouth was swollen. She glared at him through eyes puffy with tears. Mark and Jared were also in the kitchen. The boys were not bound to anything and appeared to have consumed a large amount of his beer. The table top was littered with green and brown glass empties.

Clayton bumped the door shut with a hip and came further into the kitchen. "Okay. Obvious question. Why is Fiona bound and gagged?"

"She was gonna kill us all. Starting with you, I think, was her plan."

"Wow."

"Yeah. She had a gun."

Mark nodded at the kitchen counter.

Clayton stared at the gun. "I repeat, wow. She have a

reason for this insanity?"

"She's fucking crazy."

"Right, well. That sort of follows, I guess."

Fiona strained hard against her bonds, causing the chair to wobble. Her jaw worked as she tried to speak around the gag in her mouth. The words were only half-intelligible, but the anger and frustration came through loud and clear. She was staring right at Clayton, her eyes wide and beseeching. He had a fleeting moment of doubt. It was possible, of course, that something else was going on here. Maybe Fiona was the victim and the boys were just trying to silence her. It was clearly what she wanted him to think, what her eyes and body language were trying to communicate. On the other hand, this was the same girl who'd goaded that cop into attacking him for no other reason than spite. And he had a good sense of what kind of guy Mark Bell really was. He was a fuck-up, but one with a strong moral center. He wasn't a scumbag, in other words.

Mark tipped back a swallow of Heineken. "Take the gag out, if you want. You ain't gonna hear anything but bullshit, though."

"I suppose you're right."

"You bought more beer."

Clayton grunted. "I can't remember the last time I ventured into town and returned *without* beer. Oh, wait. 1998. Had a couple weeks there where I was thinking about going into rehab."

"What happened?"

"Girlfriend dumped me."

Mark drained the last dregs from the Heineken bottle and set the empty on the table. "Oh. Yeah. Girls can fuck you up."

Clayton's smile was rueful. "Truer words never spoken."

Jared belched. "What's in the box?"

A small metal lock box was tucked under Clayton's left arm. It didn't weigh much, because there wasn't much in it. Some of its contents did rattle around when he moved. He set the box on the table and watched them for a moment as their eyes fixated on it. Even Fiona craned her neck around and stared at it. There was a strange kind of reverence in their expressions. Not one of them had any clue what was inside the box, but they all seemed to be regarding it as some kind of holy object. He couldn't blame them. They were caught in what appeared to be an impossible situation, facing a foe that was ancient and powerful, a genuine agent of the forces of darkness. A fucking demon. Not some fairytale monster or bogeyman, but a real thing. In such circumstances, it was only human nature to hope for some miraculous and magical solution.

He carried the beer cartons over to the fridge and talked as he began the task of restocking his diminished booze supply. "Until today that box hadn't been opened in more than ten years. It's been in a safety deposit box since about a week after my dad put a gun to his head and blew his fucking brains out."

Jared picked up the box and shook it, making its contents rattle again. "What's in it?"

Clayton pushed bottles toward the back of the fridge, making room for more as he ripped open the second carton. "Like I was telling Mark the other night, my father had some knowledge of the thing you geniuses let out of that basement a couple weeks ago."

Jared frowned. "What, did he put it there?"

"No, that happened long before he got involved. And a lot of what he knew he learned secondhand. Which is why I thought it was all bullshit, just stupid stories he told when he was drunk. Should have known better. The stories were too crazy to be anything he'd come up with on his own. Outside of his business ambitions, he didn't have what you could describe as a big imagination." The second carton was empty. He ripped apart the glued-together tabs and folded it flat. He dropped the broken-down carton in the trash basket and took a seat at the table, positioning himself as far as possible from Fiona. She twisted her head and glared at him across the table. "My dad was one of the bigger movers and shakers locally for a long time. Made a lot of money. Left me a lot of it. I could tell you how much, but it'd be sort of embarrassing. A guy like that, involved on an intimate level with the local power structure, he has a lot of favors he can call in when something bad happens. Well...something bad happened and dad called on Luke Harper, the mayor at the time, and Harper took care of it."

Mark got up and went to the fridge. "Who needs a beer?"

Clayton and Jared answered in the affirmative. Mark popped the tops off three bottles of Guinness Extra Stout, came back to the table, and passed them around.

Mark sat down. "So...this bad thing that happened...what was it?"

"That house you kids broke into? My father murdered a woman there on December 6, 1984."

"Whoa. What?"

Clayton drew the lock box closer and folded his hands over it. "He confessed to the murder the night he died. It was a few hours before he...you know. Anyway...he was drunker than I'd ever seen him. I was embarrassed for him and figured it was just more of his bullshit. Again, should have known better. I'd never seen him so distraught over anything, just crying and blubbering while he tried to tell me about this terrible thing he'd done."

Mark shifted in his chair, making the chair legs squeak. "So why did he kill this woman? And why did he tell you about it so long after the fact? Why not just take the secret to his grave?"

Clayton's face bore a cloudy, unfocused expression. He wasn't looking at any of them as he continued, his mind somewhere back in time. "He'd already made up his mind to kill himself and wanted to confide in somebody while he still could. He wasn't a bad man. He did some bad things, but he was still human, still had a conscience, and the murder, I guess, weighed heavily on him all those years. It was part of why he did what he did."

"Just part? What was the rest of it?"

"The rest of it was living with what he knew about the demons and that house. My dad did a lot of looking into occult stuff in the years after the murder. He didn't tell me this himself, but it's all in here." He tapped the lock box with an index finger. "The whole sordid tale."

Jared went to the fridge and came back with another beer. "Okay, so your father killed a bitch. How did he know about the demon?"

"Luke Harper told him."

"And how did Luke Harper know?"

"Because Harper was one of the men who did the original demon summoning. He and his partner called and bound Andras. They thought the demon could be useful in their business dealings."

"That's crazy."

"Well, no shit. Clearly we're not talking about stable people here. We are, in fact, talking about dangerously deranged people with delusions of grandeur. Who seriously thinks you can do mess with shit like that without facing serious consequences somewhere down the line? These guys eventually realized they were in over their heads and tried to banish the demons. Andras got sealed up in the basement. His henchman, Flauros, got tucked away inside a corner of Luke Harper's head, where he stayed until Mark's father put a bullet through the old guy's brain and let him out."

Jared looked pale. "So we have to get rid of two demons? Shit."

Mark groaned. "We are so fucked."

Clayton dug into a hip pocket and pulled out a small key. "Maybe. Maybe not."

He unlocked the box and flipped the lid open. Mark and Jared leaned over the table for a closer look. Inside was a stack of crumpled sheets of old notebook paper. Neat handwriting in slightly faded ink filled the pages from margin to margin. Clayton pulled the papers out. Beneath them was a handgun and several loose bullets, the source of the rattling noise.

Clayton passed the papers to Mark. "It's all in there. Everything I told you and more, including instructions for binding demons." He pulled one of the bullets out and showed it to them, holding it between thumb and forefinger. The cartridge was shiny and silver. "This is one way.

Actual silver bullets, made special for my father by a local gunsmith."

Mark shuffled through the papers and frowned. "You can kill a demon just by shooting it?"

Clayton shook his head. "No. You can't kill a demon at all, at least not by any means my father ever found. But a silver bullet can expel the demon from a human host and banish it back to hell, where it will stay until summoned again. Very effective, but the downside is it has to be a kill shot. The human host has to die."

Mark's hands clenched around the papers. "My dad..."

Clayton dropped the bullet back in the box. It made a soft metallic clank. "Right, and that's why it should be our last resort." He nodded at the papers. "If you read through to the end of that, you'll see the other way to get the job done."

Mark's brow furrowed as he flipped to the last pages and read. "What is this? Some kind of spell?"

Clayton nodded. "A summoning spell. We use it to call Andras, just like those other assholes did. And where Andras goes, Flauros will hopefully follow."

Mark set the pages on the table and leaned over them. "This talks about ways of increasing the likelihood of success when performing a binding spell. 'If possible, the binding should be performed on hallowed ground, or in a place of deep magical significance.' Hallowed ground would be a cemetery, I guess, or a church, but..."

He trailed off.

They were all thinking the same thing. It was obvious in the haunted looks they exchanged. Fiona picked up on it and became vocal again, shrieking muffled curses around the gag in her mouth.

Jared slapped a palm against the table top, making the empties rattle. "Shit. The basement."

Mark swallowed hard. "Fuck."

Clayton sipped beer. "It's the logical place to do it. Andras was imprisoned there a long time. He'll be frightened to find himself drawn there again. He'll be off-balance. Confused. It still won't be easy. Hell, it'll probably still be almost impossible. But I like our odds better this way than just walking up to him and pointing a gun in his face."

Jared slapped the table again. "Shit."

Mark sighed. "We'd never get close enough for that to work anyway."

Clayton had another sip of beer. "What I was thinking, too. And, from what I understand, all the wards and seals in the basement are still in place. We just have to reactivate them, basically. Like flipping a switch. And I'm sorry, Fiona, but you'll need to be with us. You probably already guessed that. The more of you who were there the night Andras got out, the better."

"Why?"

"Well...I'm getting into hunch territory here. This isn't in my father's papers."

"Spill it."

"You all endured a traumatic event there. I think the binding magic will be more powerful the more of you we have working on it. Again, just a hunch, but it feels right."

The boys didn't say anything to this at first. But it felt right to them, too. Clayton saw it in the grim set of their features.

Mark coughed. "So...when do we do this?"

"I don't think we can afford to wait much longer. It has to be tonight."

The looks on the boys' faces made it clear they weren't happy about it. But, beyond the troubled expressions, there was a clear sense of acceptance and determination.

They were going to do this crazy thing.

Summon and, hopefully, bind a demon.

Clayton drank more beer.

God help us.

FORTY

The ongoing dark revelry at the former McGregor residence did not abate as the evening lengthened. Scenes of unhinged debauchery and depravity continued to play out in every room. The madness was nearing a point of uncontrollable frenzy, tilting toward an explosion of violence and violation the house was not nearly big enough to contain. And that, of course, was the point. Andras wanted the members of his congregation on the edge of hysteria. He wanted them burning with the need to inflict pain and spread misery. They were close. Natasha could feel it even in here, behind the closed door to Andras' private room. It made her ache. She wanted desperately to be a part of the revelry. She was so bored in here by herself. On occasion Andras would return to check on her, but each time he denied her pleas to enter the fray.

She got up again and peered through the bedroom window at the backyard. Much of the decadent cavorting had spilled over into the backyard, which was surrounded by a high wooden fence that effectively blocked the sinful activity from the view of anyone who might happen to wander by in the street. Natasha smiled at that, knowing the need to hide what was happening here was nearly at an end. The house and backyard was packed with people. Many of them were from the neighborhood, but numerous others had been drawn in from other parts of Ransom by calls from relatives or friends. A few people in this category harbored some suspicion at being invited to a party in posh Wheaton Hills, but most came anyway, overwhelmed by curiosity. The neighborhood was well known as the place where the rich new people lived. Who wouldn't want to check it out? They would show up and see the cars lined up on the sides of the street, hear the wild noises coming from the house, and stroll right up to the door without a second thought, never suspecting that in a few moments life as they had known it would be over.

A bonfire was blazing in the center of the yard. Andras had put some of the men to work earlier in the day. The men dug a pit and demolished nearly every piece of furniture from the house to feed the fire. The towering flames cast a flickering yellow-orange illumination over the mostly nude bodies of the frolicking revelers. A plump woman with very large breasts was on all fours almost directly beneath the window. Natasha placed her forehead against the window and slid a hand between her legs as she watched a tall black man ram in and out of the big woman from behind, making those huge, pendulous breasts sway wildly with each thrust. Natasha's attention was diverted as some more people emerged from the house, two men dragging a screaming woman toward the bonfire. One of the men had an ax. The woman bounced up right away when they threw her to the ground, but the man with the ax swung it in a vicious arc, severing her right arm just above the elbow. She screamed and spun about in a staggering circle as blood sprayed. The men laughed. Then they grabbed her and tossed her onto the fire. She was still alive as the flames began to consume her, thrashing and screaming as she slid off the pile of burning wood and tried to crawl to the edge of the pit. The man with the ax aimed his cock at her and began to piss on her, causing the other man to laugh maniacally. Natasha gasped and bit down on her lip, shuddering as she neared orgasm.

She banged her forehead on the glass in frustration.

She hated being stuck up here, even though it was what Andras wanted. She was his bride and needed to be protected from what was happening in the rest of the house. It was possible she might be hurt by accident should she join in the festivities, but it was a risk she'd like to take. Unfortunately, it wasn't her call.

The door opened behind her and she turned away from the window.

Andras came into the room and shut the door. "Enjoying the spectacle?"

She pouted. "I want to play, too."

He came over to her and cupped her face in his hands. "You'll have what you want very soon. In a short while, I will send the members of my congregation out into the world to do the work of the devil. We will join them."

"And what sort of work will that be?"

He kissed her lightly on the mouth, making her shiver with delight. "Murder. Violence. Destruction. Death and more death. We will be Hell's stormtroopers, slaughtering everything in our path, with no thought of mercy for the weak and the innocent. Indeed, we will relish their screams the most. And you'll be right there next to me, killing in the name of Satan." He kissed her again. "What do you think of that, darling? Will it be worth the time you spent locked away in here?"

She curled a leg around him and pressed close. "It sounds wonderful."

He smiled. "Good. The time is almost at hand. My only regret is that my other bride will not be with me."

Natasha tried not to smile. "Oh?"

Andras' tone turned cold. "Yes. She was not at her house. I'm afraid something may have happened to her."

"Why do you say that?"

"I found bodies. Members of her family. They had been shot. The mother and a sister. I know this because I waited there for a time, until the father arrived home from work. The man was hysterical, but I managed to conduct an interview of some substance before I killed him. He maintained he did not know what had happened and had no idea where Fiona might have gone. I believe he was telling the truth. Humans tend not to lie when they are having the flesh peeled from their bodies."

Natasha grunted. "Yeah. Uh...you're probably right about that. But..."

He put a hand to one of her cheeks. "Yes?"

Natasha didn't want to say anything further, because she didn't want to share Andras with Fiona, but her wishes were not what mattered here. Only Andras mattered. She sighed. "She might have gone to Clayton's house."

Andras frowned. "Clayton is your older friend?"

"Yeah. Fiona had this weird thing about him. Sort of a crush. She wouldn't admit to it, but I could tell. It's why she gave him shit all the time. If she was in trouble, she might go to him."

He smiled. "Thank you."

"You're going there now?"

He shook his head. "The time has come to send out my warriors. I've been waiting for just the right moment and it has arrived. I feel it. I must rally the troops. I'll send someone else to fetch her."

"I'll go. Clayton won't be suspicious of me. It'll be perfect."

Andras shook his head again. "No. I want you by my side in my moment of glory. Someone else will go. Get dressed and join me out back."

He left her then, departing quickly without another word. Natasha gathered her clothes from where she'd left them in a pile on the floor. She left the room as soon as she was dressed. She thought Andras was making a mistake by sending someone other than her out to Clayton's place, but this concern was obliterated by her relief at being out of the room. She threaded her way through the naked bodies crowding the hallway and the staircase, trailing her hands over the bare flesh as she moved. Suzie McGregor grabbed her when she reached the bottom of the staircase and slid her tongue into her mouth. Natasha let the woman kiss her for a few moments, then shoved her away and continued on into the kitchen, where the floor was awash in blood. There were dead bodies and pieces of bodies everywhere, limbs and torsos stacked in the corners to make room for more. An attractive and slender young woman was presiding over the kitchen slaughter. She directed some men who dragged another man into the kitchen and held him down on the floor. The woman then proceeded to stomp on the prone man's face with the heel of her boot. The man screamed and thrashed, but the other men held him down as she continued to stomp. A crowd of onlookers ringed the periphery of the kitchen. A woman nudged Natasha and smiled. "Isn't Carrie awesome?"

Natasha smiled. "She's hot."

It was the truth. The woman had her own little entourage and circle of admirers. It was tempting to stay and watch Carrie do her thing, but Andras was waiting for her outside. She made her way through the kitchen and exited the house through a door that opened onto a small deck. On the deck was a grill and a small table. Someone had fired up the grill. Natasha saw glowing coals and pieces of cooking bodies—a breast, a head, a cock, and various internal organs. The smell made her mouth water. A middle-aged man wearing an apron and a backwards baseball cap was tending the grill, poking at the people pieces with a long, three-pronged fork. He saw Natasha watching and gave her a wink. "These are coming along nicely. Want a taste?"

"Sure."

She tried a bite of the grilled cock. It was bliss. Then she stepped off the deck and into the yard, barely noticing that the rest of the congregation had begun to stream out of the house behind her. The view from the bedroom window had not prepared her for the sheer sensory overload of actually being down here in the midst of the revelry. The night was alive with the sounds of ecstasy and agony. Screams and moans. The crackling of the fire as burning pieces of furniture shifted and settled. Frequent bursts of demented laughter. All around her a sea of naked, copulating bodies covered the ground. More naked people danced and frolicked around the fire. Natasha marveled at how many of them there were now. It was amazing that Andras had been able to grow his congregation to this level in so short a time. There had to be more than a hundred people in the house and out here in the backyard. Maybe more. The place was approaching maximum capacity, if it wasn't there already. She was aware of the earlier attempted intervention by members of the police, but that had been a while ago, before things had really started to ramp up. It was late in the evening now, approaching midnight. To her knowledge there had been no more such incidents, which was surprising. There had to be some neighbors left who had not yet been drawn into the congregation. Surely they had phoned in more complaints. If so, though, the police didn't seem to be acting on them. Perhaps Andras had come up with some clever way of deflecting them.

Earlier in the evening...

It had been a long day for the Ransom police department and no one was feeling the stress more than Detective Matt Shannon. Fifteen years on the force and he'd never seen a day like this. It was just one thing after a goddamn other. First it was the discovery of the butchered bodies of two young men in a ditch near the outskirts of town. Those poor bastards. Local boys, born and raised. Some sick fuck had hacked them to pieces. One of them was missing a head. Then there was the relatively minor nuisance of dealing with the snooty parents of the spoiled rich brats who'd started the brawl at the bowling alley. A bunch of entitled, elitist assholes. But important assholes. And their brats wouldn't get much more than a slap on the wrist, if that. Next up had been the main event, the torching of the nursing home. Arson, no doubt about it. Some unidentified accelerant had been used, something nasty that burned hot and fast, leaving nothing behind but a pile of charred, smoking remains. It was the first mass casualty event in many a moon in Ransom, and easily the worst in the town's history.

And now this.

A cop was dead. Not a good cop, to be honest about it. Officer Decker had been the kind of belligerent asshole who gave all cops a bad name. A number of complaints had been logged against him in the ten months he'd been on the force.

In truth, Shannon had been looking for a reason to terminate him. Well, it didn't matter anymore. The dumb thug had been run down by a group of joyriding kids.

He watched the surveillance video from Decker's cruiser again. It was numbingly familiar by now. The whoop of the siren. The old Cadillac pulling over and the cruiser pulling in behind it. Then Decker acting like an asshole, pulling his piece on a routine traffic stop. Screaming like a fucking idiot. Then...here comes the truck. Splat. Decker's dead. The guy gets out of the car, gives his weird speech, takes off.

Shannon knew the guy. Long ago, they'd been friends.

He sighed. "Clay...what happened to you, man?"

He was still debating what to do about Clayton Campbell when he heard the shouting from the squad room. He came out of his office, banging the door open. He understood that everyone was stressed and tempers were short, but these men had to start acting like professionals. "What the fuck is—"

A cop with a gun in his hand wheeled toward Shannon at the sound of his voice. He felt the impact of the bullet before his ears registered the report of the gun. He staggered backward against the door frame and looked down to see blood pumping from a wound in his gut. Another shot punched through his shoulder. Then there were more shots. The squad room descended into chaos. Two cops in full uniform were firing at other cops. The rest of Shannon's men had been caught by surprise and were scrambling for cover. Several of them took hits and went down. Someone at last managed to return fire and one of the assailants went down. Shannon began to slide down the door frame as the strength left his knees. He fumbled for his sidearm as his butt hit the floor. The remaining assailant, an officer named Barton, saw him going for his gun and came striding toward him.

Barton aimed his gun at the center of Shannon's face. "Andras says hi."

Shannon could only watch as Barton's finger began to squeeze the trigger.

It was the last thing he ever saw.

* * *

Andras was standing on the roof of the shed at the back of the yard, where the rear of the property was bordered by woods. Natasha stared up at him, admiring the dramatic figure he cut as he stood there with his hands on his hips, the dark outline of his body visible against the barren limbs of the trees, the silvery white moon over his head. Multiple sets of hands gripped different parts of her body, raising her off the ground, toward the roof of the shed. She gripped the edge of the roof when it was within grabbing distance and hauled herself up to stand next to her groom. He pulled her into an embrace and kissed her passionately, making her knees buckle. There had been a time when kissing Mark had made her weak in the knees, but that had been nothing compared to this.

Andras broke the kiss off and grinned.

He turned away from her and moved to the edge of the roof. He pumped a fist into the air and let out a war cry. The sea of tangled bodies below shifted and separated at the sound of their leader's exhortation. They stood and staggered toward the shed, getting as close as they could, pressing up against each other. Andras pumped his fist again and let out another whoop. The people on the ground mimicked him. They sounded and looked like some primitive tribe preparing for battle. They worked themselves into a frenzy as Andras pumped his fist again and again. Then he waved a hand, motioning for them to be quiet. A reverent hush fell.

Andras stalked the front edge of the roof as he spoke. "Greetings to all my new friends and comrades. I say this because you are not simply servants. You are not here to simply grovel at my feet and seek approval. You are soldiers in a division of Satan's army now, the most glorious army ever assembled!" The crowd went wild at this proclamation. Andras quieted them again with another wave of his hand. "A long time ago some men in this town summoned and used me to their own selfish ends. *Me!* A Grand Marquis of Hell!" Some boos rang out. "And when they were through

251

with me, they imprisoned me for decades." The booing grew louder. "Those men are dead, but the community they helped build still stands. Tonight I declare war on that community. Tonight each and every one of you will help me tear it all down. Are you ready to fight for me?"

The crowd erupted again. Only "crowd" wasn't the right term for this gathering anymore. And it wasn't an army, despite what Andras said. It wasn't organized enough for that. This was a mob. A craftily conceived weapon of mass destruction. And it was about to go off. Natasha peered over the edge of the roof and felt a growing excitement as she watched the ranks of wildly jostling bodies and flailing limbs.

Andras smiled.

The time was at hand.

He stepped to the very edge of the roof and thrust a hand outward. *"Go forth and kill! Destroy! Fight! Burn it all to the ground! Show no mercy! Go! GO! GO!"*

The mob unleashed one last great cheer.

And then the exodus began.

Natasha slipped an arm around Andras' back as she watched the throngs of mostly naked people scale the high fence and run away screaming into the night. A lot of people in Wheaton Hills were about to die. *Good.* It was what they deserved, every one of them. She had always known Ransom was a rotten place. Andras had only affirmed that conviction.

In the distance, new sounds.

A gunshot.

The tinkling of breaking glass.

Screams.

Natasha pressed her face against Andras' throat. "Make love to me. Please."

Andras smiled and kissed her.

The distant screams continued to resonate in the night.

In a few moments, Natasha was screaming, too.

FORTY-ONE

Somewhere in the night a dog started barking. It was a big dog sound. Kent listened closely, straining to identify the direction of the sound. It was hard to tell. A lot of families in Wheaton Hills had dogs, and a lot of them stayed outside in fenced back yards at night. On occasion, one of them would get to barking in the wee hours. Often other dogs would join in, filling the night with a chorus of canine voices. It was just doggy chatter and it would usually wind down soon enough.

But not tonight.

The barking escalated in volume and became more agitated. Other dogs began to respond. The sound went on and on, with no sign of relenting. Some of the animals seemed more frantic than others, growling or emitting a series of rapid yips and barks. Kent suspected they were reacting to the party happening a couple streets over at the McGregor place. He'd received several texts about it from Brett Hogan earlier, but those had ceased hours ago. Maybe Brett had crashed the party. It didn't seem likely, but stranger things had happened.

Kent didn't really care one way or the other. He'd been trying to sleep for hours, but too many memories from what had easily been the most humiliating twenty-four hours of his life kept taunting him. All that bullshit with the cops for starters, with their questions and insinuations, which was made worse by Brett's stupid admission of their role in provoking Kevin Cooper and his friends. Then there was the ass-beating he'd taken from Cooper. Today there'd been some not-so-subtle threats from Moose via text. The big football thug's ego was smarting. Normally threats of physical violence from a guy like that would scare him shitless, but right now he didn't care. None of it compared to the grief he'd taken from his father. Cal Hickerson was ashamed of his son on multiple levels. He was a coward for persuading someone like Moose to fight his battles for him. He was a fool for trashing his heretofore spotless reputation and possibly tarnishing his chances of getting into one of the more elite southern universities. At least his mother had expressed some concern for his physical well-being, but even she had chastized him for his lack of judgment and common sense.

Kent slapped a palm against the mattress.

The goddamn dogs just would not let up. If anything, their barking was becoming more frenzied. Then he heard a sound stranger by far than the manic animal sounds. The sound itself wasn't strange. It was crystal clear and immediately identifiable. The strange thing was hearing it at this late hour. He glanced at the alarm clock on the nightstand.

12:24 am.

What the fuck?

He'd known it was late, but this was ridiculous. It had to be someone playing a prank. The obvious suspect was Mark Bell or one of his friends.

The doorbell rang again.

Next he heard someone yelling from the other end of the house. His father, understandably pissed at being roused from sleep by the unwelcome late caller. Kent threw his sheets back, sat up, and swung his legs over the side of the bed. He heard another sound from somewhere outside the house, the expected prankster giggling. Kent sat and listened as his father's shouts grew louder as he moved toward the center of the house. Something was off here. Middle of the night doorbell pranks actually weren't Bell's style at all. And simple pranksters wouldn't hang around and wait for someone to actually come to the door.

Cal Hickerson yelled some more: "*Yeah, keep laughing, assholes! We'll see who's laughing in a goddamn minute!*"

More giggling.

Kent didn't know what spurred him to act. He wasn't a brave person. But some deep down instinct told him his father was in mortal danger and suddenly he was in motion. Dressed only in boxer shorts, he got to his feet and hurried out of the room. He dashed through the house and arrived in the foyer at the exact moment his father opened the door.

The door exploded inward, kicked by someone on the other side.

His father staggered backward as a slender young woman with shoulder-length chestnut curls came into the house followed by three other grinning strangers. The woman was clad in tight jeans and a black t-shirt with a bible quote on the front. Her companions, two young men and a middle-aged woman, weren't wearing any clothes. Their nude bodies were covered in blood. Kent gaped at them, unable to fully process what he was seeing. People didn't do things like this in Wheaton Hills. You couldn't just run around naked outside. And what was up with all that blood?

The slender young woman had a gun.

She aimed it at Cal Hickerson and squeezed the trigger. A bullet tore out a chunk of his skull amidst a spray of red. He dropped dead to the floor. A scream came from somewhere else in the house. His mom. His father's murderer turned her attention on him, flashing a radiant smile that would have been lovely under other circumstances. "Hey there, baby."

She stalked closer to him and aimed the gun at his face.

Remembering what the gun had done to his father's head, Kent raised shaking hands. The girl laughed and whipped the gun across his face, spinning him to the floor. The others scampered off to find his mother. They were going to kill her. He had no doubt of that. Despair engulfed him. Both of his parents gone. His own life was moments away from ending. There was only one hope, that they be reunited in heaven. Kent was a Christian and did believe in God and the afterlife. But his mortal body remained a slave to instinct. It wanted to live. But there was nothing he could do. He was a coward. His father had been right about that. He had no realistic hope of disarming this woman and escaping this situation. It simply wasn't within him to fight back.

"Open your eyes."

He heard his mother scream again, a sound that suddenly cut off.

The woman kicked him. "I said open your fucking eyes, little man. Don't make me say it again."

Kent whimpered. "N-no."

"No? Did you seriously just tell me no?"

Kent's only answer was another whimper.

Then he felt her weight on him as she straddled him and jammed the gun's barrel up under his chin. "One more time, cocksucker. Open your eyes."

He couldn't help it then. The solid, unyielding pressure of the cold barrel impelled him to obedience. His eyes fluttered open and he stared up at the woman's leering face. "Please..."

She smiled. "Please...what?"

He sniffed. "Please don't kill me."

She laughed. "Okay."

His heart gave a great lurch. Part of him knew it was foolish to hope, but he did anyway: "Really?"

Her smile became radiant again. It was the kind of smile meant for yearbook photos, which just made it more unsettling. "Sure, baby. You just have to do one thing for me."

"Oh, here it comes."

Kent froze. Someone else had come through the open front door. Someone he knew.

He let head swivel slowly to the right. "Brett?"

His best friend giggled. "Yep."

Like the people who'd gone after his mother, Brett was naked and covered in blood. He was carrying a large baseball bat. The fat end was also blood-soaked. Whatever was happening here, Brett was a part of it. Kent struggled in vain to comprehend. He couldn't understand how someone like Brett, a good Christian boy, could wind up like...this.

Kent stared at him. "What's wrong with you?"

Brett giggled again. "You're an asshole, Kent. Nobody *really* ever liked you. Me included. I prefer my new friends.

Like Carrie here. She's cool as fuck."

The woman, Carrie, laughed. "I've got something I want you to do for me, Kent. It's simple, but important. And your survival depends on you doing it. Understand?"

"No."

Carrie moved the gun from his chin and pressed the barrel against his forehead. She did a little grind against his crotch that might have been unbearably sexy under other circumstances. "Say you love Satan."

Kent blinked. "What?"

"Say you love Satan."

Kent's mouth opened. He hesitated. It was just words. If saying them meant there was even the slightest chance he might live, it was worth it, regardless of the blasphemy. "I love Satan."

Carrie smiled. "Of course you do, sweetie. We all do."

She climbed off him and moved away.

Kent couldn't believe it. He stayed there on the floor, staring after her retreating back as she went off in search of her other companions. She had let him live. It was a miracle. Then Brett was looming over him, the baseball bat raised high over his head, looking sort of like an arrow pointing toward heaven.

The sudden burst of hope fizzled.

Kent said, "Shit."

Brett giggled. "Yep."

The bat came down.

Elsewhere in Wheaton Hills...

Something stirred Joe Simpson to wakefulness. His face was pressed into a freshly laundered pillowcase, which smelled "spring fresh", or at least that was how the label on the detergent bottle described the scent. He knew this because his wife had been buying the same brand of detergent for years. But that wasn't what was making his nostrils twitch. There was another aroma in the room. Something not exactly unpleasant but certainly out of place. His grogginess began to abate as he focused on the scent and sniffed again.

Gasoline.

How strange.

He yawned and shifted his bulk to the edge of the bed to raise a hand to the lamp. He found the switch and blinked rapidly as the light snapped on. He yawned again and pulled out one of the earplugs he wore to block the sound of Margaret's snoring.

He screamed.

An old man stood at the foot of the bed. The stranger wore black trousers, a starched white shirt, and a thin black tie. The white shirt was streaked with blood. He was holding a chainsaw. It was an old gasoline-powered model. Its blade was wet with sticky gore.

Joe sat up and saw his wife's body on the floor.

In several different places.

Joe screamed again.

The old man revved the chainsaw.

The woman crawled across the floor of the den, trailing dark blood across the carpet. She wore a silk nightgown that was slick with smears of red. The frilly hem of the nightgown rode up high on her shapely thighs. She whimpered again as she heard footsteps thumping down the stairs from the kitchen. She trembled and cried out as Lydia knelt next to her and ran a hand up the back of one of her thighs.

"Hey, sexy." Lydia giggled. "Sorry about leaving you alone. I was a little busy." Another giggle. "As I'm sure you could tell from the screams. We were just chopping up another of your little darlings."

The woman sobbed.

Lydia squeezed the woman's thigh. "She's in the oven now. That's what you're smelling. Maybe if you're good, you can have a little taste."

The woman spat blood on the floor. "Damn you."

"No. Damn you."

Lydia rolled the woman over and slammed the knife into her belly again.

The woman screamed and arched her back. Lydia laughed and pulled the knife out. She licked blood from the edge of the blade and shivered at the delicious sensation that rippled through her body at the taste. It was amazing this bitch was still alive. She'd been stabbed at least a dozen times, though Lydia had been careful to avoid thrusting the blade into places sure to cause a quick death. Still, she'd probably die soon from shock or blood loss. Which was just as well. It'd been fun drawing out her torment, but Wheaton Hills was full of people to kill. This woman was the last surviving member of her family. It'd be best to finish her off and move on to another house.

But first...just a little more fun.

She stabbed her in the stomach again, eliciting yet another scream. She sawed the blade back and forth, creating a larger hole. The woman writhed on the floor and begged for mercy. After pulling the blade out again, Lydia reached through the hole with her free hand, found some unidentifiable slimy organ, wrapped her hand around it, and squeezed.

More lovely screams.

Lydia laughed again and kept squeezing.

She was still laughing when she felt the belt encircle her throat. *What the hell?* There was no lone left in this house to fight back.

Except...

The belt drew tighter around her throat.

Suzie's breath was hot against her ear. "Surprise, bitch."

Suzie's knee was in her back then, pressing her down on top of the bleeding woman. Lydia tried to roll away, but Suzie had her effectively pinned. She couldn't understand what was happening. She and Suzie's former differences had become meaningless. They were allies, followers of Andras and sisters united in service to Satan. So why was this happening? The belt drew even tighter, cutting off her air completely. She began to panic then, clawing at the tight band around her throat with one hand and using the other to flail ineffectually at Suzie with the knife. Suzie swatted the knife away and it went spinning across the floor. The direness of the situation hit home with heart-pounding force. She was going to die soon if she didn't put everything she had into dislodging Suzie.

Suzie's mouth was against her ear again. "Yeah. That's nice. Keep struggling. I like that. You're probably wondering why I'm doing this, huh? I never stopped hating you, that's why. You never should have stopped watching your back, you dumb cunt."

The woman under her was smiling.

Seeing that hateful satisfaction in the eyes of the woman she'd been torturing infuriated Lydia. She cursed herself for not finishing the bitch off faster. The woman pressed her mouth against Lydia's throat.

Her mind reeled.

Why is this bitch trying to kiss me?

The woman's teeth pierced her flesh. Blood flowed and the woman wrenched her head, tearing out a chunk of meat.

Lydia would have screamed if she'd been capable of it.

Her head and heart were pounding.

The world began to turn fuzzy.

The last thing she heard as she died was Suzie's smug laughter.

And her last sight on earth was the grinning face of the woman beneath her.

The violence spread quickly through Wheaton Hills, consuming the neighborhood like a ravaging virus. Carrie and her entourage became bolder as they moved house to house, smashing their way in through windows rather than ringing doorbells. Ella McGregor raced through the streets in her Bentley, running down people who were fleeing their invaded homes on foot. She liked it best when they saw it coming an instant before it happened, savoring that wide-eyed look of shock that lasted for a split second before impact.

Some houses went up in flames. Fires that were deliberately set by followers of Andras. Fire trucks rolled into the neighborhood, but the firefighters were immediately set upon by groups of rampaging maniacs. Nude, blood-and-soot-covered savages that overwhelmed the firefighters and other emergency workers arriving on the scene. The flames continued to burn and the body count soared.

The night boiled with screams and desperate, unanswered cries for help.

It was a cacophony of suffering.

A glorious symphony of agony.

As the streets of Wheaton Hills flowed with blood.

Just as Andras had envisioned.

Lying on his back on the roof of the shed behind the McGregor house, with his tender young bride curled around him, the demon listened to the sounds of carnage and grinned. For the first time in a very long time, he was truly content.

Vengeance, he thought.

At last.

FORTY-TWO

Awareness returned by slow degrees. Consciousness, at first, was a murky soup of dimly perceived bits of sensory data. Someone snoring. Pain. His head pounding. A bloated bladder in urgent need of emptying. And something else. He struggled to focus. What could that be? It sounded like someone...

Mark Bell forced his eyes open.

"Oh, shit."

The surface of Clayton's kitchen table was covered with empty beer bottles. A few were clear glass, but most were varying hues of green and brown. The bottles varied in shape, width, and height. Some were tall, some were squat, some were wide. This was a testament to Clayton's eclectic taste in brews. The overall visual effect was that of a miniature glass forest. A few of the bottles had tipped over on their sides and had dribbled beer on the stained tabletop. Another had functioned as a cigarette ash repository. Dozens of extinguished butts floated in a couple of inches of nasty brown liquid. Clayton and Jared sat slumped in their chairs, their heads hanging toward their chests, both of them unconscious. The snoring was coming from Clayton, whose big belly jiggled with each exhale.

Mark groaned and sat up straighter in his chair. The movement caused the ache in his head to flare brighter. He felt woozy for a moment and closed his eyes against the glare of the overhead light. He needed to crawl off somewhere and find a place to sleep it off. He couldn't believe how much they'd drank. Every beer in the house plus a fair amount of liquor. His mouth felt thick and dry. He needed a drink

262

of something. Water. Or soda. Not booze. He wasn't ever gonna drink that shit again. He felt like he'd been poisoned. Sleeping it off definitely seemed like the best option all around.

But it seemed like there was something he was forgetting.

He opened his eyes again with great reluctance. He looked at Clayton. Looked at Jared. The sound he'd heard as he'd begun to emerge from the depths of his stupor came again. It sounded like someone kicking at something. Like someone was trying to...get loose from something.

Fiona!

Panic brought him surging to his feet and burned through the cloud of drunkenness. He jarred the table on his way up and a few of the bottles rolled over the edge and shattered on the floor. He started around the table, but his feet got tangled in the legs of the chair he'd been sitting in and he went sprawling to the floor.

Fiona was on the floor, too.

She was still bound to the chair, but she'd managed to kick it over at some point while they'd all been passed out. She was wide awake and her eyes widened when she saw him staring at her. One of the chair legs had splintered and she was trying to kick her leg free of it.

He heard a loud yawn from somewhere above him. Followed by a snort. "Ow. My head. Hey. Where'd everybody go?"

Mark tried hard to focus. The world was still spinning. He didn't know how long he'd been out. Clearly not that long based on how fucked up he still was. He braced his hands against the floor tiles and pushed himself up, staggering to his feet.

Clayton squinted at him through red-rimmed eyes. "Dude. Why were you on the floor?"

Mark pointed at Fiona. "That's why."

Clayton leaned over and peered down at her. "Oh." He sat straight again and blinked at the empty bottles. "Huh. I think maybe we got sort of carried away with the drinking."

"Yeah. Could be."

"What time is it?"

Mark wheeled around and glanced at Clayton's micro-wave oven. He gulped when he saw the numbers on the digital display. He turned around again. "Shit. It's almost one in the morning."

"Uh oh."

"Yeah."

"We should get our asses in gear."

"Yeah."

Mark knelt and hauled Fiona's chair upright. The chair wobbled on the splintered leg, but didn't fall over again. He was stunned by the hatred evident in her bulging eyes. This was a person he would have done anything for until today.

He was about to tell her that when a loud noise emanated from the front of the house. A crash followed by the sound of a door slamming open. An instant later Kevin Cooper came streaking through the archway at the far end of the kitchen. The boy had a look of terror on on his face. A naked man wielding an iron fireplace poker followed him into the kitchen. Kevin stumbled and fell to the floor, screeching as he banged his knees on the tiles. The wild-eyed man raised the iron poker for a killing blow. But then a green bottle came whipping through the air and exploded in his face. The man screamed and recoiled, dropping the fireplace poker. Jared Kelly, the bottle tosser, came out of his chair and scooped up the poker. The naked man was starting to rise, but he went back down as the poker thumped across the back of his head. Jared hit him twice more, stopping when the man's scalp split open and started leaking blood on the floor. He staggered backward and dropped back into his chair.

He stared up at Mark, panting hard. "Dude. What the fuck's going on?"

Mark shrugged. "You tell me. I have no idea. Didn't even know you were awake."

"Wasn't, until like one fucking minute ago. Jesus." He stared at all the empty bottles. "How much did we fucking drink?"

"Everything, I think."

Jared groaned. "Real genius move on our part. We're

some bad-ass demon fighters. Sam and Dean Winchester got nothing on us."

Mark looked at Kevin, who'd gotten to his feet again but was still panting heavily. "Um...where'd you come from? And why was a crazy naked guy chasing you?"

"Because an army of crazy naked people have taken over the neighborhood."

"Right. Of course."

"And somehow my parents are involved in it. Had me locked down tight most of the day, after dad bailed me out of jail this morning. Not having anything else to do, I went to fucking sleep. Next thing I know it's nighttime and people are screaming in the house. I go see what's up and it's my fucking parents, man. They're acting all crazy and shit. They're naked and there's this dead chick on the kitchen floor and they're both, like, cutting on her with fucking knives. I took the fuck off. Goddamn. I need a drink."

Mark looked sheepish. "Sorry. Drank all the booze."

"Yeah. I heard that. Damn."

Clayton pushed away from the table and stood up. He pushed aside some of the empty bottles and snatched up the metal lock box. "Okay, we've sort of fucked up here. That's a given. But instead of crying over spilled beer, let's get over to that house and do this thing."

Mark nodded. "Right. Time to stop fucking around." He grabbed the gun from the counter and started to reload it. Then he stopped and nodded at the lock box. "Hook me up with some of those silver bullets."

Clayton opened the box and started to scoop out bullets. He passed some over to Mark.

Kevin looked puzzled. "What house? What thing are we doing?"

Mark filled the gun's empty chambers with silver bullets. "The old house where this all started. The one we broke into. We're gonna trap the fucking demon there again."

"Oh. Okay."

Mark snapped the gun's cylinder shut. "All right. Let's do this."

Jared stood and nodded at Fiona. "What about her?"

"She comes with us. Get her out of the chair, but keep her wrists tied behind her back. We can't trust her."

Kevin looked even more confused now. "What? Why can't we trust Fiona?"

"Because she tried to kill me."

"Oh."

"She wanted to kill all of us."

"Shit."

Jared freed Fiona from the chair, but, as Mark suggested, tied her wrists behind her back and looped the rest of the rope around her waist several times, keeping a six foot length of it loose to use as a kind of leash.

Mark started toward the archway at the far end of the kitchen.

Kevin loudly cleared his throat. "Um, guys? You're not planning to walk there, are you?"

Mark looked at him, impatience twisting his features. "Well...yeah."

"Not a good idea. It's fucking warfare in the streets out there."

Mark realized a lot of disturbing sounds were audible through the now open front door. He'd been too intensely focused on what has happening in Clayton's kitchen to notice it until now. There was a lot of screaming going on out there. And quite a bit of unhinged laughter, the sound of maniacs running wild. It wouldn't be long until more of that chaos spilled through that open door.

"Shit. You're right."

Clayton moved away from the table, still clutching the lock box. "The garage. Hurry."

He headed toward the door by the pantry. The others followed him out to the garage and piled into the old Cadillac. Clayton started the car and reached over his head to press a button on the garage door opener. The door began to rattle upward and got stuck about a third of the way up. Clayton pounded a fist on the steering wheel. "Goddammit! Of all fucking times!"

Mark was in the shotgun seat up front. He glanced at the side-mounted mirror outside the window and caught a flicker of movement. Dark forms came scuttling in under the partially open garage door. Before he could shout a word of warning, a face loomed in the window next to him. It was an attractive auburn-haired woman. She was nude. There was a brick in her hand. Other forms crowded around the car, pulling at the doors. Fiona screamed as Clayton stabbed frantically at the door opener button. It lowered and raised and got stuck yet again. One of the car's back doors came open and Fiona screamed again. Jared launched a fist at the face of the intruder and there was a loud crack of bone as the man's nose snapped. The auburn-haired woman swung the brick and the window exploded in Mark's face. She reached through the open space and seized him by the throat with one hand and started to swing the brick again with the other. Mark remembered the gun in his hand just in time. He shot her in the stomach and felt a touch of queasiness when he saw the bloom of red on her bare flesh. But she slipped away from him, dropping the brick in his lap as she slid down the door. Behind them, the garage door finally rolled all the way up and Clayton gunned the Cadillac's engine. The car screeched backward out of the garage and smashed into another group of would-be attackers. The Cadillac hit the street with a squeal of burning rubber, everyone leaning hard to one side as Clayton spun the wheel and got the car pointed straight before gunning the engine again.

Mark sat up straight, brushing bits of glass from his lap. "Fuck! Everyone all right back there?"

Jared sighed. "Yeah. Barely. Clayton. Dude. You really need to get that fucking door fixed."

"I know. Sorry."

Mark heaved the brick the woman had been about to brain him with out the open window. "Christ. Look at all this. Has this whole fucking town gone insane?"

There were multiple fires visible in the distance. Black smoke rose into the air, forming a noxious cloud over the neighborhood. A lot of people were running through the yards and in the streets. Those fleeing the madness and the ones pursuing them. As Mark watched, a gang of men dragged a woman in a bathrobe down and ripped the garment from her body, exposing the bare flesh beneath. She screamed and writhed as they fell upon her.

Mark looked at Clayton. "Stop the car."

Clayton didn't look at him. "No."

"What!?" Mark was livid. "We have to help that woman."

Clayton shook his head. "There's only one way we can help any of these people and we don't have time for distractions."

"A woman getting gang-raped is a 'distraction'?"

Clayton glanced at him. "Right now, yes, that's exactly what it is."

Mark seethed. "Great."

But he didn't say anything else. It sucked, but Clayton was right. The people of Wheaton Hills had only one hope. And that was for Mark and his friends to successfully perform the binding spell. He thought of the way they'd spent the day, how close they'd come to blowing it, and felt shame.

A pair of headlights appeared at the bend in the road just ahead of them. The oncoming car's bright lights came on and its driver adjusted course to come right at them. Clayton kept his foot on the gas pedal and continued toward the other car at high speed. Mark pressed backward into his seat and grimaced, anticipating a crash. "What the fuck are you doing?"

There was a hint of a smile at the edges of Clayton's mouth. "Playing a game of chicken. Did this all the time in high school."

"You're fucking crazy."

"Funny. That's what they always said back then, too."

The other car was very close now. Bright light filled the interior of the Cadillac, nearly blinding them. Mark and his friends were all screaming, anticipating a bone-crushing collision within seconds. But, at the very last possible moment, Clayton whipped the Caddy's steering wheel hard to the right and the other car, a black Bentley, zipped by them. Clayton kept right on going, taking the Caddy around the bend in the road at a hairpin angle, taking the turn with just a single, light tap on the brakes. Then he was driving hellbent for leather again, with the gas pedal pressed all the way to the floor.

Mark let out a breath. "Goddamn."

Jared thumped his chest. "Man. That was fucking intense."

Clayton chuckled. "Whoever that was meant to run us off the road. Thought they were dealing with amateurs. Showed those cocksuckers."

Mark shuddered. "I repeat, you are fucking crazy."

Clayton just chuckled again.

They had a few more close encounters with the roaming maniacs, but nothing else as intense as the averted collision. Soon they were out of Wheaton Hills and on Weakley Lane. Clayton parked on the road's shoulder some fifty yards down. After pausing to collect their wits and reflect on how monumentally lucky they were to have escaped Wheaton Hills unscathed, they got out of the car and trudged across the street. Mark, armed with the flashlight from Clayton's glove box, moved ahead of them, finding the narrow, overgrown gap in the trees that led to the house. The strange stillness on this side of Weakley Lane was disconcerting after the chaos of Wheaton Hills. Though the demon was gone from this place, some trace of its taint remained, causing any wildlife to give it a wide berth.

The path twisted and Mark soon caught a glimpse of the little house. He could see the dark outline of the old Buick Special, sitting on concrete blocks. The others followed him into the clearing and they walked as a group to the front of the house, stopping at the porch steps. He glanced up at the spray-painted pentagram on the boarded-up second floor window. A chill slithered through him as he stared at the symbol. It was a blunt reminder of the nature of the evil they were facing. He thought of Natasha. She was out there somewhere in all that chaos. He felt a renewed flaring of that sense of loss. And now something else. Worry. But he had to put that aside for now. He could only pray she was somewhere safe and get this thing done.

The door they'd removed was still on the ground in front of the porch. The open black space where it had been looked simultaneously ominous and inviting. Mark knew the house was empty now, but he still had a strange sense of being watched. There was something odd about the house, even with the demon gone, as if the physical structure itself was somehow sentient. As if the house was awake and watching them, having waited patiently for their inevitable return.

Kevin spoke for all of them: "I do *not* want to go back in that house."

A long, silent moment.

"Fuck it."

Jared snatched the flashlight from Mark, climbed the steps, and walked through the door.

Mark heaved a sigh and followed him. He was grateful for the comfort of the gun in his hand. He wasn't a fan of guns, but this one had saved his ass once already tonight. He heard the others come up the steps behind him as he entered the house. The interior of the house felt colder this time. No surprise. They were deeper into fall now, the season stretching inexorably toward winter. The extra chill heightened the eerie atmosphere. Mark's skin crawled as that sense of being watched intensified.

They made their way to the kitchen, bumping into the gloom-shrouded furniture multiple times en route. Jared was already by the open pantry door, waiting there for them, in no hurry to venture down to the basement alone. He turned the flashlight toward them as they approached. Mark lifted a hand to shield his eyes against the glare. "Hey."

"Hey."

The Dark Ones fidgeted and shot occasional nervous glances at each other, with the exception of Fiona, who stayed very still and kept her gaze on the dusty floor. Kevin had taken over the responsibility of handling her, but the length of rope hung slack in his hand. It would have been easy for her to make another run for it. Mark thought it telling that she wasn't at least taking a shot.

Perhaps she was simply resigned to what was about to happen and wanted it over.

"Let's go."

Mark reclaimed the flashlight from Jared and pushed past him into the pantry. The door at the back stood partially open. The painted depiction of a sword-wielding Andras astride a large black wolf seemed more vivid than before. More intricately detailed. Probably that was just his imagination getting the better of him. He was simply noticing details that had eluded him the first time. But the impression lingered. It almost seemed as if the painting was on the verge of coming to life. He imagined it turning three-dimensional and sliding off the door to swing that sword at them. He pulled the door the rest of the way open, mercifully removing the image from sight. With one more deep breath, he started down the stairs to the basement, the others following behind him.

On the way down, it struck him again how badly the odds were stacked against them. They weren't professional monster or demon hunters. Armed with only some scrawled old notes and a gun loaded with silver bullets, they were scarcely prepared to confront, much less subdue, an ages-old entity. On top of that, he was still drunk. Even with the flashlight to guide him, he had to brace an arm against the wall to keep from pitching down the stairs.

And holy shit, but he still had to fucking piss.

The need was painful at this point. He wished he'd taken a leak out in the woods, but he'd been so focused on getting here that he'd neglected to get it done. But there was no way he could kick demon ass with his eyeballs floating. After reaching the concrete basement floor, he staggered off to a corner, unzipped, and let her rip. The strong stream of urine was loud on the brick wall.

Fiona made a sound of protest. This time he actually understood her: *Gross.*

Mark groaned in relief. "Ah...oh shit. Thought I was about to fucking burst."

Clayton and Jared followed Mark's example and watered separate corners of the room. Mark finished first and zipped up. He aimed the flashlight at the floor, letting the light play over the elaborate pentagram painted on the concrete. Smaller symbols were painted around its outer edges. One was the anarchy symbol. The rest he didn't recognize. He didn't much care what they were. All that mattered was that someone else had done most of the grunt work for them a long time ago.

Clayton zipped up and walked up to the edge of the pentagram.

The lock box was still tucked under his arm.

Mark looked at him. "Well?"

Clayton opened the box, removing the crumpled papers inside. He dropped the box on the floor and shuffled through the papers, stopping on the one he needed. He glanced across the pentagram at Mark. "Yo. The light. Get over here."

Mark approached and aimed the beam at the page clasped in Clayton's fingers. "So how's this gonna work?"

Clayton shrugged. "It's actually pretty straightforward. We call Andras. Literally. By name and by blood. Blood first."

"By blood?"

"Yeah. But not just any blood. It has to be the blood of souls touched by Andras." Clayton showed them a pained expression. "That'd, uh...that would be you guys."

Jared looked grim. "What do we do?"

Clayton peered at the papers again. "Anybody got a knife?"

Mark nodded. "Yeah."

"Of course you do, you fucking hoodlum. So...anyway... what you do is each of you should prick your thumb with the knife and spill a few drops of your blood in the center of the pentagram."

"That's it?"

"Yep. The pentagram's already enchanted. All the required sigils are in place. Think of it like an unlocked door. All we have to do is lure Andras back inside and lock it down again. Your blood will begin the process of calling the demon."

Jared held out a hand. "Knife."

Mark dug the folding knife out of his pocket and handed it over. Jared stepped into the pentagram and held his hand out toward the middle of the circle. He applied the tip of the blade to the ball of his thumb and pressed until a dark welling of blood appeared. He then squeezed the bottom of his thumb with a forefinger until the first droplets spilled to the floor. Everyone let out a gasp at the sizzling sound the blood made when it struck the concrete.

Jared passed the knife back to Mark.

Mark stepped into the circle and pricked his own thumb, wincing only slightly at the little stab of pain. The blood sizzled on the concrete again and he passed the knife to Kevin, who took it with obvious reluctance but nonetheless wasted no time in doing as the others had done. Fiona let out an emphatic grunt that caused the rest of them to exchange questioning glances.

Mark shrugged. "Whatever."

He tugged the gag out of Fiona's mouth and went to work on removing her bonds. She flexed her wrists as the rope fell in a loose coil on the floor. She snatched the knife from Kevin and, with no hesitation at all, moved into the pentagram and sliced the center of her palm wide open. A thin stream of blood pattered on the concrete. The sizzling sound was much louder this time and wisps of steam curled up toward the ceiling.

Jared squinted at her. "You're not gonna go on a stabbing spree, are you?"

"Fuck you."

She passed the knife back to Mark, who couldn't hide a small, reflexive cringe. He still didn't trust her. How could he? But now that they were down here, allowing Fiona to participate felt right. Sure, there had been no guarantee she wouldn't attack them or attempt to flee again, but he'd had a strong sense neither of these things would occur.

A sheet of straight, dyed-black hair fell across her face as she dipped her head to stare at the center of the pentagram. "Say this works. We call Andras and he actually comes. What then? How do we trap him here?"

Clayton looked at her. "Also pretty straightforward." He waved pointed at some of the arcane symbols inscribed along the pentagram's edge. "Again, the binding mechanism is already in place. We just have to reactivate it, a process we've started with the blood-calling. We finish it by...uh... well..." He squinted at the papers in his hand again. "Uh, sort of just by telling it to stay put and go to sleep."

Jared rotated his thick neck, popping tendons. "Like a misbehaving kid. Or a dog. You're shitting us, right?"

"Nope. You've activated the magic with your blood. We'll increase the wattage of the calling by actually calling Andras by name. He'll come. When he does, we say the following..." He cleared his throat and brought the papers closer to his face. "'Foul demon—"

Keven barked laughter.

Fiona slugged him in the shoulder. Hard. "Shut up."

Kevin touched his shoulder and scowled at her. "Ow. Jesus."

"Just listen."

Clayton cleared his throat again. "A-hem. 'Foul demon, hear our command. By the power of blood and the will of God, we bind you to this place. Foul demon, now we remand you into eternal darkness. Foul demon, sleep."

Mark felt another headache coming on, this one fueled by the growing certainty that what they were trying here couldn't possibly work. There was some level of genuine magic at work here, but it'd orchestrated by people who'd been dead a long time and Clayton's father had not been one of those people. The information in his letter could be based on nothing more than supposition and pure bullshit. On the other hand...

Fuck it.

There's just nothing else to do. This has *to work.*

"So let's call him. By name. Right now."

"Right." Jared raised his voice and turned his face toward the ceiling. "*Yo, Andras! Get your skeezy demon ass down here. Come on, we're waiting!*"

There was a round of laughter.

Even Fiona cracked a smile.

But Clayton was nodding. "That's the basic idea. We should all call him to amplify the effect."

Mark cupped a hand around his mouth. "*ANDRAS!*"

Fiona's voice was just as loud, but shriller: "*ANDRAS!*"

Then they all called the name in one thunderous voice: "*ANDRAS!*"

They waited.

Nothing happened.

At first.

Then the painted lines of the pentagram began to glow a dull red.

Mark took a step back. "Whoa."

Fiona cupped both hands around her mouth and screeched his name again. "*ANDRAS! We're waiting for you in the basement. Where we first met you, you cocksucker. Come here, Andras. NOW!*"

The air in the basement grew noticeably warmer. The lines of the pentagram glowed a brighter red. Something was definitely happening in the center of the pentagram.

Air shimmered.

A flickering ripple of light that flared brightly, waned, and flared again.

The Dark Ones called the demon's name again.

Natasha stared up in rapt wonder at the demon's face. He looked so beautiful. So perfect. She loved him. And she loved what he had helped her become. She'd known all along the world of men wasn't set up to nurture the hopes and desires of someone like her. She had lived in dread of a future in which she would be forced to abandon the things she truly cared about in favor of doing what was necessary to fit in and adapt to adult life. But Andras had changed everything. She had abandoned her old dreams, but it was because the demon had shown her a better way, not because she was settling for some drab and uninspiring existence, as she'd once feared. Her new life would be a grand adventure, an exploration of the furthest limits of pleasure and indulgence.

With Andras, the world would be at her feet.

She smiled and stroked his face. "I love you."

He kissed her palm. "I know."

She could smell the fires burning in the distance. A dark cloud of smoke was drifting over the entire neighborhood. She also heard screams and the occasional whoop of a siren as various emergency vehicles came screeching into the neighborhood. The screams were nice. They made her wet. People were dying out there. A lot of people. But their deaths served Andras. And knowing this rendered the sounds of their agonies delicious.

The demon began to enter her.

Natasha sucked in a breath, got ready to scream.

Andras abruptly went still.

He lifted his head, turning his face to the sky. Some of the demonic radiance leeched from his features. He tilted his head to the left. And then to the right. He looked like a dog cocking his ear to hear some distant sound inaudible to humans. At first the twist of his features conveyed only confusion. But then his eyes widened and his features went slack. He sat up, pulling out of her.

He looked...afraid.

Which terrified Natasha. She could imagine nothing in all of creation that could frighten her demon lover. Unless...

Mark.

Clayton.

Goddammit. She knew she should have talked him into letting her go after them. Mark had told her Clayton knew something, maybe had some clue about stopping the demon. And now they were out there doing whatever it was.

"Andras. I think—"

She screamed as his whole body went into a violent convulsion. He fell away from her, landing on his back with head hanging over the edge of the roof. He kept shaking and shaking, his arms and legs thumping up and down on the tin roof. Then he sat up with a loud, gasping intake of breath and stared right at her. It was still Andras. For one more moment.

Then he was gone.

She experienced a single moment of soul-wracking grief. And then she was screaming. Because she was herself again. She was free of the demon's influence. But she would never be free of her memories of the things she'd seen and done.

For the first time in weeks, Derek McGregor was also free. Dazed and barely conscious of where he was, he scooted away from her and tumbled over the edge of the roof.

He hit the ground and didn't get up.

Natasha kept screaming.

"Foul demon, hear our command. By the power of blood and the will of God, we bind you to this place."

To Mark, the words didn't feel right coming out of his mouth. They felt stilted and hokey. He was sure the rest of them felt the same way as they stood crowded around Clayton, craning their necks to peer at the faded writing on the page.

Mark lowered the flashlight. The shimmery glow at the center of the pentagram had intensified, rendering it unnecessary.

Jared tugged at his shirt collar and mopped sweat from his brow with a flannel sleeve. "It's getting fucking hot in here." His nose crinkled. "What's that fucking smell? Is that... *sulfur?*"

Clayton glared at him. "Focus, goddammit. The next part. Again."

Jared rolled his eyes, but craned his neck toward the page again.

"Foul demon, now we remand you into eternal darkness. Foul demon, sleep."

"Again."

"Foul demon, now we remand you into eternal darkness. Foul demon, sleep."

A rumbling sound emanated from the center of the pentagram, where a shape was taking form as steam leaked from the edges of a hole in the fabric of reality. The hole was a portal and the shape was coming through it. The shape came closer, grew bigger.

Clayton swallowed audibly. "Oh, hell. This crazy bullshit is working."

Fiona clutched at Mark's arm and pressed against him. This time he didn't shrink away from her. Her whole body was shaking. He couldn't blame her for being scared. He was fucking terrified. It was one thing to talk about demons in the abstract. It was easy to imagine being brave from a distance, especially with enough liquid courage. But being confronted with the undeniable reality of an ancient evil from the literal Hell of the bible was another matter altogether.

The demon emerged from the portal and the lines of the pentagram glowed brighter than ever. The creature loomed above them, impossibly tall, the top of its monstrous head nearly brushing the ceiling. It was humanoid in basic form, but a huge pair of wings unfurled at the center of its back and flapped twice, creating a hot wind that blew back the hair of the human onlookers. The head of a raven sat atop its broad shoulders. The raven head squawked at them, a sound so piercingly loud it made them all cry out and stagger backward. It squawked again and came at them.

Fiona screamed and buried her face in Mark's chest.

Mark screwed his eyes shut, tensing for death.

The thing squawked again.

Mark forced his eyes open.

The demon was right at the outer edge of the pentagram, straining to come closer, but something was containing it in the circle, some invisible force. The binding magic Clayton had talked about. It was real. It was fucking working.

Clayton had dropped to his knees. He gulped and stared up at the towering demon with an awestruck expression. His face was covered in sweat. His puffy cheeks had flushed a deep red. Mark hoped he wasn't about to have a heart attack. But he seemed to rally when it became clear Andras couldn't move beyond the containment field. He got jerkily to his feet and stared down at the crumpled pages in his hand again.

"Foul demon, hear our command."

The rest of them crowded around him again and picked up the chant: *"By the power of blood and the will of God, we bind you to this place.*"

Mark felt a weird tingle of disorientation. Something was pushing at the edges of his consciousness, looking for a way in. Andras. He remembered how the demon had manipulated them before. How it had used and shamed them. He became much more awkwardly aware of Fiona's lithe body pressing against him. Fiona clutched at him again, but in a way that was motivated by something other than fear. He felt a stirring at his crotch. He looked at her and saw a lust in her eyes that mirrored what he was feeling.

It was happening again.

Fiona's eyes glimmered. "Please. Make it stop."

Mark reached for the snap of her jeans and she arched herself up against him, standing on her tiptoes to kiss him firmly on the mouth. He kissed her back, made a growling sound deep in his throat. He knew exactly what was about to happen. He was going to fuck Fiona right her on the concrete floor. And then the rest of them would take turns with her. And while that was happening, Andras would break free of the incomplete binding and finish them.

Mark screamed and shoved Fiona away from him.

He snatched the papers from Clayton.

"Fuck you, Andras."

The raven head squawked.

The immense wings flapped rapidly several times.

"Foul demon, now we remand you into eternal darkness. Foul demon, sleep."

Clayton flashed a raised middle finger at the demon. "Nightie night, you unholy douchebag."

The demon banged its fists against the invisible field.

Jared approached the edge of the pentagram. "Look at that. He's scared."

The demon confirmed this by lifting into the air and buzzing about madly inside the circle. He looked like a trapped firefly bouncing around inside a jar.

Pretty soon they were all laughing and mocking the demon. The sound of their taunts appeared to infuriate Andras, who kept flinging himself about inside the circle in increasingly frantic efforts to break free.

"Sleep, Andras," Clayton said, investing the words with as much force as he could muster.

The rest of them said it together: "*Sleep.*"

They kept at it, impelling the demon back into the darkness that had been its prison for so many years. Its desperate, futile efforts began to abate as the chorus of commands rang out louder and with more conviction Andras stopped bouncing around inside the circle and drifted slowly downward until his bare feet scuffed the dusty concrete floor. The demon's chest heaved as he stared at each of them in turn with those disturbing black raven eyes. But the Dark Ones did not falter and the commands to sleep continued to ring out. Within moments the creature was sitting in a cross-legged position on the floor, its beak dipping toward its chest, those bird eyes growing duller by the moment.

Clayton recited the full speech from his father's papers one last time.

The demon's physical form began to fade.

And then he was gone.

Except that he wasn't. Mark knew that. He was still here. You just couldn't see him anymore. He was...asleep.

Jared pumped a fist and let out a whoop. "We did it! Holy fucking shit!"

And then they were all grinning and heaving sighs of relief. There were high-fives and shoulder claps all around. The removal of the threat and the burden that came with it made Mark feel lighter than air. Maybe everything would be all right now. Sure, a lot of bad shit had happened and some people had died. But maybe there was a chance he could repair things with the people closest to him. Starting with Natasha and then—

Something was tugging at his pocket.

He frowned in confusion and glanced at Fiona, who was pressed up against him again, except this time there was nothing artificially seductive about it.

Oh, shit.

He'd forgotten about—

The gun sight ripped free of the inner-pocket cloth. Fiona backpedaled quickly away from them, aiming the gun at the center of the group. She stopped at the staircase. A weak smile quivered at the edges of her mouth. "I'm proud of all of you. You were all very brave. I have to give you that."

Jared sneered. "Goddamn. I knew we shouldn't have trusted you, you fucking bitch."

Fiona laughed. "I love you, too, asshole."

Clayton took a few steps in her direction, cautiously extending a beseeching hand. "Think about this, Fiona. You don't want to hurt us. You're just confused. I understand that. But we can help you if you just—"

She gave her head an emphatic shake. "You're right. I don't want to hurt you. Not anymore." A single tear traced a slow path down her cheek. "But you're wrong about the other thing. You can't help me. No one can. There's shit you don't know about me. Kevin knows a little of it. Maybe he can help you understand."

She sucked in a breath and stood ramrod straight.

She jammed the barrel of the pistol up under her chin.

Mark's mouth came open in a scream as he rushed at her: *"NO!"*

BAM!

The gun's loud report stopped Mark in his tracks and he watched in shocked disbelief as a dark spout of blood erupted from the top of her head. He dropped to his knees and crawled over to her as she dropped dead to the floor. The others crowded around him as he cradled her limp and lifeless body in his arms. His tears blotted out the world as he wailed and rocked the dead girl.

The immensity of the loss stunned him.

One of us, he thought.

One of us.

Gone. Forever.

He wasn't alone in his grief. He heard other sobs. Felt comforting hands on his shoulders. Some time passed. When they were able, they carried the fallen member of their clan out of the basement and out of the house.

FORTY-THREE

With Andras contained and the spell of his influence broken, most of the mayhem taking place in Wheaton Hills came to an abrupt end, with many people coming to a dead stop in the midst of acts of rape and murder. Some were so appalled at the atrocities they'd committed while under the demon's influence that they immediately took their own lives, adding to the already massive death toll. The fires continued to burn for a time as most of the survivors wandered about in a daze. But then a few people began to rally and work together. One of them was an ex-firefighter who coached some of the others on how to use the equipment left behind by the slaughtered Ransom fire department. Others began to figure out that the authorities in Ransom were either overwhelmed or out of the equation altogether, and calls went out to state troopers and authorities in other cities. It was possible to see all this as a testament to humanity's ability to step out of even the deepest darkness and put things right again.

There were, of course, exceptions to this meager feel-good aspect of the tragedy. A few people kept right on doing what they were doing. For these few people the demon had tapped into something twisted deep inside them, something that couldn't be reined back in now that it had been set free.

Greg Fox dropped the knife he'd been holding and let the little girl go. She got up and ran screaming to her mother. The mother drew the wailing little girl into a tender embrace, whispering words of soothing reassurance in her ear as she glared at the man who'd been on the brink of doing something vile to her daughter.

Greg smiled at Carrie. "Oh, God, did you feel that?" He began to laugh through the tears as he drew his girlfriend into a trembling embrace. "Andras is gone. It's over, baby. It's over."

"No, it isn't."

Greg's eyes opened wide as she thrust her own knife into his body, angling it up under his ribs. She smiled as she yanked it out and thrust it in again. She kept smiling as Greg fell away from her, wheezing in agony as he dropped to his knees.

She kicked him in the head and he fell over onto his side.

Then she turned around, a vibrant grin on her face.

"Now, then. Where were we?"

As she walked through the streets, Suzie McGregor could still hear the occasional scream, but now the sound was a product of a deep emotional pain rather than a result of fear. She saw people hugging in the streets and in the yards, comforting each other as they wept or moaned. Suzie felt nothing but contempt for them. They were only grieving the loss of other people. Flesh and blood. What was that compared to the loss of Andras?

Nothing, that's what.

Suzie didn't much care about other human beings.

Never had.

Oh, they had their uses now and then. She enjoyed sex. She liked male bodies. You could do fun, physical things with them. But, ultimately, men were just things. Pleasure toys with a pulse. Only Tom Bell had come close to making her feel anything at all, but even that had been very superficial. Andras was her only true love.

And now he was gone.

Somehow someone had done something to take him from her. She felt an intense hatred for this mystery figure. If she ever figured out who had done it, she would kill them.

No.

First she would torture them. For a very, very long time. *Then* she would kill them.

But she didn't derive much consolation from this thought. She would probably never know who had done it. They would always remain out of her reach. Which was yet more evidence of how the universe liked to toy with her. This whole thing with Andras had been just another cosmic mindfuck. A tantalizingly glimpse of absolute freedom. And now it had been yanked away from her.

She raised her tear-streaked face to the sky as she reached her house.

"FUCK YOU! STOP DOING THIS TO ME!"

Derek was waiting for her inside. He was sitting cross-legged in the middle of the kitchen floor, in a pool of drying blood, surrounded by body parts.

"Hi, mom."

Suzie stared at him for a long time. It was strange to look at this body again and see her son rather than Andras. The same body she'd fucked with such feverish intensity for weeks. She ached to touch that flesh again, even with Andras gone.

She summoned a smile. "Hi, baby." She approached him and held out a hand. "It's been a long night. Let's go up to your room and lie down a while."

He stood up, ignoring her outstretched hand.

"No."

He balled up a fist and punched her dead center in the face, snapping her nose. She tottered backward and fell hard onto her ass. Derek stepped over her and walked out of the house. Suzie curled into a ball on the floor, weeping from the pain. The physical pain from her broken nose was bad, but what she really couldn't abide was Derek's rebellion. He was her son and she needed comforting. What he'd done just wasn't right. She couldn't take his insolence anymore. If he ever dared to show his face in her home again, she would kill him.

Why wait for that?

Yes. Why not?

She got to her feet, ready to go after him.

Then she heard footsteps coming down the stairs from the second floor.

She turned toward the sound. "You."

"Yes."

"Come here. I need you."

She held out a hand again, smiling, knowing this one could not resist her.

He did come to her.

But instead of taking her hand, he seized her by the throat.

And squeezed.

Suzie died knowing the universe had grown bored with her and was simply discarding her, the way a child grows tired of a once-favored toy and searches for some other source of amusement. She felt a moment of intense, righteous anger.

And then nothing.

Ella McGregor sat sobbing behind the wheel of her Bentley. She was parked in the middle of the street. She thought of her son, poor Kurt, and wondered what he would think of the things she'd done. She hadn't quite been in control of herself, true, but that didn't change the reality that she was a murderer many times over. She couldn't bear the notion of her sweet son looking down on her from heaven and passing judgment on her for her heinous acts.

She glanced at the Bentley's rear view mirror. The reflection of her age-lined face taunted her again. With the demon gone, the restoration of youth had been revealed for what it had always been—nothing more than a very effective illusion.

She was *old*.

An old, beaten, remorseful murderer.

There was only thing to do.

Atone.

She put the Bentley in gear and pressed the gas pedal to the floor. The car quickly picked up speed, the speedometer's needle rising past seventy. The street was coming to an end. She kept her foot down on the pedal and sent out a final prayer for forgiveness. Then she jerked the wheel hard to the left, aiming the front of the Bentley at a utility pole. There was a rending crunch of metal. Ella went flying headfirst through the windshield.

The ride back to Wheaton Hills passed mostly in silence. With Fiona dead, their triumph over the demon felt hollow. They made a detour to her house, where they left her body with the bodies of the rest of her family. Seeing that entire family laid out like that, all violently dead, was almost too much for Mark. He had another sobbing fit. They then said a few parting words to their dead friend and got out of there.

Back at Clayton's house, the boys collapsed into chairs in the kitchen, emotionally and physically exhausted from their ordeal. Clayton fetched a bottle of his most expensive bourbon from his liquor cabinet and poured each of them a stiff drink.

Clayton raised a glass. "To Fiona."

The others echoed the toast and sipped their drinks.

Mark looked across the table at Kevin. "Okay. Out with it."

Kevin frowned. "Huh? What do you mean?"

"Fiona said you might know something about why she did it. So whatever you can tell us...I think we need to hear it."

Kevin stared at the forest of empty bottles, his eyes unfocused. Then he shook his head and leaned forward to brace his elbows on the edge of the table. "There's only one thing it might be. I mean, it's not like she said, 'Hey, Kev, I'm gonna off myself and here's why.' But there was one thing she told me a while back, something she said she never told anyone else."

Mark prodded him. "Yeah?"

Keven knocked back the last of his bourbon and set the glass on the table. "She...she told me she was sexually molested by both of her parents when she was younger."

Mark's headache was coming back again. Yet again. "Fuck."

Kevin nodded. "She said it went on for years, then it stopped about four or five years ago, when she was starting to hit puberty."

Jared scowled. "Those sick fuckers. I'd kill them now if they weren't already dead."

Clayton's expression was just as grim. "You'd have help."

Kevin stared at his empty glass. "She told me the thing that pissed her off the most was how they acted like it never happened. The whole family played this big 'let's pretend' game of everything being normal for years. In the end, I guess, she just couldn't live with it."

Clayton refilled their glasses again.

They drank in contemplative silence for a while, each of them lost in their own reflections about what they had lost. Mark closed his eyes at one point, felt himself drifting toward unconsciousness. He heard footsteps on the kitchen tiles and assumed someone had gotten up to go to the bathroom or find a place to crash.

Then Kevin said, "Oh. Hi, Mr. Bell."

Mark's eyes snapped open.

He spun out of his chair and stood facing the thing wearing his father's body. He had reclaimed the gun from Fiona before carrying her body out of the Hollis house. He tugged it out of his pocket now and aimed the barrel at Flauros' chest.

At his father's chest.

Mark's friends came out of their chairs and took up positions to either side of him.

A slow, smug grin spread across the demon's handsome face. Tom Bell's face. "Fool. By all means, kill this body." He thumped his chest and laughed. "Kill your father. It will only leave me free to take another host." He smiled. "Perhaps I'll abandon the father and inhabit the son. You're young and quite fit. Your body would serve me well."

Jared groaned. "Should've known this shit wasn't over. We got rid of Andras way too easy."

Kevin looked confused. "Anyone wanna tell me what's going on here? That's Mark's dad. Isn't it?"

Clayton shook his head. "Nope. Demon. Tell you later. If there's a later."

Flauros laughed. "Andras was arrogant. He never imagined

anyone would know how to draw him back to his prison. The mortals who'd put him there were all dead and he assumed their knowledge was gone with them. I was happy to allow him his arrogance. I've spent too long chained to him. Now that he's contained, I can truly be free."

Mark fought to keep his aim steady. There was only one way out of this. It wasn't fair. He'd already lost so much. God was a right bastard to put him in this position. He couldn't do this. He just couldn't.

And yet he had to do it.

"You're a bit of an arrogant fuck yourself, Flauros."

Flauros laughed again. "Oh? Perhaps you could explain. I should tell you that after you've finished your explanation, I will begin the process of torturing and killing each of your pathetic friends as you watch." He smiled. "So you might want to make it a long one."

Mark shook his head. "Nah. I'll keep it short. Dad, if you're in there and can hear me, I'm sorry. I ain't got a choice."

Flauros chuckled. "Oh, he can hear you, I assure you. And he'll be watching as I tear you limb from limb."

"That's not gonna happen. Know why?"

Flauros' smile this time was indulgent. He shrugged. "Why, boy?"

"Silver fucking bullets, asshole."

The demon's smile froze.

Mark squeezed the trigger.

They were sitting on the porch outside Clayton's house, sipping from cans of Budweiser Jared had retrieved from the fridge at his parents' house after a trip over there to verify that his family was okay. They were. Both parents and his younger brother were all fine. They were an exception to the rule. Most families in Wheaton Hills suffered at least one loss. Too many had been completely wiped out. Mark had done a bit of looking around for Natasha and for his mother, but he hadn't been able to find them. No one answered the bell at Natasha's house and her silver PT Cruiser was gone.

There had been no sign at all of his mother and he assumed the worst. Which meant he was likely a fucking orphan.

Wonderful.

He had lost everything. He assumed he had a lot of hard days and years ahead. But right now what he mostly felt was just plain numb.

There were a lot of flashing lights in the neighborhood now. A lot of ambulances and state trooper cruisers. They were collecting the dead and tending to the wounded. They were also asking a lot of questions. Sooner or later they'd work their way over to Clayton's house and there'd be some uncomfortable explaining to do.

Mark sipped his beer again. "Anyone up for a road trip?"

Jared shrugged. "I'm up for getting the hell out of Ransom, like always. You got anywhere in particular in mind?"

Mark nodded. "I was thinking Florida. Key West or someplace like that. Someplace where it never fucking gets cold."

"Huh." Jared chewed his bottom lip for a moment, then nodded. "Yeah. I could dig that."

"Me, too," Kevin chimed in.

Mark drank off some more of his beer. "So you guys know. I'm talking about staying down there, a permanent change of scenery. I've got my dad's car and a good chunk of cash he gave me. I'm thinking I want a whole new life. A different kind of life. I'm tired of this being dark and miserable all the time bullshit. Florida sunshine feels like what I need."

Jared laughed. "Dude, I am right there with ya. Got any Jimmy Buffett on your iPod for our Florida road trip soundtrack?"

Mark smirked. "No."

"Yeah. Me neither. I think I'll always be a metal guy, wherever I go or however old I get."

Mark finished his beer and stood. "No time like the present. Who's ready?"

Kevin frowned. "What, now? *Right* now?"

"Yep." Mark glanced out at all the flashing lights. "I'm

thinking I want to slip out of here before the net closes. I *never* feel like talking to cops and that goes double tonight."

Jared took another big gulp of beer and stood. "I'm in. Let's do this."

Kevin sighed and stood up. "Guess I'm in, too."

Mark looked at Clayton, who remained seated on the top porch step and had been strangely silent throughout this conversation. "What about you, Clay? You can't want to stay here and deal with all this shit. Come with us."

Jared chuckled. "Yeah, man. You're our bud. Besides, we need an older dude to buy us beer."

Clayton smiled, but shook his head. "No."

Mark did a double-take. "What? Really?"

Clayton nodded. "Yeah. Really." He sighed. He sounded as tired as he looked. "I appreciate the offer and admit it's very tempting, but I'm too old to go off on this big adventure with you."

Mark grimaced. "Don't start with this 'too old' crap. You're our friend. And, hell, don't we need an adult to keep us out of trouble?"

Clayton snorted. "Since when have I kept anyone *out* of trouble? Usually it's the opposite." He got to his feet with a groan, wincing as his knees creaked. "No, I'm staying. But listen—if you guys really make a go of it down there, maybe give me a call in a few years and ask again. Maybe I'll say no again." He smiled. "But maybe I won't."

They argued the point a little longer, but it became clear that Clayton's resolve would not be shaken. So they said their goodbyes. It was awkward and a little heart-wrenching. Despite the little bone he'd tossed their way, Mark was sure they'd never see their older friend again. For his sake, they made it quick, piling into the Lexus after Mark backed it backed it out of the garage.

A state trooper who was interviewing a woman in the yard of the house across the street turned at the sound of the car's engine and waved at them, obviously indicating they should stop so he could talk to them. Mark waved back and kept going.

***

Clayton dragged Tom Bell's body out of his house through a back door. It wasn't easy work, but Clayton kept at it, grunting and straining as he pulled the body across his backyard and dumped it in the yard of a neighbor. He repeated the process when he removed the body of the naked man who'd attacked them earlier. Talking to the cops was going to be hard enough. It would have been a good deal more awkward with dead bodies in the house.

But the cops were coming and there was no getting around that, so there was no point going to bed just yet. He busied himself by clearing the table of empty bottles, a task that required the filling of multiple garbage bags. He cleaned up the blood from the kitchen floor. The cops came and he answered their questions. They had a little look around, but didn't find anything worth their scrutiny and soon left. Clayton wasn't worried about them connecting him with the bodies he'd dumped in his neighbor's yard. There was too much confusion. Too much chaos. The authorities would pick up the pieces and try to set right what they could, but some things would get glossed over. So there were a couple of bodies in a backyard. So what? There were bodies everywhere.

After the cops were gone, he considered having one last drink before sleep. A nightcap. Surely he'd never needed one more than tonight. But he was just too tired and went to bed instead. He turned out the lights and laid there in the darkness for a time, waiting for sleep to come.

He thought of his friends. The best friends he'd ever had.

He wished them well and hoped he'd done the right thing for once.

EPILOGUE

Six years later...

Natasha slipped on a pair of dark sunglasses as she entered Clay's Place. She was starting to get recognized on a semi-regular basis and that wasn't something she wanted to deal with right now. She just wanted to sit and chat with an old friend for a while without any distractions. Was that too much to ask?

The place wasn't busy. Not surprising, considering it was the off season in Key West and it was midday on a Tuesday. Some kind of tropical island music was playing at a low volume on the sound system. Less than a dozen people were sitting at the little tables and only two people were sitting at the bar. One of the people at the bar was likely the man she'd come all the way from Hollywood to see. His back was to her and his head was bent down, his eyes trained on the pages of a magazine. He sipped from a half-empty mug of beer after turning a page in the magazine. When he reached for the beer, his head turned far enough that she was able to get a glimpse of his face. It was him, all right. He had a deep tan now and the baggy cargo shorts and loose floral-print shirt were items that never would have been in Mark Bell's wardrobe years ago. Ditto the sandals. But the face remained as handsome as ever. And he was still lean and fit. She was mildly surprised he hadn't gone soft from his years of baking in the sun and leading a life of leisure. But it was a pleasant surprise.

Two young guys were sitting at a table by a window. One of them, a shaggy-haired kid who looked like he'd maybe just turned twenty-one (that or he was drinking on a fake ID), was staring right at her.

Shit.

She tried to keep her ego in check. Maybe he'd recognized her. But maybe he was just a horny young dude who couldn't help staring at a hot babe in a tight little black dress. Either way, she hoped he'd stay where he was and not bother her.

Natasha approached the bar and slid onto a stool next to Mark. "Hey, stranger."

Mark looked up from the magazine and did a double-take. "Whoa. Holy shit." He broke out in a grin and slid off his stool to give her a hug. "God, it's good to see you again.'

She hugged him back, pressing her face into the crook of his neck. She was glad for the sunglasses. Her eyes were misting. It was good to see him again, too. Good to feel his arms around her. "Yeah."

The embrace lingered a few moments. Eventually, Mark eased out of her arms and slid back onto his stool. He shook his head. He couldn't stop grinning. "Wow. Just wow. Have to admit I'm floored. I thought you never wanted to see me again."

She shrugged. "Yeah. Well. You know. Time passes and things change. I never stopped thinking about you. One day I just decided to track you down."

A bartender came over and asked if she wanted a drink. "Martini. No olive."

The bartender prepared her drink and set it on a napkin.

Mark sipped some of his beer. "So...how did you find me?"

Another shrug. "Wasn't that hard. Made some inquiries with people in Ransom. Nobody knew what had happened to you, but I learned that Clay opened this place down here a couple years ago and from there it was easy. Jared's Facebook page gave his location as Key West. I put two and two together and came up with Mark Bell."

Mark chuckled. "Yeah. Jared actually tends bar here."

"What about you? What do you do these days?"

"Technically, I'm employed by Clayton. I help run this place. But, really, I don't do much other than sit here and drink beer. Once in a while I'll go bake on the beach."

Natasha eyed him up and down. The tropical shirt hung open in the front over a Motorhead t-shirt. He had tattoos up and down his arms. So he wasn't as completely changed as she'd feared. It was reassuring. "Huh. So where's your beer belly?"

"Oh, I still pump the iron. And I took up running a while back."

"Well, you look great."

"Yeah, so do you. But you're a movie star. Being beautiful's part of the job description."

Natasha laughed and took the sunglasses off, setting them on the bar. She tucked a lock of dyed-black hair behind an ear and smiled. "I'm not a movie star."

"Oh, really? I could swear that was you I saw in *The Killing Kind* a couple months back. And I'm almost positive I saw your face in the trailer for Rob Zombie's next flick. But maybe that wasn't you. Maybe you've got a movie star doppelganger."

Natasha smiled again. "I'm *in* movies. But I'm not a movie *star*. Not yet anyway."

Mark raised his glass. "It's inevitable. Here's to your eventual stardom."

They clinked glasses.

"I read a little thing about you in EW, the article where they called you 'America's next favorite scream queen.' It mentioned a kid."

Natasha's smile faded a little. "That's right."

"Who's the father?"

"It doesn't matter."

"Is he here with you?"

"He's in L.A. My aunt looks after him when I'm away."

"What's his name?"

Natasha sighed and put her drink down. "I really don't want to talk about my boy. It's none of your concern."

Mark frowned. "Huh. It's just that the article said he was five-years-old. And—"

Natasha's expression turned hard. "I'm going to leave if you don't drop this subject."

The look on Mark's face made it obvious he wasn't happy about that, but he just as clearly didn't want to see her go. His shoulders sagged a little and she knew he'd opted not to pursue the matter. For now. That was good enough.

She didn't want to tell him about the creepy looks little Justin sometimes gave her when he thought she wasn't looking. Looks that reminded her more than a little of the way Andras had once looked at her. It was ridiculous, of course. One of those boys had impregnated her that long ago night in the basement. Regardless of what the demon had told her, it simply wasn't physically possible that he'd caused that life to grow inside her. That was the voice of reason. Of rationality.

But the truth was, she was afraid.

She looked at Mark, studying him, taking his measure. His expression was somber but concerned. Maybe she *would* confide in him before heading back to Hollywood. Maybe he could help her figure out what to do. Or maybe not.

Right now she just wanted to enjoy the moment.

"So what ever happened with Kevin? Heard he came down here with you guys."

Mark's smile was wistful. "Oh, you know, shit happens. He met a chick soon after we got here and knocked her up. Less than six months later he and the chick took off back to Tennessee. I hear from him now and then."

"Email?"

He laughed. "Nah. He calls me. I don't do the Internet."

"You're not online at all?"

He shrugged. "I'll surf around a little on Jared's netbook now and then, but I don't have a Facebook page or anything like that. Don't even have an email address."

"Wow."

"I know. What can I say? I'm still a fucking rebel."

She smiled. "Good."

"So how long are you staying?"

She shrugged. "A few weeks. I have a small gap between projects."

"Oh yeah? Cool. Where'll you be staying?"

"With you."

Mark laughed again. "What if I'm shacked up with some other chick?"

"Are you?"

"No."

"Well, then."

Mark grinned. "I like the way this day is starting. It doth bode auspiciously, as Clay might say."

Natasha giggled. She was already getting a little tipsy. "It doth, it doth."

Curing one of the few lulls in their conversation, Mark's attention was drawn to a news report airing on the TV mounted on the wall behind the bar. "Have you heard about this?"

Natasha squinted at the TV. "Oh. Yeah. That serial killer thing up in Tennessee."

Mark nodded and kept staring at the television. "Our old stomping grounds. I've been following it pretty closely. The perp's been leaving a trail of bodies all over the midstate area for years. Cops won't say why, but they think the killer's a woman. They're calling her 'Jane the Ripper'."

Natasha chuckled. "Cute."

"Maybe you'll get to play her in a movie someday and win an Oscar."

Natasha smiled. "Maybe."

They talked and drank a little longer. The booze loosened them up, wiping away some of the natural awkwardness caused by the long years apart. She touched him now and then to emphasize a conversational point. Some of touches lingered longer than others. Jared and Clay wandered in after a while and there were more rounds of hugs and expressions of happiness at seeing her again. There was some more catching up. Feeling the booze a little more, Natasha surprised herself by broaching the subject of that last night in Ransom. She told them she'd tried to forget it had ever happened, but a part of her always came back to the question of how the demon's spell had been broken. So they told her all about it, taking turns as they told the tale from different perspectives. It was a chilling tale, but it had an amusing coda. Clayton bought the abandoned property for a song and had the house encased in concrete blocks. "It's finally idiot-proof."

The conversation took another somber turn as the subject of Derek McGregor came up. "Like you, he got to looking for us and came down here a while back." Jared sipped from a Corona bottle from the other side of the bar, where he'd taken up what was apparently his usual position. "He was in rough shape. You know, real skinny and haggard. Pale. He was all fucked up."

Natasha's nose crinkled. "Drugs?"

Jared nodded. "Yep. We tried to help him, but by then he was beyond help. He died a little later. They found him in an alley near here. Had my phone number in his pocket. I had to identify the body. Saddest goddamn thing I ever had to do."

"Jesus. That's terrible."

"Yeah."

A brief silence ensued as they all thought about the Derek they remembered. Then a few words were said in tribute to his memory and they moved on. No one was really in the mood to dwell too long on anything so depressing. There were more laughs and stories about the more fondly remembered aspects of the past, of which there were more than any of them would've guessed.

As much as she enjoyed catching up with Jared and Clayton, she was relieved when Mark suggested they leave so she could check out his place and confirm it constituted suitable lodgings for a celebrity of her stature. They walked out of the bar and strolled hand-in-hand down the sidewalk.

She felt something relax inside her.

She hadn't felt this good in a long, long time. It was wonderful to be with Mark again. Maybe nothing much would come of it. It was possible they just weren't meant to be together. But at least this time they'd have a chance to find out.

She relaxed even more as she made her decision.

I'll tell him about Justin, she thought. *Tonight.*

Then we'll decide what to do.

Together.

About the Author

Bryan Smith is the author of numerous mass market horror novels, including the popular releases *Depraved, The Killing Kind,* and *The Dark Ones.* His full mass market backlist will be reissued by Deadite Press throughout 2011 and 2012. His first title with Deadite Press was the acclaimed novella *Rock And Roll Reform School Zombie*s. Another novel, The Late Night Horror Show, will be published by Samhain Publishing in 2013. Bryan lives in the middle of Tennessee with a vast array of pets. Visit his home on the web at www. bryansmith.info.

deadite press

"Rock and Roll Reform School Zombies" Bryan Smith - Sex, Death, and Heavy Metal! The Southern Illinois Music Reeducation Center specializes in "de-metaling" – a treatment to cure teens of their metal loving, devil worshiping ways. A program that subjects its prisoners to sexual abuse, torture, and brain-washing. But tonight things get much worse. Tonight the flesh-eating zombies come . . . *Rock and Roll Reform School Zombies* is Bryan Smith's tribute to "Return of the Living Dead" and "The Decline of Western Civilization Part 2: the Metal Years."

"Highways to Hell" Bryan Smith - The road to hell is paved with angels and demons. Brain worms and dead prostitutes. Serial killers and frustrated writers. Zombies and Rock 'n Roll. And once you start down this path, there is no going back. Collecting thirteen tales of shock and terror from Bryan Smith, Highways to Hell is a non-stop road-trip of cruelty, pain, and death. Grab a seat, Smith has such sights to show you.

"The Killing Kind" Bryan Smith - Roxie is the goth girl of your dreams. There's just one problem-she's batshit crazy and has a fetish for murder. After a petty insult at a gas station, she goes on a murder spree, hunting down those that pissed her off. But she's not the only monster on the road. There are others out there killing and raping. And everyone's headed to the same beach house. A desolate vacation getaway with no neighbors and no one to hear the screams.

"Depraved" Bryan Smith - Welcome to Hopkins Bend. You're never getting out of here alive... In the middle-of-nowhere, USA, there is a town not on any map. A place where outsiders are tortured, raped, and eaten. Where local law enforcement runs a sex trafficking ring. And the woods hold even more monstrous secrets. Today four unlucky travelers will end up in Hopkins Bend. If they want to ever get out alive they will have to become just as vicious and violent as their pursuers. Just as depraved.

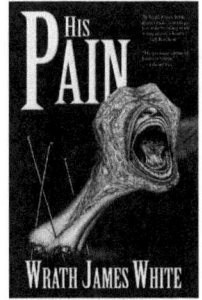

"His Pain" Wrath James White - Life is pain . . . . . . or at least it is for Jason. Born with a rare central nervous disorder, every sensation is pain. Every sound, scent, texture, flavor, even every breath, brings nothing but mind-numbing pain. Until the arrival of Yogi Arjunda of the Temple of Physical Enlightenment. He claims to be able to help Jason, to be able to give him a life of more than agony. But the treatment leaves Jason changed and he wants to share what he learned. He wants to share his pain . . . A novella of pain, pleasure, and transcendental splatter.

"Jack's Magic Beans" Brian Keene - It happens in a split-second. One moment, customers are happily shopping in the Save-A-Lot grocery store. The next instant, they are transformed into bloodthirsty psychotics, interested only in slaughtering one another and committing unimaginably atrocious and frenzied acts of violent depravity. Deadite Press is proud to bring one of Brian Keene's bleakest and most violent novellas back into print once more. This edition also includes four bonus short stories.

"Mangled Meat" Edward Lee - No writer is more hardcore, offensive, or notorious than Edward Lee. His world is one of torture, bizarre fetishes, and alien autopsies. Prepare yourself, as these three novellas from the king of splatterspunk are guaranteed to make you gasp, gag, and laugh your ass off. Featuring "The Decortication Technician," "The Cyesolagniac," and "Room 415."

"Apeshit" Carlton Mellick III - Friday the 13th meets Visitor Q. Six hipster teens go to a cabin in the woods inhabited by a deformed killer. An incredibly fucked-up parody of B-horror movies with a bizarro slant
"The new gold standard in unstoppable fetus-fucking kill-freakomania . . . Genuine all-meat hardcore horror meets unadulterated Bizarro brainwarp strangeness. The results are beyond jaw-dropping, and fill me with pure, unforgivable joy." - John Skipp

THE VERY BEST IN CULT HORROR

www.ingramcontent.com/pod-product-compliance
Lightning Source LLC
Chambersburg PA
CBHW051143030726
47504CB00004B/1010